Sean is a vegan with chicken-eating tendencies, who supports Newcastle United and lives in West London with no pets and a guitar, which he plays badly.

For my son.

Sean E. Boye

A DECENT MAN

AUSTIN MACAULEY PUBLISHERS™

LONDON • CAMBRIDGE • NEW YORK • SHARJAH

A CIP catalogue record for this title is available from the British Library.

ISBN 9781398440579 (Paperback)
ISBN 9781398440586 (ePub e-book)

www.austinmacauley.com

First Published 2022
Austin Macauley Publishers Ltd®
1 Canada Square
Canary Wharf
London
E14 5AA

Chapter 1

"Well, I know I shouldn't say this, because we don't want to encourage young men to fight, but from what I hear, you did very well," declared the nurse as she gave her patient an impish smile, before pressing her fingers against his battered skin once more.

"Oops, sorry."

It's okay," replied Luke with a grimace.

"Yes, you definitely took a risk. These days anything could have happened, God knows we see enough of that in here. But, still, you don't see too many men do what you did. No, not many good men around anymore, more's the pity," continued the Nurse wiping the blood from his wound, while Luke raised his head a little from the crisp NHS pillow and suddenly felt a warm glow flood into his broken body.

He liked being called a good man, and despite the discomfort of having staples inserted into the side of his head, he managed a self-effacing smile, like the ones he'd seen actors sometimes do in the final scene of a movie, with that "It's nothing, it's what I do" look in their eyes.

Now he wanted a bandage.

A big, sexy white one, wrapped tightly around his head with a little blush of blood showing through, and maybe a cut above the eyebrow.

That would be nice.

"Ahh," exclaimed the nurse, recognising the smile, as she gently rubbed his arm as a reward. "Yes, not that many decent men around anymore, not like you," she repeated, and again Luke experienced another dopamine hit from the compliment, except this time, a distant voice from the back of his mind seemed to mutter something that he couldn't quite hear and without warning the pain surged back through his body once more.

"You okay," enquired the nurse, noticing a little change in his eyes.

"Oh yes, thank you," replied Luke.

"Ahh, bless," she replied and then after turning around to close a few cupboard doors and do some general tidying up, the Nurse returned to check her handiwork one more time, before finally declaring that he was probably well enough to be discharged.

"And don't be such a hero next time," she added, as she began to help her patient off the trolley.

'No chance, it fucking hurt too much,' thought Luke, with a polite nod, carefully angling his body into his blood-stained jacket, before making his way out of the treatment area, and in the general direction of the exit. For the next few minutes, he limped along the bright yellow lines of the hospital floor, as if he were a broken piece in some giant board game, until a familiar "Bruv" made him stop and turn his head. Now Ravi, his older brother, Imran, Fitz and the rest of stag night, flickered into view under the bright lights of the Hospital reception area, and for a brief moment, Luke felt a spasm of shame, as he watched his friend's eyes recoil in mild alarm at the sight of his battered face before Imran spat out "fucking wankers" and they quickly hurried over to form a man circle around their fallen comrade.

"We should have been there, bro", "the tossers legged it" and "I think they came from outside London" suddenly filled the air, as everyone fought to outdo each other in cursing his attackers, until Fitz stepped forward to announce that "Even though, it had been most unfortunate that Luke had taken a bit of a slap, the real story of the night, was that he had left the club without buying the last round of shots", and in an instant angry faces were replaced by drunken grins, as the natural male instinct of "keeping everything light" was swiftly restored.

Luke was glad of it.

That was the great thing about being a guy, wasn't it? Don't dwell on things, accept what has happened, and then move on. Perfect his thoughts confirmed and feeling strangely relieved, he then proceeded to hobble off towards some seats in the corner of the reception area, to await the next instalment in the post mortem of the night before. Again, Luke looked passively on, as once more, his friends battled with each other to tell their version of the night's events, until eventually, through all the shouting, he was able to establish that sometime during the previous evening, he had apparently stepped in to help a woman, who was being harassed by two men, and after a pint glass was smashed into his nose, and various punches and kicks landed on his body and head, he'd eventually ended up in the A & E department of St Thomas' Hospital.

"Plus, someone filmed the whole thing and now it's all-over social media. You're like Tyson Fury or Raheem Sterling, bruv! You're a hero, I'm serious, look?!" declared Ravi, whose stag night it had been, before he thrust his phone towards the face of his friend. Now, as Luke's eyes began to narrow, he watched himself, with increasing unease, not only arguing with two huge men in a club, but also proudly declaring that "There's nothing wrong with Me Too."

"I'm gonna use it for my ringtone, bro'" announced Ravi, breaking into a little dance on the spot, as Fitz started singing "de ladies are gonna love you now", while the rest of the group suddenly erupted into loud laughter, performing various impersonations of Luke saying "There's nothing wrong with Me Too", until it became so loud, that the duty nurse had to lean over the counter to politely ask them to keep the noise down.

At once, contrite hands were raised and sheepish glances exchanged, and as everybody continued to whisper more details from the night before, into each other ears, Luke stared blankly at the polished tiles of the hospital floor, while faces filled with rage and fury, smashed their way into his thoughts for the very first time.

From the little he could recall, they had ended up somewhere in Hoxton, and after doing some pills on Ravi's big night out, he had been happily floating about in the middle of the dancefloor to One Kiss by Dua Lipa of all things, when he'd noticed two big guys talking to a girl in a corner of the club. He remembered that she was very pretty and from the look of their plain faces and bodies that screamed way too many nights down the gym, "the steroid twins" seemed a bit out of their depth, so at first, he thought they were just messing about and would eventually leave her alone. However, they didn't, but instead towered over her, and the more she shook her head, the more they laughed and moved closer to her body.

For as long as he could remember, he had always really, really, REALLY, hated this type of thing.

No meant no, didn't it? It was the first law of nature, for Christ's sake, and even when he had seen similar scenarios played out on T.V. or in a film, he had always instinctively covered his face with the nearest cushion or just changed the channel. How he wished he had a remote control right now; he'd thought as he looked out in anguish from amongst the happy clubbers and wondered what to do next. He was hardly a tough guy, and his record of losing both of the only fights that he'd ever had, first to his best friend Fitz in primary school and then, in his early twenties, to a Brummie with a huge beard at a house party in South Ealing hardly gave him cause for hope. Plus, he was on a pill! Maybe he could hug them to death? he'd mused from the darkness of the club, while he looked frantically around for help, but discovered to his horror, that no-one was looking, well no-one, except him, of course.

"Look, I don't think she wants to dance with your friend," he had said, sliding up next to the smaller of the two men, and almost swallowing his words through fear, before the larger man quickly removed his hands from the hips of the terrified girl to poke a thick finger into his chest.

"Who are you then? Me fucking Too?"

For some reason, he had blurted back, "There's nothing wrong with Me Too," which even at the time, he'd remembered thinking was an odd thing for him to say, especially, as he'd never really been that bothered about Politics or Social Justice in the past, so maybe it was the MDMA talking or something he had read online, but whatever it was, as the thuggish pair stood back and laughed at his reply, he suddenly realised, what he had always hated about his own sex.

Immaturity and pointless brutality.

Bet they would all be over at "mum's" tomorrow afternoon, eating Sunday dinner, as she fussed over them and told them to get their elbows off the table. Lovely boys still attached to the breast, waiting desperately for the last drop of mother's milk to trickle into their mouths, as they fooled themselves, they were proper men, decent geezers.

Well, they weren't his thoughts had thundered and stepping forward again, he asked them, more firmly this time, to leave the young woman alone, before a pint glass quickly put an end to his pilled-up gallantry, and the next thing he remembered, someone was placing their hands under his shoulders and ferrying him past the strobe lights and concerned faces.

"Bruv, you're such a hero," swiftly nudged Luke back into the present once more, and looking up from the hospital floor, he manufactured another smile, while Fitz launched into one more story from the night before, this time about a girl he'd met in the club who said that he was too fat to kiss.

Again, Luke tried to laugh along, but suddenly, he felt very tired, and leaning forward on his knees, he thought he might actually pass out, until thankfully he caught the eye of Imran, who seeing that he was in a bit of trouble, told everyone "To shut the fuck up", before calling him an uber. An hour later, he was home and after being ushered upstairs to his bedroom by his predictably distraught mother, he managed to dredge up few more re-assuring smiles together with an unreserved commitment to keep out of trouble for the foreseeable future, until collapsing onto his bed, he fell into a deep sleep.

Chapter 2

Luke moved anxiously along the wall of the office and taking a sharp left down an avenue of desks, he was just about to slip unnoticed into his seat, when suddenly everybody stood up from where they were sitting and burst into a spontaneous round of applause.

"We're so glad to have you back," gushed his line manager, Amber Jones, springing out from behind a pillar, in the middle of the room, and slightly unnerving Luke for a second, until he quickly defaulted to his now familiar pose, of sinking both hands deep into the pockets of his pants and returning his trademark grin.

Positive, neutral, not too pleased itself.

Perfect.

The Internet loved it, the Press, when they interviewed him outside his mother's house, loved it, even the nutter on the Motability scooter in Asda, who had nearly run him over recently, screaming, "you're that guy!" loved it, and therefore Luke duly nodded his head in appreciation, while the clapping continued for another thirty seconds or so, until a girl who he recognised as Tasmin, and had never previously spoken to him before, suddenly emerged from a crowd of happy faces to hand him a bottle of champagne and a CD.

"We all chipped in, and David said that you were a big Michael Bublé fan, and we didn't know which one to get you, so we got you his greatest hits. Hope that's, okay?" she said, as Luke grinned down at the CD in his hand, while Fitz's face beamed back at him from the back of the crowd.

Dick.

Luke hated Michael Bublé, and Fitz knew it but he returned a grateful smile, as everyone moved forward to congratulate him again, before chatting away for the next few minutes about seeing him all over news and in the papers and "how it was so exciting", and "had he spoken to any celebrities yet?" The questions were not unfounded, as Luke had indeed become the focus of, not only, national but world attention, since his nightclub heroics, while the You Tube video of his intervention had been clicked on over 200 million times and been trending online at number one for nearly a fortnight now. As a result, everyone from Politicians, to Celebrities from the world of Sport and the Entertainment had eagerly queued up to laud his brave actions while the rest of society, after years of cynicism, started to embrace notions of chivalry again. There had even been a spate of copycat incidents, by over-zealous males, where, in one case, a father in Buenos Aires had been attacked in a store for simply arguing with his daughter, while in Rome, a husband, after coming up behind his wife to surprise her for her 40th birthday, had been thrown in the Piazza Navona fountain by an over eager passer-by. It had been overwhelming to say the least, and on more than one occasion over the previous week or so, Luke had simply shaken his head in absolute amazement and wondered what the hell was going on. However, resolving to make the best of it, he had decided that he could only really be himself, and so continued to smile and answer his work colleague's questions as best he could until Amber intervened with a sharp "okay there's work to be done people" causing everyone to cease talking immediately and then scuttle back to their desks once more.

The noise in the office, quickly returned to its familiar volume of formal chatter, and Luke was just about to return to his lap-top as well, when Amber Jones sprang out of nowhere again to whisper "Let's have a little catch up" into his ear, before leading him out of some large glass doors and along a short corridor. Seconds later they had decamped to a meeting room, usually reserved for company executives, where his manager continued to eulogise about his bravery, and how well it had reflected on the organisation, whilst breathlessly adding that "the grand fromage's" back in head office were "sooooo over the moon" at what he had done, and it wasn't beyond the realms of possibility that by the end of the year he could become "an assistant team leader or possibly more? Just as long as he didn't take any more sick leave, of course".

Maybe more employees should get off their tits on a pill and then get punched in the head on a Saturday night, thought Luke with a grin, as he proceeded to sign the usual absence forms, before listening further to "that he was a credit to the company" and "it's a shame more men weren't like him", until thankfully an awkward pause in the conversation, finally gave him a chance to escape the half-crazed grin of his line manager and return to the "relative calm" of the recruitment industry.

"Yeah, sorry, we will get those contracts over to you ASAP."

"Really? I thought the payment runs were fine this week, okay, let me check and I will get back to you."

"Yes, the interview is booked for next Wednesday."

Luke had forgotten just how insane his job was, but despite all the pressure and the mayhem, he found that he was actually glad to be back at work, or at least vertical again. Of course, ten days or so of recuperation, had been nice, but there were only so many episodes of *Brooklyn Nine-Nine* or bags of Pom Bears a sane person can get through before becoming incredibly bored. Furthermore, his return to the coalface had also provided him with a temporary respite from his present obsession of trawling through the internet and looking for the latest example of men being demonised or patronised in popular culture.

Even now, a week or so later, Luke was still not entirely sure how he had ended up in this place.

One minute he had been quite happily receiving adulation and the odd marriage proposal from the thousands of female fans, who had recently joined his Twitter account, whilst the next, he had randomly turned on the television to watch a morning chat show, featuring Suzanne Burke, a prominent feminist and author of a controversial book called, *Why I hate men* and that seemed to be that. Now, with increasing irritation, he had listened to the veteran women's rights campaigner declare to an all-female panel, that "this Luke Casey isn't really a hero, is he?" and "surely the world has moved on from bloody white knights coming to the aid of passive females, hasn't it?", and as a result, been left, a little unsettled to say the least.

Naturally, he didn't want to be called a hero, even though he so obviously was, but now a little stung by these comments, he had quickly switched off the television and sat in a sulky silence for a moment or two until, for some reason, he had typed "why men are rubbish" into his phone, only to find himself completely shocked at what subsequently appeared in front of his swollen eyes.

Men are dangerous! Men are useless! Men just need to shut up and listen!

There was even an online petition against a male snow leopard, from a recent BBC nature documentary, who had been filmed trying to kill the cubs of a female, which although completely normal behaviour in the wild, was now suddenly viewed as another example of toxic masculinity. It was relentless, and as a result, for the next week or so, Luke seemed to spend his every waking hour, either listening to podcasts by male groups who had completely given up on the

14

whole business of romance altogether, or reading articles by women who felt that the world would be a far better place without anyone in possession of a penis. There was so much to take in, and as his thumb flicked through the furious debate, considering words like Patriarchy, Misogyny and Gender Politics for the first time in his short life, he quickly found himself very, very confused.

For a start, he didn't really accept a lot of the male commentary, which seemed nostalgic for a time when men were in charge, and any woman who sought to live outside this world, was denying her real place in society, while at same time, he also wasn't buying into the feminist perspective, that men were completely in control, and women were just pawns in an ugly, one-sided game.

He didn't feel in control.

In fact, most of the men he knew, seemed to be the exact opposite of "in control" either spending half their time down the gym or in the male cosmetic section of Boots, desperately trying to find out what women wanted, and apologising profusely whenever they got it wrong.

Hardly the super confident masters of relations between the sexes, was it? his thoughts protested, and as he continued to trawl through the hyper-polarised content of social media and related news articles, quite annoyingly, a myriad of female empowerment statements began a steady march past his weary eyes.

"Men still run the world; not sure it's going so well."

"Only boys are scared of strong women."

"A real woman can do it by herself and a real man will let her."

A real man? What the hell was that? Luke thought to himself, as a memory of an awful tinder date suddenly came to mind, where the woman in question declared that she liked "a man to be a man" before spending the next three hours or so criticising an ex-partner for being "too full of himself".

It seemed like a perpetual onslaught.

Too confident, not confident enough. Too pushy, too insecure. Too emotional, no sorry, not emotional enough. He'd even read somewhere that all men were potential rapists. What?! So, having male genitalia, was now the equivalent of being in possession of a criminal weapon, was it?! Most women had two hands, that didn't make them all potential murderers, did it? Even mothers seemed to be at it, as he'd recently heard a woman on a pod-cast describe her teenage son as "a typical sulky young man, who has no idea how to express himself". It was as if she was describing an animal of some sort, not a complicated, nuanced human being, and he was pretty sure that if a father had

15

said the same thing about his young daughter, he would have been denounced as a vile sexist.

It just seemed so unfair to Luke, and therefore, as he had laid on his sofa, scrolling through his phone with increasing irritation, the tsunami of female approval he had been receiving, since his noble intervention, was now actually having the opposite effect. It was beginning to bother him and he was certain that if he heard one more time that he was "a decent man," from anyone, especially a female, he might just scream.

Then again, maybe it was his mild OCD, making him think too much again? reasoned Luke, and so deciding to seek temporary refuge in some caffeine, he rose wearily from his desk, to wander off into the kitchen with his mug, and gaze blankly at a little flash-mob of plastic milk containers inside a fridge, until from behind him, a well-spoken voice interrupted his tangled thoughts.

"Oh, hi Luke."

"Oh err, hi, err Nicola," replied Luke, turning around quickly before taking a second to realise who was speaking to him.

"It's Nicole actually," came the reply, still smiling, but a little put out that he hadn't remembered her name correctly.

"Err, yes, of course, sorry, err hi Nicole."

"Do you need some milk? No problem, you can have some of mine. You've been away, haven't you? Anyway, doesn't matter, everyone just nicks everyone else's, don't they?"

"Yeah," replied Luke with an anxious laugh.

"Yes, it's only milk, isn't it?" continued Nicole, as she swooped past Luke to pluck out a half full carton of semi-skimmed milk with Nicole written in large black letters on its side before placing it in his hand.

"Oh thanks."

"Just wanted to say, Luke, that I thought what you did in that club a few weeks ago was soooooo brave. My god, I couldn't believe it when I saw the video. So awful, but it was completely amazing. I mean it happens all the time, doesn't it? but no-one takes any notice or bothers to help, do they? That's why what you did was so brilliant, seriously," said Nicole, as Luke tried to return something approaching a confident smile, but his treacherous heart had typically abandoned him and was already pounding out an anxious tune.

He had always fancied her, but until this moment, she had never looked that interested. He wasn't really her type; she was well spoken and he basically wasn't. However now she was placing a strand of hair behind her ear, whilst giving him that look, she usually reserved for men who sounded more like her. Jacob from head office or Harry the area manager and for a second this thought slightly unsettled Luke, as the coldness of the milk carton started to numb his fingers.

"It happens everywhere, doesn't it? even in this office. I mean there's a guy here who keeps staring at me. It makes me feel really uncomfortable. In fact, I am thinking of saying something. You know these things start small, don't they? I bet those guys who did that to you, started off by staring at girls, making them feel awkward. I mean you have to nip these things in the bud, before they get out of hand, don't you? I mean women shouldn't have to put up with this type of thing, should they?" continued Nicole, as Luke nodded his head again, before moving the milk carton around in his hands, while the numbness in his hands increased.

"You might know him. The large guy who sits in the corner and is always singing grime songs."

"What? Fitz?! Err, I mean David Fitzgerald?"

"Yes, I think that's his name."

"Err, he's a really nice bloke, I don't think...." said Luke.

"Well, that's not an excuse, is it?" interrupted Nicole, firmly.

"No, of course, but I am sure he...."

"Well, it needs to stop, and I think you showed an incredible example. You have to stand up to these people or it will keep happening, and I'm definitely thinking of reporting it."

"Err no, don't do that. I'll have a word with him, he's a mate," replied Luke hurriedly, while Nicole edged a little closer to him as she continued to complain about male harassment and how, "of course, not all men were the same, but most were, weren't they?" while Luke blinked his eyes a few times and took a deep breath. He had been hearing this kind of thing all week on various podcasts and not overly keen to hear the live version, Luke's heart now decided that he didn't fancy her that much anymore and beat less anxiously, before he mumbled something about promising to ring a client, and then scurried back to his desk with a frost-bitten hand and an empty coffee cup.

"Fuck me!" Luke mouthed to himself in exasperation, as he dropped angrily into his chair, while he mimicked Nicole's voice inside his head.

"He keeps looking at me, he keeps looking at me."

I bet if you fancied him, you wouldn't mind him looking at you, his thoughts spat back, as the conversation in the kitchen now only served to confirm his previous fears, and in frustration, he raised his eyes to the ceiling of the office, with increasing despair.

It was official.

His sex was now under attack.

He had just had a glass smashed into his nose, been kicked half to death, and was getting violent backflashes on an hourly basis, but was now wondering whether it had been worth all the trouble. Micro- aggressions, feelings trumping facts, gaslighting, permanent dissatisfaction, never ending judgment, the attacks on men just continued without end, and feeling his face redden with fury, Luke tried to look up from his desk for some relief from his internal rant only to find a big smile from Nicole beaming back at him again. *Maybe I should report you?!* Luke thought, returning a polite grin, before he sank his head back into the screen of his lap-top once more and tried to think of something else.

Chapter 3

By 5 pm, Luke's irate thoughts had nearly brought him to the point of complete exhaustion, and so it was a blessed relief when Fitz wandered over to enquire if he fancied going for a few drinks after work. Yes! came the immediate reply and after grabbing his coat from behind his chair, ten minutes later, he found himself staring at the lager taps of the Red Lion and Pineapple, and in the company of a familiar face. Thank God for male friendship, Luke thought as he picked up two pints of overpriced craft lager from the bar and wandered over to a table in the corner of the pub.

"And you know what else they're doing, bro'? In South Korea, some poor guy was sitting on the underground with his legs apart and then a load of militant feminists ran over and covered him in flour and videoed it. Geezer looked like a fucking doughnut in the end, and the thing was, he wasn't even near anyone. I mean I could understand if he was stuck between two birds and stretching out and invading their space, like some of those idiots you see on the tube, but he wasn't. He was just sitting there all by himself in an empty carriage, minding his own business, but they said he was man-spreading and deserved to be punished. What!? In 2025? It's a joke, Bruv!" declared Luke handing Fitz his pint, and taking a seat.

"I know bruv, getting out of hand, innit? But no problem for you though, you being a hero now and all that. Mate! I saw how Nicole was checking you out today. She is bare nice. Maybe I should get beaten up for standing up for a girl? Ha! Be worth all the pain for her, she is so nice," replied Fitz, as, Luke took a quick sip of his beer, before looking back at his oldest friend. For a second, he considered telling him to maybe ease up on staring at Nicole all the time, until Fitz exploded into laughter once more, as he launched into another story, this time about a social activist contractor refusing to work for a company, because the shops in the local area used plastic straws. This was not the face of a sex pest, decided Luke, and although he would definitely mention it later, when they were properly drunk, and the male ego was more amenable to constructive criticism, for the present, at least, he just wanted to drink his fury away and have a good time. So, they drank, talked and drank some more, and by the time it was 10 pm, himself and Fitz had knocked back six pints of lager, four Jager bombs, and two JD and cokes, while they discussed such varied topics as: was J Cole better than Stormzy, or could a Komodo Dragon beat a Honey Badger in a fight.

It was absolute bliss, thought Luke, and as he walked over to the bar to order another drink and sank his elbows into the metal counter, it seemed as if friendship and alcohol had finally released him from the agonies of his temporary obsession. *Thank God for that*, his thoughts rejoiced and he continued to grin contentedly to himself for another few minutes, while he watched the barman pour the slowest pint in the history of mankind, until a little bored, he gradually found his attention being directed towards two young women who were talking loudly about ten yards along the bar from himself.

"Yeah, I think it's completely wrong," said the taller woman holding a glass of wine.

"Definitely," replied her smaller friend with blonde hair and wearing a black biker jacket.

"I mean how many normal girls like us do you ever see on the cover of Cosmo or Vogue, or any websites like You Hoo? None. Right? It's not on"

"No, you're right. It's really wrong, it's body shaming, innit?" agreed the smaller friend.

"That's exactly what it is!" replied the taller woman, nodding her head, before turning to look over in the direction of a group of men standing by the door of the pub.

"That guy in the blue shirt looks a bit like Channing Tatum."

"Nah. Too small," replied the smaller friend.

"Yeah, he is a bit. Shame," said the taller woman, as they both took a sip out of their drinks and began to chat about something else, while further down the bar, Luke was now standing up and shaking his head in complete amazement.

What?!

They were complaining about body shaming, while they effectively body-shamed.... a man. Too small? his mind thundered, and suddenly lurching forward, Luke suddenly pressed his forehead against the cold metal of the bar, as it seemed all the good work of the last five hours had been undone in the space of a few words. "It's a fucking joke bruv" his thoughts now loudly proclaimed again, and in frustration, he angled his head sideways for a few seconds, to get a better look at the source of his latest outrage, until his surreal surveillance soon brought him to the attention of the taller of the two women.

"Can I help?"

"Err, No, I don't think you can" replied Luke dramatically, and then springing back on his heels, he glared at the two girls for a moment before immediately marching across the bar to grab Fitz by the arm and then drag him towards the exit of the pub.

"Bruv?!" protested Fitz through a mouthful of cheese and onion crisps, as they clattered through the doors of the bar and spilled out onto the street outside, where after a brief conversation, which included "I liked it in there" and "What would Stormzy do now?" they decided to follow Luke's new plan for the evening of "getting away from women's constant bullshit" and quickly relocating to Soho for a night out in Trisha's.

Luke loved Trisha's.

It was cool, retro and opened late, and once inside the small bar, they ordered more drinks, while the increasingly drunk, Fitz, now spent most of his time pointing Luke out to every girl in the bar, as "The guy who got decked for helping that bird" in the vain hope, that his status would rise in his friend's reflected glory. It didn't. Meanwhile Luke soon got into a conversation with a young woman wearing a feather boa about relationships, as he confidently declared that "females would never be satisfied with men, and would always give them a hard time" whereupon the woman laughed and called him a misogynist. "How can I be a misogynist?! I'm a hero!" protested Luke as he ordered another JD and coke before wandering off to have a smoke in the tiny beer garden at the back. By 3 am Luke was totally hammered and as he staggered out of the bar, and into the dim lights of Greek street, he tried to explain to Fitz that "deep down, women probably didn't like men very much", while Fitz enthusiastically nodded his head in drunken agreement, before crashing his hand into Luke's chest to declare "but they like you Luke, you're a hero bruv". This routine continued, for at least, another ten minutes, all the way down to Leicester Square, until finally they climbed into an uber, where Luke found another soul mate in their driver, who described in great detail the way in which his two ex-wives and four ex-girlfriends spent most of their waking hours, trying to make him do things that he didn't want to do. "Exactly, they don't like us" declared Luke as the cab jolted to a stop out outside his house, and he lurched out onto the pavement, to wave at the back of Fitz's head for a moment, while it sped off towards the Uxbridge Road, and he turned away to look at his phone.

"Hope you are better."

"You're an inspiration."

"Just wanted to say my boyfriend has changed so much after seeing your video, thank you, Luke."

Ahh, that's nice, darling. Is he easier to handle? Is he a better man now? Luke's thoughts scowled as he stared at his twitter feed, before letting himself in and slowly climbing the stairs of his mother's council house. "They keep calling us scum, and saying that the world would be a better place without us, but what about them? What if we said no for a change," mumbled Luke, lighting a cigarette and plonking himself down on the end of his bed. For another few minutes, his head remained hunched over his knees, while he sucked on his Marlboro lite and kept repeating "suppose we said no" until gradually a curious smile began to creep onto his inebriated face, and then grabbing his lap-top from a bedside table, he quickly tapped a few random keys, before sitting very still and staring into the webcam.

"Err, hiya, this is Luke; you know the guy who stepped in for that girl in a club in Hoxton recently and got his head smacked in by two fucking psychos. Yeah, that bloke. Remember him? Anyway, so I thought I would say hi, you know and chat and thank you for all your nice messages, and actually share a few thoughts with you and see what you think. Yeah? Cool. So, after the club thing, the interview outside my house and celebrities like Portia Ramone, saying I was a hero and all that, I was lying there on my mum's sofa, with my head the size of a fucking pumpkin, and I start watching the telly and I see all these women on a morning news show, talking about what men should do or shouldn't do and some say leave them alone, they are lovely while others say no, they are horrible, so cut their nuts off. Oh, and guess how many men were on the panel, by the way? None. Which is kind of weird don't you think? cos if it was the other way around, there would be a shit-storm, wouldn't there? and then when they do ask a man, it's the bloke who's doing the weather, and of course, he says, "oh don't get me involved," and then bangs on about a cold front coming in from Norway or something, cos he probably doesn't want to get slagged off for saying the wrong thing, which I totally get, right, but then I start to think, that there's definitely something going wrong here, between men and women, that is. And you know what? Thinking about it, there's probably always been something wrong, hasn't there? The thing is, whatever we do, men that is, we are total fucking idiots, aren't we? I mean if you asked a woman to say three things that she liked about a man off the top of her head, she seriously wouldn't be able to do it, would she? Probably take her a fucking week to think of something and even then, it would be, "oh they look good in trainers or skinny jeans". I mean all you have to do is look online and there you have it. Why men are shit and here's ten million reasons why. And okay, fair enough, most of the crap in the world is probably caused by us, but that ain't the whole story, is it? I mean, I was in a bar tonight, as you can probably tell, and these two bir…err I mean girls were complaining about body shaming and how normal looking women are not getting on the front of magazines or in films, which I get okay, but then one of them turns around and points to some geezers in the corner and says, 'What about that bloke over there?" And the other one says, now get this, she says, " Naah, too short" Too short? And I wouldn't mind but the bird who said it was tiny herself and the geezer she was coating was taller than her! Bruv! If I was Prime Minister, I would make it the law that you couldn't go out with anyone more than five inches taller than you. That would sort it out, wouldn't it? But, that's it innit! You complain about being judged, but you judge us fucking worse. Most guys are whatever, she's okay, I'll have another vodka Red Bull and things will get better, but not women. No, no, you are, err, you are, yes, you are genetic snobs, that's right, genetic snobs. We have to be tall enough, have the right shoes, speak ten languages, have a nice car. Be solvent! By the way, what does that even mean? I see that all over dating sites now. Be solvent. What? Like you want a bloke with access to a lot of glue or sommink? But it's like, you are never happy, or don't seem to be, at any rate. It's so fucked up! Like the ones on the right of the argument want us to be real men, while the ones on the left want us to be lap-dogs, it's a nightmare. Seriously! Don't call me mate, cos I wanna be treated like a lady, and you have to buy all the drinks, and you have to be a gentleman, and remember everything that's important to me, and keep me happy, cos if you don't, I will shame you and slag you off online and then probably get off with your best mate. Really? And what do men get for going along with all this? Hey? I'm not joking bro'. What? Sex? The social status of having a girl? Something to do? Yeah right! It's sooooo fucking worth it, innit? And then, even if you do settle down, you only break up anyway, and then she stops you seeing your kids, cos the courts always side with the bird, don't they? and then you end up living in your car, paying a shit load of money for somebody else to bring up your kids. Yeah, right, where do I sign? Don't think so, bruv. So anyway, I've had enough of all this, so I am saying no. Yes. I mean No. No to women. From now on, I'm not going out with any birds, or women until all this whole bullshit stops. And yes, I would rather knock one out. Well, to be quite truthful, that's what most men are doing these days, now anyway, if you read the papers, no-ones having sex anymore, except for the boomers getting STI's in the old people's homes, of course, so fuck it, we got nothing to lose, have we? You say you don't want us? Tres cool. Guess what? We don't want you either. Ha! That will teach 'em, won't it? Ha! Yeah. So that's it. No more women for Luke Casey! Well not until it all starts to change anyway. Okay, right, so it's been really nice talking to you, and thank you again for all your nice messages and I just wanted to share that with you, so I hope you have, err, a very pleasant erm day, what time it is? but yep, err bye."

Luke now remained perfectly still, and he continued to stare at the screen of his lap-top in a kind of a wasted trance for another few seconds, until suddenly lurching forward, he slurred "fuck it" before slamming his finger down on the send button.

Done, thought Luke, and as the first rays of the morning sun started to creep through his bedroom window and warm the side of his drunken face, he lay back on his bed and started to smile.

Chapter 4

Jake stared at the picture and crinkled his nose.

Stubborn eyes, hair shaved over the ears, cheekbones a little too sharp. *Bet he has a big dog called Tyson or Brexit*, he thought, as he took sip of his peppermint and liquorice tea and then clicked onto another page.

He didn't like him and he didn't like his accent either.

Farkin London, innit?

God preserve us from the football factory and nineties rave culture again.

Oi oi saveloy and all that rubbish.

Jesus! He'd seen enough of all that crap in his first job working as a hack for Spank? a second-rate lad's magazine that tried to be the porno version of Loaded, if that was possible.

Anyway, hadn't we all moved on? his thoughts hissed again, as he took another sip of his tea, while every cell in his body seemed to whisper that, deep down, he instinctively disliked cocky working-class boys.

In fact, scratch that.

He absolutely hated them.

It had taken years for him to admit this fact, even to himself, but the naked truth was, he did.

He had pretty good reason to as well.

Being educated in a public school, didn't exactly endear him to this social demographic, so as a result he'd had to endure more than his fair share of abuse when he first came to London in the late nineties, for not acting like he was raised on some sink estate in Bermondsey, snorted huge lines of cocaine, and then spent the rest of his week sexually harassing women. *Thank God Bermondsey had a decent coffee shop now*, Jake thought as he scrolled through Luke's twitter-feed and continued to shake his head.

What utter bullshit!

So called "decent blokes" lining up to support "their boy's" brave actions.

"Can't say anything these days."

"Keep going, mate, we're all behind you."

"The establishment hates people like us."

The establishment?! Really?! What was the hell was that, by the way?! Some shady organisation designed to hurt poor people? Yeah right. William Beveridge, the man who basically designed the Welfare State didn't go to the local comp did he? Alan Turing, who more or less invented the idea of the modern computer, wasn't brought up in some Northern slum living on spam fritters, was he? No, they weren't! They were educated in private schools, with middle to upper class parents, and nurtured by a system that generally brought everyone a little closer to civilisation and the notion of a better society. However, listen to this lot online, with their half-baked truths and uninformed conclusions and you would think that all the advantages of the modern world were their bloody idea! Fucking morons is what they were! Fighting culture wars that didn't exist, voting in charlatans who would sell their own grannies for dog food given half the chance, while generally dragging everything and everyone back towards the Stone Age again. For over ten years, on his mid-morning radio show, he had tried with every fibre of his being to promote good ideas from decent minded progressives, and expunge this type of retro bullshit from the national consciousness once and for all and yet here it was, back again.

Yuk.

"What do we think about this guy? "Jake now declared, before turning around his tablet around to show a picture of Luke to the eager faces of his brainstorming team.

"Who's he?" asked Hugo squinting his eyes.

"Oh, I think he's that guy who stepped into to save that girl in a club, and then got drunk and did a big rant online," replied Becky.

"Oh yeah, Luke Casey, isn't it? Was in the papers a few days ago, bit upset with women in general, I think," recalled Hugo.

"Bit of fly by night story, Jake. Probably been done to death by Five Live and the other morning chat shows. Just a nobody who got his 15 minutes of fame. Might end up on a reality show if he's lucky. No, I think we should carry on with this knife crime angle, your last show was extraordinary, got a question asked in the House." interrupted his producer, Marcus, from the other end of the table.

"Err, not sure about that, fella. Did you see the video? Very powerful for a certain audience, and he has over two million followers on twitter now and it's growing by the hour. Of course, knife crime is really important, but it's getting a bit samey, isn't it? I mean Christ. I can't talk to another crime psychologist; they all say the same thing and they know fucking less than I do. No, we need a change. What do you guys think?" replied Jake, sitting back in his chair, as the young interns all laughed at his cheeky expletive, while keeping their heads very still, so as to favour either side, until it became completely obvious who was going to win this little argument. Even if they disagreed, they certainly weren't going to say it openly to Jake O'Callaghan, top radio chat show host in the country, bestselling author and self-styled "conscience of London". They wanted careers, and had worked hard for this opportunity. First or higher second-class degrees gained from Oxbridge, favours called in by desperate parents, the right clothes had been bought, the correct pronouns included in their online profiles. After COVID and the mega- recession of 2024, it was brutal out there, so any dissent could be fatal, and although Jake liked to put it about that he wanted to be constantly challenged, and strived to nurture "an honest and open working environment", in reality he didn't. He liked things his way, so as a result everyone kept a neutral cheery demeanour, while staring at their tablets and trying to look engaged.

"I really think this is storm in a teacup territory, Jake, seriously," sighed Marcus, moving uncomfortably in his seat, as he started to hitch up the belt of his chinos.

"You're doing that thing with your belt again Marky, baby," replied Jake leaning forward on the table, as there was more laughter, while his producer rolled his eyes and extended his hand out to the nearest intern, who dutifully placed their tablet into his hand.

"Nice kid, steps in to help a girl, gets upset with women when he doesn't get enough Vaseline on his ego, excuse the imagery. Leave it to the Guardian columnists and the twitter mobs to finish him off Jake, he will be chip paper in a week. Its boy meets girl stuff and unless some fat Hollywood twat is involved, I don't think it's for us. This is trivial, beneath you. You're huge, and you don't fit this type of news. Bloody hell, we will be doing that fucking hamster who dances to his owner's ringtone next," commented Marcus after a few seconds of considering the picture on the screen, before handing back the tablet to the intern.

Jake's eyes now narrowed in frustration, as he took a sip from his cup of tea again. He didn't like his ideas being dismissed in such an offhand way, especially in front of his team, and he was just about strike back with a suitably sarcastic remark when a young girl in the middle of table started to speak.

"I can absolutely see where you are coming from Marcus, and of course, we don't want to follow every trend that comes our way, but I really think there is more to this than that, and I tend to agree with Jake on this one. On Saturday night, I was in Dalston with some friends, and this is all we talked about. How he had done something amazing, you know helping that girl in a club and then got drunk and totally ruined it. It really divided the guys from the girls as well. A few boys thought, what he said was fair comment, while a lot of the girls thought it was misogynistic, and the voice of a bitter man. I think there is something here, definitely."

"Err sorry, you're new, aren't you?" interrupted Jake, turning his head towards the young woman.

"Yes, I'm Antigone," she replied, as the rest of the table now held its breath to see if her intervention had worked or if she would be out the door with the dreaded "sometimes these things don't work out, and best of luck for the future" email.

"Antigone, of course, sorry. You see, Marcus, they are talking about it in Dalston, bro! It will be all over Hackney by lunchtime. It's dividing opinion. Isn't that what we want? Aren't we here to tell stories? I mean, that's essentially what we do, isn't it? And boy meets girl is the greatest story of them all, Marcus! Too corny? Okay, but I actually think this could be very dangerous. In his 'farkin' little video rant, he talked about women oppressing men with their choices, and not having agency in his own life. It sounds like that old trope to me. You know, women, get back in your little box, and stop disturbing the patriarchy," continued Jake, mimicking Luke's accent to more general laughter from his team.

"Err I don't know, Jake. Okay, people are talking about it, but they talk about anything, don't they?" replied Marcus.

"Well, that's the point of our show, isn't it? Talk about the things that people are talking about" declared the radio host, staring back across the table, while his producer lifted his eyes to the ceiling for a moment, as if in deep thought, before he instinctively pulled on his belt again.

"Look, he's going for the belt, he's going for the belt!" shrieked Jake excitedly clapping his hands together, as everyone laughed once more, until eventually Marcus threw his hands into the air and finally conceded defeat.

"Lovely jubbly geezer. So, let's crack on with this, people. Find out everything about this guy. Listen to the debate, check twitter, see what they are saying. Let's really go for it! I have a very good feeling about this one," declared Jake, and after taking a brief glance across the table towards Antigone, he quickly rose from his chair and left the room.

Chapter 5

Some people choose little parks hidden behind busy high streets or the silent corners of medieval churches but for Luke, the crisp section of Sainsco's was the perfect refuge from a mad and cynical world. Now, as he paced slowly along the aisle, and stopped to stare lovingly at a variety pack of bacon-flavoured wheat crunchies, all traces of tension and anxiety in his neck and shoulders seemed to drain away, while his previously scrambled thoughts gradually began to settle themselves into some kind of order.

It had been almost two weeks since his online verbal puke and the inevitable front-page backlash of "No sex please, I'm Casey"; "Hoxton hero ditches women"; or Luke's personal favourite from the Daily Sun, "If you were the only girl in the world, I'd rather have a w#nk", became the number one topic trending around the globe. It was incredible, and a lot for a young mind to take in, as previously glowing tributes from celebrities, like the A list actress, Portia Ramone and Tik Tok influencers, such as Paul Dykes, were quickly replaced by "pathetic", "toxic" and of course the ever present, "misogynist". *Misogynist?! These days, wasn't that just disagreeing with a woman?* thought Luke, and anyway, how could saying "I don't want to go out with a woman" be misogynistic, for god's sake? How was that fair?

"Oh, you want fair, do you?! What about being oppressed for thousands of years for not having a penis, sonny boy, try that for fair!"

Jesus! Now he was replying to himself in the voice of his accusers, Luke sighed as he reached forward and plucked a large packet of mature cheddar and red onion hand cooked crisps from the shelf and looked admiringly at the seductive packaging. Everywhere else on the planet, people were satisfied with an ordinary potato snack or a tortilla chip, but only in this green and pleasant land was "The Crisp" treated with the due reverence and respect that it deserved.

In fact, since Brexit, COVID, or anything else you would care to think of, a love of crisps was probably the only thing that most of the country still had in common with each other, and for a brief moment, this lightly salted patriotism cheered him up, until recent events returned to his mind again, and he sadly returned the packet to its place and walked on a little more.

Of course, it hadn't been all bad.

His twitter following was now over three million and rising, as "ordinary men" from all around the world sent messages of support for what he was trying to say, whilst significant numbers of women over 5ft 11', previously frustrated at seeing guys over 6 foot, "regularly ending up with 5ft 2' midgets", also loudly endorsed his "five-inch rule", as well.

However, despite these little bright spots, most of the commentary from the mainstream media and beyond, was still mostly negative. Even the girl who he had stepped in to help, Lucy, had tweeted that although she was still very grateful for Luke putting himself at risk for her and getting badly injured in the process, she was a little disappointed by his latest video and "hoped that he might reconsider his unhelpful message". Of course, he could see it from her point of view, especially after being harassed by those two meat-heads, but despite this, it still seemed to Luke, that everyone was purposely misunderstanding what he was trying to say.

The very last thing, Luke wanted was for women to return to a 1950's sexist hell or imprison them in some perfumed gulag. In fact, he had no problem with women doing exactly what they wanted, any time they wanted to do it, just as long as he didn't have to take any more of their crap, his thoughts protested, and for a moment he tried to appease his increasing frustration, by halting in the middle of the aisle to stare down at packets with a hundred different flavourings, in the hope of greater clarification, but nothing came back from the Delphic Maize Oracle, except an announcement over the supermarket tannoy that the chorizo and sour cream fried pitta breads were now on half price. Dismayed, Luke trudged on, as the backlash from social media wasn't the only issue that he'd been forced to deal since his nocturnal ravings; there was also the issue of sex, or the lack of it, thereof.

To be quite truthful, it wasn't as if he had been having loads of sex before his drunken vow. A few liaisons on Tinder and Bumble in the previous six months could hardly be described as excessive, but from the moment that he had declared to the world that he wasn't going to have any dealings with the opposite sex, he suddenly became obsessed by it. Like the man said, what you can't have, you want more, and to make matters worse, this new found priapism had merged with his mild OCD, so now, any time he spoke to a female, from the girl in the sports shop bringing him a pair of trainers to the woman's voice at the call centre negotiating a new deal for his mobile phone, it provoked truly terrifying images and craven desires Furthermore, he was masturbating as if his life depended on it, and when not in the safety of his locked bedroom, he seemed to find himself permanently in the disabled toilets at his work. Twice in the morning and sometimes three times in the afternoon, his sexual urges had now gotten so bad that on one particular occasion he'd actually run around a blind member of staff who was heading towards the rest room, so that he could get one in before his tea break, resulting in loud bangs on the door and a complaint to the management. Pubs, hotels, even the Gents of the National Gallery, on one occasion, when he was unexpectedly aroused in Leicester Square were now all up for grabs, as Luke sought desperately to satiate his constant desire to cum. In fact, the only conveniences, he didn't frequent were those in McDonald's or places where there were lots of kids, but this was hardly a noble act, thought Luke, to himself, as he stared blankly at a multi pack of Munster Munch on a shelf in front of him, and tried not to weep. For a moment or two, the crazy face on the outside of the packet, seemed to sympathise with his plight, and he was just about to reach up and grab it for further engagement, when from just behind him, a soft voice suddenly interrupted his tortured thoughts and made him stop and turn around.

"Oh hiya, aren't you that guy from that video? Oh, you like Munster Munch? Me too, soooo old school," said the young woman, walking forward and giving him a big friendly smile, while Luke stared back with genuine terror in his eyes. Only a few days earlier, he had been approached in a similar fashion by a young woman in a coffee shop in Hammersmith, whereupon she began screaming that he was a disgusting male and a fascist, resulting in him having to flee the premises in some distress and without getting his beloved caramel Frappuccino. Now they had followed him to his crisp sanctuary, Luke's thoughts lamented as he took a quick step back and hoped he wouldn't have to leg it again.

"Err, yeah, my mum used to get 'em," replied Luke anxiously, as he tried to establish if she was friend or foe.

"Oh, mine too. Those pesky Gen Xers, it's all nostalgia with them, isn't it? Rhubarb and custards, Branston pickle."

"Angel delight," chipped in Luke now feeling a little less threatened, but still remaining vigilant just in case it was another social activist ruse.

"God yes, you'd think they'd never left the eighties, wouldn't you? Oh, I'm Petra, by the way," said the girl holding out her hand.

"Err hi," he replied, returning a limp handshake.

"I saw the video you did."

"Oh."

"It was cool," said Petra.

"You think?"

"Of course, I like a guy to stand up for himself."

"Really?" replied Luke a little surprised.

"Oh definitely. Too many men just keeping their heads down these days, you know terrified of Me Too."

"Oh, okay."

"You looked a bit drunk though," said Petra.

"Yeah, I was."

"So, you're still not going out with women then?"

"Err, well, err…"

"No?" she enquired again.

"Err well, I'm a…" replied Luke, as Petra now quickly moved around him to grab a packet of Yoshoi sweet chilli and lemon pea snaps from the shelf, while the fragrance of her scent, mixed with the conditioner in her hair, now hung in the air beside him. He couldn't remember, the last time, he'd been this close to a female, and he wobbled slightly on his feet, as this complete attack on his senses made Luke fear that he might actually pass out.

"You really shouldn't deny yourself Luke, and it was so sexy when you stepped in for that girl," continued Petra, with a cheeky smile.

"Oh, err, okay."

"And women love a gentleman you know," she added, smiling again before she placed a scrap of paper into the palm of his hand, and then slowly walked away. Luke's head, now hardly moved an inch as his eyes followed her all the way down the aisle, until she disappeared from view, and after taking a second to catch his breath, he looked down at what was sitting in his hand.

It was her phone number.

He wanted to ring it now.

She was hot, quirky and incredibly sexy and surely nothing was worth missing out on a girl like that? his thoughts demanded until the memory of his insane vow of celibacy reluctantly dragged him back to reality again, and he grimaced once more. There was only one thing for it, he thought, and after grabbing a packet of jalapeno and cheese double crunch beer chips from the shelf, he immediately exited the supermarket in the direction of the nearest Wetherblakes pub and the familiar sanctuary of a disabled toilet to consider his problem some more.

The handle of the door felt cold, as he grabbed it with his clammy hands, but thankfully it was open, and sliding inside, he swiftly locked it behind him before quickly unbuttoning his jeans, and then standing in the bright light of the convenience with his cock in his hand. Of late, his wanking fantasies had started to resemble a Marvel movie, where any moment, a cast of thousands might turn up, which was obviously, more than a little off-putting, but now, Luke decided, it would be different. Yes, today, it would be just him and Petra, and so after closing his eyes, he started to imagine kissing her slender neck in his bedroom while she slowly moved her hand under his T-Shirt and he could smell the conditioner in her hair again. It felt so real, and he could almost taste her kisses, while his body tingled with so much desire, that at one point, he was forced to open his eyes again, only to notice a calendar of upcoming events fastened to the wall of the toilet, informing patrons that every Tuesday was Mexican Night, where you could purchase a Chicken Fajita, Taco, Quesadilla and a drink, all for £7.99.

That's pretty cheap, thought Luke, and he immediately made a mental note to keep Tuesday evenings free from now on, before the memory of Petra's deep brown eyes and the delicate shape of her face brought all of his focus back to the matter in hand again. Now all he could hear were her little sighs in his ear, and as she purred "Women love a gentleman, you know," he continued to kiss her sinful lips and was just about move his hand over her gorgeous breasts, when an angry face that dwelt in the dark recesses of his mind suddenly burst through the bedroom door, making Petra scream out in terror, as she quickly dragged a quilt over her body to preserve her dignity.

"Women love a gentleman? Do they? That's nice," cried the voice.

"Oh, grow up, Luke, it's just a compliment," snapped Petra.

"Is it?"

"Yes, you idiot."

"No, it's not! It's expectation, its control, it's everything I've been talking about, and it's not on" confirmed the voice.

"Are we gonna fuck or what?" demanded Petra now folding her arms in irritation.

"Not sure."

"Right then, piss off!" she screamed, fixing Luke with a final stare from her beautiful eyes, before disappearing into the ether with a packet of Yoshio pea-snacks under her arm.

What the hell!

Now he couldn't even go for an innocent wank, without his rebellious thoughts sticking their bloody oar in! his mind screamed, as for the next few seconds, he laboured to bend his erect penis into his tight boxer shorts, so he could finally release himself from his disabled hell and scramble out onto the high street again.

What was going on? Was he going mad? He desperately hoped he wasn't and in despair, he lit a cigarette and marched away from the pub, before glancing down at his phone again, only to see more posts from the ironically named Vaughan 2Lose, i.e., Born to Lose, a pod-caster and self-styled male activist, who had been bombarding him with messages of support, ever since his You Tube outburst. Normally, Luke would ignore, these kind of people as they were always too shouty, to make any sense, however, despite his initial reservations, he had to admit, that there was something very different about this guy. For a start the picture on his twitter feed was of a woman called *Gloria Steinem*, who Luke later found out was a celebrated feminist, and had been at the forefront of the Women's liberation movement in the 1970s.

"She's my all-time hero, because she didn't take any crap," Vaughan had declared on one of his regular podcasts, which Luke listened to now and again and when the on-line activist wasn't hurling abuse at the Men Going their Own Way brigade, "You call your mother a bitch, do you, twat face?" he was preaching about the need for men to be emotionally self-sufficient and to stop looking to women to sort out their problems, all the time. He seemed intense and reminded Luke of the kind of man who might spend a week sitting on the top of a crane dressed as Batman to make his point, but on the other hand he was smart, funny and had a kind of street wisdom that really appealed to the more curious side of his personality.

"Men need to wake up."

"Masculinity is a gift not a curse."

"There's a meeting this Thursday, Luke. We want you there, we need you there."

Luke palms started to sweat, as he stared down at the last post again and wondered what to do next. He definitely needed help, and maybe this guy had a solution, he thought, and so after hesitating for a second or two, he decided, in sheer desperation, to reply to the tweet.

"Where's the meeting?"

"Back of the White Hart pub in Harlesden, 7.30 pm, wear something beige."

"Okay. C U there."

For some reason, Luke now started to breathe a little slower, and feeling a little less on edge, he pulled apart the packet of beer chips that he'd been holding, before ramming a handful into his mouth.

They smelt of cock.

In the confusion, he had forgotten to wash his hands. Yuk, he thought, as he popped another crisp into his mouth and then wandered off towards the nearest tube station.

Chapter 6

"This is the female century, and we shouldn't be afraid," declared the man standing behind a small wooden table, as bottoms moved uneasily on plastic chairs while a sudden cough from the middle row merged with a distant roar from a football match being shown in the back of the pub. Tentatively, Luke moved forward a little in his seat to get a better look at the man who had been flooding his account with tweets for the last month. He had half expected a "big fat twat" with an unkempt beard and a Judge Dredd T-Shirt, and not a six-foot, slim, good-looking, guy aged anywhere from his mid-forties to early fifties, dressed in a very cool blue three-piece suit, and, as a result, immediately reprimanded himself for falling into the trap of thinking that anyone who spoke about male empowerment was automatically a loser. However, appearances are designed to deceive reasoned Luke, and therefore remained delicately poised on the edge of his chair at the back of the room, ready to bolt, at the first sign of anyone declaring all women were bitches, or shirts being ripped off in some north- west London version of Fight Club.

"So why do I say that? I hear you cry," continued the speaker, now strolling around the table to the front of the audience. "Because you might justifiably say, oh no, no, you've got it wrong, son. With all the crap men have been getting recently, Me Too, Toxic Masculinity, Male Privilege etc, men should be afraid, very afraid in fact: and of course, you'd have an excellent point. Women are indeed on the rampage. Re-defining relationships, laying siege to old established institutions, beating up men four times their size in action movies; it's a credible concern, I grant you. But then again, my friends, maybe we should take another look, you know, just to provide a little bit of balance, if you will. For the last 9,000 years or so, ever since some smart-arse discovered intensive farming and because of our superior upper body strength for ploughing, men got to do all the interesting stuff, like running the joint, while women stayed at home to look after the kids; there has been a certain one sidedness at the heart of the human experience. Frankly it's as plain as the nose on your face and any fool can see that for millennia, anyone with an XX chromosome has, routinely, been beaten, ignored, side-lined, burnt as a witch, locked up for hysteria, patronised, objectified, did I mention repressed? 9,000 years of looking out from behind velvet bars, living out lives of servitude and boredom, and except for inventing etiquette and beer, making the discovery of DNA possible and not getting any credit for it and having the odd exciting affair, nothing really to report. I mean, admittedly, a few women have fallen between the cracks, Eleanor of Aquitaine, Ada Lovelace, Harriet Tubman, Rosa Luxemburg, Kylie, but in the main, it's been a bit harsh and a little dull, to say the least.

Now, I can see immediately, from the look on your faces, that you've heard all this kind of talk before? Yeah, yeah, boring, clichéd woke nonsense, mate. Men are evil scum, the world would be better without us, blokes are just programmed to subjugate women.

Whatever!

Exhausting innit?

But then again comrades.......

Not too many women have ordered the destruction of empires, written the Barbados slave code of 1661 or organised the Holocaust, have they? I mean, not too many women have gone out on mental shooting sprees cos life has been just a little bit unfair to them? or tied up and tortured men to death in dirty dark cellars in the middle of a forest dressed up in their mother's dressing gown, because no-one gave them a cuddle when they were a kid? It's not really what women do, is it? Because let's face it chaps, there's a pretty good reason why men are usually portrayed as the bad guy, because until about half an hour ago, most of the time, we were. C'mon, we all know this. Yes, yes, we have created great beauty, the Pyramids, E= MC2, the first Massive Attack album, but also there has been a cost, and as much as we stomp about in the manosphere bemoaning the fact that things aren't fair for men today, deep down in our soul, we also know that, over the course of time, we have kind of taken the piss. We have, haven't we? Don't believe me? Just think about what life was like for your average woman, as recently, as the last century, say about 1910. Endless child birth, no money of her own, couldn't even vote. Okay, men did all the dangerous jobs, still do, but given the choice, I know which sex I'd rather have been" stated the speaker plainly, now placing his hands on hips, as he looked out into the room again for a few seconds to see some of the audience nod their heads in resigned agreement, before suddenly he produced a huge grin and then clapping his hands together so loudly, that it startled a very muscular man in the front row, he started to speak again.

"However! Fear not, Mon Braves! There is no need to feel down-hearted or full of self-loathing for the multitude of transgressions committed by men since the dawn of time, because, quite frankly, who gives a toss anyway, try shaving once a day; for I bring good news, in fact I bring incredible news! This might well be the female century alright, but it is also a great opportunity for us, men that is, because Me Too, the apparent scourge of masculinity everywhere, may not be the absolute disaster that everyone is saying or signalling the end of man; it could actually save our lives. Literally, and rather than criticise the movement, we should get down on our knees and worship Tarana Burke, the original leader of Me Too by the way, or Ashley Judd, because she is totally gorgeous, and lay garlands of flowers at their feet. They have saved us brothers, they have saved us because now, now, NOW we can get our asses out of the most mental contract ever agreed by anyone, EVER! Worse than Dr Faust's deal with the devil, worse than Ronald Wayne selling his 10% share in Apple in 1976 for $800, worse even than Winston Bogarde signing for my beloved Chelsea and playing twelve times in four years and getting 40 grand a week for the pleasure. In fact, the worst deal ever made, in the sum total of human existence on this planet. Gentlemen, if you please, cast your eyes over in this direction and regard with me, this poor bastard for a moment," now instructed the speaker, quickly turning around to press a key on a laptop sitting on the table behind him, before pointing his finger towards a nature programme that was starting to play on a white projector screen hanging down from the ceiling of the room.

"This, my friends, is a male bird of paradise. Now watch him closely, because although he usually hails from Papua New Guinea and Eastern Australia, as we will come to see over the next few minutes, he might just as easily come from Canning Town or Cairo. Notice, he is making a nest. In fact, he spends three days doing this. A little twig here, a few leaves there. Look at the attention to detail. He is meticulous, everything is swept clean, immaculate. No Ikea for this boy, he's been down to John Lewis! Its flawless, spotless and pristine. A wonder to behold. Now why, I hear you ask, is he putting all this effort in? are his mates coming over to watch the game? is his dear old mum popping around to pay a visit? Not flipping likely. Be lucky if he emptied the bins if they were turning up. No, my friends, there's a particular reason why this male bird of paradise is hopping around like a fucking nutter and here it comes now. Yes, you've guessed it, it's a female bird of paradise. Hello to you!" announced the speaker now saluting the screen with his hand, while everyone in the audience leaned forward to get a better look.

"Yes, here she is, just had a few cheeky white wine spritzers with her besties down a Pitcher and Piano and now she is ready to make her grand entrance. Watch as she walks in and has a good look around. Mmm…what do we have here then? not bad, not bad, liking the twig feature and yes nice use of the leaves, but hold on a goddamn minute! That lampshade shouldn't be there! the frying pan isn't Le Creuset! and oh my God, can you believe it?! he is wearing black shoes with jeans! Now, watch closer, my friends; watch as he starts to realise something isn't quite right, and the more disinterested his intended looks, the more he starts to brick it. Oh no, he says to himself, she's gonna leg it. I can't let that happen; I've spent three fucking days on this crap! What do I do? Oh no, she is looking away again. I've seen this before on the Eden channel, she's bound to piss off now. Bollocks! Think of something you fool, think of something, quick, quick! Now my brothers, watch what he does next. Watch as he starts to hop up and down in manic desperation. He is going absolutely mental, it's incredible, and now he has no choice, no choice comrades, but to pull out the big one - and voila! He has just expanded his head to ten times its normal size! Ten times, my muchachos!" the speaker repeated, quickly stopping the action, as a frozen picture of a male bird of paradise with a seemingly massively inflated now head stared back at the audience.

There was some nervous laughter from certain parts of the room, while the speaker stared back at them with a pained look on his face, before shooting his finger back towards the projector screen again.

"That is us! That is us! It is us my friends. Inflating our heads, looking like absolute idiots, showing no dignity whatsofuckingever, in a vain and desperate attempt to impress a female. Okay, to be fair, he is actually doing that inflated head thing with his wings, but whatever it is, that is us! And you know the sad thing is, a few seconds later the female bird of paradise pisses off anyway. She wasn't impressed, so all that bullshit was for nothing. Yes, I can see your heads nodding. That is soooooo us, isn't it? Hopping up and down, looking like complete and utter fools, hoping we will get chosen or find the one or our soulmate or life partner or whatever nonsense gets knocked out these days in polite society. Don't you see Mes Amis? THIS is the contract we can break! Our ancient obsession with trying to impress a female. For 200,000 years we have kicked, punched and hacked our way, towards the hopefully approving gaze of a woman with varying degrees of success, and even today in our so-called glorious age of self-awareness, it's still going strong. This is why the manosphere has gone apeshit over the last decade or so. Chads, Red pill, White pill, Black pill, Simps, Cucks, Beta, Sigma, Alpha Males, Soy Boys, Edge Lords, Lookism, Aggrieved entitlement. Seriously?! After 200,000 years of evolution and civilisation, and we are reduced to this?! Gentlemen, I say to you, that we are not birds of paradise, we are intelligent men capable of changing our destinies and now in 2025, because of beautiful, gorgeous Me Too, we can finally step out from all this madness and finally breathe."

"But surely that's the deal? I mean, that's what we are programmed to do, isn't it?" interrupted a large man in the second row, with a shaven head and a Brentford F.C tattoo on his forearm.

"No! It is EXACTLY what we are programmed to do. However, that doesn't mean that we have to do it, does it? I mean we don't fly or have the lung capacity to plumb the depths of the oceans, but we do, don't we? So why can't we defy nature on this one? observed the speaker, as another member of the audience, quickly raised his hand to make another point.

"Yeah but, it's central to who we are, isn't it? I mean how would that even work?"

"Well, it has to, my friend, or frankly we are doomed," replied the speaker, now walking slowly around behind the desk before looking out into the audience once more.

"Okay, let's look at it another way. Who do you think was the greatest philosopher of the last 300 years, possibly of all time? Descartes? Kant? Satre maybe? Perhaps, they were all giants in their field; but you be wrong my friends. It is, in fact, Peter Crouch. No, no don't laugh, I am deadly serious here. Peter Crouch, was once asked what he would have been, if he hadn't been a premiership footballer and he immediately replied - a Virgin. If he couldn't kick a ball, six-foot, seven inch, not so attractive, bit awkward, working-class background Peter Crouch, would have probably ended up in warehouse somewhere in Northolt, wearing a uniform that was a bit short on the sleeves, whilst making roll ups in his tea-break, and not married to one of the most beautiful women in Britain. You see, in that little sentence, in that witty reply, The Crouch sussed it, cos in general, a woman will only ever be interested in a man who is on her social level or above, but never below. NEVER! That's the absolute truth. It's even got a name. Hypergamy! I'm serious. Look at any study you like on the subject and it will tell you the same thing. It's a building block of the universe. A Duchess never goes out with a Brickie, well only if she fancies a proletariat bunk up, but nothing more, certainly not to settle down and have kids with, that's for sure. In fact, you could probably safely argue, that there is no such thing as love at all, as women are programmed from birth to find the right genetic profile. That's why so many middle-class women freeze their eggs, when there are billions of available men out there. That's why there are so many female tick-lists. It's sad but true. Women are the sex selectors and are looking for the best genes, the best outcome, so most men are completely fucked from the start. You're all familiar with the Pareto principle I presume? the so- called 80/20 rule, yeah? 80% of women are chasing 20% of the men? Well, that's a fact dude; and it's not only a fact, but it's pretty much a provable fact; I mean we see it all the time, don't we? How many girls have you dated or tried to date and they wished you had a bit more money, had a better job, were a bit taller maybe? It's nature's dirty little secret and what's more, whether they like to admit or not, most women are disappointed in men. It's true. They are hard wired to be critical of anything with a dick, because they're looking for the right one, aren't they? This is why 40% of men never have the chance to have kids and pass on their genes. With women, the figure is closer to 20%. I'm telling you, it's brutal out there and to bugger things up, even more, men also have to be all knowing, all conquering and stinking rich and if we are not, our women, in the main, will look at us every morning like something they have stepped in. Interestingly, this is also why many women would rather be in harem with a man she does want, than in a relationship with one she doesn't. It's true, I'm afraid, and to drive this point home even further, note that this behaviour doesn't go both ways. Not too many rich, powerful, unattractive women ending up with Chris Hemsworth, is there? Don't see a lot of that, do you? which by the way, also explains why so many men are pissed off about their wives and girlfriends earning more money than they do. Yeah, that little one. The one that no-one really talks about anymore. Maybe happens to some of you here? Of course, most men pretend to be really cool about it, you know I don't mind, I celebrate her getting more money than me. But you sure about that, dude? Have a good look behind the eyes. It's still a massive problem, lurking under the surface, as society and biology whispers in their ears, 'Surely, it's the wrong around, isn't it?' And there's a point, because in general, most women, in that situation, do eventually lose respect for their men. How many house-husbands have ended up being two-timed by their more successful wives? I'm ashamed to admit it, but I've shagged a few. But is this the fault of women? Of course not. Women are not the enemy here, my friends, it's just a dirty biological game that we have all been forced to play for the last couple of hundred thousand years, but now, at last, we can change all that.

Comrades, we have nothing to lose, but our gold neck chains!

We don't have to fear the female century, we don't have to fear it all, because there is no threat to masculinity, none whatsoever; and furthermore, we can destroy the Patriarchy, whatever the fuck that is, cos if don't you seek women's approval, why would you need to control them? Finally, men and women can be equal, as the good Lord intended. Equal pay, equal stake in society, equal opportunity to self-actualise our lives. Job done. No more hostility between the sexes and no more irate 2nd or 3rd wave feminists discussing hegemonic masculinity, so anyone called Raewyn or Andrea is now looking for a new job. Brothers, there is a revolution coming, but it's not the one that everyone thinks. It's not the liberation of women, but rather, it's the liberation of men; and you know it would be quite nice, if we actually started one for a change, cos most of the revolutions in history, the good ones anyway, the French, the Russian, the Civil Rights movement, were all started by women, until, as usual, the men piled in afterwards to take all credit, and sent anyone in a skirt back home to put the kettle on. Christ, no wonder they think we're dicks. You know, in the end, my friends, I hate to say it, because I love his music, but I think James Brown was wrong, he was so wrong. It's not a man's world any more and more importantly, it doesn't take a woman to fill it!" declared the speaker quickly raising his hands in the air, to indicate the end of his speech, while a small ripple of applause from the audience, struggled to compete with loud shouts from the bar next door, as West Ham had just equalised.

However, as the speaker moved forward to sit on the end of the desk to take questions from the floor, many of the men in the room started to look around a little bemused, as it seemed they had just been instructed to avoid women, when in truth they had probably turned up, secretly hoping for a few tips to get closer to them. However, in contrast, from the back of the room, Luke was beaming with delight and clapping his hands in wild approval.

It was like the first time he heard Definitely Maybe by Oasis or watched The Sopranos. He got it. Way before helping that girl in a club or "pissed up" rants on YouTube, he'd always felt that something was wrong, out of synch. Why should he buy the first drinks? Be great in bed? or adhere to the thousands of little unwritten rules that society deemed appropriate before, during and after going out with a woman? He had previously assumed that he was just contrary or it was a bi-product of his mild OCD, but now someone was saying what he actually felt, and like a singer who was articulating a slice of your life in three minutes of perfect pop, Luke somehow felt, as if he was reborn. Soon the noise from the back of the pub subsided, and a forest of hands immediately shot into the air to clarify what the speaker had just said.

"So, can we still have sex with women?"

"Of course. As long as it's consensual,"

"What about meeting the one?"

"The one is usually someone who is the most like you. So, meeting the one is basically an exercise in masturbation."

"Aren't you really just a misogynist?"

"No. I'm a misogamist – I hate relationships."

Luke had so many questions, but, as usual, didn't feel confident enough to ask, so he just listened, a little awestruck, as the speaker continued to expound his view that the old romantic narrative was one of the most dangerous ideas in modern society, before quickly adding that this wasn't the fault of women, as ultimately it was only men could sort out men's problems. For the next hour or so, the questions kept coming from the audience and the debate continued in a similar vein until the speaker glanced down at his watch, and started to bring the meeting to a close.

"We do this every second Thursday, so please keep coming and tell your friends, and tell your friends to tell their friends, because we need to keep talking, to keep thinking about this. It's about our future happiness, chaps," said the speaker slowly moving around the table, as he started to disconnect his laptop, before raising his head again to add, "oh and remember, women are not the enemy," prompting the regulars to grin at the speaker's usual sign off, while everyone, including Luke started to make a slow progress out of the room. He had briefly considered going over to have a chat, but deciding it was probably easier to send a congratulatory message later via twitter, he was just about to walk out of the door, when, "Mr Lysistrata, I presume" suddenly stopped him in his tracks.

"Err, pardon?

44

"It's an old play by a Greek bloke called Aristophanes, about a group of women who wanted to stop a stupid war, so they decided to stop having sex with their men until they did," declared, the speaker now shooting out a hand.

"Oh right, did it work?"

"Absolutely. Women are unstoppable when they work together. I'm Vaughan, by the way, It's Luke, isn't it?"

"Err, yeah."

"Yeah, I recognised you when you first came in. You look better in the flesh," said Vaughan, now standing back with a smile.

"Oh thanks."

"Sat at the back, ready for a quick getaway, just in case we were a bunch of nutters?"

"Err, ha, err, no, no."

"It's okay, I would have done exactly the same myself," replied Vaughan with a grin before quickly adding, "Fancy a drink?"

Luke had originally intended to slope off and catch the 220-bus home, as he had work the next day, but like seeing a great band that no-one had ever heard of, in some obscure pub and then getting a chance for a chat afterwards with the lead singer, he suddenly decided that this was an offer he really couldn't refuse.

"Sure," he said, and so after Vaughan did a bit of tidying up and collected his laptop from the table, they made their way to the front of the pub, where they joined five or six other men, from the meeting. Predictably, everyone recognised Luke from the newspapers, and after slapping his back in congratulation for his late-night rant and then fighting to buy him a drink, everyone settled down to chat away about the unfairness of his treatment by a one-sided mainstream media etc, until by about 11.30 pm most of the crowd had drifted away, leaving just the two men.

"Fancy another? It's open until 2 am," Vaughan suggested with a big grin, as two Cuba Libras suddenly appeared, and Luke smiled before the conversation quickly turned to more weightier subjects.

"Is gender a social construct?"

"Can you be a millionaire and still consider yourself as working class?"

"Are dogs overrated?"

It was a blast, especially for Luke, who was usually, more acquainted with talking about whether Ronaldo had been better than Messi or if the American version of Storage Wars was better the English one. Of course, Luke loved his mates, especially Fitz and Ravi, but with them, the trivial was always king. Of course, every now and again, you might have a chat about the unfairness of society, or some random injustice where someone you knew might have been unfairly stopped by the police but this would be swiftly countered by "did you see that badger online who put a condom over its head". *Keep it light, nothing too serious* was the mate's mantra, which hitherto, Luke had always subscribed to, but now, especially, in the light of his more recent experiences, he found that he was no longer satisfied with that kind of approach. So, they shouted, disagreed, drank and shouted some more until it was time to leave and they lurched out of the bar to exchange mobile numbers and drunken hugs on the pavement outside.

Now, as the cold night air stung his nostrils, and he watched Vaughan stagger off down the Harrow Road in search of a three-piece chicken dinner with burger sauce, for a moment or two, Luke sucked on a cigarette and wallowed in a kind of empty bliss, until without warning, an overwhelming feeling of elation suddenly surged through his body. It was, as if, he had just been released from a kind of malign gravity, which, without his knowledge, had been gently holding him in place for years. Was this Freedom? Awareness? or maybe too many Cuba Libras? Who the hell knew thought Luke, but whatever it was, it felt amazing, and now pacing around and sucking manically on his cigarette, as he waited for his uber, Luke also felt something else for the first time in his twenty- seven years.

He felt purpose.

Chapter 7

Alex McDonald sat in the front seat of his car and shook his head, as he wearily dragged his thumb across a new crop of news stories that had just appeared on his phone.

Trump pushes over elderly Mexican after rally at US border.

Strawberry Jam cures dementia.

French couple face jail over sand theft from beach.

Nothing was happening.

Brexit? The odd pandemic? Putin invades Ukraine? What a load of overblown bollocks! well maybe not the invasion of Ukraine which had some kind of validity, but rest of it was nothing more than irritating noise. Culture wars to give assholes something to do, rather than watch porn all day, and a bit like Theoretical physics or Art, it seemed as if all the exciting stuff had been done years ago, sighed Alex before chewing on his gum and watching the trouser leg of his bodyguard, flap in the morning breeze. It was hardly Cambodia in the seventies or the Iran/Iraq war in the eighties, was it? Back then, millions died and no-one gave a fuck, while today all they do is give a fuck and no-one really dies.

Except from boredom, thought Alex as the ping from another random news item forced him to glance down at his phone again.

Man punched in face in Dundee.

"Christ," he mumbled to himself. *When I was a kid, if a man hadn't been punched in the face in Dundee, then that was news*, he mused as he brought the phone closer to his face, to give the unfortunate victim a cursory look, before quickly deleting the post with an angry jab of his finger

He missed the old days, before social media, identity politics and the bloody cancel culture, when you could drive in a straight line, get things done. Back then, no-one gave a toss if you cut a few corners or stamped on a few heads, just as long as you got the job done. Now it was all role models and influencers;

47

wankers who couldn't find their arse in a pair of jeans if you paid them double, and when they weren't desperately trying to "out-woke" each other with stories of giving quinoa to food banks, they were bragging about their new basement conversion in Fulham, which had just put twenty percent on the value of their house.

Suddenly, he wanted a drink.

A tall glass, Stolly vodka, squeeze in the lime, pour on the tonic, hear the ice crack. He could taste it. Maybe chop out a few lines, light a B & H, listen to some Roy Ayers. Alas not now, not ever, and quickly raising his eyes to the ceiling of his car, he let the urge ravage his body for a few seconds longer, until unable to endure any more, he leaned forward to switch on the car radio, to maybe listen to another voice, other than the one barking inside his head.

"Oh my god, this is priceless. So, women or girls as you like to call them, cos of course females are just pretty little things to prance around for our own amusement, aren't they? but aside from your obvious sexualised image of women, you think that girls have taken things too far and its time men stood up to them. Okaaaay. Can I just ask one question? What century are you living in, Dean from Basildon?" asked the radio host.

"Look Jake, I ain't saying that am I? I'm not saying that women are sexual objects. All I am saying is this, Luke or whatever his name is from that YouTube thingy has a point, doesn't he? Men are getting a hard time these days."

"Oh, of course, women have the upper hand in all things, don't they? I mean let's not forget the gender pay-gap, the enormous disparity in domestic responsibilities, the rise in domestic violence, objectification, marginalisation" continued the radio host.

"What?" replied the caller, a little confused.

"Yes, it is overwhelming, isn't it? so anyway, Dean, please tell me, before I forget, why you are wearing sunglasses on the tube, again?"

"Because I don't want to look for female approval," confirmed the caller.

"Really? Ha! Well, I'm sure the women of Basildon are beside themselves with grief now. Oh no Dean doesn't want us, anymore. Oh Lordy, our lives are over, forever! So, for the benefit of our listeners, Dean here, is following this puerile trend started in South Korea I think, where men are now wearing sunglasses everywhere they go, and I think the general idea is, so they don't get accused of harassing women or some such nonsense. In fact, I am looking at a picture now, it's on the show's website, if you can be bothered to have a look, and it resembles a really bad version of Reservoir Dogs. Yes, not very good, bit sad if I am being honest, and if you look at their twitter-feeds and other related web-sites, it's actually quite difficult to establish, what they are all so angry about in the first place. So, Dean from Basildon, can you enlighten us, if you haven't already walked into a lamp-post, wearing your nice new sunglasses? What are you actually angry about, fella?" enquired the radio host.

"The way men get treated, that's what. Where it's one rule for bir...I mean for women and then there's one rule for us. It's unfair, and so that's why I am wearing sunglasses, in protest against how men get treated."

"Nearly said the B word there, Dean. I think we know where you are coming from, fella? So, let me ask you something else. Did someone dump you Dean? Is that it? Did some nasty woman not want to hear any more of your sparkling repartee? Is that it, darling?"

"You can laugh all you want, that's all you lot do anyway, isn't it? Anything a straight bloke does is always wrong innit? I mean all you gotta do is just look at the ads on the box. Every one of them makes men look stupid. You know, I saw one the other day where a bloke was rewarded for being able to put a cover on a duvet, it's pathetic."

"Okay, can I ask you something, in all seriousness Dean?"

"Err yeah, alright," said the caller.

"Can you put a cover on a duvet?"

"You see this is what I mean, of course, I can! Your attitude is just typical, Jake. Everywhere you go these days, if you're a man, you're somehow automatically an idiot."

"Well, I'm sorry to say this Dean, but a lot of men are idiots, and I'd like to include myself in that category too. Look seriously, do you think women actually care what you do, or how you act? They don't. Seriously fella. All they care about, all they really want, is freedom and equality and the ability to walk down the street without being harassed or assaulted."

"Well, they'll be all right now, then, won't they?" replied Dean, with a laugh.

"Oh brilliant! We can't harass you or belittle you, so now, we'll just ignore you instead. That says a lot for men, doesn't it? You know Dean, it sounds to me like you don't have one original idea in that head of yours. I could read word for word what you have just said off a thousand of these *Men Going Their Own Way* websites or from this guy Luke Casey and his twitter boys. You are part of a cult fella, and a very dangerous one at that, from the sound of it. Jesus, give me strength; you know, Dean, if I was you, I would take off those sunglasses and maybe see the light for a change. For millennia, men have done unspeakable things to women and it's still happening today, if you hadn't noticed. Pick up any newspaper and there'll be a case of a woman being killed or beaten by some man. So, rather than complain and whinge, don't you think, it's time that men just put their silly egos to one side for a moment and apologised unreservedly for what they have done and are still doing and maybe listen to what women are saying to them. About male privilege, unfair pay, coercion, gaslighting, sexual assault. You know, Dean, I used to think like you, be a low-level misogynist. Didn't treat my wife too badly, gave flowers to my mum on Mother's Day, watched the odd Rom-Com without complaining too loudly, but at the same time enjoyed sexist banter with the chaps down the pub. Wow she's hot, she's a B word, I bet she likes a bit of this or that. I was pathetic really. But then I stopped, talked to my wife, read a few books, embraced the whole Me-Too movement and it was great. I didn't feel any less male or under threat, in fact I felt the complete opposite. It was liberating, progressive even. So, if you listen, really listen Dean, then maybe you might just learn something instead of throwing all of your toys out of the pram. God, I bet Dean voted Brexit, and look what a bloody disaster that was! It's the same old, same old, I'm afraid. Well, my friend and the other misguided fools who think like you out there, sorry to inform you, but it's the 21st century, in case you hadn't noticed; and so instead of moaning about what you have lost and how you are being treated, maybe you should think about joining us. It's not so bad actually, the nasty women won't bite, and we can all just get along nicely, equally, side by side, you know smiling at each other, moving forward together and without the bloody sunglasses and without idiots like Luke bloody Casey and his pointless posse! Anyway, I'm Jake O'Callaghan, and I will be right back after the break, to talk some more about this. You know the number, 0635-70-70-777, so come on give me a call, tell me what you think."

Luke Casey?

Alex vaguely recalled something from a front page a few weeks previous, and now switching off the radio he quickly tapped the name into his phone and stared at the face on his screen. Young, nice looking, should be in Ibiza not trying to change the world, he thought as he swiped through the headlines and the subsequent fallout after his infamous late-night video rant.

Now, as he chewed harder on his gum, Luke's face started to creep under his skin, and suddenly, he could feel his heart beat faster in his chest. It reminded him of the seventies, and bolshy men, who lived on a diet of nostalgia and prejudice, and nearly brought the country to its knees. Thank God those clowns were swept away by Maggie and Blair, and the working classes had been anesthetised with Reality TV, cheap clothes and a nice little vigil when something awful happens?

God, the Poor loved a vigil, didn't they?

Princess Diana dies or a kid gets stabbed, don't find out why it happened, just light a few candles, tie some flowers to a wire fence, and then chuck in a few little Teddy Bears for good measure. Sometimes he wished that he'd had shares in the company that made those little teddy bears, he'd have made a fortune, he thought, as a cruel smile slipped onto his weathered face, before he brought the phone closer to his face and stared into the eyes of the young man again.

"Who the fuck are you?" his thoughts demanded, and as the blood began to race excitedly through his veins, he suddenly sat upright in the seat of his car and chewed harder on his gum. Now, finally, there was something he could really get his teeth into, other than gammon Brexiteers or second-rate Dictators. Not since Saddam and all the Iraq bullshit had he felt this alive and in celebration, he popped another piece of gum into his mouth, before picking up his phone from the seat next to him and bringing it close to his ear.

"Hey Pippa, sorry to ring you on a Sunday, but be a love and get me Jake O'Callaghan's private number, will you? yeah Jake O'Callaghan, the radio chat show guy, yes, him, lovely, quick as you can." said Alex before quickly ending the call and tossing his phone onto the seat again. Now, outside, the leaves started to lift from the pavement and placing his hands on the steering wheel, he stared blankly out of his car window for a moment, until in the distance he noticed an old lady button up her coat and turn her back against the early autumn wind.

Chapter 8

Luke bounced a pen off his bottom lip as another email appeared from Amber Jones, requesting that all his spreadsheets should be completed by close of play today, or at the very latest, first thing tomorrow morning. Normally, he would have been given a week to do them, but not now. More work, more supervision, more criticism. "Oh, hi Luke, we have been monitoring your calls, just routine you understand, but we think that you should use a less familiar tone with the clients, they are not your mates down the pub, are they?"

No Amber, they're not, well spotted, thought Luke, but then again, he shouldn't be surprised. He hadn't taken their advice, he hadn't apologised for his late-night rant, and although it would have definitely been the sensible thing to do, the image of his contrite, pleading face on a YouTube video, quickly persuaded him otherwise.

Say sorry and move on, wasn't that the drill?

Over the years, like everyone else, Luke had watched hundreds of Film stars, Singers, Influencers, and Politicians eagerly genuflect in front of the altar of media outrage. It was expected, demanded even, so why shouldn't he do the same? Why was he so special? Then again, why should he? He wasn't some highly paid Actor with agents, and brands to consider, he was in recruitment for God's sake. Okay, he had been famous for fifteen minutes or so, but that wasn't through any design of his own, and as far as he was concerned, his only crime was stating the bleeding obvious.

Well, obvious to him anyway.

Maybe he should give back the Michael Bublé CD? Luke thought with a little grin, before he looked up from his desk, and tried to avoid another icy stare from Nicole.

Not that it mattered anyway.

The media circus had long departed from his front door and aside from the odd furious look in the street or cold shoulder from a work colleague, he was pretty much back to being a regular Joe again.

Except, of course, he wasn't, was he?

That meeting in Harlesden, had changed everything for him, and now instead of watching box sets or UFC until four in the morning, most evenings he could be found on his twitter account tapping away about changing the narrative of being a man in the 21st century and annoying the hell out of anyone who thought having a penis was some kind of medical condition.

"Take control of your life."

"Stop seeking female approval."

And of course, "Women are not the enemy."

Vaughan provided the ammunition and Luke fired the shots; it was a beautiful combination.

Fitz called it a Bromance.

Maybe it was, but then again why couldn't two straight men enjoy a close friendship without it being seen as sinister or the subject of ridicule? Two women do it and its, called *Sex in the City*, or *Thelma and Louise*, but two men? and it's a bit unclean, possibly sexual. *Fucking gaslighting if you ask me,* mused Luke as he gave his pen another nibble.

However, if he was to be totally honest with himself, he would have to admit that he had been more than a little dazzled by his new friend. Vaughan was just about the most amazing person that he had ever met, and seemed to live his life, with an unapologetic swagger, unafraid to feel or say things, that most people of his own generation could only read about.

It was like Vaughan was still living in the 1990s, and for Luke, this was the ultimate decade. In fact, it was just about his favourite period of all time and he constantly bemoaned the fact that being born in 1998, he had been too young to hear the first Suede album when it came out, go to illegal raves, or see Pulp at Glastonbury, when you could still bunk in and it wasn't £400 a ticket. In contrast, Vaughan had lived through all that, and so talking to him, in drinks after work or walking around the Tate Modern, was like having your own personal Samuel Pepys chatting in your ear, but instead of stories about the Great Fire or the Plague, he spoke of late-night parties in a field in Hampshire with Spiral Tribe or doing lines of cocaine with someone vaguely famous in the Good Mixer pub in Camden Town.

Obviously, Vaughan 2 Lose, wasn't his real name and after a few pints one afternoon in a bar in Kensal Rise, he had revealed to Luke that he had taken his nom de plume from the lead singer of an obscure band called *Department S* from the eighties, and was in fact called Danny Ward, born and bred in a West London estate. From there, after being expelled from school at 15 for punching a teacher, and working in a string of "no hope jobs", labourer, barman etc, he'd finally ended up as a club promoter in the early nineties, engaged in what Vaughan liked to call "a bit of this and a bit of that", before pretty much going legit, by the mid noughties opening a string of businesses including a florist, and an online gambling site.

It was a classic CV of a chancer from that period and Luke suspected that "doing a bit of this and a bit of that" probably involved some drug dealing, which Vaughan alluded to now and again in his conversations, but as he said "growing up skint in eighties London, no-one was offering me a job in Goldman Sacks, so you had to make your own luck."

Luke couldn't really disagree with this logic and instantly seduced by his new friend's street wise philosophy, it wasn't long before he was not only referring to himself online, as *Mr Lysistrata*, after the Greek play of the same name, but was also using *Donita Sparks*, the feminist lead singer of the nineties band L7, who famously, once threw her used tampon into a crowd at the Reading Festival, as the picture on his twitter account. Of course, it was Vaughan's idea, but this didn't matter to Luke, as there was no ego or no competition involved. Vaughan just wanted to share what he knew and as a young apprentice, Luke was hungry to learn.

He'd also started to read again, as *The Ragged Trousered Philanthropist by Robert Tressell,* the working class Das Kapital, *Meditations by Marcus Aurelius*, the Stoic handbook and *The Female Eunuch by Germaine Greer,* the feminist classic were all thrown in his direction by his older mentor, while songs such as *Keep on Keeping on by the Redskins, Ship Ahoy by Marxman, Poison Flour by Dr Alimantado,* and *The System by Tom MacDonald* were played on repeat on his Spotify playlist. It was overwhelming, to say the least, but as Luke sifted through this new cultural input, he started to regard the world in which he now found himself, built on trickle-down economics, the judgement of social media and risk averse parenting, as more than a little pointless.

Now Luke wanted desperately to abandon the present paradigm of the working class being considered unconfident, and unintelligent, and re-visit a time, as in the latter part of the last century, where kids from the local estate read Clockwork Orange, Plasterers loved John Coltrane, and the currency was intelligence again. However, this seemed like a distant land now, and recalling his own youth, he shuddered, as he remembered applauding an advert where a well-known bank "advised" people of his own age not to use silly email names such as "Luckyboy 52", or something similar, if they wanted to get ahead in society. At the time, the message had made total sense to him, i.e., make the most of your opportunities and be the very best version of you, but ten years later, he wasn't so sure. Now it seemed like control or even worse, a dark, insidious voice muttering inside your head, designed to make you shut up and conform, and probably half the reason why his generation felt so impotent and lost in the first place. *It was such bullshit* his thoughts snarled and he continued to chew on his pen and stare at another boring spreadsheet with increasing exasperation until the buzzing of his mobile phone on the desk in front of him, dragged him back to reality once more.

"Yeah," said Luke, sharply.

"Oh, is this Luke Casey?" replied a woman with a well-spoken voice.

"Yep."

"Oh great, hi. I'm Rachel from *Sisters Doing it for Themselves*, it's a mid-morning chat show for women."

"Okay," replied Luke, narrowing his eyes and wondering if this was yet another wind up from Ravi.

"Yes, well, I hope you don't mind me calling but I got your number from a friend of mine who works at the Daily Sun," said Rachel.

"Err yeah, that's okay, no problem," replied Luke still not completely sure that he wasn't being set up.

"Err, great, well ever since your intervention in the club, which I thought was great by the way and then of course, your You Tube video which provoked, well global interest."

"Yeah, but that was weeks ago," interrupted Luke.

"Yes, it was, but people are still talking about it, which is amazing, of course and because you're the one who started all these fantastic conversations, so to speak, we were hoping that you might consider coming on the show next week, and being our special guest," said Rachel.

"What?!" exclaimed Luke.

"Yes, I appreciate, it's short notice, but I think it would be really good to hear your side, you know, now everything has calmed down a little, you know get the male angle."

"The male angle?" replied Luke, now realising that the call wasn't a hoax, and quickly walking off his section to continue the conversation in the corridor outside by the lifts.

"Well, yes, from the male perspective," said Rachel.

"The male perspective?"

"Yes, from a guy's point of view."

"Err, yeah, err okay, err can I get back to you," replied Luke, hesitantly.

"Yes, yes of course, you obviously need time to think about it. You have my number?"

"Yeah, I have it on my phone," confirmed Luke.

"Ok lovely and please, please get back to me, I think it would be amazing," gushed Rachel.

"Yeah sure, err thanks," replied Luke, swiftly ending the call, and for the next thirty seconds or so, he leant against the corridor wall, and listened to the opening and shutting of the lift doors, while he desperately searched for an oasis of calm within himself, until inevitably his mind started to bark at him again.

He couldn't go on a TV show, not after everything that has happened? No chance! His mum would kill him! The Press turning up at her work unannounced again and then contacting her friends for a comment. It had been a nightmare, especially after his little online rant. No, it wouldn't be right, thought Luke, folding his arms, as a man with very bushy beard edged past him in the hallway with two cups of coffee.

Then again, if you wanted to get your point across, television was still the best place to do it.

What would Vaughan say?

He knew what Vaughan would say.

"Do it, geezer, you know it makes sense. He who dares Rodney."

However, Luke wasn't sure.

He definitely needed more time to think, and so returning to his desk, he quickly emailed Amber that he had a family emergency, before deciding to head for the only place, other than the crisp aisle in Sainsco's, where he felt safe. Ravenscourt Park.

Ever since his youth, it had always been his bolthole, a place to work things out, when the world had proved too much to bear. *Why didn't he have a dad? Why was he anxious all the time? Why did he support Queens Park Rangers?* Yes, this would be the perfect place to go, and work out what to do next decided Luke, and so after exiting the office, and dodging the traffic on Hammersmith Broadway, he soon found himself marching purposefully up the Dalling Road, towards his destination. Ten minutes later, he had arrived close to the park and was just about to cross over the road, when out of the corner of his eye, he saw a figure walking towards him and for some reason, he didn't cross, but instead, remained on the pavement. For another twenty yards, Luke continued at a normal pace, until, just as he was about to pass by the person, he slightly turned his head, and looked straight into her eyes. Now, in an instant, all thoughts of television appearances, male empowerment and more or less everything else instantly departed from his mind, as a little dazed, he stumbled on for a few more steps, and then like a dumbstruck Orpheus, he couldn't resist looking back, only to discover, to his horror and delight, that the object of his desire had done exactly the same thing.

She stopped. He stopped. She smiled. He tried to smile, and now frozen in time, they stood like ancient statues, while the early rush hour traffic thundered past their blank faces before the young woman finally decided to break the spell.

"So, were you checking me out?"

"Actually, I thought you were checking me out," replied Luke, nearly laughing out loud, that he'd actually managed to blurt out something vaguely resembling the right thing.

"Oh right. So, this isn't street harassment then?"

"Probably," replied Luke anxiously, as he inched forward another step, and quickly remembered that the government had only just recently made it an offence to approach women on the street, without their consent, so he could, technically, be breaking the law.

A pause. A smile, a pause, a little shift forward again, until the young woman took the initiative again by declaring "God, I hate all this crap, it's Katie, by the way," and then walked the final few yards with her hand extended.

"Luke," came his subconscious reply, as his eternal clamminess dampened the softness of her hand.

"Err, I've been running."

"No problem," she replied, smiling, as Luke could now feel the tension pour through his helpless body like an unwelcome shower of rain.

He wanted to leave and he wanted to stay.

Why did the women he really fancied always make him feel like this?

Maybe Men should be able to sue for this level of emotional intrusion, he thought, as his mouth now ceased to function, and his eyes pleaded for help.

"You live around here?" asked Katie breaking the brief silence yet again.

"Askew Road."

"Oh, I know it."

"You?" asked Luke.

"Around the corner. Stowe Road."

"Oh, I know it."

"Cool. Err, maybe she should swap numbers," suggested Katie, after another awkward pause.

"Yeah! Definitely!"

"Great," replied Katie with a smile.

"Err, cool, err, so where's my phone, oh yeah, here, okay, err, so what's your number? I will just, err put it, err, in my phone, erm," replied Luke now feeling like Hugh Grant in *Four Weddings and a Funeral*, except a more cockney version. Nervous indecision in a posh accent sounds plausible, almost endearing, but in a native London accent it just comes out as thick, and so after three attempts and praying that she didn't give him her email address as well, because then he would have definitely passed out, he finally typed her number into his phone.

"Well, okay, I have to be off, things to do, you know," said Katie.

"Oh right, me too," replied Luke.

"Well bye, text me if you fancy," added Katie, smiling again, before she quickly turned around and walked off towards Goldhawk Road, so in seconds she was completely out of sight.

Only five minutes earlier, Luke had wanted to sit down and watch the ducks in some dirty water, and agonise about going on a TV morning chat show, but now he didn't have a thought in his head, well except Katie, of course. Suddenly he was gripped by an urge to run, and run until his heart could finish singing its song, and so after shooting an enormous smile towards the grey metallic sky, Luke quickly jammed his hands deep into his pockets, before marching straight past the park and in the general direction of he didn't have a clue.

Chapter 9

Jake kissed his wife on the lips, before quickly looking over her shoulder at his two boys sitting at the table in the middle of the kitchen.

"Hey you two, what do we say to lovely mummy for making a yummy breakfast?

"Thank you, lovely mummy, very much for making our yummy breakfast," chorused back the two boys mechanically, as they giggled together at their morning ritual.

"Wow! said with such sincerity, chaps! You'll have me crying next," replied Jake as he leapt from the arms of his wife to run over and mock fight with his sons, until he suddenly stopped and raised a closed hand to his mouth to make a pretend cough.

"Er hum, and what do we do now?

"Go and play Fortnite," shouted back Edward, his eldest son.

"No, we certainly don't. What we do is get off our lazy derrieres and do the washing up. It's not a hotel, boys have to do half the job as well. Come on, you're six and nine now, so no excuses, c'mon, up," ordered Jake, before walking back to the arms of his wife as his sons began to slide off their seats and move reluctantly towards the sink.

"Why don't you do the washing up, then too, Daddy?" enquired Otis, his younger son, as he squirted the washing liquid into the bottom of the basin and started to run the kitchen tap.

"Because Daddy has to go and be brilliant on his radio show darling, and if he does the washing up, he will be late." replied Jake's wife as she wrapped her arms around her husband, and he moved forward to kiss her lips again.

"He's right, you know," said Jake, crinkling his nose.

"Anyone can clean a few plates, darling, and anyway I will have plenty for you to do when you're back tonight," his wife whispered, into his ear while she lifted her heels out of her Birkenstock sandals and fixed him with a sinful look.

"Mummy and daddy are being silly again," the boys chirped, and clattered the cereal bowls against each other in the basin, as the radio host laughed and then after reaching around his wife to lift his bag from the back of a chair, he suddenly took a step back to take a good look at his family, for a moment.

God, he loved them.

He loved them so much, that sometimes he felt as if his heart would collapse under the sheer weight of his happiness. *How the hell could Luke Casey and all those Neolithic reactionaries think that men and women shouldn't be together?* his thoughts demanded as he stared into the gentle face of his wife and kissed her one more time until an image of the W3 bus stuck in mid-morning traffic, demolished his little moment of contentment and he launched himself towards the front door with a shout and a wave.

Seconds later, he had hustled through his front gate and making very sure not to stray into anything that might remotely resemble a swagger, he strode off towards the bus stop, hoping that most of the Crouch End rush hour would have passed by the time he got there, and his journey to work might not be as hellish as it usually was. It was only a ten-minute walk from his house, but as he was running a little late, he started to pick up a good pace, and was just about to take a left on to Ferme Park Road, when a ping from the depths of his jean's pocket broke his rhythm, and he wrenched out his phone to give the screen an irritated look.

"Been listening to your show, think you are utterly brilliant, we should meet ASAP to sort out this Luke Casey business – Alex McDonald."

Now, in an instant, Jake came to a complete halt in the middle of the pavement, and after nearly colliding with a woman behind him who was pushing a double buggy of twins, he quickly raised a hand in apology, before bringing the phone closer to his puzzled face.

What? The Alex McDonald?

No way.

Surely someone was fucking with him he thought as he began to slowly walk off towards the bus stop again, while, all the time, glancing down at the message on his phone. Conrad maybe? an old friend from school who was always messing about or maybe Marcus? Then again it wasn't really their style, he reasoned as a long equine face, with thinning strawberry blonde hair suddenly spread across his mind, like a poster from a 1950's horror film.

Everything about Alex McDonald disturbed Jake.

Aside from being the Cardinal Richelieu of Fleet Street, issuing edicts against those who displeased him and ruining the careers of anyone foolish enough to get in his way, he had been the virtual architect of the Iraq War, pushing the agenda way before even Blair had got his sticky hands on it. He'd made it happen, and like Goebbels, he was a master of swaying millions to a bad idea.

Jake had hated the Iraq War with a passion, it was his bugbear, as his wife would say, and although he had gone on the million-man march back in 2003, and got into a few heated debates in the pub after one too many pints of real ale, eventually, like the rest of the country, he had hidden in his beer and talked about what Saddam did to the Marsh Arabs and left it at that. In reality he wouldn't know a Marsh Arab, if he sat on the end of his nose, but at the time, it had been enough to camouflage his shame, and if that wasn't enough, there was also the small matter of the suicide of the army whistle-blower, Sergeant Kelly David, who had leaked to the press, that the war had been unnecessary and based wholly on fabricated intelligence. The establishment predictably closed ranks and denied everything, but the subsequent pursuit of a rank-and-file soldier through the courts and the media by the media mogul, until the poor man blew his brains out in his kitchen, while his two young children were asleep upstairs, was vicious even by McDonald's low standards.

In fact, many times, in the privacy of his own home with friends, and after a few glasses of red, he had declared that if Alex McDonald had died in 2002, in all probability, the Iraq war would never have happened and Sergeant David would still be alive today. So, what the hell did he want? Jake's thoughts hissed as he sat down in the back of the bus and listened to Night of the Living Baseheads by Public Enemy on his headphones, while he tried to think of something else.

Then again, he did say that I was brilliant, no utterly brilliant, and this was from the man who turned a sub-standard hack like Pedro Griffiths into a global superstar, hosting morning news shows and doing interviews with the rich and famous. Maybe, he could do the same for me? and I am twenty times more talented than Pedro fucking Griffiths, interrupted an increasingly enthusiastic voice inside Jake's head, as the W3 jolted to a stop, and he stepped off to walk towards Finsbury Park underground station. Okay, McDonald was a bastard, but then again so was everyone else who got anywhere in life. He was just better at it than most people; and anyway, hadn't Jake done the same kind of thing himself? whispering into the ear of a powerful producer that a good friend of his wasn't really up to it, before taking over his show and becoming the biggest star on chat show radio. That was the way of the world, wasn't it? he thought squeezing onto the Piccadilly line, and staring at a poem on the wall of the carriage, that seemed to say something about forgiveness.

Anyway, McDonald was completely awful, was he? reasoned the radio host, before standing aside to allow an older lady to take a vacant seat. His campaign, a few years earlier, for a new EU referendum had been first rate, nearly swung it, while he'd also read somewhere that the billionaire was now the head of a charity helping people with mental health issues and depression. Fair enough, after what he had done to Sergeant David, that was like putting Gary Glitter in charge of the nursery, but then again it did show some regret on his part, thought Jake with a smile, and he continued to think positive thoughts about Alex McDonald for the next few stops, so by the time he reached Holborn, he had completely rehabilitated the media mogul in his mind and was nearly wetting himself with anticipation, as he charged up the escalators of the station to get a better signal on his phone.

"Yes, it is getting ridiculous, let's meet." he typed with excited fingers, as he loitered by the entrance of the underground station amidst the late rush hour crush, and was just about to send the text, when something deep inside his lizard brain urged him to think again. Now, as he stared down at the screen of his phone, Jake was suddenly reminded of that scene in a thriller, where the hero opens the door of a basement and everyone shouts, *don't go down there, you dick.* Yes, it was risky. Involving someone like Alex McDonald in your life was always complicated, but then again what wasn't? Jake's thoughts confirmed, and so after taking a deep breath, he mouthed "Fuck it" to himself before pressing the send button on his phone, and the message on the screen, turned a light shade of blue. Now the radio host tried to force out a celebratory grin, but still feeling a little uneasy, he turned around much too quickly to exit the station, only to find himself crashing straight into a very tall man, wearing dark sunglasses and a T-Shirt declaring "Women are not the enemy" on the front.

Chapter 10

"So, ladies, we have a very special guest today. A very nice young man, polite and extremely good-looking "announced Cheryl, clasping her hands together and smiling into the studio camera.

"Yep, I can vouch for that, very tasty,"

"Yes, well calm down, Lacey dear, we don't want a repeat of last Friday night, or in fact any Friday night with you and any men under the age of thirty, do we?" interrupted Cheryl, as Lacey just shrugged her shoulders and smiled wickedly into the camera, to general laughter from the mainly female audience.

"Or indeed under twenty-five, naughty girl," reprimanded Cheryl, before she looked into the camera again and continued with her introduction. "Anyhoo, as I have said, we're very lucky to have with us today a young man who has recently grabbed the headlines, not once but twice in fact. First, for stepping in bravely to help a young woman getting harassed in a club in London, and in the process becoming the new understated hero to millions of women across the globe, receiving plaudits from such celebrities as Hollywood actress Portia Ramone and the best- selling author Mercy Folarin-Thomas, and THEN! for releasing a late night You Tube video, where he said that, despite all his good deeds, he didn't really want anything to do with us girls anymore," declared Cheryl as loud jeers and boos rang out from the studio audience, before the chat show quickly placed her hands out in front of her to calm everyone down.

"Ahh, now come on, ladies, let's be fair, come on, he's allowed to change his mind, isn't he? and what's more he has nearly five million followers on twitter, which is more than all of us here put together, especially you, Lacey, I think you had about three at the last count, but anyway, his video has caused a worldwide sensation, with men from Huddersfield to Hong Kong, following his lead and saying "No to women." Yes, we have seen all the pictures online, haven't we? Men with sunglasses on the tube, wearing T-Shirts with all sorts of slogans on them; it's all got very heated and now it's even being referred to in the press as the new He Too movement, so whatever you think about it, let's give a big Sisters are Doing it for Themselves welcome to Luke Casey everyone."

Why the hell had he agreed to this? was Luke's first reaction as he, blinked into the studio lights, to make his way towards a large table in the middle of the television studio and tried not to throw up. Then again, he only had himself to blame. He didn't have to tell Vaughan that he'd been invited on the show, he could have kept quiet and said nothing, but, in the end, he couldn't help himself and once he had told his older mentor, he then spent the next three days being bombarded by texts, until completely exhausted, he had finally come around to the idea.

Of course, he wanted to make a change, and like most men, he was sick of women either haranguing him or sticking up for him, but God in heaven, there had to be an easier way to make your point than this, he thought, as he moved towards the outstretched hand of Cheryl White, one half of the eighties pop duo White and Black, and now main host of the most popular chat show for women on TV, and nervously took his seat. Soon, the applause mixed with a few boos, started to peter out, and as he stared back at the familiar faces of the four panellists, for a brief moment, he feared that he might just turn around and run out of the studio, until in a faltering voice, he forced out the first line that himself and Vaughan had agreed on.

"The man at the head of the table? Bit patriarchal, isn't it?"

Immediately there was laughter from the audience, before the panellists looked at each other with a little surprise, and Cheryl leaned across with a serene smile, to place her hand on Luke's arm.

"Now don't get ahead of yourself there, sweetie, you are not in charge here or anything, we just want a good look at you."

"Yes, peer into your eyes and see what makes you tick," laughed Alicia Garrett, ex radio 1 DJ from the noughties and host of the online dating show, *Swipe Right.*

"Anyway, what's all this patriarchy malarkey? My Alfie came out with that the other day, and he's only flipping 12,". protested Lacey Wright, ex-glamour model and star of *Lacey's World*, a highly successful show about her life and her former boyfriends.

"It means that men are in charge, Lacey dear," replied Cheryl.

"Ahh that's nice," replied Lacey.

"Well not really," shot back Judith Robson, ex ITN news-reader and long-time feminist activist.

"Okay, okay, let's not get on to that quite just yet. We'll have plenty of time to fight the gender wars later, Judy love," replied Cheryl, before she turned her head to look at Luke again.

"So, thank you so much for coming, and I just want to ask, before we start, are you fully recovered from that awful incident in the club, love?"

"Err yes thanks, all good now, erm you know still a little pain here and there, but otherwise, okay," replied Luke, now briefly returning to his pre- rant charm, as the audience "aaahed" their sympathy, while shapeless faces with hate filled eyes barged into his thoughts once more.

"Oh, that's good, I really hope they find the horrors who did that, I really do, but anyway, let's forget about them and talk about you and the big stir you have caused recently. Oh my God! So where do we start pet? Right, first up, can you tell me and the millions of adoring females out there, after all your heroics, helping that girl against those two bullies, why did you go and blow it, with a rant at four in the morning after too many Bacardi Breezers ? I mean, why, cupcake? What's the problem? Why don't you want to go out with us anymore? What have we done love?" asked Cheryl.

Vaughan was spot on, Luke thought as a hush now descended over the studio audience and he looked back nervously at the expectant faces of the panel, except for Judith, who looked a little bored.

This would be the first question.

They had discussed a few options; keep it light, so you can get your point across in a gentler way, and it has more effect, or maybe just turn the question back on them.

They had decided on the latter.

"Well, why not," replied Luke, as the audience half laughed at his response, while the panel narrowed their eyes in confusion and leaned back in their chairs.

"No, I'm being serious here, why should I go out with a woman?" added Luke.

"Err because it's fun," replied Alicia hunching her shoulders, as if the answer was blindingly obvious.

"So's snowboarding," replied Luke.

"You can't compare going out with a woman to snowboarding," replied Alicia.

"Maybe you're doing it wrong, love," added Lacey, to more laughter from the audience.

"Oh, don't be silly, there are lots of reasons to go out with a woman, Luke," declared Cheryl, throwing her arms in the air.

"Ok name them," replied Luke, now relaxing a little.

"Err, well someone to be with, you know someone to talk to," offered Alicia, again.

"You can get that from good friends," said Luke.

"Yes, yes, you do, granted, but it's not the same, is it? Flipping hell, we've got a right one here. C'mon girls, what reasons are there to go out with us? There must be loads? asked Cheryl, turning back towards the studio audience for some help.

"Commitment," "Intimacy," were shouted back enthusiastically, while one girl at the front screamed "Sex" to more general laughter.

"Yes sex," shouted Lacey to huge cheers and clapping, before adding, "As long as it's good."

"There we go. Men have to be super-hot in bed, yeah?" replied Luke looking straight at Lacey, while remembering Vaughan's previous advice, *they will do you on sexual inadequacy, but don't take the bait.*

"Well, it definitely helps," replied Alicia as the audience erupted into laughter again, while Luke shook his head and started to forget his nerves.

"What about the woman being good in bed?"

"Well, it's a morning show, Luke, I don't think we need to go into all that," replied Cheryl, as a few boos were now heard from the audience.

"Anyway, I reckon, it's the man's job," replied Lacey to more laughter from the audience.

"Is it? Exactly! This is the problem. Female expectation of men," replied Luke.

"I think she was joking there, Luke," interrupted Alicia.

"You sure about that," countered Luke.

"I don't think we expect anything, except of course, common decency and respect," broke in Judith.

"And the odd mini-break to Barcelona," replied Alicia to some more laughter.

"Ooh I love Barcelona," replied Lacey.

"I disagree. There has to be more than boy meets girl," countered Luke, sitting a little back in his chair, and relieved that he had remembered to get another pre-agreed line in.

"Oh no don't say that," replied Lacey.

"Actually, he could have a point," replied Judith.

"Okay, okay, you don't wanna go out with a woman, so would you rather go out with a man then chuck?" interrupted Alicia, now accentuating her northern accent to further laughter from the audience, as Luke suddenly felt his body tense at the question. He knew they would ask him this and Vaughan had prepared him over the last few days, by asking him time after time, if was he gay, in mock interviews. However, like most of his generation, Luke had absolutely no problem with the idea of being gay or indeed being gay himself for that matter, but when the question was asked by a woman, it somehow felt like a judgement or an awful accusation, so he immediately hit back.

"No, I am not gay. You know I get a lot of this. So, I don't want to go out with a woman, therefore I must be gay. It's ridiculous, and for the record, is there anything wrong with being gay, by the way?"

"Err well of course not," replied Alicia.

"So why use it like a weapon then?" asked Luke.

"She's not, she is just asking a reasonable question," replied Judith, stepping in to defend her fellow panellist, who was now looking a little bit flustered and wondering if she had damaged her brand with the LGBT community.

"Well, I disagree and by the way, if I was a woman saying all this, you would be shouting about how empowered and independent I was, but as a straight guy, there has to be a problem? I don't get it." said Luke, shaking his head.

"Well, that's why we are here, petal? To persuade you that the love of a good woman is everything," interrupted Cheryl, trying to bring the conversation back to a happier place, while the camera caught Luke smiling and Cheryl patted his arm again.

"Lovely, that's what we like to see, lots of smiles. So, Luke darling, ooh I've just noticed, what nice curly hair you have. Have you seen it, girls? lovely, anyway back to what I was saying. So, from what I understand, there is a particular reason, why you don't want to go with women, is that right."

"Yes. I don't want to spend my life, living up to female approval, I don't want to play the game," replied Luke. sitting forward in his chair and deciding to ignore the blatant objectivization by his host.

"Approval? I don't understand," replied Cheryl looking genuinely confused.

"Trying to live up to what women want of us, what they want us to be."

"Ahh, okay, so you and your followers are all exercised by the idea that..." replied Judith sitting up and suddenly looking interested for the first time, in where the conversation was going.

"I don't have followers," corrected Luke.

"Well okay, people who agree with you then. So, you say that you don't like the idea of female approval or whatever, and in your video, you referred to women as genetic snobs, is that right?" probed Judith.

"Yes, that's right."

"All women?" continued Judith.

"Yes, all straight women."

"So, men have no part in this then, it's just women who control the process," continued Judith.

"Well, you choose us, don't you? I like him, but I don't like him. You are the sex selectors in nature," explained Luke.

"But this is natural, isn't it? That's been going on for thousands of years, how does that make us snobs? I mean what about toxic masculinity? replied Judith folding her arms."

"What about toxic femininity?"

"That's ridiculous, you can't compare the two," said the ex-newscaster.

"Can't I? What about Jada Smith?"

"Well, that was a long time ago and remember it was Will Smith's choice to assault Chris Rock," replied Judith.

"Oh, right? But you don't say that when a man is accused of gaslighting a woman do you? If she does something violent or irrational, then it's nothing to do with her and he is completely to blame, isn't he?" replied Luke with a grin.

"Actually, I quite like a little bit of toxic masculinity, as long as it's not too toxic," laughed Alicia.

"That's not funny, Alicia," reprimanded Judith, before turning all of her attention back to Luke again. "Anyway, these are isolated incidents, because if you look at every statistic, every study, it's men who degrade women, assault them, control them. Every day, around the world, hundreds of women are killed by men, and this is our fault now I suppose?"

"Now, now Judy love, Luke's not one of those, he's one of the good guys," interrupted Cheryl.

"Oh, am I? one of the good guys? You see that's what I mean. Men spend all day trying to be the good guy, because that's what you want until, of course you decide that you want something else," shot back Luke, now feeling increasingly irritated by Judith's remarks."

"You know, this is soooooooooo boring, just sounds like the old trope of women never being satisfied yadda, yadda, yawn yawn, but this is not the case at all. In reality, women are sexualised by men, objectified by men, and if we protest in anyway, then we are shouted down and pilloried. Forget choosing, Men have the most important thing, and that is power," declared Judith.

"Well, if we are talking power? then I think all of you here, have more power, wealth and influence than most of the men in this country, "replied Luke, now looking around the table at all the panellists.

"Oh, I really don't think so. I think the gender pay gap proves that," countered Judith.

"You're wrong actually. If you look at the stats, these days women are more likely to get a college education than men, more likely to get a decent job, and the only real gender gap happens either, at the top of society, with all male CEO's etc, who are a tiny, tiny proportion of men or if a woman decides to have a baby. In reality, it's men who are more likely to get killed at work, commit suicide, be a victim of homicide, go to prison, be homeless. Look at any study you like, most of the people at the bottom of society are usually men. You can see it for yourselves every day if you want. Who is living on the streets? Usually a man, isn't it?" declared Luke.

"Well, as usual, I think that's a giant simplification. Women are overwhelming the victims wherever you look, I mean…."

"Well, yes, yes, Judy love, I can see your point, but getting back to something else for a second, I just want explore what Luke said on one of his podcasts recently. You said that Chivalry is the smiling face of the Patriarchy, which is a very nice line by the way, but what you did, helping that woman in the club, that was chivalry, surely?" interrupted Cheryl, turning to face her guest again.

"No, I was just helping another human being "corrected Luke.

"So, no chivalry at all," replied Cheryl.

"Nope, why should we? If we want to be equal, all that has to go. No buying all the drinks on a first date, no opening doors, no air kissing."

"No air kissing?!" declared Lacey, as boos rang out from the audience again.

"Why should I? I don't air-kiss a man, do I?" replied Luke.

"Well of course, the COVID thingy stopped all that for a while, but that seems a bit extreme cupcake, if you don't mind me saying so," replied Cheryl as the boos grew even louder.

"Yeah, too right, I think men SHOULD buy all the drinks. Do you realise how much it costs to look like this? Tanning, shaving your bits," declared Lacey, now motioning towards her famously well-proportioned body.

"Then don't shave your bits," suggested Luke.

"Ooh I couldn't do that," replied Lacey.

"She has a point, Luke; it does cost a lot for women to look good," replied Alicia.

"C'mon, you don't dress for men, you dress for each other," said Luke with a grin, as he suddenly recalled another quote from Vaughan.

"I do?" volunteered Lacey, putting her hand in the air.

"No, you don't,", replied Cheryl laughing.

"Actually, no we don't, he's right, we compete with each other," agreed Alicia.

"Exactly," said Luke.

"Fair enough, we can probably do without the chivalry, I suppose, there's not much of it around these days anyway, but what about babies, love? Last time, I looked, we did need men and women getting together for the, you know, future survival of the human race! Just a small point, but I thought I'd bring it up," declared Cheryl now throwing her hands in the air again, to more laughter from the audience.

"Like we need more people? The place is packed already, if you hadn't noticed," replied Luke folding his arms tighter across his chest, and remembering that this was the one thing, he and his older mentor disagreed on.

"Well, actually the birth-rate is going down, so we need more people, not less," shot back Judith from the end of the table.

"Okay, okay, that's probably another topic for another time, but what about relationships dear? we can't get rid of them, now can we?" broke in Cheryl, looking directly at her guest again.

"I think we can. Most relationships have an end date, don't they," replied Luke, ticking off another phrase, himself and Vaughan had agreed to include somewhere in the interview.

"Oh god, here we go," replied Alicia.

"Excuse me," gasped Cheryl.

"Well, love is a drug, isn't it? It's even got a name. Oxytocin, it bonds us together and it lasts about 18 months," explained Luke.

"I wish. Doesn't even last that long," replied Alicia shaking her head.

"Exactly. It's a drug, like heroin or cocaine," added Luke.

"No dear, you can't compare love with something awful like heroin," replied Cheryl.

"Why not? You get hooked the same. At the start everything is perfect, and then when you break up, it's terrible, like withdrawing from a drug."

"Well, sometimes," replied Cheryl.

"A lot of the time. Look, love doesn't conquer all," said Luke to more boos from the audience.

"Yes, it does," protested Lacey, now looking more than a little outraged.

"Well, I just think men should appreciate women," interrupted Cheryl.

"Really? Why? Why should we appreciate you? God, I really hate that kinda of crap, you know," said Luke, looking around the studio and getting increasingly more irritated by the responses of the panel.

"Careful Luke, this is a mid-morning show, little kiddies," warned Cheryl.

"Who cares. You know little kiddies or at least male little kiddies should know this. Disagree with women at your peril. You just want me to come here, smile and joke and maybe get my point across in a subtle, unaggressive manner, don't you?" replied Luke, now looking straight at the chat show host.

"Well, what's wrong with that," asked Cheryl.

"But that's your way, not my way. It's like we are replacing a patriarchy with a bloody matriarchy. I don't want to live in a Bonobo republic," said Luke, sitting back in his chair.

"Ahh, so now we finally have it. Typical. You can't have complete control over our minds and bodies anymore, so now you think, the only other option for society is hordes of women will now start storming about controlling men. Bonobo republic? female Bonobo monkeys controlling the males with sex, that's your fear, isn't it? God, it's so predictable," replied Judith shaking her head.

"It's true though, isn't it? Be that perfect guy. Try harder. Make us like you. Be a better man for us. You know what they kept saying to me after I helped that girl? oh you're one of the good ones. You've even said it on here, today. Really? So, Man equals bad, and woman equals good, does it? It's totally insane," said Luke getting redder in the face and now sitting up in his chair.

"Well of course, you're entitled to your opinion, Luke, but if you don't mind me saying so, I don't think you will get a girl with that kind of attitude," cautioned Cheryl.

"Really? fantastic, where do I sign, err cos if you haven't noticed, I don't really want one, do I? Yeah, so for all those prospective girlfriends out there, I'm skint, I have a really small penis and I won't buy you dinner. I think those are the cardinal sins, aren't they? Oh, yeah and sorry I don't have nice shoes," said Luke now folding his arms.

"I like a man with nice shoes," added Lacey.

"Okay, okay, look, lets calm down here, for a second, please. I think I finally see the problem. What you are missing Luke, if you don't mind me saying so, is….", said Cheryl, desperately trying to bring the conversation back to a calmer place.

"Jesus, are you gonna womansplain it to me? Am I a bit thick?" interrupted Luke shaking his head and leaning forward on the desk again.

"Well in these matters, men can be a bit slow on the uptake," replied Cheryl.

"Imagine if I said that about a woman? You would all freak," spat back Luke.

"No, no, look, look, just wait for a second. What I think women are really saying is: we want to be treated properly and fairly but also, we want a bit of romance too. You see Luke, I mean what's wrong with that?" explained Cheryl.

"Everything! You can't have a win/win. If you want the total equality, you gotta lose the romance, can't you see that? You gotta work out if you want a seat on the bus or a seat on the board." declared Luke recalling another quote from Vaughan.

"Oooh can't we have both," gushed Alicia.

"No, you can't. That's the problem, innit?. You think we are scum but then you want us to love you too. It doesn't work that way."

"Women don't think men are scum," protested Cheryl.

"Don't they? Have you been on the Internet recently? Every article, every podcast, every book, every advert has an empowered woman wagging her finger at a speechless man. T-Shirts saying, 'We know our place!', every sentence you write or speak, screams that you are not happy with men."

"Oh dear," replied Lacey, folding her arms, as she sat back from the force of Luke's delivery.

"Well, it's about time frankly, after all the nonsense we've taken off you lot over the years," replied Judith now raising her voice and pointing her finger back at Luke.

"Good for you Judith. But you know I think even if we were equal, no gender pay gap, no discrimination and men and women were totally and utterly equal, I bet you anything you like, women would still have a problem with men. It would be like, err, don't like this, I think we are a bit too equal now." snapped back Luke.

"Oh, for god's sake, not again! All women are nags, permanently unsatisfied, another boring sexist trope," shouted Judith now raising her eyes to the ceiling of the studio.

"Or is it just the truth? Personally, I don't think it's worth it. A man needs a woman like a fish needs a bicycle," said Luke.

"I think you'll find that's an old quote from the sixties about men actually," replied Judith with a smug grin.

"Really? Thought it was the seventies? Shows you how things have changed since then, doesn't it? Anyway, here's the deal. We are not here to cherish you, protect you or maybe even love you. We are here to co-exist with you. Happily, if that's possible. As far as I'm concerned, you are bi-pedal female carbon-based units, end of," replied Luke sitting back in his chair again, and referencing a quote from a science fiction book that he'd recently been reading.

"Oooh that's a wicked thing to say, I think you are very disrespectful to women," said Lacey, as most of the female audience had now started to get to their feet, to shout and boo at Luke.

"I'm disrespectful? That's a laugh. Ever since I've been on here, I've been called sweetheart, honey, dear, had comments about my hair and I've had my arm rubbed a hundred times! Imagine if a male presenter did that to a woman?" replied Luke, now pulling his arm away from the host.

"It's just the way we talk, it's not meant to...." protested Cheryl.

"Isn't it? You prove my point again and again. More rules for us and none for you. Whatever we do, we're always wrong, aren't we? Always! It's a joke, bruv; and actually, what do we get out of it anyway? men that is? seriously? What? Sex? intimacy? they fade after a while. I mean look at most couples, they look miserable, stumbling about in sexless routines."

"That's not true," replied Alicia.

"Yes, it bloody is, anybody can see that. You know what we should do, we should respect each other's civil and human rights and then just leave it at that."

"That's ridiculous."

"Is it? I'll tell you what's ridiculous, Alicia, every bloody November, loads of men give up booze, grow moustaches and run around like a bunch of idiots trying to be ironic and oh so self-deprecating. Now that's ridiculous! declared Luke, recalling his own personal distaste for the Mo'vember mental health initiative.

"What you going on about now? That's for charity!" cried Lacey.

"No, it's not! Not even close! Don't you understand?! Those men are doing it so women will like them a little bit more. Seriously. They basically make themselves look like dicks, so girls will think "Oh, you're one of the good ones". Well, it's pathetic, if you ask me, cos I have been "one of the good ones", and let me tell you, it sucks arse."

"Now Luke, can you please stop," replied Cheryl looking nervously around the studio, as the rest of the women on the panel had now folded their arms again and were staring up at the ceiling of the studio to ignore their studio guest, as the jeers and boos from the audience grew louder and louder. However, Luke was now in full flow and completely ignoring the protests of the chat show host, he leaned forward in his chair to continue his rant.

"In fact, you know what we should do? Forget the booze and just give up women for a month, know what I mean. Yeah, forget the dodgy moustaches, bruv, and let's have a women-free month. Might as well, no-one is getting laid anyway, read the papers, my generation are having less sex these days, so let's glorify it. I have done it for five weeks, and its no big deal, you get used to it, so yeah let's have a women-free month then. In fact, let's have a woman-free February. Yeah, February, perfect. Poxy Valentine's Day. I hate Valentine's Day, fabricated love festival, where all you do is argue over the restaurant and get fucking grief for only buying flowers again. Why do we have to make the bloody effort? what a load of crap that is. Done deal. There you are, problem solved. I now declare women-free February," declared Luke, sitting back in his chair again.

"I have to apologise to everyone for our guest's bad language," interrupted Cheryl, looking seriously into the camera, as the audience started to heckle and jeer again.

"I thought on your Podcasts, you said that women weren't the enemy," enquired Judith, with a knowing smile.

"They're not, but they're not the bloody solution either," spat back Luke, folding his arms again.

"You know, Luke, maybe it's not women who need to be away from men, maybe it's just women need to be away from YOU!" interrupted Alicia, before causally placing her chin on the palm of her hand, to huge cheers from the studio audience, while Luke started to rise from his chair and speak again.

"Yeah right, like I haven't heard that one a thousand times before. Anyway, I don't need to be around here anymore, do I? It's like a religion with you lot innit? In fact, I know just how bloody Galileo felt years ago, standing in front of the Pope and his mates trying to explain that the Earth goes around the Sun, and no Lacey, Galileo isn't that geezer who came second in the X factor."

"Cheeky sod," replied Lacey, as the booing continued to get louder while Luke turned and stared into the angry faces of the studio audience for a few seconds, before shaking his head once more.

"You know what? This is pointless, totally fucking pointless."

"Now excuse me, young man," said Cheryl trying to grab his hand, but Luke had quickly stepped away from the table, and now standing with his hands on his hips, he began to stare directly down the lens of the camera.

"Here's the way it is. Men don't need women, in fact we are far better off without them period, and the quicker they fucking realise that fact, the better it will be for everyone in the end," and with that he pulled the wire from his ear and threw it on the table, before marching out of the television studio.

Chapter 11

"I told you, didn't I?" exclaimed Jake triumphantly. "I told you, Luke Casey was dangerous. And now we know, don't we? He's not the messiah of male empowerment, he's not some misunderstood prophet, he's not even a cheeky chappy, dodgy but "wiv a heart of gold". No folks. He's a threat. A threat, pure and simple. You know, for weeks, I've had friends repeatedly telling me, c'mon Jake, he is a good guy, stuck up for a girl in a club, didn't he? and we all have a whinge about women, now and again don't we? That's all it is, fella. Well, is it? Really? Did yesterday's appearance on *Sisters Doing it for Themselves* look like a whinge to you? Seriously? Oh, and before I get the usual 'Go Luke' brigade ringing in about "he's standing up for men", and "how most women hate men anyway", which is a such a sad joke when you really think about it, your hero was sober this time, chaps! Yes, in full control of his faculties, and not out of his face in his bedroom at four in the morning but clear-headed, and so we finally got to see, what this Gandhi of male liberation is really like.

A nasty, aggressive, angry, vicious misogynist.

A woman hater of the first degree.

Have you ever seen anything so childish, so petulant, so divisive? I watched it again with my wife last night, and I have to say, it was bad enough for me, but she was actually frightened by what she saw. It's like an address at a Nuremburg rally, she said, except this time, it's not Jews but women who are at risk, and then after reading the posts on his twitter-feed afterwards, she was genuinely fearing for the general safety of women in society. Fifty percent of society is being targeted! It's that serious, my friends, over half of the human race is being 'othered' and this is supposed to be 2025. Frankly, I am speechless, which as you know is a rare experience for me. But hey. Maybe I'm wrong? I mean, is my wife overreacting here? Am I just another tree-hugging beta male, looking for female approval? You tell me, give me a call on 0635-70-70-777, this is Jake O'Callaghan, back after the news."

Wow, that's original, you prick, compare me to the Nazis, that's never been done before, has it? thought Luke, instantly recalling Godwin's Law, where any argument in the 21st century, usually ended up with someone being compared to a 1930's fascist, before clicking off the link that he had been sent by Fitz, and then plunging his hands into his underwear, in a desperate search for some kind of reassurance. Normally, this would be a prelude to yet another erotic diversion, but after all the abuse he had been receiving since his now infamous performance on the morning chat show, the very last thing on Luke's mind now, was a wank.

Whichever way he looked at it, it was a mess, and as he lay on his bed and stared at the ceiling, his body froze repeatedly, while images of his angry face from the previous day, continued to dance around his tortured mind. Ironically, it had been the very last thing that he'd intended to do, as beforehand, it had been agreed with Vaughan, that he should do everything in his power, to avoid losing his temper, as it would dilute the message, and just make them look like those nutters online who wanted to ban contraception and get women back in front of a kitchen sink. Anything but that they had said, sitting in Vaughan's front room in Harlesden, while they had planned out in precise detail what Luke was going to say on the programme and more importantly, how he was going to say it. Well, so much for detailed planning, Luke thought as the front pages of every newspaper in the land now screamed out "Pathetic!", "No Sex February" and "It's Not a Man's World, Are You Joking?", while the Twittersphere predictably went into meltdown. The pro-Luke camp, of course marvelled at his TV performance and embraced the whole idea of no-women February, while the anti-Luke party thought he was a Neanderthal, who wanted to drag everyone back to the dire misogyny of the past.

In truth, Luke wasn't all that fussed about these comments or those from the likes of Jake O'Callaghan or Portia Ramone, who immediately referred to him on Tik Tok as "worse than a sex offender", because these were celebrities who regularly demonstrated to the world, that they had no relationship to real life whatsoever, but what really got to him now, was the support he was getting from the crazies from the other side of the argument. Men like Bobby Baxter, leader of Defending Albion, a Xenophobic hate group, who regularly targeted minorities and the LGBT community and tweeted "well done Luke, we are all behind you," or Francoise LeBlanc, leader of France First, an ultra-right-wing political party, who commented "at last a European man is standing up to the cultural Marxists and the Feminists who are destroying our society, I salute you, Luke Casey".

He had nothing in common with these people and yet they were calling him by his first name as if they played in the same five aside team or drank together in the local pub. Vaughan had instantly responded with the tweet "Piss off, pondlife, we don't need help from the likes of you", but despite this, the damage had been done. In the fragile, literal world of the 21st century, association was guilt, and where before his "chippy podcasts" had been vaguely tolerated by the commentariat, now the so-called liberals and progressives, who to Luke seemed to be as bad, as the extremists they sought to destroy, quickly piled in, as the cancel culture got into full swing.

"Where does he work?"

"What's the name of his line manager?"

"Let's boycott the organisation until they sack him," appeared within seconds of his appearance on the show, and so by the following day, it was no surprise to Luke, that he received the inevitable email from Amber Jones informing him that he was suspended from his job, with immediate effect, pending an enquiry, for "views that were incompatible with the aims and direction of the company."

Suppose that promotion is out of the question now, Amber? thought Luke as he grimly plunged his hands deeper into his underwear again, seeking further comfort from his increasing despair until another ping from his phone made him raise his head from the pillow once more. Probably more abuse, thought Luke as he craned his neck over to look at the screen, but a "Hey, was that you on the chat show?" immediately brought Luke's hands out from the recesses of his underwear and sitting up in the middle of his bed.

Katie.

Amidst all the madness of the last twenty-four hours, Luke had completely forgotten about her, and now staring intently at the text, he anxiously rubbed his cheek with his hand, as he wondered what the hell, he was going to do next.

He could say it wasn't him.

I mean they hadn't really got a good look at one another, during their chance meeting the previous week and so he could definitely say it was someone else. Then again, he would probably recognise Katie from space, and now that his ugly mug, was plastered all over every newspaper and website in the country, there definitely wouldn't be too much of chance of him getting away with that one. Furthermore, it didn't help matters, that they'd been texting for days, and although he wasn't supposed to be seeing anyone, and other than the Pope, was probably the most celebrated celibate on the planet, once he had started sending messages to Katie, he found that he couldn't stop.

For Luke, good texting was similar to a game of tennis, where you needed the ball to come back fast and an inch over the net to make it interesting, and whereas most girls, he knew, just lobbed the ball up, and sent something bland back once every three hours, and therefore when you tried to hit it back, it usually ended up over a fence for a dog to play with or some local kids to steal, this was not the case with Katie. She was like Serena Williams meets Dorothy Parker quick, witty, intelligent, and as her texts boomed back over the high part of the net, he found, that when he responded in kind, he was funnier, gentler, more himself.

Well, so much for that then, thought Luke, as now a little dejected, he picked up his phone and replied with a simple "Yeah" before slipping back onto his bed to await his fate. Usually, she'd get back to him within thirty seconds, even if she was working, but as he turned around for the hundredth time to stare at his phone, nothing came back, well except a message about car insurance and he didn't even have a car. This awful silence continued for another twenty minutes or so, until he was just about to abandon all hope and order a large shish kebab, chips, large chicken supreme pizza, onion rings, large bottle of diet coke and a large chocolate chip cookie from Just Nosh to heal his broken heart, when another ping from his phone made him look up from his bed again like a lovestruck meercat.

"No way, such a bad boy, so I won't see you in February then?"

Won't see you. That sounded a bit more positive, thought Luke, as all plans for his takeaway therapy were temporarily banished from his mind, while he eagerly tapped the screen of his phone.

"Are you sure you wanna see me, now I am the most hated man on the planet."

"Don't flatter yourself, big boy, there are loads of assholes ahead of you."

"I don't think being behind Prince Andrew is much to brag about."

"Are you sad?"

"Very."

"Poor petal, shall we meet for a drink?"

"Please! where?"

"Fancy Ravenscourt Park in an hour? we can sit on a bench, with a bottle of wine and shout abuse at passers-by."

"Perfect."

"But we must wear double denim." 😊

"Done," texted back Luke with a huge grin, and after charging about his bedroom looking for his best pair of Levi's and then borrowing a jean jacket off his mum, fifty minutes later, he found himself, on a park bench, dressed like a refugee from a Status Quo concert and clutching a bottle of Mateus Rose with the price tag still on.

Minutes later Katie arrived dressed in skinny blue jeans and a fitted jean shirt with a red scarf around her neck, and rising from his seat, he was just about to air- kiss her, before he remembered, that this was now against his new rules, and so instead restricted himself to a quick handshake before they both sat down on the bench.

"You dick," laughed Katie, shaking his hand and after taking her place beside him, she suddenly looked away for a second, while Luke glanced at the side of her face and felt his stomach tie itself in a thousand knots again. He'd forgotten just how pretty she was and as a result tried to mumble something which sounded vaguely cool until "you look handsome" and "oooh Mateus, my favourite" quickly put him at his ease. Before long, they had finished off the Mateus, and opened a bottle of Sancerre that Katie had brought with her, as they soon discovered that as well as loving Kendrick Lamar and Wolf Alice, they both liked Harry Potter, although Luke said that he might have liked the books and the films even more, "if Hogwarts had been a Comprehensive", making Katie laugh so much that her head crashed into his shoulder, so he could smell the conditioner in her hair and the faint smell of wine on her breath. Suddenly he wanted to lean forward and kiss her, and must have looked as if he was going to do just that, because as soon as their lips got closer, she suddenly pulled away from him and started to speak.

"So, we are having a glorious time, drinking lovely wine, getting on famously, but what are we doing here? I mean aren't you supposed to be Mr Lysistrata or something? No sex please I'm Luke Casey, or is this just typical guy bullshit, designed to get your wicked way with women, like David Bowie when he was pretending to be gay."

Luke bowed his head.

He loved Bowie, well frankly who didn't, but even the thin white Duke would have had a problem with Luke's latest incarnation. The elephant wasn't only in the room, it was the room! How could a guy who, had told the world that he wasn't going to be seeing women anymore, be on a date...with a woman.

He should really have thought this one through, it was bound to come up, his thoughts scowled, as he searched his slightly intoxicated mind for a suitable reply, before, thankfully Katie, leaned back on the bench and started to speak again.

"Unless, of course, you want us to be friends, which is fair enough, I suppose, but I don't really go in for that type of thing, and anyway men and women can't be friends, can they?" she added, as Luke took an anxious sip of his wine, and tried to tap into his own inner Google Maps for a route out of this particular emotional cul de sac.

However, she was right.

Men and women could never be friends.

He'd seen Fitz try it on many occasions and come off very badly each time, while even the guys who hung around his mother, trying honestly to be "mates", but it was obvious to a blind man that they wanted something more. It was nature's cruellest trick, and try as you may, to persuade yourself that it was possible, in the end, he had to agree with Vaughan that the only real friendships a hetero-sexual male could ever have, was either with other straight men or lesbians, where the possibility of sexual attraction was off the table. Luke had even read scientific articles which virtually confirmed this fact, but now hearing it from Katie's lips, it sounded more like a death sentence.

"So what's this all about, Caseypants? Because right now, I want to kiss you," now rudely interrupted his thoughts, as Luke managed to mumble back, "and so do I," before staring mournfully into his plastic cup again.

"God, this is like dating a priest," replied Katie with a laugh.

"Well yeah, of course I get it, but this whole romance thing is, you know err, well of course, romance and religion have now outlived their usefulness in society, because (a) they are part of the Patriarchy and (b)..."

"Bloody hell, Luke, that sounds like something, you've read on a website! Look I saw a recording of that chat show thing you did the other day, you looked tres handsome by the way, and I actually agreed with some of the things that you said. Men have been getting a bit of a bad time of it recently and that Judith, oh my God, my mother knows her, and she's always been a bit of an uptight bitch apparently, but darling, don't you think that you're taking this all a tad too far? You know ' It's not a man's world and it doesn't take a woman to fill it' bollocks on your podcasts," interrupted Kate, making drunken quotation marks with her fingers and then laughing again.

"Well, it's not bollocks, is it? Things have changed," replied Luke, now starting to get a little irritated by her dismissive tone and realising, that like most men, he wasn't overly keen on the girl that he really liked, getting too drunk.

"Yeah, a bit, but not massively. I mean come on, sweetie. It's still way better to be a man than it is to be a woman" said Katie, taking a sip of her wine.

"You sure about that? You work in PR, don't you? I bet you earn three times as much as most of the men in this country," replied Luke moving away from Katie a little on the bench.

"And I bet they earn ten times as much as some poor farmer in central America. It's all relative. I mean the world isn't fair, is it? Okay, I went to public school, before you bring that up, like everyone seems to do these days. So, I got a better start in life than most people, but what could I do about it? say to my mother, err sorry mater, but could I possibly go to the local comp down the road, instead of Roedean, because I don't want to increase the privilege that I already have? I was only 11, for God's sake."

"No, I get it, but that's not what I am saying. It's just that everything at the moment, revolves around men trying to please women. I'm even doing it now! Trying to show the best side of me, or the side that you'll like. You know, I'm easy going, a few indications that I am not too thick, couple of funny stories. It's all about approval and I hate it." protested Luke.

"But that's how it works isn't it? We like someone, so we want to show them our better side. Its natural darling. Anyway, it's not just men looking for approval, it's women too, you know. God, women are completely wracked by huge insecurities, if you hadn't noticed. Am I thin enough? funny enough? got a good enough job? Fuck, just look at social media, it's young women who are doing all the self-harming and I don't see that many men experiencing anorexia?" replied Kate now gently placing her hand on Luke's arm.

"Actually, there are quite a few," replied Luke, now remembering some of the experiences of the men on his twitter feed.

"Well, yeah, but only the err…"

"What, only the weak ones?"

"No, I wasn't going to say that," replied Katie.

"You sure?" replied Luke pulling his arm away.

"Jesus! Think you might be over-dramatizing things here a bit, Luke," said Katie, shaking her head and shifting her bottom away from him on the bench.

"Oh right, so when a guy complains, it's over dramatics, is it?" snapped Luke.

"You know, I can get your cynicism anywhere and I don't buy it, I really don't and actually I don't think you do either,"

"Oh, so you can read my mind now, or is that female intuition, I always forget?"

"That just sounds bitter Luke."

"I'm not bitter, it's...

"Look, I don't want to be rude here, because I do like you, but we're not getting anywhere here, are we?" interrupted Katie, as Luke now looked a little unnerved by the fury in her eyes, while he desperately searched his mind again to find the right words to express how he really felt. However, the tank was empty, and therefore, he simply lowered his head and stared sheepishly into his wine again, until Katie suddenly rose to declare "You know what, maybe text me when you have some idea," before shaking her head and then quickly walking away.

For the next few minutes, Luke sat and watched, as she slowly disappeared out of gates of the park, and for some reason, a song that his mother always played called *Don't Come the Cowboy With Me Sonny Jim, by Kirsty McColl* suddenly came into his thoughts.

It was about a man trying to be something that he wasn't.

He did want her.

In fact, every particle in his body now felt like chasing after her, to say sorry, whilst promising never to talk such bullshit again, but he didn't. Was it pride? Or fear? Or perhaps, subconsciously, he enjoyed all the melancholy and the bittersweet pain of love. Who knew, but whatever the hell it was, one thing was for sure, his life was now slowly becoming a complete disaster. If it wasn't the catastrophe of the chat show, it was getting suspended from his job, as even Ravi, who was just about the most stable person that he knew, had recently split up with his fiancé, Emma, over an argument about Hobbits, of all things. Apparently, Ravi was a Lord of the Rings nut, and Emma had insisted that he should stop going to conventions dressed as Frodo Baggins and grow up, but he had refused, so now the wedding was off.

Maybe men and women were cursed, Luke thought, and leaning his back against the bench again, he looked out towards the darkening sky, as his heart began to sink in time with the setting of the evening sun.

For a few moments more, he remained in this glorious state of self-pity, until his ringtone of *Cast No Shadow by Oasis* suddenly pierced the silence and he quickly shoved his hand into the pocket of his jeans.

Now he prayed with everything he had, that it was Katie so he could tell her what an idiot he had been and that they should definitely meet again and talk it through, but as he brought the phone to his ear, his hopes were quickly dashed by the sound of another familiar voice.

"Oi superstar, where the fuck have you been? Have you seen it online and twitter? Dude, it's completely blown up! You need to get your arse over here, now!"

"Err Hi Vaughan, err yeah, you know I'm a bit tired, and…."

"You wanna change things or not?!"

"Yeah okay, see you in an hour," replied Luke and now slowly rising from the bench, he placed the wine bottles in the bin, before walking slowly back towards Goldhawk Rd.

Chapter 12

"Yeah, I think I might do it," said a young man smiling into the camera, and wearing a T-Shirt that declared 'I'm crap in bed'.

"So, you're not going out with women in February? Why is that?" enquired the female BBC reporter.

"Because I like what Mithras are saying, it makes sense, and yeah why not? why should we do what we are told? Maybe it's time for a change, you know, take back a bit of control." replied the young man with another smile, before putting on his dark sunglasses again and then walking off into the winter rain.

In their make-shift office above a charity shop in Acton High Street, Luke and Vaughan stared in silence at the news report on the laptop for a few seconds more, until jumping to their feet, they both screamed "Yes, before proceeding to run around the small room as if they had just won the lottery.

Only a day earlier, on February 1st, their organisation, Mithras, set up immediately after Luke's appearance on *Sisters Doing it for Themselves*, and named after a Romano/Persian deity, who was the head of a male only religion in the 1st Century CE, had officially announced the start of "No women February," on a video on their website. Here Luke, now the official face of the new movement, had called for a "Male Lysistrata" for a month, urging his fellow men to "Stop having sex with or trying to date women for 28 days, in protest at a system that damages us all". Furthermore, in a speech that lasted over an hour, and was clicked on by over 80 million users worldwide, Luke called for civil behaviour and respect towards women at all times during the protest, whilst specifically discouraging the wearing of moustaches, fezzes, or any other type of self-deprecating behaviour from participants, because "we don't have to make ourselves look like dicks anymore to get our point across, do we?" The broadcast, together with the organisation's logo of a bird of paradise wearing sun glasses with its wings folded across its chest, was reputedly seen in over a hundred different countries and had an immediate effect, as men from France to Burkina Faso, quickly took to the streets to pledge themselves to a month of celibacy.

For the next few days, societies across the globe remained in a strange kind of limbo, as everyone tried to work out whether this was a stunt or something more serious, while firms like Ray Bans and Foster Grant reported a global shortage in sunglasses, as shares in these companies hit a fifty-year high.

Predictably, Luke and Vaughan didn't have to wait too long for the backlash, as first Jake O'Callaghan, now the de facto leader of the anti- Mithras platform, railed on his radio show against Luke Casey and "his battalions of ridiculous men", while various faith leaders hastily assembled outside Westminster Abbey to heavily denounce the move, stating that from the beginning of time, God had intended for men and women to be together, and therefore the actions of Mithras were not only wrong but "a sin against humanity itself". This last comment, greatly amused Vaughan, a committed atheist, and prompted him to immediately tweet back, that "if Adam and Eve were around today, they would have never made it to the tree of knowledge in the first place, as they would have probably met online and split up by their third date anyway", which only served to fan the flames of opposition to the protest.

However, despite the outcry, the "Love ban" as it was being called by the press, was still receiving solid support, and was especially popular amongst younger men, who had started to join the movement in their thousands, instantly dismissing the advice of their mainly older peers as out of touch and patronising. "Try living in our world boomer bollocks", yelled one popular podcaster, as he ridiculed the reactions of older men, especially those, like rock legend, Keith Watts, who had recently shot a YouTube video, dressed in his trademark leather jacket and black Stetson, to beseech younger men in a mid-Atlantic drawl to calm down and restart the dance with the opposite sex, "because men and women are beautiful with each other, man". This message of conciliation between the sexes, was initially well received by most of the mainstream media until it was quickly pointed out that the veteran guitarist had reputedly slept with fifteen year-old girls on a tour in the 1970s, whilst also penning songs such as "Down on Me," extolling the virtues of oral sex whist driving a fast car and "Don't wanna hear your Shit, Girl", whose title spoke for itself, thus forcing the rock star to immediately refute the accusations, before stating that the matter was now in the hands of his lawyers. Other established celebrities received similar treatment, as men from Generation Z, now derided their older peers, as having had the luxury of living at a time, where they seemingly got everything, and abused the privilege. From increased judgement from women to the lack of decent jobs, no housing, and an impending environmental catastrophe, it seemed, that it was now the majority of those born in the remaining years of the last century who were having to pay the heaviest price.

This sentiment was further amplified by other young male artists with huge followings on You Tube, Instagram and Tik Tok, such as the world's most successful pod-caster Babs Stone, who had been recently criticised online for not buying an "expensive enough" present for his partner's birthday or the Grime artist, Crisis, who had been formerly accused of being "emotionally unintelligent" by an ex- girlfriend. These stars, now, not only made sizeable financial donations to Mithras, but went further, and also posted a joint video in support of the new campaign. "The damn process no longer works for men anymore, and in particular black men, because if we raise our voices, we get accused of being aggressive, like our brother Luke experienced, on that morning chat show, the other day. We know that feeling bro' because all we get is shit, spending our every waking hour wondering if we said this right or did, that wrong? Fuck it, it's too exhausting and from the way it's going now, any guy could end up doing some serious time for just stroking his girlfriend's butt on the street without asking permission first."

Feminist groups quickly hit back at these comments calling them "pathetic "and "misogynistic", and just another example of a blinkered patriarchy, while adding that maybe they should ask permission before "stroking their girlfriend's butt". However other female voices, were not so critical and tentatively welcomed the general idea of separation of the sexes, as a possible solution to a centuries old problem. "Could Luke Casey have a point?" was the lead article in the New Statement, by a leading millennial feminist, Lucy Cartwright – Soames, who agreed in principle that men and women were drastically different, before outlining what a world governed solely by women for women might look like. This sex separatist theme was also quickly taken up by others including a club promoter in Copenhagen who organised a night called Unconsciously Uncouple, which proved to be hugely popular, where all kissing was strictly prohibited and participants were encouraged to get drunk and celebrate the separation of men and women, while dancing to a soundtrack of *I Can Get Along Without You Now by Viola Wills, Go Your Own Way by Fleetwood Mac* and *Love Removal Machine by The Cult.*

Obviously, not everyone agreed with this analysis, including many female commentators, such as the radio host, Donna Marley-Muir, who on her popular afternoon show, denounced "the bloody feminists, who have pushed things much too far, for far too long and therefore it shouldn't be surprise to anyone, that men wanted to go their own way, now". This view was further endorsed by large groups of women, mainly over 40 it must be said, including some ladies on Mumsnet, who made a special cake with Lukes's face on the front to express their support. The pressure was now starting to build everywhere, and so by the end of the first week of "No Women February", over five million men worldwide had committed themselves to the new campaign, as the first reports of women being routinely deserted by their male partners, started to appear on social media. In one video, a young man in Mississippi working in a famous fast-food outlet was confronted by his newly dumped girlfriend and his own mother, who then proceeded to march up and down the store counter to accuse him of being "fucking weak" and "an idiot" as he shouted back that he just wanted to be "emotionally self-sufficient right now", while in a less amusing case, a woman in London who had petitioned the Home Office for three years and succeeded in getting her dissident academic husband freed from an Iranian jail, was deserted with a text, saying that he needed more time to process his masculinity.

Of course, the traffic wasn't all one way, as predictably women reacted in kind, and male partners and boyfriends were routinely abandoned, in a pre-emptive strike strategy, with the hashtag, "Dump the Loser" and as a result, Mithras was now inundated with complaints from ex partners, seeking redress for their new state of affairs. However, Luke immediately went on the offensive and made a robust defence of himself and the organisation against these allegations, stating on twitter that, although he didn't wish for anyone's distress, "if the relationship was strong enough in the first place, a few words from me shouldn't have made any difference."

Therefore, by the middle of the second week, the battle lines were now clearly drawn and as St Valentine's Day, itself, soon approached, a mixture of excitement and uneasiness hung in the air, with even the Prime Minister and his wife announcing that they would be having a special Valentines dinner together and urging everyone else to do the same. Similarly, the Jane Austen society and the National Theatre, decided to follow suit and join forces "to make this Valentine's Day, the best one ever", with Period Balls and Pop-Up events appearing all over the high street, showcasing the most romantic scenes from the literary and film world.

Brief Encounter, *Romeo and Juliet* and *Dirty Dancing* were all performed by casts of very good actors, but despite their enthusiasm and passion, the initiative seemed a little out of step with the general mood, as Mithras and other commentators mischievously pointed out, that for the most part, all these love stories usually ended up in abject failure. "Romeo and Juliet topped themselves, the couple in Brief Encounter were married to other people and the rich girl in Dirty Dancing would probably have left working class Swayze for a dentist after a couple of months," commented Vaughan on the Mithras Website, as this cynical sentiment now carried over to the big night itself.

Usually, one of the busiest evenings of the calendar, this year's St Valentine's Day remained unusually quiet, and even more subdued than the previous years, affected by the COVID outbreak, as Waitrose and Marks and Spencer were forced to cancel their Valentine's dinner for two meal deals, while Agent Provocateur and Victoria Secrets, both reported desperate sales figures, in what was usually their most profitable time of the year. It was a disaster and the following day the newspapers reflected the gloom, with "St. Valentine's Day Massacre", "Valentine's Day Is Over" and "Casey Kills Cupid", while the Daily Sun listed "10 things that you didn't know about Lysistrata". At the same time, sales of supermarket alcohol and fast-food outlets reported a steep rise in sales for February, as most men chose instead to visit each other's houses or meet in local Parks to seek refuge from the female population.

By the third week, attitudes began to harden from the other side of the argument, as several women's groups around the world, decided to test the male resolve, by announcing LetsSeeHowStrongTheyAre Tuesday where it was decided that participants would wear their most sexually provocative clothing permissible to work, therefore turning underground platforms and high streets into catwalks of erotica. To counter this, Mithras bellowed "We are not animals" from their website, in an attempt to discredit the long-held assumption that all men were "ruled by their dicks" whilst encouraging participants, to wear dark sunglasses at all times and listen to anything by Joy Division or the Cure on their headphones to protect themselves from the sensual storm, that was about to rage all around them. Unfortunately, this stoic advice didn't work for everyone, as many men, after three weeks of enforced celibacy, experienced severe reactions to the stunt, with numerous cases of panic attacks and increased blood pressure being reported, while a man in Belarus was rumoured to have died from a heart attack after encountering a young woman dressed as a sexy Vampire. However, not everyone was happy with this strategy, and although seen by many women as a bit of fun, many feminist organisations questioned the morality of turning yourself into a classic trope of objectification to make your point. "Surely playing up to men's unrealistic sexual ideals of a female has only made the situation worse."

Furthermore, in a not wholly unexpected twist, men who had hitherto received very little attention from women in the past, were now finding themselves a little more in demand. All over the world, overweight, shorter or generally perceived unattractive men, who would normally be mostly celibate because of their physical characteristics, were now beginning to receive compliments from women and sometimes "a whole lot more". "I have never had so many looks at work from hot chicks," cried one male online while another announced that he had recently hooked up with a girl, he had never dreamed he could attract, as thousands of men previously deemed undesirable by a majority of females, were now starting to get lucky.

This new turn of events immediately angered the men participating in the month-long campaign, who complained bitterly online, that they had just seen a hot ex-girlfriend going out with a "complete minger" or a very attractive woman was seen kissing a "fat twat", as the abstaining males urged their shorter, overweight, and unattractive brothers to resist, because the greater goal of emotional emancipation was "surely the bigger prize". Understandably, these entreaties fell mainly on deaf ears, as the so-called "ugly mob", who had now formed their own social media groups, tweeted back, "Yeah right Chad. Where the fuck was the solidarity when we being rejected for all those years", thus referencing the derogatory name previously used in male chatrooms, for those in the "top 20% of men" who were considered to be the ones usually successful with women. In response, Luke expressed deep sympathy for his previously forgotten brothers, before releasing a statement on the website urging solidarity amongst all men. "In the future, masculinity must not be equated in direct proportion with our success with women. Gone are the days when manhood is defined by how many birds you can pull."

"No to female approval, yes to emotional self-sufficiency," was now the new battle cry, and so by the end of the month, it was estimated that almost 15 million men worldwide had participated in the "No women February" campaign, prompting Governments to start to take notice, as questions were regularly asked in the House of Commons, the European Parliament and the US Senate about the economic and social effect of the worldwide sexual withdrawal, and what could be done about it.

Think- Tanks and Academics quickly joined the discussion, to caution of the continued problem of a falling birth rate, whilst warning of a significant and lasting drop in global well-being and growth, if men stopped being interested in women. "Humans are one of the very few species of mammal who pair bond, and as a consequence, Civilisation has been one long love letter from men to women, as without women, why would men have bothered to leave the caves, in the first place?" stated a group of prominent social anthropologists, and while accepting Mithras' view that women were, in general, hyper-critical of men, they saw this as nothing to be concerned about, as essentially "Men needed the dissatisfaction of the female to survive, and the unfairness of the romantic narrative was and is a vital evolutionary tool for progress".

Predictably, both these arguments were roundly rejected by feminist groups, who stated that "it is not the main function of women to support or influence men, but rather to fully engage in the building of societies with their own agency," while LBGT groups also complained that the whole argument was, as usual, seen purely through "a CIS gendered lens" and was therefore very misleading. "Was Michelangelo, a gay man, trying to impress a woman, when he painted the ceiling of the Sistine chapel?" they asked justifiably as the argument seemed to continue on without end.

However, on the stroke of midnight of 28th February, it did end, and staring into his webcam, Luke proudly announced the end of the sexual Ramadan, while congratulating those who took part for their fortitude and self-restraint under extreme pressure exerted by "the usual people who like telling us what to do".

"This is not the end," Luke declared with a grin, before quickly adding, "My brothers, the revolution has only just begun."

Chapter 13

Katie stared at Luke's face on the front of his latest pod-cast entitled "Why do women want us to be funny", and allowed herself a little smile.

"You're not funny in the slightest ☺", she texted, as seconds later she received something very rude in return, which made her laugh, and as usual she felt a warm glow inside. Stupid really, but despite all of his Mithras malarkey, it still felt good to be connected to him. Of course, they'd agreed to be friends, which was about as much use as a chocolate tea-pot, but what else could she do?

So, she had started dating again.

Just because he wanted to keep it in his pants, didn't mean she had to, she'd reasoned, but despite this, she hadn't told him of her lovers, not that it was any of his business anyway, but for some reason she didn't want him to know.

It was completely ridiculous.

She wanted him, she was pretty sure, that he wanted her, but with half the world looking on, it seemed hopeless. Maybe she and Luke were in some weird religious love pact, like Peter Abelard and Heloise, the twelfth century priest and nun, kept apart by religion and impossible circumstances?

That didn't work out too well.

Poor old Peter had ended up being castrated in the end, by Heloise's irate uncle, she recalled with a slightly wicked grin, and come to think of it, she knew quite a few women who wouldn't mind seeing Luke's testicles detached from his body right now.

"Total misogynist", "Worse than Harvey Weinstein", and "That weirdo" were some of the nicer comments she had overheard from her friends recently as even her mother, who was usually quite balanced in her views, regularly referred to him as "that horrid man", whenever his face appeared on the television.

"You don't know him like I know him governor," Katie thought as she popped another Malteser into her mouth and started to crunch. Anyway, at least,

Luke and his new army of men dressed in dark sunglasses and swaggering all over the high streets were demonstrating some kind of honesty, which is more than could be said for most of the men from her own background. Proudly wearing T-Shirts with "This is what a feminist looks like" on the front, and their pronouns and "be kind" tags on show for all the world to see, before spending half the evening trying to get into her knickers, the sad truth was, that these well-bred activists usually did very little to truly help the plight of ordinary women in the real world. In contrast, Mithras seemed to be a completely different story, as within months of "No Women February", the male empowerment movement with its ten million strong, global membership, had become a significant force in politics and was making great strides, petitioning Government ministers behind the scenes, to provide free childcare to all families and a weekly wage for women who stayed at home to look after their children. Furthermore, only a few weeks earlier, some senior members of the organisation had famously talked down a man who had threatened to jump off a tower block with his two young children. *Men only really listen to other men*, was the name of a new domestic violence initiative organised by the organisation and was producing some startling results, that even their harshest critics were forced to acknowledge. They had even tried to address issues surrounding online Porn and how destructive it was, especially for younger men, although considering the irony of their previous celibate initiative, they had ended up advising members to limit use to once a week, and "maybe rely on your imagination a bit more instead". However, as usual, these very laudable actions would almost always be accompanied by yet another annoying slogan. "Reject romance and the violence will go away.", being the latest, and so despite her general support for many of the things that Mithras were doing, she really couldn't go along with this one.

Love is real.

Call it kismet, serendipity, or simple fate, but she firmly believed that an invisible force existed in the universe specifically designed to bring people together.

Like when she turned her head and saw Luke for the first time, and in that one look, they had downloaded everything about each other, and it all made sense. Exactly the same as her mother and father had done, thirty years ago earlier, when there were less choices and people had the courage, to say, yes, yes you are for me, let's do it now!

Not like today.

Who cares less wins?

Yuk

What a terrible place for her generation to find themselves, with only the online dating horror-show to keep everyone vaguely interested. That wasn't love, it was more like shopping, and disengaged shopping at that. Of course, she'd tried it herself, had to, only game in town, wasn't it? but it had made her sick to her stomach. If it had been up to her, all-online relationships would be annulled immediately and everyone told to go back and do it the proper way. A bit of effort maybe. Real love was hard work, wasn't it? she thought before a random ping interrupted her internal rant and made her glance down at her phone again.

"Hey pumpkin, thought we might go to the Portobello Road tonight, for a late drink? x."

"Sounds perfect, darling, but not feeling great, might have an early night," she tapped back with slightly guilty fingers, before adding a kiss and placing her phone back on the coffee table. All thoughts of Luke and Love had now sideswiped her, and so pointing the remote control at the television, she settled back into her sofa just as "It's Jake O'Callaghan's I've had enough" bellowed out into her front room. Everyone at work, had been talking about the show, she thought, putting another sweet in her mouth, and as she looked closer at the small bearded man on the screen, she suddenly remembered that her brother had mentioned that he'd worked with a guy who went to school with the new rising star of late-night TV chat shows.

"So, what do you think?" asked Jake, looking out into the studio audience and shaking his head.

"A few months on from 'No women February' and how funny was that by the way? Thousands of women abandoned by their partners, because men are apparently getting a raw deal. Can I say that again, because it still beggars' belief, doesn't it? MEN are getting a raw deal! Hilarious! So, anyway, what do we think Ophelia?" asked the chat show host, now quickly turning his head towards one of his guests.

Oh my god, I met her at a party a few months ago, thought Katie placing a cushion into her tummy and recalling she wasn't that funny.

"Well actually, Jake, I'm a little bit exhausted from a whole week of oppressing men to be quite honest with you. My husband or "him indoors" as I like to call him these days, has had to take the bins out and do a bit of washing up, which is obviously a form of torture for him and now he is just sitting in the front room with a pair of dark sunglasses on, whilst every now and again chanting "Women are not the enemy", at the wall – It's confusing the dog."

"Is the dog male?" enquired Piers, another guest and fellow comedian.

"Yes."

"Was he wearing sunglasses?" probed Piers.

"Thankfully not, they kept sliding off his ears," replied Ophelia raising her eyes to the ceiling.

"Well, at least, he's not as barking as you might have thought," said Jake to more laughter.

"Nice one, Jake."

"Thank you, Piers, always nice to get positive feedback from you. But hey, enough of my rubbish jokes, because tonight we are going to have a different take on Mithras. My God, I still can't get used to saying that name. Can you believe it? They've called themselves after a 1st century Romano/Persian deity? Incredible!" said Jake, shaking his head before looking at his guests again.

"Well, it could have been worse. They could have been called after Miranda, the goddess of Anorgasmia," replied Piers.

"What's that?" asked Ophelia.

"A failed orgasm," replied Piers.

"Blimey, I think I pray to her every night," exclaimed Ophelia to more laughter from the studio audience, before quickly adding, "Oops sorry hubby, only joking."

"Well thank you, Piers, your grasp of ancient mythology has always been the one thing that has impressed me about you, the most."

"Actually Jake, I just made that up," replied Piers with a grin.

"Typical, but hey, talking of failed orgasms, we keep hearing about Luke Casey abstaining from seeing women and not seeking female approval and all that jazz, but let's find out, what he did before he entered the priesthood of the God, Mithras and when he actually had a girlfriend." declared Jake to some "ooohs" and "aaahs" from the studio audience, while Katie's shoulders now instantly tensed, as she quickly pressed down on the remote control to raise the volume.

"Yes, yes, we've done a bit of digging and we've found her. So, let's give a big welcome tonight to Luke Casey's ex-girlfriend, Mia Reynolds, everyone. Yeah c'mon, big round of applause, you snowflakes and boring Gen Zers, clap like you really mean it, c'mon" insisted Jake as he stood up, while a petit woman with brunette hair walked shyly from the wings of the studio before shaking the hands of the resident comedians, and then sitting down on a chair opposite the host.

"Hi Mia," said Jake.

"Oh hi," replied Mia.

"May I say, if it's not too creepy, how lovely you look tonight,"

"Oh, thank you."

"Oh my God, you look amazing. Lurv the dress, hun," joined in Ophelia, as Katie stared at the television screen and crinkled her nose.

She did look amazing. Nice hair, she obviously liked a straightener and a pretty face that wouldn't have looked out of face on your average TV reality show, thought Katie, as she smiled at the little twinge of jealousy zipping around her body, before tucking her legs a little further under her bottom.

"So, thank you for coming here tonight," continued Jake.

"Oh no problem," replied Mia.

"So, when did you first go out with Luke, then?" asked Jake.

"Err when I was nineteen."

"And how long did you see him for?"

"About two years."

"And what was he like?"

"Well, he was okay at the start, but he was always a bit moody, you know wrapped up in himself," replied Mia as she pulled a strand of hair away from her face.

"No change there then," mouthed Katie as she reached across to her coffee table to take another Malteser out of its packet.

"Not very romantic then?" chipped in Piers.

"Erm no," replied Mia.

"Did he bring you flowers, serenade you under balconies, write furious, passionate poetry?" asked Ophelia.

"Ha! no," replied Mia.

"Not even plastic flowers from Poundland?" asked Piers, before Mia smiled and slowly shook her head, to more laughter from the audience.

"So, you are not surprised by how things have turned out then?" asked Jake.

"Err no, not really. I mean don't get me wrong, he was okay, but yeah, he was always a bit angry about stuff, you know his dad leaving him at a young age and all that," replied Mia

"Well, my dad left when I was pretty young, but that didn't make me want to destroy thousands of years of romance and divide the planet, did it? But let me ask you another question, Mia. Was he ever off hand with you, inconsiderate, not engaged in the relationship?"

"Well, I suppose, you could say that. He would cancel dates we had arranged and not spend loads of time with me."

"How could he not want to do that? You're lovely, Mia," added Ophelia.

"Oh, thank you, but yeah I remember once we were supposed to spend a bank holiday together and he went off to a festival instead with his mates."

"Did he give you notice?" asked Jake.

"Well yeah, he told me a few days beforehand, but it wasn't very nice, if I'm being honest," replied Mia.

"No, it wasn't and I think that's where men get it so wrong Mia. We don't realise that we have to put something back into a relationship. Seems to me, as if Luke just wanted to do what he fancied, and forget about you."

"Yeah probably," replied Mia, lowering her head.

"And what did you think when you heard him say, that men are not here to cherish or protect women?" enquired Jake.

"Well, I thought that was a bit disrespectful of women to be quite truthful," said Mia in a quiet voice.

"I agree, and do you think it's no longer a man's world?" asked Jake with a smile.

"Ha! no, it's definitely a man's world," replied Mia, as the camera stayed on her face for a few seconds until the audience erupted into loud applause again, and Katie moved uneasily on her sofa. Vulnerable, she sucked deeper on the chocolate sweet, before suddenly feeling a little fat. she spat it out into an ashtray sitting on her coffee table, while the camera continued to focus on Mia's face and a picture of the Mithras logo appeared on the top of the screen with the wings of the bird of paradise now unfolded and covering its eyes. Irritably, Katie poked the remote control at the television screen and then sat in silence with her arms crossed for a moment or two, until reaching over for her phone, she tapped, "Hi sweetie, changed my mind, meet you in Trailer Happiness in an hour?" before smiling again and popping another Malteser into her mouth.

Chapter 14

"Come on, girls, let's go to Maxwells," declared Donna McCauley, with a big grin, before raising a glass of champagne to the very high ceilings of her river front apartment in Wapping.

"Oh no Donna love, let's just stay here and get pissed. Your place is like a bar anyway, look at the size of it and we have chicken dippers," replied Kay laughing, as she held up a small piece of fried chicken dripping with a dark coloured sauce.

"They are not chicken dippers, you old slapper, they are very expensive teriyaki chicken mini-bites covered in a raspberry and avocado sauce from Testino's if you must know, but anyway I wanna meet some men, cos unlike you lot, I am thankfully single, and still think about sex, so I've called an uber, and we are going," confirmed Donna, before taking another swig of her champagne, and then walking off into the bathroom to check her hair, while her friends pulled various faces at each other from across the apartment. Given the choice, they'd have preferred to stay put, eat catered food and listen to Luther Vandross all night, but when the main news anchor of Empyrean TV, the top cable news network in the UK, wanted something, she usually got it, especially when she'd had a drink or two. Therefore, after another chorus of Never too Much by Luther, forty -five minutes later, everyone found themselves in Maxwells, the new exclusive members only club at the back of Goodge Street station, sipping watermelon mojitos and looking on as their old school friend flirted with any man who came within ten feet of their table. She had just turned 56, but you wouldn't know it, as only the previous year, she had been voted "rear of the year", which although the news anchor had turned the award down for its blatant objectivization of women, according to Kay, when telling the story to her friends later, "Made her happier than if she'd got the Pulitzer Prize, whatever that was."

For the next hour or so, the friends continued to drink and chat as the club started to fill up with the rich and vaguely famous and while more cocktails were ferried over to their table, Donna began to scan the room for possibilities.

"Oh look, isn't that thingy? the guy off the soap?" asked Kay pointing to a man in his thirties standing beside an ice sculpture of Nelson Mandela.

"Oh no darling, he's a fucking idiot, and terrible in the sack by all accounts. My friend had a night with him a few months ago, and she said she'd rathered have sat on her middle finger," replied the news anchor, shaking her head, before Kay placed a straw in her mouth and giggled into her drink.

Her oldest friend could be brutal, and although she had a heart of gold and would do anything for you, sometimes she could go a little too far, she thought, as Donna pulled another face as she continued her assessment of the eligible men in the room. "Oh, too tall", "Looks too much like a banker" and "Where did he get that hair?" she declared until her eyes finally settled on a group of younger men standing at the other end of the bar.

"Oh, oh look, look, isn't that whatshisname?"

"Who, love?" asked Kay, squinting her eyes, as she looked into the crowd.

"You know, that guy! The guy who started the anti-women month, recently. Oh my God, what's his name? he was everywhere. You know, him. Erm, Luke something, isn't it?" replied Donna, as she desperately tried to interrogate her slightly tipsy brain.

"Oh yes, yes, you're right Luke Casey."

"That's right, Luke Casey and standing next to Josh Middleton and Mason Meyer?"

"Oh, I like Mason Meyer, he's got a rude mouth," said Kay, taking another sip of her drink, before adding "Yeah, I suppose he's quite nice, shame he is unavailable though."

"No man is unavailable, honey, deep down they are all dogs," replied Donna, taking another mouthful of her cocktail, making, Kay giggle again.

She had seen her friend in this mood many times before, especially after a few drinks, and it never ceased to amaze her how brazen she could be when she wanted a man, particularly one who was apparently out of her reach. She was absolutely fearless and therefore it was no surprise to Kay, when Donna suddenly whispered "All dogs" into her ear again, before lurching out of her seat and making a beeline for the bar. The music pounded through the club, as the news anchor, approached the three men standing in a little group, and then after carefully positioning herself behind Luke, she leaned in, to grab a handful of his left buttock.

"So big boy, how come you don't wanna go out with us, women anymore then?" she asked as the Mithras leader suddenly lurched forward, and spilled his drink on the ground.

"Bloody hell, that's a bit uncalled for, isn't it?" replied actor, Josh Middleton, star of the Tangerine Anarchist movie franchise.

"Oh purlease, get over yourself, and anyway I am not talking to you, am I?" replied Donna, ignoring the actor's reproach, while beaming a big smile in the direction of Luke.

"Oh, so it's okay for a woman to just grab a guy, is it?" protested Josh.

"Think that's a bit rich, coming from you, isn't it darling? I heard, from a very reliable source, that you shagged half the makeup department on your last movie." shot back the news anchor

"Excuse me?" replied an outraged Josh.

"You heard, and anyway Luke here doesn't look like he minds, do you love? We are only having a bit of fun, aren't we?" grinned Donna, as Luke now stared back into the slightly glazed eyes of the celebrated journalist and his heart began an anxious thud. A few months ago, he had been a recruitment consultant who was pinching people's milk from the fridge, and now he was getting his bum squeezed by someone he had spent his whole life watching on T.V. *This is so fucking weird* was his one solitary thought, before, understandably, Josh and Mason Meyers, the star of the evening soap, Beasley Street, now narrowed their eyes in his direction, expecting a robust response from their new found leader.

Only problem was; he wasn't that bothered.

He didn't feel vulnerable, objectified, or even the victim of an assault, and if anything, he felt rather complimented. In truth, he quite liked Donna McCauley and a famous interview a few months previous, where she had decimated the arguments of Bobby Baxter, leader of the Albion First party suddenly came into his mind, before he stared back into her drunken eyes again.

However, he knew he had to do something.

His new found celebrity friends had been emboldened by his message of male empowerment and self-sufficiency and like millions of other men, had crowded around Mithras, with a desire to seek a new meaning in a world that seemed to increasingly reject or marginalise them. Therefore, now was probably not a good time to back down, Luke thought, as he folded his arms, and fixed his eyes on the news anchor once more.

"Well to be fair, that was a little bit out of order."

"Sweet Jesus, not you as well?! Let me tell you, I've had my arse pinched from Monday to Sunday by every sleazy twat from Rochdale to Belgravia in my time. I know everything there is to know about sexual harassment matey and this is not it. Not even close, it's just a bit of laugh," snapped Donna.

"Well, it's not, is it?" replied Luke relaxing a little and placing his hands in his pockets.

"Too bloody right it ain't, suppose I do that to a girl?" interrupted Mason Mayers.

"Suppose I do that to a girl! I think, Mason darling, you would do it all the time, if you thought you could get away with it." replied Donna mimicking Mason's Essex accent, before shaking her head at the soap star.

"You what?" replied a deeply offended Mason.

"Oh yeah, I remember your sort from the eighties, John Leslie and all those other pervs. You don't change sweetie, you're only interested in getting your leg over, and quite badly in most cases, I might add - and for your information it's a woman Mason, not a girl, we're not girls, are we?" corrected Donna with a wry smile.

"Okay, suppose I did that to a bipedal female carbon-based unit, then? Hey? That's it, aint it Luke? That's the new name for a bird now?" replied Mason winking at the Mithras leader and quoting from his now infamous interview of a few months earlier.

"Birds? Even better, Mason. What a feminist you really are! You know I am getting sick to the back teeth of all this He fucking Too bollocks recently. Its such crap. You've got nothing to complain about for God's sake. You still run everything and treat women like shit, so if I want to grab any guy's arse, I just will, okay? because as far as I am concerned it's just paying you tossers back for all the rubbish you have given us over the last 10,000 years or whatever it is. And anyway, why don't you pay your bloody taxes instead of moaning at me, Mason darling," replied Donna now folding her arms.

"Oi, I did pay my taxes, it was just the accountant filled out the wrong form," protested Mason, who had recently been implicated in a celebrity tax scam that had been exposed by one of Donna's colleagues in an Empyrean TV special investigation,

"But of course, I don't mean you, cupcake, you're very nice," added Donna now ignoring the objections of the soap star before turning all her attention back to Luke again.

"Err well thank you, but I would appreciate it, if you didn't do that again," replied Luke, this time with a little more firmness in his voice.

"Oh honey, I wouldn't dream of it," declared Donna with a cheeky grin, and then waiting for a beat, she smiled at Luke again, before quickly moving her hand around his back, to squeeze his bottom for a second time.

Now, as Luke lurched forward again, Mason, Josh and indeed anyone within a five-yard radius of the group, immediately started to shout and point at the veteran TV journalist, while the door staff soon became involved, as well as Kay and her friends who rushed over to see what was going on. For the next few minutes, chaos reigned, until finally, in frustration, the news anchor shouted "You're all fucking wankers, except you, of course, Luke," before storming off towards the exit, followed by her slightly bemused entourage. Predictably, as the drama unfolded, someone had managed to film it on their phone and not only captured the melee by the bar, but almost all of the "bum pinching" incident itself, and therefore within hours, a video had been uploaded onto YouTube, followed by the usual circus of support and recrimination from the media and the wider public at large.

"If a man did that, he would be decapitated."

"She needs to be arrested."

"I am not condoning it, but it's hardly the same thing, is it? What about the thousands of assaults on women that go unpunished every year?"

Another day, another controversy, Luke thought, as twenty-four hours later, he was inevitably contacted by the police and asked if he would like to press charges. For as long as he could remember, his Aunties, his mother's old school-friends, even the next-door neighbour, had squeezed, hugged or routinely rammed his head headlong in the general direction of female breasts of various sizes, after one too many Baileys Irish Creams, or glasses of white wine. Okay, sometimes they might hold on a bit too long, especially the older ladies, but he had never really minded, and at no point had he ever felt under any kind of threat.

Donna McCauley was drunk, big deal, his arse would recover.

But that wasn't the point, was it?

These days, everything meant everything, as echo chamber screamed against echo chamber, so after an avalanche of outrage from Mithras members, particularly Vaughan texting "we can't really let this one slide", Luke reluctantly went down to Shepherds Bush police station, and provided a statement. For the next week or so, the controversy raged in the press, and faced by a charge of sexual assault against their top broadcaster together with the damning evidence of the online video, Empyrean TV had no choice but to suspend their premiere star. Undaunted, Donna McCauley, then went on to release a statement through her solicitors, which stated "Although it is always wrong to lay hands on someone without their consent, at the time, I didn't think Luke Casey seemed to mind, and it was more his friends, who took offence, which was pretty ironic, coming as it did from a serial womaniser and a known tax dodger. Maybe Luke should choose his friends more carefully in the future?"

Obviously, this did little to defuse the situation, as right-wing commentators, such as Bob Biddle predictably pursued the "one rule for women and one rule for men" angle while Suzanne Moore chipped in with an article applauding Miss McCauley, for "giving men a bit of their own medicine, for once", before stating that maybe now men might appreciate how humiliating and degrading their behaviour had been over the previous Millenia and look to change their ways.

For Luke, it was a grim business though, and except for Katie texting, "if I had known you liked older women, I would have worn pearls" he found little in the confected fury of the latest social media meltdown to smile about. Ten days later, Donna McCaulay appeared at Westminster's Magistrates Court, wearing huge Elton John-type sunglasses, now regarded as the "official female riposte" to the dark sunglasses of the Mithras movement, as she pleaded not guilty to the charge of sexual harassment, while accepting a £250 fine and confirming that she would not be repeating the same offence again.

"They should be so lucky," she shouted outside the courtroom, before immediately decamping to a huge A list "Women only," celebrity party given in her honour at Romeo's in Shoreditch, where bottom pinching was not only allowed but positively encouraged. Luke thought it was quite funny, but his fellow co-founder of Mithras was less impressed and issued a statement on the movement's website demanding that, not only should Donna McCauley be sacked from her job with immediate effect, but also placed on the sex register, as this would have been the probable outcome, if the offender had been male. Furthermore, Vaughan complained of the "absolute hypocrisy" of the veteran journalist who had previously been very vocal about inappropriate relationships between older men and younger women, but had herself just propositioned a man half her age. "Okay for a MILF but not a DILF," he thundered, as Twitter and Instagram became battlegrounds again, and the Government was forced to defend what was seen as a light sentence for the TV star, while reiterating its commitment to building a society that served both men and women equally.

However, despite this, the Donna McCauley case, only seemed to amplify male anger.

Something was definitely beginning to stir.

Chapter 15

The Book of Mithras or the Commandments as they became more commonly known, were a set of general guidelines for men in the 21st century, written by Vaughan and Luke in the period just after 'No-women February' and were initially designed, as a bit of a riff on the 2018 book, *12 Rules for Life,* by renowned clinical psychologist Jordan Peterson, who both men greatly admired, but also as a good excuse to annoy those on the other side of the argument, who seemed to spend their every waking hour attacking the organisation. However, despite their flippant intentions, once published, the book soon developed a life of its own and quickly became the bible of the new male empowerment movement.

The rules were:

1. *Thou must **NOT** seek female approval. This is the most important of all the laws of Mithras. Do not feel shamed by women for not reaching their expectations in any sphere of modern life, whether it be in your career, how much money you make, or even your sexual performance. Rather fight for Women's civic and human rights, as fellow human beings and leave it at that. And always remember - **Women are not the enemy.***

2. *Thou must not treat your wives and girlfriends like your mothers. Have greater emotional self-sufficiency and take responsibility for your life.*

3. *Thou must avoid antiquated male stereotypes. Be exactly who you **REALLY** are. Listen to no-one but yourself. Men can cry, or not cry, be sensitive or emotionally remote, it's all your choice.*

4. *Thou must consider that most relationships have an end date. Accept this fact. Love is a drug, so try and understand what the drug is doing to you. In general, there is no happy ever after. Do not be scared by this thought, it is not Nihilism. Life is still the most amazing adventure.*

5. *Thou must not have sex with a woman or anyone else for that matter without their expressed consent. Forget embarrassment or spoiling the moment, just make sure, especially if you've had a drink or two. Remember to access your inner James Stewart from the Philadelphia Story, at all times. In other words, always be a Gent.*

6. *Thou must never slut shame.* **EVER!** *A woman can do the same sexually as a man in all circumstances, and be judged in exactly the same way. Therefore, do not refer to a woman as a Hoe, Slut or any other derogatory name - unless of course, she specifically requests it.*

7. *Thou must never air kiss a woman. We are equal in every regard, so there is absolutely no need for this convention. We wouldn't do it with a man, so why do it with a woman?*

8. *Thou must be a good father. If you have children, do half of everything. Domestic chores, pay your child support etc, and bring them up with love and kindness, while at the same time, providing them with the tools to deal with the bullshit of modern life. Remember you are a parent first, and a friend second, so maybe forget tattooing their name on your arm, and just help with their homework instead—it's less painful.*

9. *Thou must not control or be controlled. If you feel either urge, desist immediately and simply walk away.*

10. *Thou must never propose marriage on one knee or indulge in any other out-dated notions of chivalry or romantic love. Women are not Goddesses to be adored, cherished or protected. Remember the Muse is dead.*

11. *Thou must* **NOT** *consider that being successful with women is a measure of your manhood. Reject this notion; only around 20% of men manage this bogus ideal anyway and, in the end, it never makes them happy. Furthermore, if you think "gaming," or "negging," a woman is a good idea? Forget it. Your days are over, time to grow up.*

12. *Thou must not equate any sort of bravery with Romance. Forget "faint heart, never won a fair maid", and leave courage and spontaneity for something more important. There is more to life than Boy meets Girl-* ***Remember Friendship is the higher love.***

Luke and Vaughan had originally intended to include 22 "Commandments", detailing everything from "thou shalt not put down the toilet seat," (shouldn't the same etiquette be extended to a man?), to "thou shalt not be the one to get out of the bed, if there's a noise downstairs," (why should men get battered by burglars) to Vaughan's personal bugbear, "if you are under 30, thou shall not date older women" as he was getting more than a little irritated trying to compete with " younger bastards who had a better six pack than him".

However, in the end they had settled on 12 Rules and to their complete astonishment, the book stated to sell by the truckload, at one stage, out- selling 50 Shades of Grey, the erotic sensation from 2011, thus provoking a comment from Suzanne Burke, who stated in her weekly column, that "women buy books about sexual pleasure and men buy books about being told what to do, tells you something about men doesn't it." However, Vaughan dismissed this as "just more man-shaming" and despite intense criticism from every corner of the mainstream media, the "Book of Mithras" proved to be the right book at the right time and pushed the popularity of the movement to an even greater audience.

Furthermore, with all the support and interest in their ideas and proposals it soon became obvious to Luke and Vaughan that books and podcasts were not nearly enough and actual centres where men could meet and discuss their problems would have to be established. Therefore, with the revenue from the book and increasing donations from men and in few cases, some women, Mithras Centres quickly mushroomed all over the country, so males could now talk freely about their experiences and difficulties in modern life, without the hindrance of the female gaze. Predictably, as soon as they opened, the new venues came under fierce attack from women's groups and the left-wing press, who complained that these all-male environments, harked back to the sexism of "men only" clubs of the nineteenth century and would only cause greater division between the sexes. However, Mithras quickly pushed back against these accusations, stating that "Women have their spaces, so why can't we? And why shouldn't men have a place to meet and talk about their issues without it being considered sinister or ridiculous?" before publishing on their official website, a strict code of conduct for all members, which prohibited, on pain of immediate expulsion, amongst other things, derogatory language such as Bitch, Hoe or Slut, or any open aggression or hatred towards females. Furthermore, Mithras declared that all men were welcome, not simply, Hetero- sexual, but Gay and Trans men also, while at same time, women were cordially invited to visit their buildings at any time to ensure everything was operating in a proper manner.

Unfortunately, these concessions seemed to have very little effect, as almost immediately the Centres found themselves, picketed on a full-time basis by feminist groups, who set up a permanent protest outside most of the movement's premises and tried, on many occasions, to bar men from walking in "like nuns outside an abortion clinic" as Vaughan would later comment. Unsurprisingly, these actions did little to improve matters, and only increased the general antipathy from a large majority of the male population, which combined with the recent controversy of the Donna McCauley case, made any chance of an immediate reconciliation between the sexes, recede further and further into the distance.

The first to feel the effects of this increasing discord, were the online dating sites, such as Tinder and Bumble who started to report huge falls in business, while Fridays and Saturday nights in towns and cities around the UK, were now virtual wastelands, with many men choosing to actively avoid the company of women, and just socialise with each other. "This is worse than the COVID" screamed one newspaper, as it showed pictures of empty town centres, while Donna McCauley in an introduction to one of her daytime programmes, made an impassioned plea for things to return to normal, as "we all love each other really, and it's just banter, isn't it?" but it was to no avail. The mood was changing and changing fast, as events like Glastonbury, Wimbledon and even the traditional Ladies Day at Ascot, were severely impacted with thousands of men staying away, while in early July, seven of the ten male contestants of Love Island decided to walk off the set of the popular reality TV show, citing irreconcilable differences with the excesses of female expectation, thus causing the show to be cancelled. The Love Island 7 as they were now being called, were not alone, as this collective cold shoulder, even extended to the very young, as teenaged boys, emboldened by the campaign, refused to attend or take girlfriends to the end of year School Proms, and before long the internet was awash with videos of parents arguing with each other on door-steps or on street corners, while they defended or attacked the merits of their son's decision. Vaughan, in particular, was ecstatic at this new development, long considering the School Prom, to be emblematic of "the complete bullshit and double standards of the whole romance business and was just another American export that needed to be thrown back into the Atlantic", although later he would have to row back on some of his remarks, and issue an apology to many of his Mithranian brothers in the United States, who were, understandably, a little aggrieved at his remarks. However, despite these little disagreements, the movement was now proving unstoppable, as experts desperately scratched their collective heads to try and get to grips with the new phenomena.

Male empowerment, was it necessary?

Surely men were in control anyway?

Was this just a reaction to Women's rights?

There didn't seem to be any clear answers to these questions, and not for the last time in history, the world seemed to move beyond the ken of the chattering classes as the zeitgeist ploughed on regardless, without them.

The world of business quickly realised this too, and although, for the previous five years or so, they had been committed to a "more progressive and inclusive" message, now, after the relative chaos caused by Mithras and rising male frustration, worldwide, predictably, they sensed a new direction of travel. First to jump on the bandwagon, was cosmetic giant, Draco Strabane, who produced a new after-shave for men called "Co-Exist", together with a popular advert showing a cool, good looking guy walking through a bar of beautiful women and ignoring them, to simply meet up with his male friends outside. Other firms followed suit, as the needs and views of "the ordinary guy" suddenly became the new driving force of money and finance.

Inevitably the world of art, started to reflect these changes too, as male artists, previously forced by a woke, creative establishment to walk on egg-shells for many years, now started to make their voices heard again. Here, celebrated Spanish artist Javier Mendez collaborated with British art bad boy Darnell Tucker, to produce an exhibition simply called "Man", which was a video installation plotting the trials of being male in the 21st Century. Filmed exclusively on a smart-phone, this controversial piece depicted amongst other things, a mother dressed in a Nazi uniform using over-affection and risk averse parenting to raise her son, before handing him over to his wife, also dressed in a Nazi uniform, and then shown to be in a constant state of dissatisfaction, until in the final frame of the piece, she executes her husband with a hammer for not giving her an orgasm. This predictably caused huge uproar and large demonstrations appeared immediately outside the gallery to have the exhibition shut down, as claims of extreme misogyny and the uses of old sexist tropes of the malign female influence on men were levelled at the artists. However, Javier Mendez dismissed these criticisms, by simply stating, "If a female artist had said this, it would be seen as interesting and thought provoking, but I say it and its disgusting and dangerous. How is that fair?"

Music too, was making its presence felt in the new thinking, as *He ain't Heavy, He's My Brother by The Hollies, No Woman, No Cry by Bob Marley, Bad Boys by Wham and of course Love is a Drug by Roxy Music* quickly entered the charts again, while Mithras joined in the fun by issuing a list of acceptable love songs for the new century. So, *Youth by Daughter, Love is a Losing Game by Amy Winehouse and Rainy Night in Soho by The Pogues*, which happened to be Vaughan's favourite, were seen as positive, as they talked of the pain and ecstasy of romantic love. However, *Without You by Nilsson, God Only Knows by The Beach Boys*, and *Everything I Do, I Do for You by Bryan Adams,* were considered off limits as they described men, either with no agency, or having to be saved by the love of a "good woman".

Furthermore, it wasn't only music from the past that was having its effect, as new artists such as the ironically named, neo-punk/grime band *The Misogynists*, brought a younger and more unashamedly stoic perspective to the fore, with their debut album, *Love is Over-rated* including the tracks *Male Lysistrata, Let's Break up for Christmas*, a future festive number 1 and the seven-minute epic, *We are not Bonobos*, which was a stinging attack on modern manhood, sedated by sex and consumerism. The album, itself, went double platinum in its first week of release and as well as providing the soundtrack to the summer, it also stayed at number 1 for most of the year, as other *"Cock Rock"* bands and singers, so named by the music press, as all the members were men, like the grime artist *T Apocalypse* and *The Helicopter Mums*, also entered the charts. Meanwhile singer-songwriter *Ned Conroy* provided some quiet reflection for this new genre with his acoustic compositions such as *I Suppose I'm Wrong Again? What Is a Man?* and in particular, *Street Play Day*, a song about being only allowed to play on his street every third Sunday in a month, while supervised by concerned mothers dressed in yellow tabards, thus giving a much-needed voice to young men, who felt a general claustrophobia about being brought up in a sanitised and feminised world. Very soon, men of every colour and background flocked, in their thousands, to gigs by these new artists, and when Reading and Creamfields refused to book any *Cock Rock* bands, because of their "so-called" misogynist content, male only festivals or events immediately sprang up at secret locations all around the country to cater for this new audience.

Now, in what was being referred to in the press as *The Summer of Bruv,* and in circumstances reminiscent of the early days of the rave culture in the late 1980's, every weekend saw thousands of men travelling around the country in cars, vans, and mopeds, pursued by armies of policemen sent by the Prime Minister to break up these illegal parties. However, unlike in the previous century, this time, there was a fair amount of collusion between the Police and the Ravers, as many of the officers, were themselves Mithras members and so regularly tipped off the organisers if there was going to be a raid on a field in the middle of Dorset or a warehouse in Rotherham. To further complicate matters women's groups and social justice warriors started follow these illegal raves around the country and sought to disrupt them, as Mithras urged complete restraint on behalf of their members and encouraged all men not to physically engage with the protesters. Alas, despite this directive, inevitably alterations between protesters and ravers began to occur on a regular basis, as videos started to appear online of men being routinely assaulted or having milk shakes thrown on them by angry woman. Obviously, this provoked a huge backlash from the majority of men, as Mithras issued a statement on its website to condemn the on-going violence. "You can hit us, but we can't retaliate, can we? We can't chat you up on the street, but we have to laugh along, if we are ever accosted by a drunken hen night. Double standards! This is why men can never compete with women on an even playing field, because whatever we do, we will always look like bullies, won't we? Maybe, it's time society stopped condoning women pushing, slapping or throwing drinks on men whenever they felt upset by their behaviour. It's pathetic and it has to stop." Naturally Women's groups, hit back immediately stating that "although no-one deserves to be physically attacked, it's laughable for Mithras to make any comment on violence between the sexes in a world where every day, women suffer at the hands of men."

Nonetheless, the chasm between men and women was only getting wider and so by the end of the Summer of 2026, Vaughan appeared to sum up the general mood, when he famously tweeted, *I could never be racist, because my sex isn't the real problem, is it? In fact, Men are only separated by social class and melanin, whereas males and females are divided by just about everything else.*

There was, it seemed, no going back now.

Chapter 16

Alex sat behind his desk and slowly chewed on his gum. while he stared at the Jack Russell lying on the carpet in front of him, who after looking back for a few seconds towards his master, returned all his focus to licking its own balls once more. At least someone was happy, sighed the billionaire, as he placed his hands behind his head and sat back in his black leather chair.

They had fucked with him, and despite all of his endless resources, and an army of woke celebrities, they had fucked with him and they had won. Even his new protégé, Jake O'Callaghan, was getting nowhere, and despite all the taunts of clever comedians on TV shows and podcasts, most men were still rejecting the instructions of "the establishment", while gleefully sticking up two defiant fingers to anyone who disagreed with Luke Casey and his Mithras revolution.

He should have guessed.

When a change comes, it comes, and there's no use fighting it. Alex had seen it with Brexit and Trump, and he could nearly have kicked himself for not seeing it again this time. Hadn't he been the first punk in his school, when everyone else was wearing flares? Cracked on to dance music, while all the trendy wankers at university were still dressed in old Clash T-Shirts? And then at the end of the 1980's, backed the third way in politics, about the same time, as all his mates were heading towards some elusive Socialist Utopia? Still, it would keep, thought Alex, there was way too much power standing guard against the likes of Mithras for them to make a lasting impact, and anyway Jake was a talented boy, his time would come.

He liked dealing with men like Jake.

Gobby public school boys with potable integrities, who liked their working class at a safe distance, either from the past, nobly fighting the fascists on Cable Street or in the present, totally skint and helpless in a food bank. He didn't even have to work that hard to get him on board, as after a couple of pints in the Chelsea Potter in the Kings Road, and regaling the radio host with a few drug stories from the 1990's about a couple of famous bands he knew, he had quickly melted Jake's snowflake heart, so by the time they had gotten onto the shorts, he had managed to persuade him that (a) he was not the monster who had started a war that virtually wiped out a quarter of a million innocent women and children, and (b) he should have his own show on UK terrestrial T.V.

He was nearly skipping after that.

Then again, all that "talent "and Mithras were still winning, sighed the media mogul staring blankly at the ceiling for a few seconds, before leaning forward to tap a key on his lap-top.

Here was the real power behind Mithras, thought Alex as a picture of Vaughan appeared on his screen.

He wasn't surprised, his contacts inside the organisation had already told him as much, and he'd even become a regular subscriber to Vaughan's weekly podcast Nothing 2 Lose.

He was funny, clever, insightful.

Five years ago, he would have given him a job.

But not now.

Now he was out of time and he didn't even know it.

He didn't even use his preferred pronouns in his bio.

Silly Boy.

Didn't he know, that this was the new masonic code, the hidden handshake, to say I'm like you, I'm one of the elect. Personally, Alex couldn't give a toss about she/her, or they/them, as any fool knew biological sex was real, but that wasn't the point, was it? It told you, who wanted the right kind of progress, and the noble little ravings of men like Vaughan were simply the last cries of a wounded wolf in a shopping mall, thought the media mogul as he reached over his desk and picked up his mobile phone.

"Hey Suze, can you do an interview with this Vaughan 2Lose character? Yeah, the bloke in Mithras, who's always photographed with Luke Casey. Yeah, find out what he's really up to, dig a bit, get something juicy. You know the craic, and pretty sharpish, if you don't mind. Anything you need, don't ring my secretary, ring me directly, yeah? This is very important, cheers hon" said the billionaire before he placing his phone back on his desk and folding his arms. The future of the world couldn't rest in the hands of cocky upstarts like Luke Casey, or clever Svengalis like Vaughan 2Lose, all looking for an ill-considered form of freedom. A freedom with no compromise, with no knowledge of how things really worked. That kind of unfettered liberty was as dangerous as the Ebola virus, he thought smiling to himself for a second or two, until his eyes suddenly widened in terror and he was thrust back into his chair, while the uniformed figure of Kelly David marched confidently into the room for his daily visit. He was late, but grinning like a schoolboy, the Sergeant quickly approached the desk and then moving his hands to either side of his head, he slowly pulled his skull apart, so gallons of blood, now started to pour out onto the carpet like a crimson waterfall while Alex jammed his eyes tightly shut and tried not to scream.

Chapter 17

"This is no way good enough," shouted Jake, slamming his hand down on the table in front of him, before glaring back at the startled faces of his team.

What a bunch of fucking dipshits, his mind barked, as an overwhelming urge to grab an axe and smash the meeting room into a thousand pieces, suddenly gripped the chat show host, until realising that, not only was a good bollocking, a thing of the past, but some cock might secretly video his rant, he slowly lowered his head and took a deep breath.

Keep it together Jake, remember what happened to that CEO on a zoom call recently his mind counselled, and so after taking another moment, he produced an amiable grin from somewhere, before looking back towards his team once more.

"Okay, sorry everyone, didn't mean to shout, but come on, where the hell are we going with all this?"

"Well, maybe we could arrange a fund-raiser?" suggested Simon

"Or another march?" added Meghan

"Or perhaps do one of those ice bucket water challenges, from years ago? You know, something fun to highlight our side of the argument," offered Becky looking around the table for some support, before, Jake placed his chin onto the palm of his hand and heaved one of his trademark sighs.

"Well, it's just one of those things, Jake. Mithras are doing well because they are tapping into something that's been around since the Ark. Dissatisfaction with women. Apologies to the women here of course, but sadly that's how a lot of men are, you know." declared Marcus trying to console his old radio colleague from the other end of the table.

"Err, actually I think they stress that women aren't the enemy," interrupted Hugo brightly.

"Oh, so you agree with them, then?" snapped Jake as he turned to look accusingly at the slightly overweight young man seated in the middle of the table.

"Err no, of course not, Jake, but err, I am just saying what they are saying, you know, I don't necessarily think…."

"This is what I am talking about! This bloody sympathy. There is no sympathy is there? Their message is toxic, divisive, right? interrupted Jake, angling his hand towards the hapless researcher, while all the heads in front of him began a vigorous nod before the radio host returned his chin to the palm of his hand and sighed again. Only recently he'd had to fire two male members of his staff, after finding out that they had secretly joined Mithras and he still had his suspicions about that a few others around the table, including the pointless Hugo.

There was no doubt it.

He was losing.

Luke Casey, Josh Middleton, Mason Meyer and all the other celebrity half-wits were not only winning, but they were owning the argument. Every day, bolshy Scallies, gobby Geordies, and loudmouth Essex boys, were calling in with cult like devotion, all repeating the same "women are not the enemy" and "we don't want their approval" mantras, with only chinless wonders from Muswell Hill to counter the onslaught, bleating, "I think women deserve more respect" and "we must listen more".

It was like he was back in the dorms again, getting taunted by the cool kids and his only friends were the social misfits who were good at physics or members of the chess club. He'd even brought Mason Meyers on his TV show the other night to expose the laddish misogyny of the new movement, only to hear one of his resident comedians, Cinesias Spence, who was normally hilarious, suddenly reveal that before having sex with his girlfriend, he masturbated first, so he wouldn't impose his primal urges on her. "Why don't you just shag her twice," the soap star had declared to huge laughter from the audience, as even the feminist commentators had little time for dear, sensitive Cinesias, and sniggered from their Sunday columns, as the online world continued to side with Mason and his Mithras posse.

Brilliant!

Now they are chuckling along with the thickest celebrity on the planet and he was left looking as out of touch as an Anglican Bishop thought Jake as he tapped the table with his pen, while the faces in front of him continued to strain for a solution, until finally a familiar voice punctured the silence.

"We could do a documentary,"

"Err yeah, Antigone, but didn't Channel 4 just do one of those?" replied the chat show host, but this time without the usual irritation in his voice.

"Yes, they did, but it was only half an hour long, and it was more of a 'what's going on with modern men', rather than anything Mithras are up to. What I mean is that we do a deep-level investigation, find out what's really going on. As far as I can see, Mithras have taken a bit of a battering from Suzanne Burke and Portia Ramone and a few of her film star friends, who no-one is really listening to anyway, but otherwise they have been given a free ride."

"Well, I think I have had a little go as well, Antigone," replied Jake, playfully sticking out his bottom lip.

"Of course, that goes without saying, Jake, and you have been totally brilliant. But it's just you, isn't it? I mean a few people have grumbled about this and that, but nothing really impactful. Mithras are winning the argument and we need to change that; Luke Casey and people like him are dangerous."

"Yes, they are dangerous, fucking dangerous! I've been saying this for months now," replied Jake, suddenly sitting up in his seat with renewed vigour, while he noticed the delicate shape of her slender neck,

"Well, whatever we do, it has to be a better outcome than the interview with Luke Casey's ex. No disrespect, Jake, but that did more harm than good," interrupted his radio producer from the end of the table again before Jake's shoulders slumped once more and he took a consolatory sip from his coffee cup.

Marcus might be an annoying dick, thought the chat show host, but he was right on this one. Mia had turned out to be a bit of a fantasist and in reality, had only dated the Mithras leader for a few weeks, before basically stalking him for the next two years and Luke's mother rant online about her turning up unannounced to family events like christenings and 40th birthday parties had left the TV host with egg on his face and he would do anything to avoid that again.

"Okay agreed we don't want any more of that, but yes maybe a documentary could work, but a bloody good one, like a Michael Moore. Let's really get inside this thing, there has to be something? You get more than four men together and there's always some scandal, some nasty behaviour, I mean look at your average cricket club for god's sake. What do you think Jake?" continued Marcus with increasing enthusiasm.

"Uh, really? a Documentary? Bit last century, isn't it?" replied Jake now staring off into the distance and looking very unconvinced again.

"Yes, I totally agree, but then so is a book and look how successful the Book of Mithras has been? We would have to do it properly, no mistakes, get a top director," said Antigone now staring directly at Jake.

"Definitely, definitely. Someone like Adam Curtis, Can't Get You Out of My Head kinda thing, but with that Nick Broomfieldy vibe, like on his Tupac and Suge Knight doc," joined in Simon.

"Yeah, loved that," replied Hugo.

"Well, I was thinking someone younger, less tied to the past. Maybe Mark Eastwood?" replied Antigone.

"Who?" asked Marcus.

"Yes of course. He would be perfect. He gets people to say the most mental things, and he always gets the dirt. Did you see that thing he did on Boris Johnson?" replied Simon.

"Yeah, totally sick," replied Hugo.

"You won't get him. He lives in a council house in Wigan or Northampton or somewhere up that way, only lives on the minimum wage apparently." countered a young woman with a blue fringe and a nose-ring sitting opposite Simon.

"Really? his documentaries make millions," replied Hugo, now a little put out.

"Suppose he wants to keep it real. Yeah, yeah, you're right, Jocasta, he won't do it, he only does things that interest him," agreed Simon.

"Well, if he's that good, I will make a few calls," replied Marcus nodding in the direction of Jake.

"You won't get him. Seriously Marcus, he even turned Corbyn down. Makes Banksy look like fucking Nigel Farage," continued Simon before Jake gave him a disapproving glance from across the table.

Only he and Marcus did the swearing in the meeting and Simon dutifully lowered his head and started scribbling something on the pad in front of him, while the chat show host stared off into the distance once more.

"I could talk to a guy I know in Channel 4," offered Marcus after a brief silence.

"It's okay, I know a man," Jake replied now smiling again, before he sat back in his seat and took another sip of his coffee.

Chapter 18

The fifty or so people assembled in the bar of the football club raised their heads and smiled, as the man in front of them, stared down at the faded carpet underneath his feet for a few seconds before he looked up sheepishly again and started to speak.

"Err, err, yeah, ha, err, not very good at this type of thing really, but I just wanted to say a few words you know, about me and Maria's 25th anniversary. So, you all know how fuck...oops there are kids here ain't there? sorry, err how messed up I was, doing things I shouldn't and all that."

"Pill head," came a shout from the back of the crowd.

"Well, you should know, Jim, you sold him most of 'em," cried another voice, to general laughter, while the speaker, now stepped back and waited patiently for the noise to die down, before starting to speak again.

"Yeah, yeah, well, that was a long time ago, wern it, but anyways, you all know how I was and where I was headed, and it wasn't good, not good at all. But then I met Maria, and I have to say that night when I saw her down the Golden Gloves in Fulham, twenty-seven years ago, was just amazing. I mean, she looked stunning as she always does, and I just knew when I saw her, that she was the one for me, well you do, don't you? But as amazing as that night was, that was the second-best day of my life, cos the best day of my life was when two years later, she stupidly said that she would be my wife, and then that was the start of everything, really. Our two lovely children, Callum and Natalie, who are here today and who we love very much, and then getting a house and all that. And course we've had our ups and downs like everyone, I mean who doesn't really, but I can honestly say, that without Maria, God knows where I would be right now? No honestly, I'm really serious here. I know people say that all the time, but hand on my heart, I really don't know where I'd be without her. She saved me, pure and simple. Happy 25th anniversary darling, I owe you everything."

"Sounds like he's shagging his mum," whispered Vaughan in Suzanne's ear, as the journalist now lowered her head, desperately trying to suppress a laugh, before thankfully, everyone else around her started to clap loudly, and then move forward to congratulate the happy couple.

"That was naughty," reprimanded Suzanne with a mischievous grin, as they both turned around and walked towards the bar, to get some drinks.

"Really? Think I've had enough of middle-aged men telling me how much their wives have saved them, know what I mean?" declared Vaughan, before quickly raising a twenty-pound note in the air.

"Cynic. They seem nice though," offered Suzanne.

"Actually, Brendan and Maria are lovely. They might even be in love, whatever that is, but look at the rest of them. Seriously thinking their lives are incomplete without that special someone. Ridiculous. I reckon about ten percent of relationships actually work and that's only through blind luck. Ten percent! I mean that's the same amount of people in the world, who are left-handed. I'm left-handed but I don't get loads of right-handed people coming up to me saying Oh wow, Vaughan, I wish I was left-handed."

"Point being…"

"The point being, Miss Burke, is that ninety percent of people who are in mostly boring, mechanical, relationships, usually wishing they were somewhere else, seem to drive themselves almost insane to be in this so-called glorious ten percent and I just think, they should give it a fucking rest, know what I mean?" declared Vaughan, accepting two drinks from the barman, whilst showing the journalist the faintest hint of a cheeky smile.

Jesus, he loved to talk, didn't he? she thought as she studied his profile, and watched in amused silence while he nodded and winked at a succession of middle-aged men and women who began to walk past the bar. This was not exactly what she had expected from her interview with the Machiavelli of men's liberation, but when he asked if she fancied going to a party to conduct the interview, it felt as if he was testing her, even daring her. Are you just another boring hack? same questions? same conclusions? No, she wasn't. But she wasn't stupid either. Neutral ground was always best, and she was just about to refuse until he added, "Cos if you are gonna do a hatchet job on me for that war mongering bastard, McDonald, then we might as well have some fun too."

Suzanne was sold, and although she was well aware that he was tapping into her inner mischief, she found, to her surprise, on this occasion, she didn't really mind. Anyway, her heart was way too frozen to be melted again, but she liked his smile, it was warm and a little dirty, and she even liked the way that he swaggered about with an almost knowing arrogance. She would really have to sleep with him, she thought as she took another sip of her drink and stared into his dark, brown eyes again.

For the next hour or so, the two of them continued to chat by the bar about Mithras and the general aims of the organisation, until they were eventually joined by Jimmy Jazz, Davie B and Andy Papps, Vaughan's oldest friends. Where the hell did men get their bloody names from? What was wrong with Shazzer or Tay Tay?, the journalist thought, as more drinks were bought, before inevitably, the men gathered in a circle around her, so the testosterone pantomime could begin in earnest.

"Why can't we say bird anymore? I mean, I wouldn't mind if women had a dodgy name for us," protested Jimmy Jazz."

"What? Like Dick you mean?" replied Davie B.

Suzanne laughed.

Normally, she wasn't that enamoured by boysy repartee. It was mostly boring and very predictable, but as she sat perched on a bar stool and sipping on her vodka and tonic, she had to admit that Vaughan's friends were fun and despite their constant desire to be "diamond geezers" they reminded her of the people that she'd grown up with in the North- West of England. Generous in spirit, gritty, authentic and although she knew these same people could also be cruel, prejudiced and incredibly narrow minded, for the present, she allowed herself a few hours off being the guardian of all things woke, to just have a good time. By midnight, everyone had melted away, leaving just herself and Vaughan, and when he suggested that she come back to his place for a "brandy and Lucozade", she smiled and said lead the way.

"So why did you want to interview me and not Luke, he's the poster boy for Mithras, isn't he?" asked Vaughan, as Suzanne, moved her hand over the contours of his chest, and then traced her finger down to his almost flat stomach.

"Ooh I think I would much rather talk to Iago than Othello."

"Ouch. That's a bit Jodie Harsh. Luke's his own man, you know."

"I bet he is. But aren't you two on this same journey together, then?" replied Suzanne smirking.

"If you like."

"You boys and your duos. Butch and Sundance, Mick and Keef…"

"You girls and your disapproval of men being exclusive from female power. Bromance Nazis!" replied Vaughan, as Suzanne stuck her tongue out and then looked into his eyes once more.

"So, Vaughan 2 Chippy, what have you got against us little old women, then? I have read your Book of Mithras, and its rules. Hasn't it all been said before? Make you bed, sort your life out. Bit sixth-formy don't you think?"

"Is this the interview, Miss Burke?"

"Ha! of course," laughed Suzanne.

You usually conduct your interviews like this?"

"Are you calling me a tart, kind sir?"

"Never! Commandment Six. Never slut shame," replied Vaughan raising a solemn hand.

"Answer the question."

"Okay. Do you know why I started all this pod-casting malarkey, way before Luke or Mithras turned up?" replied Vaughan now sitting up a little in the bed.

"Oh goody, a story," grinned Suzanne quickly folding her arms.

"Yeah, yeah whatevs. Anyway, about fifteen years ago, I was coming back from Ibiza. I'd been out there for a week visiting a mate of mine who lived on the island. Bit of a DJ, well thought he was, more like a drug dealer with a good record collection, but anyway I'm coming back on the plane, and there's this party of women, sat next to me, all quite young, probably in their mid-thirties, all having a brilliant time, you know chatting, drinking the duty free, nothing lairy or anything, just funny. So, we get chatting, and I started to have a drink with them and they were absolutely hilarious. Seriously. They'd been on a hen night for the weekend and for the whole flight, they told jokes, teased each other, talked about their kids. I mean they were all married except for the girl whose hen night it was, but it was great. I mean most flights are rubbish, aren't they? but this one was a really good you know, one of the few you'd actually remember. So anyway, we land and we get off and they are still smiling when we say our goodbyes and I walk ahead of them to get my luggage and then, just as I am about to walk out of the terminal to where everyone is waiting, I look around to check where the next train back to London is leaving, when suddenly I see the girls that I was chatting to on the plane come out of the baggage area and they are all laughing, until suddenly, as one, they all stop smiling. Like dead in the water, as if someone had punched them in the face or something. So obviously, I look over to see if there is a problem and as I walk closer, do you know what I see?"

"Piers Morgan" replied Suzanne.

"Worse. Their husbands. So, anyways I move a little closer, just in case they are all horrible wife beaters or something, but I find there is no problem, in fact the men are all smiling, and they have even brought the kids with them. But the women are not smiling, well except for the one getting married, she is still okay, but these women who five seconds earlier, were as happy as Larry, were now looking like a bulldog chewing a wasp. So, naturally, this freaks me out, so I move closer again to find out what's really going on, and then I hear the women start to have a go at the men about how the kids aren't dressed properly and where's the car, yadda yadda and they looked so pissed off. I mean, sooooo pissed off! and what's even worse the men were just grinning like fucking idiots and that's when it hit me. Something is fundamentally wrong here!" declared Vaughan, suddenly raising his finger in the air, before placing both of his hands behind his head on the pillow to indicate the end of the story.

There was now complete silence in the bedroom, while the journalist sat up and crossed her legs, as if she was seriously considering the merits of what she had just heard, until a puckish grin appeared on her face and she suddenly burst into howls of laughter.

"That's it? That's your inciting incident for the biggest social earthquake since Black Lives Matter? Some women didn't wet themselves with excitement when they saw their husbands! Really? They are not smiling, my little cupcake, because they know, they will have to do all the bloody work for the next 52 weeks. No wonder the men were smiling, a weekend of looking after the kids probably nearly killed them," replied Suzanne staring down at Vaughan's grinning face."

"Yeah, yeah, heard it all before, and you know what else I noticed?"

"Oh, do tell, oh intuitive one?"

"The women kissed the kids first before their husbands or partners."

"It gets worse."

"It's not nice, Suzanne."

"Who cares?"

"We do."

"Jesus, Vaughan, you are stretching it a bit now, love."

"Am I? so tell me why, when they saw their husbands, did they stop smiling?

"Maybe they were dicks," replied Suzanne.

"Maybe, they're weren't."

"Well, that's marriage, I am afraid."

"Exactly, so why go through all the bloody the pretence in the first place. What was it Lampedusa said in *The Leopard?* Fire for a year and ashes for thirty? He wasn't wrong, was he? And anyway, we all know, women love their kids more than their men, it's nearly tattooed to their flipping heads. It's seriously fucked up and so yeah, that's the reason why I started doing a podcast. To liberate my own sex," said Vaughan, now folding his arms.

"Like you lot need liberating."

"Wanna bet? You ever listen to a man who's been in a long-time relationship, Suzanne? They all talk as if they've been a survivor from a Siberian gulag, or a twenty-year famine. You know, "it's really hard, but you just gotta get through it, you know really work at it". That so big nose? Well, if it's that fucking hard, why bother in the first place?"

"Nonsense. Men live much longer, when they're with a woman" replied Suzanne, shaking her head.

"Exactly! And the stats show, that for women, it's the total opposite! They live longer, when they're on their own. It's a bad deal for chicks! You should be on my side on this one, Suzanne. In fact, I would go, even, so far as to say, that relationships are just a human's way of weaning themselves off the love drug. About two years in love, four years to enjoy the security and then two more years to realise you don't really love them anymore and you are ready to meet someone else," confirmed Vaughan with a grin.

"Jesus! you're so romantic," swooned Suzanne.

"I am, as it goes."

"Yeah right."

"Actually, Men are the guardians of romance, I'll have you know," announced Vaughan, before turning his head to look at the journalist.

"God in heaven! Not another slogan!" replied Suzanne, throwing her hands in the air.

"Well, it's true. Women know nothing about romance, because romance is about the chase, isn't it, so how could they know? You know what women know a lot about? Sex. They are the guardians of sex. Men know sod all about good sex" confirmed Vaughan.

"Well, we all know that, don't we?" replied Suzanne

"Precisely, and that's why men are the guardians of romance," repeated Vaughan.

"Stop! I'm not listening," protested Suzanne, now putting her hands over her ears.

"Okay, who writes all the love songs then?" persisted Vaughan

"More bullshit!" spat back Suzanne, closing her eyes.

"It's mostly men."

"Don't be stupid," replied Suzanne, opening her eyes again.

"I'm not being stupid. I looked it up,"

"I bet you did."

"The only love songs I could find written exclusively by a woman were: *I Will Always Love You by Dolly Parton, The Man with The Child in His Eyes by Kate Bush,* and *Love and Affection by Joan Armatrading,* " revealed Vaughan, folding his arms.

"What? That's rubbish!" cried Suzanne, now abandoning her original plan to ignore his latest line of bullshit, before crinkling her forehead, as she desperately tried to think of other female-penned love songs.

"You sure?" added the journalist, as her mind suddenly drew a complete blank.

"Totally."

"Bullshit. You're wrong! What about *Crazy in Love by Beyonce?!,*

"Nope. Co-wrote it with two other geezers," replied Vaughan shaking his head.

"You sure?! Okay, okay, got you now, smarty pants. *Someone Like You by Adele?!,* that's sooo gotta be her" announced Suzanne clapping her hands together with glee, before bursting into song, and taunting Vaughan with the first few lines of the famous hymn to female heartache.

"Sorry, she wrote it with a guy called Dan Wilson" shot back Vaughan with a grin.

"What really?!" exclaimed Suzanne, now bringing her singing to a halt, as she looked sideways in disbelief.

"Google it? In fact, my in-depth research has revealed that unlike men, who write songs such as *It Must Be Love, Your Song or Can't Take My Eyes off You,* celebrating the joys of emotional love, women tend to write songs about either being generally dissatisfied with men, like *You're Not Quite Harry Styles by*

Dylan or just wanting to stab them in the face a hundred times with some scissors, as in anything by P.J. Harvey."

"With very good reason, matey, because it's usually men who are the cause of all the crap that women have to put up with, half the time. Jesus! I can't believe I'm having this conversation?! It's total misogynistic rubbish!" spat back Suzanne shaking her head and getting more annoyed, before adding, "*What about Rhianna, We Found Love?*"

"Written by Calvin Harris, and a man wrote *I Will Survive by Gloria Gaynor* AND Gerry Goffin wrote the lyrics to *Natural Born Woman by Aretha Franklin.*"

"What? Really? I love that song," replied Suzanne, now frowning with her arms crossed again, while Vaughan gave her a smug grin, before laying his head back down on the pillow once more.

"Anyway, it's all shit. You lot don't mean a fucking word of it. I mean look at Billy Joel, he wrote *I Love You Just the Way You Are* for his wife, then three years later, the twat left her to go out with a supermodel, so who really cares what you idiots write," announced Suzanne squeezing her arms tighter together, as Vaughan laughed out loud for a few seconds, before leaning across to try and kiss her lips. However, Suzanne had now sat up in the bed again and was instead glaring down at Vaughan with unforgiving eyes.

"What petal?" enquired Vaughan a little surprised at the sudden change of mood.

"Enough of your bullshit 2Lose."

"Excuse me?" replied Vaughan with a grin.

"I'm not buying all this tough guy shit. I know lots of men who dislike women, I can smell it from fifty yards, and that's not you," declared Suzanne, placing her hands on her hips.

"I could be wearing a different cologne to mask my internalised misogyny?"

"I doubt it."

"Fair enough. I only use a roll on, with an anti-chafing ball. You have gorgeous breasts, by the way."

"Forget the breasts."

"It's hard, they're lovely. You seem upset pumpkin?"

"I am."

"Pour quoi?"

"You're a fraud."

126

"You think?"

"Hundred percent. It's all a big front, because despite all this Mithras nonsense, it's obvious to anyone with half a brain, that you like women" snapped Suzanne.

"Of course, I do. I'm just not that convinced that you like us. I think women like the idea of men" replied Vaughan.

"Oh, that's such rubbish."

"Is it? As far as I can see, the only males, women really like, are their dads and their gay friends."

"Not true."

"You sure about that?"

"Okay, you might be a tiny bit right," conceded Suzanne, after a moment of consideration, before she sat back on her heels and took a long look into his eyes again. She could so fall for this guy; he was definitely her type. Selfish, funny, nice bum, and moving forward to kiss his lips, her hand slipped inside his white boxer shorts to caress his hard cock, while he slowly moved her knickers to one side, before gently touching her with the tip of his finger. God she was so wet and raising her head, she sighed again before looking deep into his eyes once more.

They were clear, direct, she could fall for him, she really could.

But she couldn't.

Well not now, anyway.

"No, no darling, stop."

"Whaaat!" cried Vaughan quickly moving away from Suzanne, before staring back with desperate eyes.

"I don't want to."

"Oh, okay. Is it something I did, I mean, you know I was joking about...?"

"No, not at all, it's just me."

"Anything I can say to change your mind."

"Not really."

"I can sing or I could recite you a Blake poem."

"No," replied Suzanne laughing.

"John Donne? Rumi? Barry White?"

"No, no darling, it's nothing you have done. I'm just not ready, that's all."

"Okay, fair enough," replied Vaughan lying back on the bed and placing his hands behind his head again.

"Are you okay?"

"Yeah, of course. It's totally your choice. I get it, it's no problem. Honestly."

"Are you sure?" asked Suzanne with half a smile.

"Well, obviously, I did fancy…"

"I know, but I didn't know myself, until now," interrupted Suzanne, now resting her head on the palm of her hand.

"But that's the point, isn't it? Women always know when they are gonna have sex, men never do. Ha! No wonder we're such assholes," laughed Vaughan, staring at the ceiling.

"Is your pride very hurt, cupcake?" asked Suzanne.

"Bollocks to my pride, honey bunch," replied Vaughan laughing again "I've just taken a bloody Viagra."

Chapter 19

Luke tried to stop looking at his phone.

He had only just powered it up and now it said 97%.

He wanted 100%, and angrily he grabbed it again and plugged it into his charger, before he standing back in the middle of the meeting room with his hands on his hips.

Of course, he knew what was happening.

It will pass, it will pass.

No, it fucking wont, his mind screamed back.

Sometimes he wished that he could have lived thirty years previous, when OCD was just a rumour, no-one knew what OnlyFans was and dinner ladies could afford to buy a house. Now an image of him having sex with a dinner lady holding a ladle of mashed potato and a cigarette hanging out of her mouth, barged its way into his half-crazed thoughts, as he rubbed his eternally damp palms together and began to pace around the empty meeting room. He'd tried mindfulness, meditation, yoga even, yet despite all this, he was still smoking thirty cigarettes a day, and masturbating like he was getting paid for it, and for the life of him, he couldn't understand why?

By rights he should be happy, elated even.

Men were finally taking charge of their lives; female approval was seen as unnecessary, the England football team had, the previous year, won the 2026 World Cup, with ninety percent of the squad declaring themselves as Mithras members, while even Ernie Featherstone, the diminutive, middle aged tech billionaire and owner of the Pittsburgh Giants Basketball Team had recently split from his six foot, 28-year-old "trophy wife", Krystyna, stating that women should never be seen as a reward for a successful life and from now on he would be looking for someone closer to his own age…and height.

The world had suddenly changed on a sixpence and what had started in the pandemic of 2020, was now finding its logical conclusion in 2027, as "being alone isn't nearly so bad," was the new mantra, for most men, and although there were repeated criticisms from older generations that romantic partnerships were a metaphor for life and you had to take the rough with the smooth, no one under 40 really seemed to be listening. Even the love locks on the Brooklyn and Rialto bridges were being removed, so why, after all this progress, did he feel this bad?

Luke had no idea and raised his eyes to the ceiling again, in search of some kind of an explanation, just as the door of the meeting room suddenly burst open, and Vaughan came walking in.

"Oh, alright?"

"Oh hi, err, just preparing a meeting," said Luke, a little shocked at the abrupt intervention into his troubled thoughts, before quickly pointing towards some notes on the table in front of him.

"Okay, so you want I should come back? just wanted to write something for my sub-stack," asked Vaughan with a warm smile, while he held up his laptop.

"No, it's fine," assured Luke, as the two men quickly exchanged friendly glances with each other before settling down at the large table in the middle of the room and starting to type. Six months ago, they had been conducting business above a charity shop, but now since the enormous amounts of money coming into Mithras accounts from membership fees and wealthy men tired of being called a sex pest every time, they tried to say something nice to their secretary, they could now open their new headquarters in some of the most expensive real estate in London.

Vaughan had chosen the site, because apparently it was situated "next to the old Blitz club, and just down the road from the Roxy", which obviously had something to do with the past, where everyone did a lot of spitting or running away from skinheads, thought Luke, but despite the dodgy nostalgia, with five floors of meeting rooms and office space, Covent Garden proved to be the perfect HQ for the new movement.

An easy silence descended over the two men, as Luke's heart now beat a little slower and his previous mania started to dissipate into the perfumed air of the meeting room while they both tapped away on their lap-tops for a few minutes more until Luke raised his head up from what he was doing and started to speak again.

"Oh, by the way Vaughan, I've been given an offer to go and set up a few Centres in the States. Spoke to Josh, the other day and he says he can reach out to some of the top people he knows out there, you know get us in the door."

"Reach out?! Flippin' hell! It sounds so victimy. Why can't people just say 'contact' anymore?" replied Vaughan, with a grimace.

"Ha! yeah but anyway, Josh thinks we can get some really big players in Hollywood and the Tech business involved, so we can properly get to the next level, you know really expand Mithras, make it a proper brand," gushed Luke excitedly, deciding, to ignore Vaughan's usual irritation with the lexicon of the modern world, before turning around in his chair to face the older man.

"Oh right, cos, that's exactly what we want, isn't it?" replied Vaughan laughing and shaking his head.

"Bruv, this is how things are done today, you know influencers and celebrities. I know you don't like it, but to be fair, it works. I mean, how does anyone know about anything unless someone with the right platform tells them?" replied Luke, now, with a little irritation in his voice.

"By ideas Luke. C'mon, do we really need another poxy celebrity to help us?"

"Of course! Look at Deacon Hiddlebatch."

"I'd rather not," replied Vaughan.

"What?! He's massive bro. When he refused to get any pictures taken with his top off, loads of men joined Mithras and then when he walked off the set of that Rom-Com, cos he didn't like the plot-line and said he didn't want to be saved by the love of a good woman, that was mega, you said so yourself."

"That was for his career Luke."

"No, it wasn't. He got sued by the streaming service for £150 million, he could have been bankrupted, until everyone started to cancel their subscriptions," protested Luke.

"Ha! Don't worry, he still does okay mate," replied Vaughan, looking back towards the screen of his lap-top again and smiling, while Luke sat back in his chair again and rubbed his face in frustration. He'd been having this conversation with his friend for months now, and it was starting to get seriously boring to say the least.

Why couldn't he see?

How didn't he get it?

The power of celebrity was everything these days.

Everything!

Where would Me Too have been without Portia Ramone or Black Lives Matter without footballer, Frederick Boyega, who had famously walked off the pitch in a Champions League Final the previous year after being racially abused. That was where the real power lay, Luke thought, and you only reaped the benefits by working with the system, not smashing it. It was blindingly obvious, Luke thoughts complained, but despite this blind spot in his old mentor's thinking, he still placed great store in Vaughan's opinion and so smiling again, he decided to try and navigate a middle course once more.

"Well yeah, I do get that, ideas are important, of course, that's how you get things started in the first place innit? but to be fair bruv, we also need the influencers as well, you know to get our message across. I mean people go on about celebrities all the time, about how false and shallow they are, but actually when you get to know them, it's not like that at all; they are just like you and me, really,"

"Well, you would know about that, a bit more than me, mate," grinned Vaughan

"Pardon?" replied Luke defensively.

"Oh, come on dude, even you'd have to admit it. All you do, these days, is hang about with Celebs. Ha! I bet you've even got Stephen Fry or Ed Sheeran on speed dial now! 'Err, sorry dahlink, can't make the party tonight, cos I'm having a ruby with Fitz and Ravi, gotta keep it real you know, but yah, will definitely make Soho House this Saturday."

"That's not fair, it's not like that," replied Luke now a little shaken by the force of Vaughan's sarcasm.

"Okay, I might be taking the piss a bit, mate, but there's some truth, in there too, don't you think?" replied Vaughan giving Luke a little wink.

"No, there isn't! It's not us versus them! Josh might be well off, but he's a really good bloke once you get to know him, I mean he's done loads for Mithras, stuff you've never seen, bruv" spat back Luke, now getting more annoyed.

"They always do Luke. The Josh Middleton's of this world and every other bright young thing in history. They jump on any bandwagon slow enough to pick them up mate, you know little distractions to keep them occupied. One minute they are fucking die-hard socialists, while the next they are buying an island in the Caribbean. Geezer, these are the tossers who sleep out in £500 arctic sleeping bags for one night in Trafalgar square to raise awareness about the homeless, while Dame Maggie Whatever reads 'em a bedtime story to get them to sleep." said Vaughan, now sitting further back in his chair.

"Actually, that did help, Josh went on that, and it raised millions," replied Luke defiantly, remembering the famous 'sleep out for the homeless' campaign from a few months earlier.

"The only thing it raised, was the blood pressure of the poor bastards who ACTUALLY have to sleep rough. People like that don't care mate, they are social tourists, like those bloody Trustifarians I used to know down Ladbroke Grove when I was a kid. Get a bit of working-class cock for a few years, and then marry the doctor or the banker that they were always destined to end up with, in the first place. Except now of course, they have a few more interesting stories to tell at their shabby little dinner parties, when they are middle aged and past it. I used to tell my mates, to steer clear of 'em, they will use you and spit you out, but no, they said, she's cool, until sure enough, a year or so later, it was, 'I really valued our time together, but please don't bother me again, cos I've kind of grown out of that stage of my life now, and could you just leave your key on the side, on the way out.' It was brutal, and some of my spars nearly went nuts over it. Seriously. You know Dave B?"

"Yeah."

"Poor fucker tried to kill himself over one of those posh bints. As if it wasn't hard enough already being black and skint in the nineties. They will always let you down mate, trust me, it's all fucking performance with them, nothing changes," spat back Vaughan bitterly.

"Yeah, okay, I get that, but it's totally different today, people are better. I'm telling you, it's not like in your day. Josh is a really good person"

"Well as long as he's a good person, Luke," replied Vaughan sarcastically

"Fucking hell! You're too pure, bruv. Everything has to be perfect with you, doesn't it? No sell out and all that rubbish. You know, I checked out all those bands you revere so much, the Velvet Underground? the Doors? The Chemical Brothers, and guess what? They all came from the suburbs! And Spiral Tribe? The guys who ran all the raves in your precious eighties and nineties? They were posh boys Vaughan. All public school. I looked it up. In fact, the real working classes were probably listening to Michael Jackson or Whitney Houston, when all the middle classes were ramming themselves into the Hacienda. Seriously. I couldn't believe it when I read about it. It's never been perfect; you live in a dream world, bro!'" scowled Luke, finally losing his temper and now standing up from the table.

"Ahh, wanna hug, son?" replied Vaughan with a cruel look on his face, and now turning around to look at the screen of his lap-top again, he started to type, as Luke grabbed his notes and walked out of the room.

Chapter 20

"I would have preferred meeting in a pub," complained Carl, as Alex put a spoon of sugar into his cappuccino and slowly cast his eyes towards Ronnie Scott's Jazz Club, sitting on the opposite side of the street.

"I like it here."

"Bit gay, isn't it?" replied Carl, as the media mogul took a sip from his coffee, before smiling benignly at the well-dressed man seated in front of him. He had just spent the previous afternoon trudging through Carl's 'Men Walking Their Own Path' or MWTOP website, and after reading the usual tripe about "women needing to retake their natural place in society" and "because men have created the modern world, they should rule it", he'd nearly had his fill of reactionary bullshit for one life-time, until he reminded himself of the greater goal, and tried again.

"I saw the James Taylor Quartet in there thirty years ago, brilliant."

"Mmm. sounds wonderful," replied Carl, now scratching his nose and pretending to watch the passers-by.

Perfect. Well spoken, homophobic, piss-taker, thought Alex bringing the cup of coffee to his lips and for a second, he seriously considered forgetting the whole thing and slipping his bodyguard a grand to give the cheeky prick a bit of a slap, when the younger man started to speak again.

"So, it seems we are after the same thing."

"Are we? I would have thought you would have been all over Mithras, you know take back control, and that kind of thing?" replied Alex, deciding to give the activist another chance.

"I'm afraid not. I mean, yes, there are a few things we agree on, and at the start, it did look rather promising, I grant you, but once you dug a little deeper, they are all still basically, feminised men. A bunch of socialists, if you ask me, and worse than the feminazis. You see, we want something very different. There is a huge diff...."

"I am sure you do, but, as my representative must have explained, what I am after is a scandal, something massive, that will bring Mithras and the rest of this little carnival to its knees," suddenly interrupted Alex, not wanting to hear the agenda of another sad little narcissist with an inferiority complex for the hundredth time.

"Well, yes, Sebastian did mention that. By the way, how do you know him? he's an old friend," asked Carl, a little put out at the apparent invasion of his cherished inner circle.

"I know a lot of people. So can you, do it?" replied Alex, enigmatically and taking another sip of his coffee.

"I am sure it can be arranged, for a price, of course," confirmed Carl, with a smile, before glancing out into the street again for dramatic effect which nearly caused the billionaire, to burst out laughing into his frothy coffee.

Fucking idiot thinks he is in a film.

Next, he will pass me a piece of paper with a number on it and mumble "that's where you can reach me," before quickly walking off towards the nearest tube station. This is why he had to meet a bell end like this in person thought Alex as he leaned across the table and glared at the man opposite.

"Now listen to me, and take very special notice, because I don't like to fuck about. Don't worry about the money or the arrangements; I will sort all that out. All I want, is your people inside the movement, to be ready, to do what I ask, when I ask it. Yes?"

"Err, of course, that's a given," replied Carl, now losing a hundred percent of his poise as he felt himself visibly shrink under the blackness of Alex's stare.

"Seriously, I don't want any amateurs buggering things up," repeated the media mogul.

"No, no, of course not, there won't be, they're all top boys," confirmed Carl meekly.

"Good, just make sure they are. Right, you know how to get hold of me?" said Alex starting to put on his overcoat.

"Err, yes, the phone you gave me. Thanks. Oh, and the money?" enquired Carl, sheepishly.

"It's already in your account."

"Oh great," replied Carl brightly, before Alex suddenly rose from his seat, to look around the street.

"Soho has changed, I heard Madam Jo Jos has shut down"

"Madam Jo Jos?" asked Carl.

"Yeah, great club, you would have liked it. Lots of men going their own way in there, back in the day," replied Alex with a smile, before he buttoned up his coat and then walked off in the direction of Leicester Square.

The buzz- saw rattle of a moped driving past, pierced the afternoon air, as from across the street, Suzanne squirmed about in her chair while she tried desperately to squint through the condensation on the window of the coffee shop to get a better look. Was that Alex McDonald? What the hell was the Lord of the Undead doing in Soho? and who was that man he had just left outside Bar Italia? the journalist thought, leaning forward in her seat again to peer a little closer, while her friend opposite continued to complain about her ex-partners refusal to let her share custody of their cat.

"Yes, yes he sounds like a dick," replied Suzanne mechanically, offering one of her napkins to stem the steady flow of tears, while she searched her mind for a clue to the stranger's identity. She knew him, she definitely knew him, and seeing the waiter approach their table with their coffees, she managed to break free from the attentions of her friend again, to quickly look over to where the man had been sitting before, but he had gone.

Chapter 21

Antigone came over and sat by the side of the bed, while Jake grimaced and continued to flick through the pages of his tablet.

"Can you believe this?!"

"I know, I saw it on the news last night,"

"Luke Casey voted Man of the Year by Time magazine!" fumed Jake as he turned around his tablet to show the offending front page to his mistress, before reading further from the article. "Time magazine for god's sake! Martin Luther King. J.F.K, bloody Barack Obama and now Luke fucking Casey."

"And Adolf Hitler," replied Antigone.

"What?"

"Yep, Hitler in 1938, I looked it up, and Stalin."

"Really?" replied the chat show host with genuine surprise, as Antigone nodded her head and tried to suppress a grin.

"Oh. Well, he's in good company then. Jesus wept! How the hell has it gotten to this?" exclaimed Jake, tossing his tablet back on the bed, and shaking his head in deep frustration.

"Well, I suppose, he has been the standout figure in the world this year."

"Oh God, not you as well."

"I think he's a dick as well, obvs darling, but he is popular," smiled Antigone, before crawling into bed next to him, and kissing him on the lips.

Jake kissed her back.

She tasted divine.

Maybe only betrayal tasted this good, Jake thought as a snapshot of his wife and two boys instantly flashed into his mind, while his heart tried it's very best not to throw up. Funny thing was, he hadn't even really noticed her before her intervention in his brain storming meeting, a few months earlier. She wasn't stunningly beautiful like the other interns, Becky or Meghan, but she was pretty, and the more he looked, the prettier she became, until one afternoon, he'd asked her to go for a drink to chat about work and she leaned across and kissed him, and that was that. He could have said no, but he didn't really want to, and so, as a result, he now found himself in a Marriott at 2 o'clock in the afternoon, staring at a hotel kettle and wondering how many cheating husbands it had seen over the years?

"I bet you think he's cute, as well, don't you?" said Jake gently touching her cheek with his hand, and trying to take his mind off his unpardonable infidelity, for a moment.

"Well, he does have a rough charm. But not really my type darling. Too much chippiness."

"Chippy can be sexy."

"Chippy is chippy. Anyway, I like you," replied Antigone, as she kissed him again and stroked his beard.

"I can't see why; I'm middle aged and washed up," complained the chat show host.

"You're the most intelligent man on television cupcake."

"You think?"

"Of course,"

"You really think that?" asked Jake again.

"Such vanity. Of course. You're by far the cleverest man, I have ever fucked and the sexiest" confirmed Antigone, as they kissed again, and the dopamine rush of the compliment poured through chat show host's body for another moment or two, until the dirty boots of his guilty conscience stomped into his mind once more, and he sat up in the bed to scowl again.

"So why are we losing then?" demanded Jake.

"It's just a blip, darling," answered Antigone, untangling herself from his body and preparing herself for another rant.

"A blip? I wish. Luke Casey and his bunch of M-Exiteers have taken the high ground, haven't they? and we are all left, just looking like twats," replied Jake, throwing his arms up in the air in exasperation, while Antigone stared at his freckled back and allowed herself a little smile. M-Exit, or Male Exit, was now the new expression on the block to describe the societal effects of Mithras and the male empowerment movement, and she didn't think it would take too long, before her lover would start using the term too.

"Sexual assaults are way down, there is less violence against women. Men who have joined Mithras are reported to be 60 % happier than those who haven't, while even stabbings in London have decreased by 85%, because of something the fucking psychologists are now calling it the "Casey effect" about young working-class men taking back control of their lives or some such shit. I mean okay, obviously, less women being assaulted and fewer young men getting stabbed to death, is a good thing, but it doesn't help us, does it?" continued Jake, before he looked back and saw the beginnings of a smirk appear on Antigone's face.

"Okay, next he will bring about world peace and sort out global warming and then we'll all be fucked," added the chat show host, throwing his hands into the air again, before they both laughed and kissed some more.

God, he loved being with Antigone, he thought, as he felt, her fingers lightly touch his skin and then slowly move down his body. So, she didn't always agree with everything he said, in fact most of the time she took the piss out of him, which was a little annoying, especially as, up to this point, in all three of his former relationships, he'd mostly gotten things his own way. Then again, maybe that was the problem? Control has its limitations, because with Antigone, he had finally found the freedom, to feel foolish, ridiculous even. Fair enough, there was nearly twenty years between them, but that wasn't very much, not when you had the same thoughts, then age was only a number, wasn't it? In the end, it was how you felt, and she felt amazing," mused Jake as he cupped his hand over her small breasts, and felt his cock harden against her thigh until inevitably, the face of his wife barged back into his mind once more to expose his craven hypocrisy. How many men had he ridiculed on his radio show over the years for their unfaithfulness? How many male Politicians, Sportsmen, Celebrities had he roasted for running off with a younger woman? Just like his own father had done. Was it in the blood? Were sons forever fated to walk the same paths as their fathers, whether they wanted to or not" his thoughts enquired before he stared at the kettle in the corner of the room again and tried not to feel sick again.

"You, okay?" asked Antigone with an anxious smile.

"Err, yeah, of course," replied Jake, now busily searching around amongst the bed clothes for his tablet, to hide his shame.

"Good, grumpypants, because I have some very good news, that you will be very happy to hear," continued Antigone, clapping her hands together and looking at the side of her lover's face.

"What? Hugo's decided to leave."

"No darling, I'm serious. I've been talking to one of the researchers on Mark Eastwoods documentary and he says it's going brilliantly, and they're getting loads of undercover stuff, really embarrassing to Mithras, but he was also telling me that they have just been approached by a woman, called Dolores Brady, who has told them that she was quite badly beaten up by this Vaughan 2 Lose guy, you know the one who set up Mithras with Luke."

"What?!" replied Jake excitedly, now instantly forgetting his latest bout of self-loathing, and turning his head to stare straight into mistress' eyes.

Antigone nodded back.

"Jesus. When did this happen?"

"About twenty-five years ago," replied Antigone.

"Twenty-five years ago? Jesus Christ, Antigone! How can anyone prove that? it will be his word against hers," cried Jake, instantly deflated, and slamming his head back against a pillow.

"But no darling, apparently, it's very convincing."

"I'm sure it is, but you know what they will say? He didn't do it and why didn't she come forward at the time. Ninety percent of my callers follow Mithras like a religion. Luke Casey could behead the Queen or blow up a children's hospital and he'd still be a top man."

"This is not Luke Casey," said Antigone firmly.

"Well, it's the same thing."

"No, it's not! This Vaughan guy is old, from the eighties and nineties when men got away with murder and laughed about it."

"I come from the nineties."

"You are much younger, darling, be serious. This will really hurt them. Luke is clean, we have checked, but Vaughan is not so clean, and every person we talk to about him brings a bit more dirt to the surface, especially when we talk to women. He is the key, trust me," replied Antigone now leaning forward to kiss his lips again.

"You are lovely, Antigone," said Jake reaching out to touch her face.

"Call me Anny, everybody else does."

"I don't want to be everyone else."

"You're not," whispered Antigone, as she pressed her mouth against his lips once more and moved her hand slowly up his leg.

Chapter 22

"Well yeah, I'm a loser, plain and simple," explained the man in his mid-forties, sitting back in his seat with folded arms, while the other men in the meeting looked on, in respectful silence.

"Why is that?" asked Luke.

"Cos I'm a Postal Worker," replied the man.

"So, like a Postman," asked Luke.

"Yeah."

"So, is that a problem?"

"Too fucking right, it is. I got an ugly wife and a cheap car."

"So, if you weren't a Postman, you'd have a nicer looking wife and a better car?" probed Luke, now blinking his eyes at the bluntness of the man's reply before moving forward in his seat to place his elbows on his knees.

"Yup."

"Well, where I come from, Postmen have a nice wives and pretty good cars. They even have a children's programme named after them, called Postman Pat," said Luke with an impish smile.

"Postman who?"

"Postman Pat," confirmed Luke.

"Really? Then I need to come to your country pretty fucking damn quick," replied the man, as everyone in the meeting started to laugh, while Luke sat back in his chair and allowed himself another smile. Of course, he was bullshitting. He didn't know any Postmen back in the UK, and for that matter, he hadn't seen Postman Pat on the television for years. Maybe, like everything else, he had been privatised or updated and replaced by Andy from Amazon, who knew? Not that it mattered anyway, when you were thousands of miles away. No-one cares about the details when you are a stranger in a strange land, just as long as you smiled a lot and had a shower once in a while, and Luke was pretty sure, he could do both of those.

It had been about six weeks since his little spat with Vaughan, and together with his increasing anxiety, Luke had come to the final conclusion, that what he needed the most, to preserve his sanity, was to get away from all the nonsense of London and the UK media, and therefore, taking Josh up on his offer, he had come to America, to expand the brand and open up a few more centres for Mithras. If you crack America, you crack the world Andy Papps had said in a meeting at the Covent Garden HQ, and although he had whinged for a few weeks about selling out and "the yanks fucking up the message", Luke had managed with the help of Andy, Jimmy Jazz, and Davie B to persuade Vaughan that it was a good idea, and so next thing he was on his way to San Francisco.

Obviously, it was a gamble, as like many of his own age, he had never really been abroad for any length of time, except for the usual fortnight in Zante or a stag weekend in Prague, but as soon as the wheels of his 747 hit the tarmac of Northern California, he instinctively knew that he had made the right decision. Now, instead of receiving constant abuse from an establishment media who hated his guts or being heckled in the street by blue haired social activists with nothing better to do, he was working 16-hour days, establishing new Mithras centres in Seattle, Portland and Oakland whilst giving talks to large meetings in the Bay Area and generally proselytising the message that men should reject their former addiction to female approval and embrace a new way of thinking. Predictably, his speeches went down a storm with his own base, but much to his surprise, he discovered that the rest of America, well the straight male part anyway, was still stubbornly attached to the old romantic paradigm.

For decades, the average American male had considered it as an article of faith that, success with women was directly related to his success as a man, and although this instinct was present in most societies, in America, as with everything else, sexual selection had been taken to its absolute extreme. No wonder Bernard, pronounced B-nard, the postal worker, was so self-critical, but far from being discouraged by this fact, Luke felt strangely exhilarated by the challenge, and was certain, that if he could succeed in a place, as addicted to impressing females as the United States, then he could probably find a lasting solution to man's great misery anywhere, or at least get them to pronounce their Christian names properly. It's Bernard, not B-Nard bruv thought Luke with a grin, as the meeting now stopped for a break and after watching everyone leave their seats and wander off towards the kitchen for a coffee, his eyes were soon drawn towards a new message that had just pinged on his phone.

"Wanna go to a party? Levi Jones will be there, he is dying to meet you, I will send a car – Chris."

Luke beamed.

Chris Clarke was a Hollywood screenwriter and friend of Josh's who had been showing him around San Francisco ever since his arrival, and as well as being heavily involved in the US arm of Mithras, he was a really cool guy, who seemed know everyone in the Bay area party scene. No high-end social gathering was complete without Chris and although Vaughan would have probably referred to him as "another champagne cork bobbing about in the stream," thankfully. his old mentor wasn't there to spread his old school misery about, so Luke texted back "Absolutely" before getting up to make himself a drink.

Five hours later, as promised, a car arrived and duly whisked him off to somewhere called DNAs in another part of the city, where once inside, he was immediately greeted by a shout of "Hey Luke geezer" from Chris in his worst American/London accent, thus prompting an instant round of applause from everyone inside the club. After being voted Man of the Year and all the other publicity surrounding Mithras, Luke was now getting strangely accustomed to this type of reception, and so after waving and producing his trademark grin, the DJ started to play *The Misogynist's* new single *It's Not a Man's World, Baby* while male fists punched the air with testosterone joy. No-one quite does adoration like the Americans and such was the enthusiasm at his presence in the club, that it took nearly twenty minutes or so of fist-bumping and high fiving through a packed dancefloor, before he was finally able to make his way over to where Chris and his crew were standing.

Now more backs were slapped and more introductions were made, as everyone grabbed their drinks and started bonding as if their very lives depended on it, until after about ten minutes, a familiar voice suddenly brought all conversation to a halt. "You cost me an Oscar, muthafucka," declared a tall middle-aged black man, wearing a Paul Smith suit and a red Stetson, as Luke turned around to come face to face with one of his all-time heroes. Even in bad films Samuel Levi Jones was brilliant, and as Luke shook the hand of the veteran actor, while thanking him for his "incredible gesture" in recently turning down the Oscar for Best Actor in the smash hit, film *My Favourite Colour*, he thought he might actually. piss his pants. However, the great man continued to smile and was typically gracious as he told Luke it was a pleasure to do it and "a small price to pay to persuade all men to talk about who they really were for a change, and anyway I still got to keep the muthafucking Golden Globe and the Bafta, so it wasn't all bad".

Luke grinned, and for the next half an hour or so, he jammed his hands into his pockets, and tried not to look like too much of an idiot, while the veteran actor went on to chat about the movie some more, before revealing to the assembled group, that the title for the film itself, had, in fact, been taken from a recording of a Mithras meeting taken by "none other than Luke here" and therefore all the praise should really go to him. Luke had actually heard this story before from Chris and immediately recalled the incident in question, where a distraught Mithras member had confided to a weekly group session he chaired, that his former wife had exerted so much control over his life, that in the end, he didn't even know what his favourite colour was anymore. It was the perfect title for a film, which most critics, including many female ones, were now referring to as a modern classic, and told the true story of Paul Douglas, played by Samuel Levi Jones, a normal guy, going slowly insane over the course of a ten-year marriage, as his wife constantly tried to improve him, whilst busily conducting numerous affairs behind his back, eventually leading to him taking his own life. *Gas lighting doesn't only go one way* was the film's controversial tag line, and predictably, was heavily criticised for demonising women, who, in most cases, were overwhelmingly the victim of such behaviour. However, many men identified with the issues raised by the film, and therefore as the drinks and the drugs started to flow, it wasn't long before the conversation started to focus on some of the major themes from the movie.

"I loved the bit when she tries to get Paul to wear a belt with his jeans, I had a girlfriend who used to do that."

"Yeah man, why do you they want to improve us?"

"No idea. I mean, we're not fucking potential, for Christ sakes."

Of course, they had a point, thought Luke, nodding his head to another complaint, as even Marlene Dietrich, the famous actress and feminist icon, had said that "most women set out to change a man and when they have changed him, they do not like him", but after an hour of being besieged by producers, writers, actors, who all raved about Mithras and the welcome male push back after years of having to keep their head down and "take it in the ass," from the Me Too movement, Luke was starting to flag.

Tonight, of all nights, especially after meeting his hero, Luke fancied some time away from being the "Spartacus" of male empowerment, so taking advantage of a moment when everyone decamped to the dance floor for a techno version of *PIL's This is Not a Love Song,* Luke quickly slid off to another part of the bar to hide behind a large plant pot and have a quiet drink. For the next ten minutes or so, Luke nodded his head to the music and sipped on his JD and coke, until inevitably, his hideout was discovered and he found himself being approached by a young woman with a bobbed haircut and a cheeky smile.

"So, you're the guy that wants to kill romance then?"

"Yep," replied Luke, with a little irritation, at the sudden incursion into his temporary refuge.

"Oooh, you look all mean and moody," observed the young woman, taking a sip from her drink.

"Is that a crime?"

"No of course not. My name is Jennifer by the way."

"Good for you," replied Luke returning a perfunctory smile, before tapping his foot to *When a Man Doesn't Love a Woman by T Apocalypse.*

"Well, that's a little rude, isn't it," said the young woman, after an awkward pause.

"Why?"

"Well, I have come over here to say hello, and all you can manage to do, is be facetious."

"Did you know that's the only word in the English language where all the vowels are present and run-in sequence? My friend Vaughan told me that," added Luke still tapping his foot.

"Of course, everyone knows that, but it doesn't explain you being so rude," protested Jennifer.

"Well, you came over to me."

"Yes, and the least you could do, is be civil," teased Jennifer.

"So, when a man comes up to a woman unsolicited, he is seen as a pest, but when a woman does it, she has to be indulged? Yeah right."

"Oooh, so serious. I was just coming over to talk," explained the young woman.

"No, you weren't."

"I so was," protested Jennifer, before Luke smiled and folded his arms.

"Okay I wasn't, but do you realise how hard it is for a woman to come over and talk to a man?"

"A lot easier than a man walking over to a woman I would imagine."

"Really?"

"Really! We don't take rejection very well,"

"Oh, you poor things."

"Or patronisation," said Luke.

"Is that even a word?" replied Jennifer.

"It is now."

"You know, I think, I'm going to buy you a drink," declared Jennifer, now moving towards the bar.

"Suppose I said thank you for the offer, but I am fine?"

"Err, well, I would say, my apologies, because I didn't realise that I was harassing you and I would leave you in peace," replied Jennifer a little surprised.

"Thank you," said Luke, plainly.

Jennifer now stared back at him for a second, to make sure he wasn't joking and realising that he wasn't, she bowed her head, before replying politely "Enjoy your evening," and then quickly walking away.

Triumphant, Luke, now smiled as he watched her awkwardly re-join some friends on the other side of the club, until quickly turning around, he hid behind the large plant pot again.

He had absolutely no idea why he had just done that?!

She was very pretty, funny and also quite famous, as he had instantly recognised her as Jennifer Yeager, who had starred and been very good in *My Favourite Colour* and now he had just told her to get lost.

Totally ridiculous!

Maybe he preferred annoying women to sleeping with them?

Maybe this was his deal with Katie, who he still regularly thought about, and every other girl he seemed to like.

Then again, maybe he was just a cock, reasoned Luke with a deep sigh, and so after fingering a wrap of cocaine that Samuel Levi Jones had previously dropped in his pocket, he cursed his instinctive belligerence for a few seconds longer, before trudging off in the general direction of a toilet cubicle to seek solace from his contrary thoughts.

The club was now absolutely packed and therefore after squeezing past more happy faces and accepting numerous pats on his shoulder, he was just about to walk through the door of the restroom, when suddenly he found his way barred by a petite woman with delicate cheekbones and furious eyes.

"Oh, thanks for the pig's head by the way."

"Err pardon," replied Luke as he blinked against the flashing lights of the club, to just about make out the face of the actress, Portia Ramone.

"Oh brilliant, one of your Mithras boys sends me a pig's head through the post, but it means nothing to you?! Just as long as you're having a good time with your little buddies," cried the actress, standing next to a friend, who was now holding up a phone up to the side of his face to film the whole encounter, while Luke looked sideways and smiled.

He had been here before.

Be polite, say nothing, move on, was the drill, but as he placed his hands in his pockets and tried to look a little bored, something about the film star's cut glass English accent now started to cut through him like a stiletto. Previous to his visit to America, Luke wouldn't really have described himself as a class warrior, well nothing compared to Vaughan and all his mates that's for sure, but in his short time in San Francisco, he had become acutely aware, of just how much class really mattered back in the U.K. It was like a tight-fitting waistcoat that constantly dug into your ribs, where only the accumulation of fame or fortune could undo a button or two, so you could actually breathe. Even "mind the gap" on the London Underground was said in an RP accent, Luke thought as he stood and watched almost trance-like, while Porta Ramone's thick red lipstick moved up and down in front of his mildly intoxicated eyes, spewing out entitled consonants and privileged vowels until deciding that he wasn't "back home anymore," he suddenly, glared down at his well-heeled assailant.

"Oh, just fuck off, will you?"

"Excuse me?" replied a genuinely shocked Portia Ramone.

"You heard, you pointless idiot," added Luke as he winked at her friend holding the phone, and continued to grin contentedly at his little blow against one of the "Wokest" of the Hollywood elites, before a sudden movement from the diminutive film star suddenly removed the smile from his face, and he quickly ducked his head. Fortunately for him, the resulting porn star martini missed and instead splashed all over a man behind him, as the next minute, all hell seemed to break loose with huge doormen and fellow clubbers quickly joining the fray.

"You certainly have a way with the ladies, don't you," said Jennifer walking up to Luke, who had somehow managed to untangle himself from the melee, and was now looking back at the mayhem he had crafted with an inscrutable smile, as fingers and phones jabbed out in every direction, and everyone made sure that the cameras caught their best side.

"Who'd have thought, when you saw her in the Black Wizard trilogy, that she would have turned out like this? I used to like her as shy little Titania," said Jennifer, with her arms crossed, as she continued to watch the uproar unfold.

"Really? I always thought she was a bit of a control freak," replied Luke.

"You wanna go? I know a great little bar in the Mission district," enquired Jennifer with a mischievous grin.

"Really? That's where I'm staying now,"

"Cool. So, you gonna turn me down again, Mithras man?" asked Jennifer.

"Not a chance," replied Luke, as they both turned around and scurried towards the exit of the club.

Chapter 23

Mark Eastwood stepped onto the red carpet with Dolores Brady at the London premiere of his documentary, simply entitled, *Mithras,* before announcing to the waiting reporters, that, not only, was this was this "easily the best work of my career" but all proceeds from the first week's viewings of the film would be donated to various domestic violence charities around the world. Naturally, the mainstream media lapped it up, and as well as unanimously giving the film a five-star rating, they gleefully dined out on the more controversial moments in the new film. These scenes, filmed by undercover reporters posing as Mithras members, included the use of so-called "Anger Rooms" where members could go into padded cells and smash up old crockery and discarded computers to release their fury against the opposite sex, as well as "Conditioning Sessions", in which men who expressed a fear of attractive women were placed in a small space and then visited by an erotically dressed woman, later found out be a prostitute, to reduce their fear of beautiful females. The scene with a mentor, issuing instructions through a microphone, behind a plate glass screen, such as "embrace the lust" and "face the fear, face it now my brother" to a terrified young man in a side room of Mithras HQ were particularly embarrassing for the organisation, as accusations of "Stepford Dads "and "Anger Room Horror" quickly filled the pages of most of the newspapers for the next few days.

Understandably Mithras dismissed these reports as misguided, and sought to immediately limit the damage to their reputation, by stating on their official website, that these practices had been well known in the organisation and to the wider public for some time now and were only ever employed, when members, themselves, specifically requested it. "Fear of women, has been identified by many eminent psychologists, as a huge contributory factor in violence and hatred against women, and INCEL culture in particular, and therefore anything that tries to address these issues should be welcomed, rather than ridiculed and condemned out of hand" declared Femi Adeyemi, the new chief spokesman for the movement, but despite limited support for this practice from some female commentators in the media, the general response was negative and comparisons to suspect practices in Scientology, Opus Dei and the Masons were immediately drawn.

"Yes, it's official listeners. Mithras is a cult. Maybe Luke Casey and Vaughan 2Lose should move to Death Valley and misinterpret the Beatle's White Album" bellowed Jake O'Callaghan as his show was immediately inundated by male callers denouncing the comparison between Charlie Manson and the leaders of Mithras. However, despite the general outrage, these mini controversies, paled into insignificance at the central revelation of the film, namely the savage beating of a woman called Dolores Brady in the late 1990's by the co-founder of the biggest male empowerment movement, the world had ever seen.

"Violent shame of Mithras leader", "Animal!" and "Women ARE the enemy" had screamed out from the front pages of every major newspaper, a day before the film's premiere, as the media caravan quickly moved to Harlesden, where Vaughan stood outside his house to vehemently deny the central accusation of the documentary. Smiling and relaxed, he explained, to an assembled media that he had indeed known Ms Brady over twenty-five years previous, and although it had been a fractious relationship, due, in large part, to the incompatible nature of their personalities, he had never assaulted her or any other woman for that matter, and would vigorously contest any such claim in the courts. He also added, that he considered "Mithras, the movie", to be a hit-piece and just another desperate response from an establishment, that doesn't want to see their power diminished by people actually thinking for themselves and furthermore the real disappointment in this matter, was that someone of the quality of Mark Eastwood has got himself involved in this type of thing, but considering that he'd heard that Alex McDonald had threatened to end his career if he'd refused to make it, it was probably understandable in the circumstances.

Now, as more questions continued to be thrown in the direction of the co-founder of Mithras by the hordes of reporters standing outside his gate, Suzanne clicked off the BBC news website and stared at the screen of her lap-top for a few seconds, before she reached over and pressed her finger down on the P key. What a lot of P she chuckled to herself, as she watched line after line of the letter fly across her screen, until the taste of his lips and the memory of his hands moving over her breasts, made her stop and turn her head away.

It had been perfect.

She had regretted that she'd stopped him before in the bedroom of his flat, as it was the first time in God knows when, she had felt that kind of desire.

Was this the touch of a woman beater?

Wouldn't be the first time.

Most men had it in them and she had been pinned against enough walls by enough so called "good guys," in her time to know that. But Vaughan or Danny or whatever his name was, had felt different. He was so gentle with her, and when she had asked him to stop, he had stopped, immediately, no question. Of course, it didn't mean that he always had. Men were the arch deceivers, it was in their blood, but still, every savage comment about him on her twitter feed, now felt like a dagger plunged into her heart.

"Vaughan 2 Bully."

"Mithras Monster."

"Women's number one enemy."

It was relentless, and although, she had given a robust holding comment of "Now watch them destroy this poor girl", she knew that this wouldn't keep them off for long, and eventually she would have to attack him, eviscerate him, crumble him to dust.

Her heart sank again.

After their near miss in the bedroom, they had met a few more times, swapping passionate kisses outside tube stations, before having an ironic seventies' dinner date at an Angus Steak House, and then smoking a spliff outside the old Turnmills club in Farringdon, just for old times' sake. It was the most fun. He'd even given her the headline for the piece that she had written about him for Alex McDonald. "The Toxic Feminist", and then roared with laughter, the next day when he'd read all the mean things, that she'd said about him in the article. It felt like love, or as close as you could get to that devious mind-trick but she had wanted to wait, until things became a little clearer. He agreed, and said that it would make a good plot for a French Rom-Com, "The Chauvinist Pig and the Harpie". It would, but not now, Suzanne thought staring blankly across her living room, as she suddenly realised that any chance of their future happiness had just been smashed into a thousand tiny pieces.

Bloody Alex McDonald had gotten his way, as usual.

Vaughan was right about that one, as only recently, she'd been reliably informed by one of McDonald's assistants that Mark Eastwood had indeed, initially turned down the film, only for his agent to be told, that his client would spend the rest of his artistic life on a QVC channel, if he didn't bend a knee. They all did in the end, didn't they? and now with Jake O'Callaghan and his minions shouting the odds from the side-lines, Jail him! Ruin his businesses! Picket his home! the hate mob was in full swing again. She'd seen it all before, of course, even been part of it herself, and was well aware that the Left could be just as dirty and judgmental as anything coming from the Right, sometimes even worse. What a crap world she thought as her fingers moved onto her keyboard again and she found herself staring at the face of his victim.

Dolores Brady.

She was pretty, bottle blond, smaller than her, more pert, size 8 probably.

Was she jealous, as she compared herself to Vaughan's former lover?

Perhaps, she thought as she looked closer into the eyes of her rival.

They looked fragile, a little haunted maybe, too eager to please.

Was she lying?

Wouldn't be the first time.

She'd seen it many times before; women could be bitches, when they wanted to be.

See a successful ex, feel a little bitter, why hasn't my life gone so well? Go for his reputation, that was the weapon of choice for a female, wasn't it? Throw enough mud, something's bound to stick, her thoughts fumed, and she sat back in her chair and glared at the photograph again with pure hatred in her heart, until gradually, she felt something rising in her throat and began to feel a little sick.

What the hell are you thinking, you stupid cow?!

The days, when men could rely on women to turn on each other, are gone! Totally gone!

Even for Vaughan.

This was a new time, a new direction.

Now there was a genuine sisterhood, where Queen Bees, like Thatcher blocking the path of other women were no longer an option and catty remarks about the size of your dress, a thing of the past.

"God, what is she wearing?"

"Who does she think she is?"

"Try missing some meals bitch!"

153

To her eternal shame, she had done it herself, a hundred times, until late one night in a bar, a foul minded Editor, after taking a good look at her breasts, had leaned across to drunkenly declare, that "Women hated each other, even more than they hated men and that's why they will never go forward".

The old wanker might have been right then, but he wasn't now.

Her teenage daughters were a different breed, they had now joined the dots, and supported each other, her thoughts confirmed, as suddenly an image of her younger self, being pushed up against an office cupboard and a hand moving up her skirt now elbowed its way back into her mind once more.

At the time, she had done nothing except call the man a creep and run away.

Well, I have stopped running now, she thought to herself, and leaning forward in her seat, she started to type.

Chapter 24

"So how long had you known her," asked the Detective.

"About three years,"

"So, it was a relationship."

"I wouldn't call it that."

"Were you seeing other women?"

"Yes."

"So, you were in the habit of picking up girls then?" probed the Detective.

"It was the nineties. Everybody was in the habit," replied Vaughan scratching his nose, while his eyes scanned the grey paint of the interrogation room.

"So, on the night in question, you say that you were drunk when she brought you back to her flat?"

"It was my flat, I told you," replied Vaughan increasingly irritated by the transparency of the detective's questioning.

He had been here before.

Pissed off working class man from an estate and a copper with hate in his eyes.

Then again, it could be worse.

He could be a copper.

Then he really would be fucked, he thought, smiling to himself, before he clasped his hands together on the table in front of him and stared back at his interrogator.

"Oh yes, sorry you said," said the detective with a pleasant smile.

"We'd taken some pills; we were out of it." volunteered Vaughan

"So, you could have punched her and not known?"

"Ever taken a pill?"

"Err no," smiled the detective.

"You sure? you look like a bit of a head to me."

"Positive."

"Well, you don't wanna punch anyone when you're on a pill, especially the ones I did. You could hug fucking Ian Brady on the shit I used to get," replied Vaughan, now sitting back in his chair.

"How can, you be sure? it was over twenty-five years ago, now," asked the detective leaning forward.

"I remember."

"And you didn't hit her?"

"No," replied Vaughan sharply, before spending the next hour or so either repeating himself or answering more ridiculous questions that went nowhere until finally, they decided to let him go. However, three days later he was charged with assault and after being placed in a cell for fifteen hours for no reason, he appeared in court the next day to declare firmly, that he was not guilty. The Judge gave him bail, and as he walked out of the court into a sea of phones and cameras, his QC, Nick Nottingham advised him, not to say anything and keep a low profile. Cool with me, he should know, he cost enough, thought Vaughan, squeezing past the eager faces of the Press into a near-by cab. Then again, it wasn't his money. A Malaysian businessman who owned a mobile phone company had donated £ 1.6 million, while the actor Levi Jones chipped in a £100,000, which on top of all the fivers and tenners sent in from everyone else, raised over £10 million in thirty-six hours. *Only sport and women could bring men together like that,* Vaughan thought, now walking into the kitchen of his flat, as an ancient memory of him hugging a banker in a pub in Ludgate Circus when England scored their fourth goal against Holland in 1996 suddenly popped into his head, before he stood on a chair to search the back of a cupboard for a packet of cigarettes, that he had recently hidden from himself.

He'd decided to give up.

Why not?

His life had been going well.

Mithras was thriving, men were mostly in a better place and acting with some genuine confidence for a change, and he was even in love or something close to it, so why not, try and live a longer life?

"Yeah right," he mumbled to himself as he sucked on the cigarette and felt his head spin from the nicotine hit, before the face of Dolores Brady flashed his into his mind once more. The pink sequinned dress that she always wore, the tattoo of a butterfly on her shoulder and her perfume. Even after twenty-five years, he still remembered that scent, cloying, musty, foul.

Jesus, he'd always hated it.

It was like the stench of his past and the sound of "oh yeah Danny boy, bit of a blagger, tell you a good story, always buy you a drink."

That idiot was dead, and so were his sins, long live Vaughan 2Lose.

Well, maybe not, now.

Woman beater, the ugliest words in the English language.

A stain that could never go away, like Japanese knotweed wrapped around your reputation, impossible to shift.

"No smoke without fire."

"You know what he was up for?"

"Yeah, looks the type."

Funnily enough, he'd always pictured himself a little differently.

Possibly, Fred Hampton, the Black Panther, famously shot by the FBI in the sixties for his socialist views mixed with Terry McCann, the fictional London bouncer from the eighties television series, *Minder*, or maybe, at a push, the 19th Century poet, Baudelaire but without all the right-wing bollocks and better hair.

He wished.

Now he was branded a hitter of women, just one up from a nonce.

John Lennon had done it and they'd named an airport after him, but he had written *Imagine* and *Strawberry Fields Forever*, while all his own talentless arse had ever produced was the odd podcast and a few angry tweets.

Nope. There would be no rehabilitation for the likes of him, thought Vaughan, sucking harder on his cigarette, as out of the corner of his eye, he noticed a photographer crouching on top of his garden wall, through his kitchen blinds.

Suddenly he felt like praying to his catholic God.

Last time he'd rung that number, was thirty years ago, so he could hardly be considered a pest. That time, a ladder had given way, and he'd been left hanging sixty foot above the Cromwell Road. until a Scottish plasterer called Murray had been sent to grab his arm and haul him up to safety.

Who would come this time?

Probably no-one, he thought, as the door -bell rang and remembering that he was a die-hard atheist, Vaughan flicked the dying embers of his cigarette into a half-drunk cup of coffee, before placing his hands in his trouser pockets and walking towards the front door.

"Are you a woman beater, Vaughan?"

"Any comment Mr. 2Lose, since you have been charged?"

"Where does this leave the credibility of Mithras?"

Vaughan lowered his head and walked briskly past the dozens of press reporters standing outside his gate, as he had seen countless shamed celebrities do in the past.

Eyes fixed ahead and running for the open door of a waiting car.

It never looked good, nor would this.

"Fucking picks, are you alright?" said Carl over his shoulder, while Vaughan quickly slammed the door shut and the car drove through the bulging eyes and flashing cameras.

"Don't worry, we'll get through this, Guv. Typical crap. Guy gets a bit of publicity and next minute half the female population comes out and says he abused me," continued Carl, as reporters started to run beside the window of the moving car and Vaughan leaned forward in his seat.

"It was only one, Carl, put it in perspective," replied the older man.

"Err sorry fella, but two other birds have just come forward to say that you touched them up at raves in the nineties" shouted back Carl, edging around a stationary lorry.

"What?!"

"Yeah, it's a fucking stitch up, but par for the course, I suppose," replied Carl shaking his head as he finally drove clear of the obstacle and headed towards the Harrow Road, while Vaughan sat back in his seat, and mulled silently over the latest revelation. He had spent most of the nineties "banged out of his head" on Ecstasy, to the point that he had no real recollection of the whole of 1992, except for throwing a half-eaten pasty at a Tory election campaign car in the Northcote Road in Clapham and even then, he wasn't completely sure if that was him, as it could well have been a trip. It was a crazy time and everyone was inappropriate back then. Girls had come up behind him while he was dancing, he had definitely done the same thing to them; from Club UK in Battersea to The End in Tottenham Court Road, it was all badly behaved.

"Err, shall I book an Anger Room for you, Guv?" suddenly interrupted Vaughan's thoughts, as Carl looked back from the front seat again, with a cheeky grin.

"Might be a good idea," Vaughan replied, managing to crack a little smile, as he caught his driver's eye in the rear-view mirror. He liked Carl, trusted him, which was a bit strange as he had only known him for a few months, but you get an instinct about someone pretty quickly don't you, or at least he did. Granted he sounded a bit posh, and said "birds" a bit too much for his liking, plus his habit of calling him "Guv" all the time, short for the Governor, felt a bit like kissing his arse, like those dicks who kept repeating your name in a conversation, to make you feel at home. Still, despite all that, he was a breath of fresh air, thought Vaughan, especially now Luke had buggered off to the States to go partying with Josh Middleton and all the other celebrity idiots who had hitched a ride on Mithras.

"By the way, thanks for this, thought I might have to call an uber to get out of there," said the older man moving forward to tap Carl on the shoulder.

"No wucking furries Guv. Oh, and I told Stevie, Paul and Big Phil to meet us at the ranch, so we can plan what to do next, hope you don't mind?"

Vaughan gave a nod of his head, and after leaning back in his seat, he closed his eyes, while Carl glanced in the rear-view mirror again and started to smile.

Chapter 25

Luke had never seen anything like it.

A huge encampment dropped slap bang in the middle of a desert, filled with painted faces and bicycles, which on first impression, resembled an arty refugee camp or a music festival located somewhere on a distant planet. Obviously, he shouldn't be here, but when Jennifer had screamed at him at a Hollywood party, "Oh my God, Luke, you've never been to Burning Man?!", it was basically out of his hands. He was starting to feel like a cliché wrapped in an inevitability, tightly packed into an old chestnut, but from the moment he left the club with the actress to go to the Mission district, his fate was pretty much sealed. She was part Caitlin Moran, part Ariana Grande, part Cher, and was unlike any woman that he had ever met before.

He'd even had a kiss.

The last time he had kissed a girl was on a drunken tinder date outside Green Park tube station, and that had tasted of white wine and salt and vinegar crisps, while his kiss with Jennifer, in a quiet bar in Santa Monica, surrounded by sun burnt alcoholics, tasted of everything that he had ever loved. Salted caramel, the chorus in The Masterplan by Oasis, Ravenscourt Park in May and as their lips touched, for a brief moment, he found himself thinking about Katie again, until the actress whispered something funny in his ear and she was gone.

How the hell did that work?

How could you be completely besotted with a person one minute and then five seconds later.... not? No wonder men and women were doomed thought Luke, as in despair, he looked down at his phone again for some consolation, only to see more frantic messages from Femi and Andy Papps regarding Vaughan's recent arrest. Some friend he was, he mused, pitifully shoving his phone back into the pocket of his shorts, before his mind returned inevitably to Jennifer once more. At least, he hadn't broken his celibate vow, and despite some close shaves after "far too many drinks", he had insisted on sleeping on the actress' sofa for the last three nights, as his desire to consummate his love, grew almost unbearable. Her cat had even caught him having a wank. Was that abuse? Probably in California, but despite the rumours online and in the press, he was "still intact", and this fact, alone, was all that sustained him, as he bowed his head in shame, before shuffling after the film star and her merry pranksters, into internet Billionaire Alan Dawn's "Capitalism Kills" party, located at the far end of the festival in his specially constructed gold lame Yurt.

Although, the original idea of the Burning Man festival had been radically egalitarian, where everyone was supposed to be treated the same, human nature quickly intervened, as over the previous five years, the incredibly rich and the impossibly famous had managed to fashion a little part of the desert, that was exclusively their own. Therefore, as Luke stepped into the enormous space, with all the waiting staff, still wearing face masks and gloves, from the mini - pandemic of 2024, it resembled something you might see at the Oscars, as from every side of the party, the cream of American progressive society started to appear There was non-binary chart-topper, Dana Simmons, the cosmetic influencer, Logan Jones while the celebrated Trans poet, Blair Rhymes was holding court at the other end of the room. The scene could have quite easily been plucked from the imaginations of F Scott Fitzgerald or Philip K Dick, but sadly without any of the humour and style, that made those writer's visions of dystopian decadence, previously so appealing, and so, as a result, for the next ten minutes or so, icy stares now followed Luke everywhere he went, until having had enough of all the silent abuse, he finally made his way to the bar, in search of a pint of strong lager or at least a JD and coke. However, all he received for his troubles was an organic gin fizz and to make matters worse, as he looked down at his phone, a text from Vaughan now appeared in front of his guilty eyes.

"Where the hell are you? Heard you've gone to Burning Man with an actress. Are you fucking serious?!"

He had never felt like such a fraud, and quickly taking a huge gulp of his drink, he shoved his phone back into his pocket again, before an older lady standing a few feet from him suddenly interrupted his gloom.

"Oh, surely it can't be that bad darling?"

"Err, it's nothing, it's okay," replied Luke, forcing out an awkward smile.

"You're that guy from Mithras, right?", enquired the older lady, as Luke nodded his head back mechanically, anticipating yet another man-hating outburst, whilst busily scanning the Yurt for a possible getaway.

"I thought so. Oh, I really like what you are doing by the way, so don't worry, I'm not going to bite your head off, or anything dear."

"Oh, okay," replied Luke, still scanning the exits.

"You know, it's funny, but these days, I find myself sympathising so much more with the men, which is so strange, because I used to think there were all such awful bastards," continued the older lady.

"Err, really?" replied Luke, relaxing a little, but still not entirely sure.

"Oh completely. So much has changed, don't you think? When I was a young girl, there used to be a perfume advert on the television, showing a man chasing a woman down the high street, who is obviously wearing this particular brand of scent, and then when he eventually catches up with her, he gives her some flowers. It was very popular at the time, you know impulsive, romantic, all that kind of thing, but today, that same guy would be seen as a sex pest or something worse and probably be arrested. It's awful, don't you think? I mean to be brutally honest; I look at younger women today, and I can't actually believe I'm saying this, but I am a little appalled. They all seem to be running around like shoals of mackerel, seeking safety in numbers, but when they are by themselves, they looked absolutely terrified. I mean, look at Portia Ramone?"

"I'd rather not," replied Luke, with a grimace, remembering his recent encounter with the Hollywood actress.

"Exactly. She does all this empowered female thing, but most of the time she looks like she is on the verge of a nervous breakdown. It's like they are making a virtue out of being a victim most of the time. I really don't understand it, I really don't. I mean where are the Katherine Hepburn's? the Nina Simone's? the Siouxie Sioux's?"

"Susie who?"

"She was a punk, dear."

Weren't they all? thought Luke, as an image of Vaughan ranting about how Punk was more important than the theory of relativity suddenly came into his mind before he took another sip of his drink, and continued to listen.

"These were strong females, in a time when women were actually oppressed. Jesus, some of the crap I had to endure, the girls today would literally faint. I'm serious. Back then, I was a second wave feminist, still am for the most part, and don't get me wrong, I still think women get a tough time, but not nearly as bad as it was, not even close," said the older woman, shaking her head.

"What about Believe All Women?" replied Luke with a mischievous grin, recalling the initiative from a few years previous, to always believe the testimony of a woman in any case of abuse.

"Oh please. I think Amber Heard put that one to bed dear. How ridiculous was that, by the way? Believe all women?! You have to look at the facts, don't you? This is what I mean. The obsession with victimhood, has gone too far. I mean of course, we need Me Too, no doubt about it and I think we always will; men can be such awful pricks sometimes, you know, but we also need Mithras as well. Yes, definitely and maybe after all the craziness of the last decade, men might have to go off by themselves for a little while and find some space from us, but remember, even though the music has stopped for the moment and no-one wants to dance with each other anymore, in the end, we have to come back together, that's what we are supposed to do. We have to DANCE! It's nature's greatest wish!"

"Suppose we don't." replied Luke, now a little taken aback by the sudden show of passion from his newly – found bar companion.

"Well life won't be worth living young man, and then we will really descend into the abyss" confirmed the older woman, before she quickly waved at someone across the party and was gone.

Luke stood at the bar smiling for a few seconds at this unexpected intervention, until Jennifer made her way across to him and took a sip out of his drink.

"I can't believe she's still going, I remember seeing her bouncing around in a pink tutu on MTV, when I was a little girl."

"Who was she then?"

"Beth Cherry, silly."

"Oh, of course. She thinks we need to dance again" said Luke with a smile.

"Not the way she used to do it," replied Jennifer laughing as she raised her hand in the air and started singing *Unlimited Love*, one of Beth Cherry's biggest hits.

"I liked her," replied Luke.

"Okay? So, I can wear a pink tutu if you like, Caseyman?" replied the actress, dancing around in front of him for a moment or two before suddenly whispering "come with me," into his ear and then pulling him towards the exit of the Yurt. Luke began to laugh, as he half protested at his sudden removal from the party until seconds later, he found himself outside on the dusty playa with Taylor, bassist in the techno punk band My Vagina, Byron, a semi famous visual artist and five or six more of the "Jennifer Posse" who were huddled together with huge grins on their painted faces. Now all previous feelings of self-loathing for not helping Vaughan in his hour of need, quickly vaporised into the hot Nevadan air, as his curious mind gobbled up, another slice of life that he had never come across before, except in rock biographies or documentaries on Sky Arts. Like Edie Sedgewick and Andy Warhol in the Sixties or better still Kate Radley and Richard Ashcroft in his beloved Nineties, as poor Jason Pierce looked on in despair and wept into his crack pipe.

Who was he?

Richard or Jason?

He seriously didn't have a clue, however if the truth be told, in this exact moment, he didn't really care, as long as he was with Jennifer, and therefore, forgetting everything else, he skipped happily alongside the actress as they made their way to the next "amazing event".

"We won't have to queue," the film star excitedly announced as she led everyone around the back of a huge domed tent that stood in the middle of the festival, where they met a tall, handsome guy called Trent, who then guided them past two enormous security guards and into the jaws of the canopy.

"What's this?" asked Luke as everyone quickly hustled their way through the back entrance and started to giggle furiously.

"You'll see," replied Taylor with a wicked smile.

And he did, because just as Luke wandered a little further into the semi-lit space, everywhere he looked, people were having sex.

"The orgy dome," Taylor whispered as she floated past his ear to catch up with Jennifer and Trent who were now marching out in front.

Not many, Benny, thought, Luke remembering an old phrase that Andy Papps used all the time, while bare bottoms seemed to rise in every direction before his startled eyes.

Young people having sex, old people having sex, middle-aged people thinking about having sex, threesomes, foursomes, moresomes, it was insane.

"Oooh look, an Eiffel tower," commented Byron, as he saw a girl on her knees being penetrated from behind while giving oral sex to a man who was standing up.

"Err, I think you will find that's a spit roast," replied Luke with an air of authority, as since his sex embargo, and the subsequent "thousands of hours" watching online porn, he now considered himself somewhat of an expert on the position. However, this flippancy was quickly replaced by increasing panic, as realising that, not only, had he not had sex in nearly two years, but also, he was now in the middle of an orgy, Luke started to feel like a recovering alcoholic who'd somehow found himself locked overnight in an off licence, and as a result didn't know whether to laugh or cry. Even his mild Pure O was unsure, as all of his previously profane thoughts, were now suddenly being played out in real time, in front of him, and in his confusion, he feared that he might actually start urging people "to cover up" or "desist from using that kind of language.", as a contrary response to his new found circumstances. This could definitely be a cure rationalised Luke, remembering to make a mental note of this new type of confrontational therapy for future reference, until Jennifer suddenly appeared in front of him, and placed both of her hands on either side of his face.

"Amazing, right? This is Mithras. No relationships, no judgement, no lies", declared the actress, before Luke looked into her sparkling eyes and returned a weak smile.

He had just been undone by his own bullshit, was his next thought, and while Jennifer started to move her hand down his body, he glanced over to see Taylor, who now had Trent's cock in her mouth as Byron's head was buried between her legs.

He had never felt so turned on in his life and pressed his lips against Jennifer's mouth while a soundtrack of hundreds of people cumming buzzed in his ear. He'd have preferred *Dilemma by Nelly*, he thought, as he moved closer to the actress and started feel the heat of her body against his, until taking a casual look over her shoulder, he suddenly noticed a young woman, pull a man's penis from the vagina of a women lying next to her, before placing it inside herself.

Jesus, that was rude, Luke thought to himself, while the man, now looking completely unconcerned, simply carried on having sex with his new lover.

He was a life support machine for a cock and he didn't care.

Should he care?

It was only sex after all.

A need, like food or drink, not some sacrament, that required special attention. Love is a drug, most relationships come to an end, isn't that what Mithras said? It was a commandment for God's sake, so it must be true, Luke reasoned as he noticed that Jennifer had just pulled his shorts halfway down his legs and was now kissing his chest. He had dreamed of this moment for almost every second of the past six weeks, and eagerly started to kiss her back, while she started to rub her body against his hard cock.

She was so wet.

He wanted to be inside her, he wanted to feel her legs wrapped around his waist and taste her gorgeous lips, but as he moved his hand down Jennifer's back, without warning, Beth Cherry's face suddenly barged into his mind.

"We need to dance again."

"What? Do we?"

"Yes, we do, Luke."

Maybe she was right, and come to think of it, this didn't feel very much like a dance, did it? thought Luke, as pulled away from the actress, to stand back and look around at all the fucking. "Hey Luke, it's okay, really," said Jennifer reassuringly, as she started to move towards him again, but this time he wasn't so convinced.

This felt wrong and leaning down to pull his shorts over his erect penis, he suddenly declared, "I've just remembered; I have to ring Vaughan," before running as fast as he could towards the exit of the dome.

Chapter 26

"Listen to this, Carl," said Big Phil as he leaned forward and started to read from the screen of his laptop. "Women don't want us to be men, they just want to cut off our dicks and place them around their necks in a necklace, like trophies of war. Mithras needs to wake up! Saying women aren't the enemy? Ignore them on Valentine's Day? Getting a shaving advert banned? waste of fucking time! You'll be destroying every copy of *Frozen* next. They need teaching a very big lesson, one they will never forget. Grow some fucking balls Luke Casey, those bitches wont rest until they have destroyed every man on the planet. We need to strike hard, and strike now."

"Wow, he sounds like fun. What's his name?" asked Carl with a grin.

"Anton, apparently, he's only nineteen. Been talking to him for last two weeks. He's bi-polar or autistic or something, and hates his mum, cos she's pissed off to Spain with her new boyfriend and left him with his Nan."

"Mmm... bit young, but keep him talking Phil, could be useful. He can't trace us, can he?"

"No chance, thinks we're in the States. Also, I called the website Fuck Mithras, Freedom for Men," replied Big Phil.

"Very nice, very nice," replied Carl, patting his colleague on the back, as he continued to walk amongst his fellow agent provocateurs, cracking some more jokes and looking over a few more shoulders until a quick glance at a text on his phone, completely changed his mood.

"What the hell are you doing? People siding with Mithras. Get serious. Target more celebrities!"

Now the smile completely disappeared from Carl's face, and he shook his head in frustration before quickly texting a message back.

"We are! We are doing what you asked. Even sent a pig's head to Portia Ramone."

"Wow, that's original. Not nearly enough. Target young woke female celebrities. Felicia Lorenz, Tatiana Mason -Wright, Ayala Bloom, make them march against Mithras. No excuses, you are being paid enough."

"Tosser," mouthed Carl to himself, before he shoved the phone back into his jacket pocket, and stomped over to lean his back against the office wall. Alex McDonald was right, they were getting paid enough, maybe enough for a proper male revolution, that would show up Mithras for the charlatans they really were, and make their male empowerment movement look like a toddler's tea-party. That day was near, he could feel it, but still, he didn't like being talked to like "a fucking bitch", jumping every time someone in power raised their voice to him and in time, the media mogul would see that and give him the respect he truly deserved. However, for the moment, the bastard was still paying the bills, Carl reasoned and so pushing himself off the wall, he walked back into the centre of the room and stared at the back of his crew's heads for a few seconds, until he started to speak again.

"This is an absolute joke! Phil, where is that report I asked for two days ago? Paul, get on your twitter accounts and start targeting those woke actresses we talked about, and Stevie, get off the porn sites, for fuck's sake," shouted Carl with his hands on his hips, as in an instant, the three men jolted in their seats, and quickly turned around to look anxiously into the eyes of their leader.

"Err mate, there's no need to be like that, we are doing what we can," replied Big Phil, with a little defiance in his voice.

"No, you are not, MATE, cos if you were, MATE, then I wouldn't need to raise my bloody voice, would I? We need to ramp up the pressure, we are here to fuck Mithras up, don't you get it?"

"Err, yeah, of course Carl,"

"Are you sure, Phil? because I'm getting the distinct impression that you think Luke and Vaughan are cool guys, you know, bit mainstream but deep down they are just like us,"

"Err no Carl. Err no, of course not."

"You sure, Phil? Because every time I see you, you're always joking with Vaughan, aren't you? giggling at his stupid little stories."

"Well, he is funny," replied the big man looking around to his other colleagues for some support, before Carl leaned down to stare directly into the big man's face.

"Is he? Didn't realise you were that close, Phillip? Is this before or after you suck his cock?"

"Well, erm, it's not..."

"Not like that? hmmm... Well, that's what it sounds like to me, fella. These are NOT cool guys, Phil. In fact, they are the worst type of men. Respecting women, "old school geezers" with a feminist edge. Oh, let's play the woke game with a little twist, shall we? Where does that get us? More pointless compromise, that's what. Men are here to rule, that's what our biology tells us, that's why we exist, or do you want the feminisation of the world to keep barrelling on until every fucker with a dick has to squat before he takes a piss."

"Err no Carl, of course not," replied Big Phil more firmly.

"You sure?" probed Carl.

"Yeah, definitely," he confirmed.

"Good. So, get to work on these woke celebrities. Felicia Lorenz, the singer? Make it vile. She has just lost the Mercury prize and I read somewhere that her mother has recently been diagnosed with Parkinson's or something. Send some flowers, don't get better soon, all that kind of thing. Make it something that even the Daily Sun would shake their head at, and make sure it comes from Mithras members. I want a shit-storm chaps" barked Carl, now standing up straight again, and placing his hands in his trouser pockets.

"Yeah, yeah, okay, mate, got it," replied the big man, who now emboldened by his leader's little rant quickly turned around in his chair, and started to type furiously, while Carl continued to loiter about at the back of the room with his arms crossed, for another ten minutes or so, until completely satisfied that his verbal rocket had done its job, he walked out of the room and headed for the lifts. He loved ripping people to shreds, sometimes it was nearly as good as sex, he thought with a vicious grin and after walking along a short corridor, he quickly sped up to the fifth floor of Mithras HQ, where he continued to amuse himself by lurking outside the glass door of a meeting room, as he watched his boss, stare down at the forest of placards in the street below.

"Oh dear, oh dear. Our Mr. 2Lose doesn't look happy at all, does he? Quel dommage," thought Carl with a little snigger, before he pushed open the door and swaggered into the room.

"Fucking wankers" he declared pulling up a chair from the large oak table that sat in the middle of the floor, while Vaughan made no reply, but instead remained motionless, staring blankly out of the huge plate glass windows.

"Yeah, we need a big response this time, Guv" continued Carl, sitting down and reaching over towards a plate of biscuits on the side of the table.

"You think son? Really? Because at the moment, I think, we should probably just keep our fucking heads down, know what I mean?" spat back Vaughan as he suddenly turned around to glare at Carl, who was just about to put a chocolate digestive in his mouth.

"Err, yeah, of course Guv, yeah, I get that," replied Carl lowering the biscuit and genuinely taken aback by the violence in the older man's eyes.

"Remember I'm the one on trial here, it's my fucking neck on the line."

"Yeah, yeah of course. Must be a nightmare fella. Erm, sorry Vaughan, I wasn't thinking, so wrapped up in all the madness that's going on at the moment. Yeah, should stop and think, my bad. But you know, you don't have to get involved directly, Guv. Me and the boys will just go online and wage the war there, push back hard, you know, get our retaliation in first" suggested Carl, as Vaughan's face now started to relax a little, and he gave the younger man a conciliatory smile, before he sunk his hands into his trouser pockets and stared out of the window again.

War? Retaliation? Push back? How the fuck did it get to this place? All he had ever wanted, was for men not to be completely terrified of the opposite sex, which most were in his experience, and to finally acquire something approaching their own agency, without causing women or society too much grief in the process. Fat chance of that now, Vaughan thought as the noise from the protestors outside filtered through the office windows again.

Vaughan 2 Hate! Vaughan 2 Hate, Vaughan 2 Hate."

Now, there was no way out, he was in far too deep.

A pantomime figure loved by nutcases and Nazis, or serenaded by fifth rate comedians who told jokes about starving immigrants, and thought Obama was a communist. *He would definitely get that documentary by Louis Theroux now* he mused, as he continued to scowl at the faces in the street below. The usual suspects. middle class woke tosspots, telling poor people how to live their lives. He hated them and their celebrity neo feudal storm-troopers, like Jake O'Callaghan, Portia Ramone, and Suzanne Burke, well maybe not Suzanne, but he definitely hated the rest of them.

"Yeah, fuck it, let's fight back. Do what you have to do, Carl," now announced Vaughan, after another moment of furious contemplation, before immediately spinning around on his heel and marching towards a bottle of Jameson's that sat on the end of the meeting room table.

"Now you're talking, Guv. Fuck those bi…I mean fuck those women," replied Carl meekly, as he quickly remembered to stop himself from using a banned word in the presence of the Mithras Leader.

"Nah, you were right the first time, Carl. Fuck those bitches," Vaughan hissed and now raising the glass to his lips, he grimaced as the whisky started to slowly burn into his throat.

Chapter 27

Antigone moved forward in her seat to gently stroke Dolores' hand before it was quickly jerked away and the older woman started to sob again.

"No, no I can't bear it, I can't,"

"I know, I'm so sorry," whispered Antigone.

"But this is not happening to you though, is it?!"

"Well, no, but I do get it."

"Do you? I don't think you do," cried Dolores as she pushed herself back into the chair, and pulled a tissue from underneath the sleeve of her cardigan to wipe her nose.

Only three days earlier, a video taken from a camera phone in 2010 had been uploaded onto a porn site, not only showing Dolores snorting lines of cocaine but also having sex in the toilets of a North London bar. The Press had a field day, with its usual lurid headlines of "Vaughan to Party" and "Sex and Coke shame of Mithras accuser", while on social media "yeah right, I believe her after that", clashed with "why should a woman be judged by her lifestyle, this changes nothing."

"You are allowed to have fun you know; doesn't mean you deserve to be beaten up," said Antigone with a sympathetic smile, as she moved forward to stroke Dolores hand again.

"But that's not the point, though, is it? People put two and two together, don't they? She's a slut who's had sex in a public toilet and does drugs, so how can we believe her? I mean, it's started already. Have you seen the papers? Even at my son's school, some little brat told him that his mummy was a slag. Trying explaining to a six-year-old, what a slag is?!" exclaimed Dolores pulling her hand away once more.

"I didn't know that," said Antigone.

"I might have to move away as well, now; it's getting too much, I don't think I can do this."

"But you must Dolores, think of all the women who are supporting you. It's so important, we must see it through."

"I'm not a hero, Antigone, I'm just a dozy bint from the Holloway Road who got caught shagging in the bogs."

"You so much more than that, you're an inspiration. You can't give up now," urged Antigone, moving forward in her seat again, as the two women hugged for a few seconds, until Dolores pulled away and tried to force a smile on her tear-stained face, but exhaling suddenly, her body recognised that she had come to a final decision.

"I'm sorry Antigone, I can't do it, I just can't. I have to think of my son, now," she replied and after wiping the remaining tears from her face with the side of her hand, she mouthed sorry to Antigone again, before picking up her bag and walking out of the hotel room.

The following day the headlines of the papers and news websites barked predictably at an eager public, as left and right-wing commentators either denounced or supported the move, until a week later, the inevitable happened, as without the testimony of Dolores, the police didn't really have a case, and Vaughan was a free man once more. Again, the Internet blew apart, with both sides railing against at each other until their fingers were raw, while Vaughan, against the advice of Carl and his cohorts, who wanted to throw a large party at the O2, decided to keep a considered tone, thanking everyone for their support, before immediately committing himself and Mithras to ending violence against women once and for all.

However, Vaughan's acquittal, now touched on a very raw nerve that had been exposed in society for some time, so as a result, other male groups were not so measured in their response, and before long, thousands of men were coming forward on TV, Radio and Podcasts to relate stories of being wrongly accused by an assortment of women for various crimes and misdemeanours. Echoes of the Johnny Depp/Amber Heard trial from 2022, quickly resurfaced, as tales of violent wives, false charges of sexual assault, being "Titled Nined", a reference to the law surrounding male students being accused of sexual misconduct on University Campuses in America, careers being ended for having consensual drunken sex with a female colleague, the list was endless, as for the next few weeks, the airwaves seemed to become a carnival of justified male fury.

Naturally, this was met by an equally vociferous female opposition as marches were hastily arranged in nearly every major city in the world highlighting the thousands of assaults on women that go unprosecuted every day while Mithras Centre's worldwide were now picketed on a full-time basis by women's groups. Furthermore, Portia Ramone and other high profile female celebrities also founded The Sisters of Khutulan, named after a 13th century Mongol noblewoman, famed for never having been beaten in combat by a man, as they declared that they would be seeking £5 million in reparations for every woman on the planet, in recompense for "all the shit that we have had to put up with over the years."

These actions only heightened the tension and as a result relations between the sexes were now at their lowest point at any time since Mithras and the male empowerment movement began, as men and women began to seriously shun each other in every part of their lives. Pubs, clubs, and restaurants remained empty, as relationships broke up in their hundreds of thousands, even more than during "No women February", while those couples which remained, were now being regularly accosted in the street by activists from both sides of the argument, urging them to spilt up immediately and not "fraternise with the enemy".

The literary world was affected too, as this renewed conflict brought fresh interest in a 2018 work by the eminent American biologist and feminist campaigner Paula E. Jones called Why do we need men anyway? which soon found itself at the top of the New York Times, best -seller list. The book, which charts the biology of men and women over the last 200,00 years, argued that as (a) the Y chromosome which turns the female egg into a male one will probably die out in 125,000 years and (b) it was now possible to reproduce life without the presence of male sperm, as a recent healthy baby hamster produced in a laboratory from two mothers had shown, was there, in fact, any need for the men at all? Predictably many male commentators pushed back against these claims, commenting online, that it was actually a male scientist who had produced the baby hamster from the two mothers, in the first place, while celebrated comedian and Mithras supporter, Dave Chateau controversially tweeted "As we've only got 125,000 years left, fuck it, we might as well just have a good time. Forget women bro', they're just a buzzkill anyway."

For the next few months, this back and forth between the sexes continued unabated, with neither side backing down, until just as it seemed that it couldn't get any worse, the debate was further inflamed by Dr Abel Francois, a renowned Belgium scientist who stated in what became known as "the Francois Prediction" that in precisely 120 years' time, babies will be produced outside of the womb, menstruation and the menopause will be a thing of the past and the human sex urge would be solved by a pill; thus resulting in not only, men and women deciding to willingly separate from each other, but also, half the population of earth, namely the male part, eventually decamping to the planet Mars.

This hypothesis, released in an obscure medical journal, sparked howls of derision from large sections of the media, including Suzanne Burke, who commented in her weekly Sunday column, that it was obvious that the "esteemed" Dr Francois had taken the book Men are from Mars and Women are from Venus a bit too literally, and while she and many other women would be quite happy to see the scientist and his followers "bugger off," to Mars any time they fancied, men could still sleep soundly in their beds, as they was no plan to get rid of them any time soon – although she did express a great interest in any future cure for the menopause as "the hot flushes were starting to get on her tits."

Alex smiled as he finished reading the piece in his bed, while his wife slid into her slippers, before telling him not to "fanny about" as their daughter's boyfriend, Magnus was coming at 1 pm for dinner.

The billionaire chewed harder on his gum.

Magnus.

God, not another limp handshake and concerned looks over the roast beef and Yorkshire puddings, he thought as he tossed his newspaper onto the bed and placed his head back on a pillow again. Maybe Mithras were right, and it was the men who needed saving after all. Still better than the old days, when you basically had a heart attack, every time your daughter stepped out of the front door. These days you actually feared for the men. Poor bastard, he thought, as another image of Magnus, with a pitiful look on his face, flashed into his mind again, before he glanced down at the newspaper and read the headline once more.

Mithras Girl In Hiding.

Now all his plans could seriously go south, because some silly slag had a few lines and sex in a toilet a million years ago, thought the billionaire to himself, as he chewed harder on his gum, and the idea of cocaine entered his brain for the millionth time.

Oooh a nice line would be heaven now.

He could feel it run down the back of his nose.

Nice little buzz.

No chance.

Be lucky to get a cup of Jasmin infused green tea these days, he sighed and for a few seconds the media mogul, retreated into a little sulk, until inevitably his eyes returned to the front of the newspaper again.

Still, it wasn't that bad, and could actually be a good thing. Public outrage at another trial collapsing because of slut shaming, even if she was a slut. Not good for Mithras, not good at all, but what was needed now was an extra push, thought Alex, quickly grabbing his phone from the table beside the bed, and starting to text.

Chapter 28

"So, you think it's okay for some idiots in Indonesia to start smashing up statues of 8,000-year-old earth mothers, do you? said Luke rubbing the side of his nose, before he glared back at Big Phil's over-sized head.

"Well yeah, I think it's fair enough. I mean the whole of society is based on a mother obsession, isn't it? You said yourself, you know, devouring mothers having an unhealthy influence on men, stunting their emotional development by treating them like fools when they are kids, and then doing the same when they are adults."

"Well yes Phil, so the answer is for men to take full responsibility for their lives and get a bit of emotional self-sufficiency for a change, but not declare war on their fucking mums, for God's sake," replied Luke.

"Look, there's no need to swear fella, we are all friends here," interrupted Carl.

"Oh, right FELLA. Are we?" snapped Luke as he leaned back into his chair to glance over at a Soviet - era style poster tacked to the far wall, showing a defiant woman with a closely cut bob poking a man in the chest with her finger and shouting "I'm never wrong", and in an instant Jennifer came back into his thoughts again. It had been nearly three months now, since he had run out of the orgy at the Burning Man festival, and somehow made his way back to a motel near San Francisco, to eat pringles and listen to old love songs on his Spotify to explain to him why his broken heart would stay broken. He had even tried calling her a few times to try and explain, but the actress never answered, but simply texted back that he was "a fucking hypocrite who talked a good talk, but when it came down to it, he was just a conventional guy who played by the rules like everyone else" and therefore never wanted to see him again.

Maybe she was right, but then again, it wasn't a crime, was it, not to want to consummate his love for her in front of five hundred people with painted faces, who were all having sex, by the way? It did seem a little unfair, but in reality, he probably, only had himself to blame. She was way out of his league, and he had always known it, so he moped around San Francisco for a few more weeks, throwing himself into meetings and fund raisers, to try and keep it together, until he'd decided to take his mother's advice to stop messing about and finally come home. It was the right move; lost love is like gravity and the further away you are, the less pull it has on your soul, and although in the first few weeks of his return, he thought that he might have to move to the outer rings of Saturn to cure his aching heart, the meeting room of Mithras HQ, seemed far enough for the present.

"Look, it's not a big deal, it's good for publicity. A few earth mother statues get destroyed, who cares? They are ugly looking things anyway, always freaked me out," now returned Luke from his short-term melancholy, as stared back over the table towards Carl.

"You what?"

"Relax fella, it's just a stunt," added Carl with a smug smile.

"Yeah, and anyway bruv, they were well fat," added Big Phil.

"Oh okay, so if they were fit and a bit more attractive, it would make a difference, would it? By the way are you listening to this?" enquired Luke, now looking down the end of the table, towards his old mentor for a comment, but all he received in return, was a disinterested burp, as Vaughan returned to sipping from his can of lager.

"Err, well it sounds to me, like Isis when they smashed up all those Buddhas," continued Luke, as he crinkled his forehead at Vaughan's indifferent response, before returning all his attention back to Carl and his crew.

"Err I think you will find that was the Taliban."

"Really? Oh, thanks for that Paul. Can't you see this is insane?! We should be denouncing these guys, not laughing about them. Are you reading the papers? It's getting more extreme every day. Men and women are actually fighting each other in Spain, and some nutter in India, threatened to blow up the Taj Mahal, because it's a symbol of romance. I mean this is not what we do is it? We are not in the business of attacking women, are we?" asked Luke, leaning forward in his chair.

"Well, they started it, with the whole Dolores thing," said big Phil.

"Well, that's over now, isn't it?" countered Luke.

"Not as simple as that, fella. We've moved on a bit, since you were away in the States. There are big forces allied against us now. The media, celebrities,

Jake O'Callaghan and his Woke mob and you can see our centres are picketed 24/7, we have to fight back," explained Carl.

"Well, I disagree. We need to keep doing what we have always done, and push for peaceful co-existence with women," replied Luke, and wincing a little from Carl's reference to his recent absence from events in the UK, surrounding Vaughan's arrest.

"Women are not the enemy? Not too sure about that now? Think that ship has sailed, Luke. Seriously. We have to get a bit dirty. The feminazis like Suzanne Burke and Portia Ramone don't play fair, do they? Do you know how many men have lost their jobs for being Mithras members since Vaughan's release?" asked Carl.

"It's not that many," replied Luke.

"You need to look again, fella; it's getting into the thousands."

Luke instinctively shook his head in disagreement, but even he might have to concede that Carl could be right on this one, as every day more members were complaining about being sacked, not taken on, or harassed at work for being a member of the organisation. However, despite this, Luke was absolutely certain that more antagonism was not the solution to the problem.

"It's just a phase," replied Luke unable to think of anything else to say.

"Look, I get you want to do the right thing, but today you have to talk to your constituency, to your audience. That's what the 21st century is; one massive echo chamber. That's how the algorithms are set up, no-one listens to anyone they don't agree with anymore, c'mon even a child knows that that, Luke. Confirmation bias is the new law, all the journalists are activists, cancel culture rules the roost. Pull down a statue here, no platform your opponent there, get what you want at all costs, because at the end of the day, it's about winning, fella."

"Winning what, Carl?" asked Luke, irritably, before folding his arms.

"Our place in society, get some respect. Stop them from turning us into women," interrupted Big Phil, thumping his fist on the table.

"Women don't want that, for Christ sakes," replied Luke, shaking his head.

"Don't they? Everywhere you look, men are being told to be less masculine, every razor advert telling us to be soft and compliant. Think about your male privilege. What privilege? I come from Stoke on Trent, mate. Most of the women up there, have more power than any bloke, I know right now. I'm serious," interrupted Paul, from the middle of the table.

"So what? we're gonna start attacking women in the street now, are we? Suppose that will teach them," replied Luke throwing his hands up in despair.

"Well, we were thinking of something less drastic. A male strike for a day," declared Carl, leaning back in his chair.

"A what?"

"Maybe a week," chipped in Paul.

"You're joking, right?" replied Luke, incredulously.

"Well, they're always telling us how much we need them, let's see what will happen, when we walk away. Pilots, Construction workers, Farmers, Fishermen, Oil Drillers. Society would grind to a halt," continued Carl with a grin.

"Be great. They say, they want inclusion and equality in the work-place? Cool. Let them lay a few bricks, for a change then," said Paul.

"No chance. They only want equality in the nice jobs bruv. Never hear them complain about not enough female representation on a fishing trawler, do ya?" laughed Big Phil.

"Yeah, yeah, okay, we all know that, don't we? But you lot aren't actually serious, are you? A male strike? We will be laughed all the way to Court. What about doctors? Most of the surgeons are still men, you know. You gonna let people die?" replied Luke, looking over at the faces of the four men sitting opposite.

"Don't worry, it will be all organised beforehand. It was done before in Estonia, last year. The doctors went on strike there for a week, and it went okay, minimal damage," explained Carl, clasping his hands together on the table.

"Minimal Damage! Are you listening to yourselves?!" bellowed Luke, furiously thrusting himself into the back of his chair.

"Actually, there is a really important point here Luke, if you take the argument to its natural conclusion." said Paul, after a few seconds of uncomfortable silence.

"What point?" snapped Luke.

"The future mate. Look, I did my PhD on this. From now on, all the tough stuff is gonna be done by Robots and Artificial Intelligence, yeah? So, there'll be no place for the traditional male anymore, except maybe to entertain, as a footballer or a singer, which is a bit humiliating if you think about it, but that will be about it, for us. I mean, you have said so yourself, more women go to university than men, much more, and now loads of men are dropping out, it's getting worse, you've seen the stuff online about this. By 2030, there will be two female graduates for every male. Just think about that for a moment. Twice as many women, trained for academia, law, medicine, most office careers, plus they are getting preferential treatment in the work-place, with promotion etc, because everybody thinks it's all really sexist and we're still living in 1973, but we are not. They just keep repeating this narrative to keep control, and shame anyone who tries to challenge it, because the real truth is; they are the ones with the advantage now. It's brilliant actually. By every metric they are predicted to outperform us over the next fifty years. The gender pay gap, is only for older people these days, the Boomers and Gen X, all the stats confirm it, but no-one has the nerve to say it, for fear of being called a misogynist. I mean, look at the women in my generation now, the late millennials or Gen Z? If they don't have kids, which increasingly they don't, they are earning way more than men. We're out of date, Luke. Seriously. Even their biology, makes them less immune to illness, so fewer died during the COVID thing and the last pandemic. We are doomed, mate. Think about it. Male suicide, prison, gang violence, drug abuse, steroids, having less testosterone, which is a real problem by the way, shit jobs, no chance of a family, fucking homelessness. I mean it, men are going the same way as the Neanderthal's if we don't get ourselves sorted out now." replied Paul.

"And their orgasms could kill a man," added Stevie joining the conversation for the first time.

"What?!" replied the rest of the table, as even Vaughan stopped sipping from his can of beer and now looked over in interest.

"If a man experienced the female orgasm, it could kill him. I saw a documentary about it on Channel Five "continued Stevie, nodding sagely for a few seconds, until Carl shot him a dirty look before quickly leaning across the table to address Luke personally again.

"Jesus, shut up Stevie, will you? Look, you need to have faith, fella. It will work, we have a plan, just trust us on this."

However, Luke was unconvinced, and continued to argue for another approach, but despite his objections, he was out-voted five to one, with even his old mentor declaring in favour of the proposed action and therefore the following week, a two-day male strike was announced by Mithras, with Vaughan declaring on a chat link to millions of members that it was time for men to stand up for their rights in an increasingly matriarchal world. "We don't want a patriarchy, but we don't want a matriarchy either," was the new rallying call, as everything from construction to transport soon ground to a halt.

In some parts of Europe and USA, the reaction was mixed with about five to ten percent of the male work-force joining in, resulting in only minor delays in airports, train stations and hospitals, but in Russia and South America, male participation was high, and medical assistance, especially in some areas was virtually nil. Thankfully, in the end, very few deaths could be actually attributed to the dispute, but the subsequent fallout from the action started to have severe repercussions for Mithras as the majority of the media with the exception of a few right-wing publications urged governments to shut it down, as it was now considered to be veering completely out of control. Within weeks, new laws were introduced, worldwide, to protect vital services, while in the UK, a COBRA meeting was convened, where it was decided that greater attention would now be focused on the activities of the organisation, who in the words of the Home Secretary, Davinder Singh "were moving ever closer towards the mindset of terrorism".

Now, in the dim light of his car, Carl afforded himself a smug grin while he flicked through the moral outrage on his phone.

"MithrISIS,"

"Barbarians,"

"Lock them up."

The Wokies were going totally insane and he loved it.

The male strike had, of course, been his idea, genius really, and then the constant barrage of abuse against prominent women engineered by Big Phil and the rest of his crew had turned the world so crazy, that all fingers were now pointed at Luke and Vaughan, as the whole Mithras dream sank deeper and deeper into the mire. Perfect plan, perfectly executed, although if you listened to McDonald, you would think, that everything was going tits up. Then again that's how he keeps you keen, isn't it? Clever bastard, thought Carl, as he rang the number on a piece of paper and raised the phone to his ear.

"Hi Anton."

"Brad?"

"Yeah, it's Brad," replied Carl, in an American accent.

"Oh, it's so good to hear your voice finally," said Anton.

"You too Buddy. So, everything's ready. Primed to go off at 8 pm."

"Oh, brilliant mate. So where do I go?"

"Err like we told you before, remember?" replied Carl shaking his head.

"Oh yeah, sure," said Anton.

"In the side room, where the cleaners keep their equipment, which is right of the stage, remember?"

"Oh yeah, I remember, got it. And where do I pick up it up from again?" asked Anton.

"How many times buddy? We'll deliver it to you."

"Like Amazon," laughed Anton.

"Yeah, just like Amazon. So, make sure you don't go out, okay?"

"I never go out," replied Anton.

"Good, and then just put it in your backpack and take the 6am train from Winchester to London Waterloo on the 24th, and then do as we planned? Oh, and make sure you're wearing a Mithras T-Shirt when you go out, Anton, that's very, very important, bro'"

"Yeah, I hate those She Males."

"It will be so ironic and take a selfie too."

"Yeah, great idea."

"And remember to take it in the side room, before you send it," added Carl.

"Will do."

"Perfect. You'll be hero for all time, to all men," added Carl.

"You think?"

"For all time Buddy."

"Oh, cheers mate, oh and Brad?"

"Yes Anton?"

"Thanks so much for this." replied the younger man, before Carl quickly ended the call and then moved his hand anxiously across his face.

This was some serious shit.

Alex McDonald had made him go to Soho again, and while handing him a midget cup of coffee had simply said "Trust me". Arrogant prick. A bomb? You want me to plant a fucking bomb? "Yes," he answered smiling, like a lizard, before he added, "It won't go off."

"Oh, that's alright then, I'll only go to prison for 20 years instead of the rest of my life!"

"Don't worry, my people will sort it out, just get me the man. You have a man, don't you? Like I asked?" he had replied as he chewed his fucking gum.

Of course, he had a man. Well, more like a boy, but who cared, probably doing the crazy bastard a favour. Give him his fifteen minutes in the sun. Notoriety, that's what those lunatics craved, wasn't it?

Was he any different?

Yes, he was.

He didn't want approval, he wanted something much more important.

Power.

Women loved power, but didn't have a clue, how to use it; like a sword, that only men could lift.

This was the real war.

The Hindus had it right.

Men are order and women are chaos.

Carl had no desire to live in this new feminine world of compromise and emotion, he was a proper misogynist. Not like Vaughan, a pathetic charlatan or all the other posers online, who disagreed with women, but secretly loved them. He didn't. He hated them. He hated them all.

Chapter 29

The police received a phone call about 9am to say that an extremist called Anton Richards was in the newly opened Invictus conference centre on the South Bank and in possession of a bomb and intending to detonate it during a meeting of leading feminists that was to be held there later that evening. By the time the call had been verified by police intelligence, officers had rushed over to the conference centre and found Anton in a storeroom by the side of the stage with enough Semtex in his backpack, not only to kill all the delegates expected to attend, but also cause significant loss of life to those in the first five rows as well.

"It was only an act of god, that the two wires at the back of the bomb had come loose," declared the lead detective at the press conference, the following day, as he further revealed, that the chief suspect Anton Richards, a 19-year-old unemployed man from near Winchester, had been detained at the scene, and as well as being in possession of a bomb, he was also found, to be wearing a Mithras T-Shirt that said "No surrender to the Matriarchy" at the time of his arrest.

The next day, most of the newspapers led with this quote as they roundly condemned the male empowerment movement of being nothing more than a terrorist organisation, whilst providing further details of the police search of the accused's bedroom in his grandmother's house. Here, as well as unearthing some extremely misogynistic material on his lap-top, the authorities also discovered copy of a "Book of Mithras" on the top of a wardrobe, signed personally by Vaughan 2lose, together with the inscription, "Never give up, keep fighting". Naturally Mithras, immediately released a statement on their web-site to unreservedly condemn the actions of Mr Richards and while confirming that he was indeed one of their members, clearly stated that "the actions of this one individual in no way reflected the values and general aims of the movement".

Vaughan, also released a statement to say that he, too, totally condemned "this inhumane act" and although he couldn't remember signing this particular copy for Anton Richards, or "the Mithras Bomber", as he had now been dubbed by the press, he confirmed that the message inside was meant to inspire and obviously not to be taken literally. "How many crimes had been committed by people reading the Bible?" Vaughan then added thus prompting headlines of "Mithras leader thinks he is Jesus" as Alex McDonald ensured that every day, all of his media outlets continued to apply the pressure on Mithras and their outspoken leader.

Understandably, public opinion was rapidly moving away from the organisation and so after an emergency meeting at Mithras HQ, it was decided that, as Vaughan had now become enemy number one in the eyes of the public, Luke should handle most of the publicity from now on. Therefore, a few days later an interview with a "sympathetic," journalist, was hastily arranged by Carl, so people could re-engage with the man who started the movement, and hopefully bring some stability back to the situation. However, the reporter in question was Cameron Reid, a far-right blogger and linked to some very unsavoury anti- women groups in America, who after the interview, proceeded to completely misrepresent Luke's views, turning an innocent comment about the dangers of identity politics and the need for people to listen to each other more, into a headline that read 'Women want men to die'.

Obviously, Luke tried to immediately distance himself from the article, but after more push-back from an outraged media, plus a petition of over one million signatures to ban the organisation, a week later, the headquarters of Mithras was raided by the police, and the premises closed until further notice, while a full investigation took place.

This move only served to divide the movement even more, as some members wanted to return to the energy of the early days focusing on male development and co-existing with women, while others were now advocating more radical strategies to confront what they saw as a feminised establishment oppressing the natural rights of men. It was clear everything was now descending into chaos, and so after another pointless argument with Carl about doubling down on their position and calling for another male strike, Luke stormed out of the offices in Covent Garden and fled back to the only refuge that existed for a Gen Zer in a cruel and hateful world.

His mums.

At least nothing could go wrong here, Luke thought, accepting a cup of tea from his mother, as for the next few moments, the Mithras leader stared blankly at the TV, desperately trying to dispel the events of the last few days from his tortured mind, until "It's Jake O'Callaghan's I've had enough," suddenly boomed out into the living room, to disturb his peace. Instantly, his mother sprang forward towards the remote control, in an effort to shield her son from his long -time nemesis, but Luke, now weary of all the hyper-polarisation and general acrimony, smiled and said "it will be alright" before they both settled back in their seats to watch the show.

"Thank you, thank you and good evening to all you lovely people. So, in a week when repentant men everywhere started to burn their T-Shirts and snap their sunglasses in two where next for the global domination of Mithras?" declared Jake with a wry smile as boos and jeers instantly rang out from the studio audience.

"Come on, come on, let's not be nasty, now. I mean they had such a refreshing message, didn't they? God in heaven! what the bloody hell was that all about, can anyone tell me please?! Made Brexit seem vaguely plausible, didn't it? Anyway, thankfully the great separation of the sexes is now less likely than ever, as human nature and common sense seems to have finally won the day. I mean people are basically good, aren't they? No really, they are. They mostly help each other, are altruistic for no reason, look on the kinder side most of the time, and that includes Mithras members by the way" continued the chat show host, as loud booing started again, prompting the chat show host to immediately raise his hands and call for calm once more.

"No, no, seriously, now, come on, please stop, I mean it. Let's not be like the extremists we fight against on a daily basis, let's think for a second. Some of the messages from Mithras did have a hazy kind of validity, didn't they? In a Me-Too age, where men felt they were suddenly losing all that lovely power, it was a bit difficult to get used to, wasn't it? What do they say? Equality feels like oppression to the privileged, and, of course, new ideas bring new fears, it's natural, so it wasn't a great surprise that reasonable men were seduced by the message. You know, if we can't have it our way, then it's the highway for us. I kinda get it, but then again, we can't look back, now, can we? so seriously my friends, this is not really the time to gloat. Good men joined Mithras, no doubt about it. In fact, some very good friends of mine did, and for the very best of reasons, and by the way, we are still friends, which is the way it should be, I think. But in the end, it didn't really work out or at least it's looking like it's not working out anyway, so in a kind and civil society, we have to let people make mistakes, don't we? yeah? I do think so, and that's why I am happy to introduce on a special, one guest only show tonight, so yes, no comedians or any of the usual business, I will be talking to just one person. One human. One male bipedal carbon-based unit, if you will, and so, without any further ado, please put your hands together and give a big Friday night welcome to Josh Middleton everyone," declared Jake to huge applause, as Luke leaned forward to put his cup on the coffee table while his mother shot him another anxious glance. Now, the studio audience continued to clap and cheer wildly, while the camera followed the renowned actor, as he made his way across the set, and after the usual waving and acknowledging a few wolf whistles from the female members of the studio audience, he finally made his way towards the chat show host.

"Hope you didn't feel too objectified there, fella?"

"Oh God, don't start all that again" replied Josh to more laughter, before he settled into his seat.

"So, Josh, where are we now?" asked Jake breezily.

"Well yeah, it's definitely been a journey, hasn't it? And I think, as you said in your introduction, there were a few things about the world and men's place in it that I wasn't too happy about and Mithras seemed to have some of the answers."

"Of course, that's how these things usually work, isn't it?" sympathised Jake.

"Yeah totally. You want someone to express the anger you feel sometimes and Mithras were part of that. I mean, for better or worse, they said things, that at the time definitely chimed with me."

"But now? They tried to ban Mother's Day. I mean fricking Mother's Day dude?!" said Jake shaking his head to some more boos from the audience.

"Yeah, crazy I know, and then obviously all the stuff with the Vaughan 2Lose trial, the male strike and the bomb that nearly went off."

"Yeah, that was a bit mental, wasn't it?"

"Absolutely, and of course, I didn't want to be part of anything like that," replied Josh lowering his head.

"Did you know Mr 2Lose? sorry, I still can't get used to saying that name." asked Jake.

"Not really. Met him a few times at some fund raisers, but, if I'm being totally honest, he was a bit too loud for me, old school ranter, you know the type," replied Josh, before Jake looked directly into the camera and after raising an eyebrow said, "Oh yeah I know the type," to more laughter from the audience.

"Yeah, but joking aside Jake, the one I got to know really well, was Luke. He was the one I responded to, you know after helping that girl in the club and some of the things he said, like men standing up for themselves and being a bit more emotionally self-sufficient."

"Of course, but surely, everyone needs that Josh, not just men? enquired Jake.

"Yeah, yeah of course, I see that now. it's about all of us, isn't it? Men and women." confirmed the actor.

"So, is there still a future for men and women, then?"

"Absolutely," replied Josh.

"Phew thank the Lord for that, I can start moisturising again. So, Josh, this is all lovely and very positive, so I hope you won't find me too intrusive now, if I ask you just one thing?" enquired the chat show host with a grin.

"Okay, go on then" replied the actor a little apprehensively.

"Are you sorry about the last two years?" asked Jake.

"Ha! err well yeah, I mean men say that word a lot, don't they? and of course, mostly for good reason, but I think right now, err…" replied Josh, as he suddenly stopped talking and slowly lowered his head again.

"You, okay?" enquired Jake with genuine concern.

"Yeah, yeah," replied Josh, as complete silence now descended over the studio, and for second or two the actor seemed a little lost, until regaining his composure again, he slowly raised his eyes towards the camera, and said, "I'm sorry."

Now, the studio audience went completely wild and as Jake clapped his hands and Josh nodded his head in appreciation, Luke leaned forward to take another sip of his tea.

Chapter 30

Suzanne widened the picture on her phone with her fingers and studied the face of the man standing next to Vaughan and some other nameless Mithras members, outside a pub in West London.

Yes, it was definitely him.

Simon Pinner, founder of the UK arm of Men Walking Their Own Path.

Of course, she exclaimed to herself.

Simon bloody Pinner.

Only five years previous, she had interviewed him as part of a piece, that she'd written for a Sunday newspaper, called "Male rage in the 21st Century" and consequently been forced to listen for hours as he rattled on about the gradual erasure of men from mainstream society and if women didn't see the error of their ways, everything was going to end in some female inspired apocalypse. Usual pseudo alpha- male cobblers, from a niche voice on the fringes of society, she'd thought at the time, and rightfully assumed that he would probably wander off into obscurity to scream at his lap-top in some basement and live on garage food for the rest of his life. So, what was this little twerp doing with Mithras then? and more importantly why had he met up with Alex McDonald in a café in Soho, a year and a half earlier? the journalist now asked herself as she took another sip of her vodka and tonic.

Even McDonald would have nothing to do with someone like Pinner, be like Stalin hanging out with Jason Donovan, she mused, and remained pre-occupied with this question for a few minutes more, until inevitably all of her attention was drawn back to the picture on her phone again.

Vaughan was laughing.

He had such a great laugh, she remembered, put everything into it, unlike the reserved and knowing titters of half the bourgeois fools she usually came into contact with. Even months down the track, she still mourned his loss, and despite all the acrimony of the trial, the male strike and the bomb, he remained unmoved, "in a cool squat" in the far reaches of her mind, waving an eviction notice in her face, while she waited in lustful expectation for his nocturnal visits after "the kids" had gone to bed. It was her guilty pleasure, and as she reached down, to welcome his urgent kisses and muscular embrace, it was like loving every second of *Kind of Blue by Miles Davis*, whilst being fully aware that he knocked seven bells out of his wives, or watching *Vertigo* for the thirtieth time, safe in the knowledge that Hitchcock was a sexual degenerate who was prepared to ruin the career of any actress who wouldn't sleep with him.

Can you ever separate the Art from the Artist?

Tough one.

Maybe Nick Drake was the only high-profile male beyond reproach, because he was beautiful, probably never had sex and been dead for nearly fifty years.

Was that the perfect man?

Who knew, but in the end, she'd decided to block Vaughan or Danny or whatever the hell he was called. Okay, he hadn't been convicted of a crime, but her daughters needed a good example and dating a "maybe woman beater", however much she liked him, just wouldn't cut it. She'd be writing letters to mass murderers on death row next, she thought as she tapped the space bar on her laptop, and sighed at the fragility of her sex. If wasn't hormones, it was unsuitable men; in fact, all men, except for lovely Nick Drake, of course. Shame he wasn't up for a quickie behind the bike shed. Suppose you can't have everything. Perhaps she could slip a Viagra in his Nesquik, when he wasn't being moody and unattainable, Suzanne thought, before returning all her attention to the picture on her phone once more.

And who the hell were these new guys?

Where was Davie B, who made her laugh, and Jimmy Jazz who tried to chat her up behind Vaughan's back? Where was Luke for God-sakes? Whatever she thought of Vaughan and Mithras, they were not the same as the Simon Pinner brigade. These were committed misogynists, openly hostile to women, and embracing the crazed INCELs who regularly gunned down innocent people because they couldn't get laid. Imagine how angry you would be if you got shot by fucking idiot just because he couldn't get a girl, she thought, as she desperately tried to equate the reasoned yet slightly eccentric arguments from a committed socialist like Vaughan with the super alt -right principles of someone like Pinner. It didn't fit and she smelt a rat and she was pretty sure of the rodent's name.

Alex MacDonald.

Chapter 31

Luke kept scrolling down his twitter feed, as images of drunken celebrities posing with even more intoxicated hangers on, continued to parade past his jaded eyes.

Same old same old.

Big smiles, hugs, and fist bumps, as everyone tries so hard to pretend that they are at the best party of their lives, when in reality, nothing really happens, unless, of course, you count Mason Meyers getting pushed into the fountain in the middle of the club by his now ex, ex, ex-girlfriend, Jessica, after a huge argument and in the process probably ruining three grammes of quality cocaine, that he usually kept in his sock.

Not good and in the end Vaughan had probably been right.

Causes and politics were always just a game for the rich and famous.

Spend a week in favela surrounded by security, take a private jet to protest against climate change, or maybe wear rainbow laces in your boots, while gladly "trousering" a millionaire pay packet from your club owners in Saudi Arabia, where the rights of gay people were seldom respected.

I suppose, it was ever thus, thought Luke rubbing his chin, and although he had been complicit in the never-ending celebrity circus himself, and probably gotten as much out of them as they had out of him, the whole business still left him with a nasty taste in his mouth, and for the first time in his short life, he never felt more a part of the proletariat as he did right now.

Maybe he was turning into a socialist after all, he grinned to himself, placing his phone back on his desk before turning his head towards the police, outside the large windows of his office, busily sifting through boxes of documents behind a taped off area. They had been here nearly a week now and despite the earnestness of their manner, had found virtually nothing to incriminate the organisation other than a few receipts for Pizza which didn't tally up with the petty cash. Hardly the missing weapons of mass destruction predicted by Jake

Callaghan and his Woke commentariat, but then again this was never supposed to be an investigation but rather a form of theatre to show something was being done, reasoned Luke as he smiled at an officer carefully scrutinising a random page of foolscap, before returning once more to his lap-top. He tapped away for another ten minutes or so, until looking up from his screen again he suddenly noticed Vaughan appear in the doorway of the room.

"Oh, err hi," said Luke.

"Idiots will find fuck all," declared Vaughan, looking out into the main area of the office, with a sour look on his face.

"Yeah, its mad, isn't it?" replied Luke, hesitantly.

"You're wasting your time, mate We shredded all the good stuff, months ago," Vaughan now shouted again at a few officers, hunched over some documents in the corner of the room, who duly smiled back, before the older man closed the door and flopped down into the nearest chair he could find. Instinctively, Luke looked over and produced a weak smile, but continued to type, while an uneasy silence settled, like a filthy dust-sheet, over heads of the two men.

Ever since his return from America, Luke had seen very little of Vaughan, and other than a few brief conversations about another one of "Carl's great ideas", there had been a noticeable distance between the two of them for some time now. In truth, it was to be expected. Running all over the West Coast of America chasing after Jennifer, wasn't exactly the best way for Luke to show support towards his friend in his greatest hour of need, and although, at the time, he had managed to make a few videos with Deacon Hiddlebatch and Samuel Levi Jones, championing his case, it wasn't nearly enough and Luke knew it. So, for the next ten minutes, they both said nothing, whilst glancing at each other, every now and again like estranged lovers, until the Vaughan decided to break the silence again.

"Saw in the papers, that dick Meyers got pushed into a fountain by his Doris."

"Ha! yeah," replied Luke.

"Thought you would be there," added Vaughan with a knowing smile.

"Nah."

"Fallen out with them?"

"Not really, Josh did invite me, but I just didn't fancy it."

"You should've gone, mate, get what you can out of the fuckers, before they up sticks and trot along to their next well-meaning cause," snarled Vaughan warming to his theme, and sitting up in his chair, as Luke politely nodded his head back, while preparing himself for another story/lecture from his old mentor.

"When I was your age, we used to meet these rich kids all over the gaff, down the Ministry, the Blue Note, the Dogstar in Brixton and they would be all over you, kissing your arse, putting on the accent, getting their taste of the ghetto. Bit sad actually. All that effort to get away from who they actually were. Anyway, every now and again, they would invite us back to their drum for some after-club naughty behaviour, and I always made sure I left with a souvenir or two. Ha! I fucking nicked an entire sound system from some loaded prick in Chelsea once, sold it to a bloke down the pub for a oner, hilarious."

"Well, that's a bit wrong, isn't it?" replied Luke, sitting back and feeling genuinely outraged by what his friend had just revealed.

"Not really. A fair trade innit. He got the joy of hanging about with a gutter jockey like me, you know "bagged" a few interesting anecdotes for when he gets older while I got a nice pair of speakers. Done deal. Probably telling that story right now in some wanky bar in Fulham or Highgate to some twat called, Giles that he went to Cambridge with."

"Sounds a bit bitter to me," replied Luke, shaking his head, as he returned to writing an email.

"Well, that's where your generation gets it wrong innit?" snapped Vaughan.

"Oh, right? so a guy who happens to have a bit of money, goes to club and meets up with some people who he doesn't know and then invites them back to his flat, which is a pretty nice thing to do, to be fair, and then you steal his speakers? Yeah, right Vaughan, that makes complete sense," spat back Luke raising his voice and now completely abandoning any former feelings of guilt regarding his behaviour during his friend's recent arrest.

"You boys love saying that don't you, hey? "To be fair", "To be fair". Fuck me, your generation wouldn't know "Fair", if it jumped out of the bushes and tried to suck your dick."

"It's just an expression we use."

"Oh, is it? That's nice. Like "reach out" or "my bad "I suppose, or starting ever sentence with "so" or always going up at the end of your sentence, seeking some kind of fucking approval. Upward inflection, I think they call it. It's not healthy son, not healthy at all," replied Vaughan with a cruel grin, before folding his arms across his chest.

"You know what I think?" said Luke, now turning around to face the older man, and giving up on the pretence of working on his laptop.

"Yeah, what do you think, Luke? cos I would be really interested to know if you had any original ideas in that fucking head of yours instead of nicking mine all the time,"

"You're paranoid bruv. They are just people, ordinary people like me and you, who happened to have done okay for themselves, that's all," replied Luke, trying desperately to ignore the barb of Vaughan's latest insult.

"Ha! Well, "To be fair", if that's what you think Luke, then you're a bigger twat than I took you for."

"Oh, thanks for that."

"I'm sorry, was I being obstreperous? replied Vaughan, laughing out loud again and shaking his head, before Luke, now desperately wanting to avoid another argument, began to unplug his lap-top and gather up his things.

"Nice response, snowflake."

"God that's original, Vaughan."

"Fucking true though innit. You know, I was mentoring one of you lot the other day. He was about your age and he wouldn't get off his arse to get a job, said he was vulnerable, you know depressed. Which is fine, but I told him sometimes, after all the CBT, all the medication and all the hugs and affirmations from every bell-end in the universe, he would still have to walk towards the bullets, you know, sort things out for himself, which is pretty sound advice if you ask me, and do you know what the fucking muppet said? He accused me of bullying him, said I was telling him to man up," replied Vaughan.

"Well, weren't you?" said Luke.

"Was I fuck! I was telling him to face up to reality. You know stop tattooing motivational messages in Chinese or Latin on your arm like 'It's not the falling down it's the getting up' or wacking 'don't limit yourself' on the screensaver of your fucking phone, and actually start doing something about it, for a change."

"It ain't so easy! Ain't so easy as that," cried Luke now raising himself from his chair as he felt the fury begin to rise through his body and his palms start to sweat again.

"Ain't it? Well, maybe that's why half of you, end up having so many panic attacks then? Hey? Any criticism, any obstacle, and its ooh no, please don't make me face up to things, see things as they really are. Oh no! and now you are saying something that I don't completely agree with, ooh, ooh, help, help, police officer quick, quick, I'm being triggered, I need a safe space, where's my fucking therapy dog?! Fucking arseholes! You know, come to think of it actually, it's not your fault at all, probably ours. The generation who never heard the word, "Yes" bringing up the generation who never heard the word, "No". Maybe we should've let you play out on the streets a bit more, you know open up a few more adventure playgrounds, let you graze a knee or two, I don't know, but whatever it is, you lot have succeeded in building a world of complete and utter bullshit. Where a fucker who makes a cup of coffee is now called a barista, a prick who just stays at home during a pandemic is a local hero and any celebrity who starts an online campaign is some kind of legend," said Vaughan, shaking his head and folding his arms again.

"We know that! don't you think we know that?" shouted back Luke, gripping the arms of his chair and feeling his face redden with anger once more, before Vaughan suddenly stood up and started to walk towards him.

"But do you, Luke? I mean do you son? Cos, I don't think you do mate. You know what I had to do with that idiot in the end? I had to apologise. I'm not joking you. I had to say sorry, and then in a soothing yet reassuring voice, I had to tell him that I fully respected his needs and recognised his vulnerability, and you know what? It fucking worked. The dick head was happy again. He was still in the same shit as he was before but now because I had poured ten spoons of sugar on his head, he was as happy as a pig in his own manure. Makes me want to scream! You know sometimes I wish there were the Mongols out there, or Huns or even fucking Klingons, who would sweep across Europe and America and wipe you useless, bearded, fragile wankers off the planet once and for all.", spat back Vaughan, now staring at the younger man with uncontainable fury in his eyes.

"Oh right, that makes total sense Vaughan. Wipe us all out, yeah that will definitely work," replied Luke, shaking his head before quickly reaching down to grab his laptop and marching out of the room.

Chapter 32

What a prick, Luke thought as he stormed down the stairs of Mithras HQ and pushed open the glass entrance door to find himself on the street outside and searching for his cigarettes.

He hated Vaughan now.

Totally fucking hated him.

If his generation were fragile, then it was the fault of tossers like Vaughan, who had left them with such a fucked-up world to inherit, Luke's thoughts now barked, as he quickly took a left down Long Acre and tore off in the direction of who knows where. Now, as the increasing rage surged through his veins, the misshapen faces of his attackers from a few years previous suddenly barged into his mind again, and with a baseball bat, Luke started to smash their stupid, violent heads until thick blood and bits of brain began to ooze out of their eyes and ears. It felt good, really good, and he was just about to take another imaginary swing into their pulverised skulls, when a ping from his phone brought his febrile day dream to a temporary halt.

"Hiya 😊 Katie."

Wow. He hadn't heard from her in ages, and quickly dropping his fantasy baseball bat, his heart instantly sang out with joy, at the very welcome sight of her name on his phone.

"Hi, you don't know how good it is to hear from you."

"Are you okay?"

"Absolutely not. Fancy meeting for a drink? Like now?!"

"Yeah, okay I will finish early," texted back Katie, and after Luke replied with a big smiley face, forty minutes later, both of them found themselves leaning over the deck of the Tattersall Castle, a converted bar on a ship in the middle of the Thames, sipping gin and tonics and doing their very best Vaughan 2Lose impressions.

"Everyone who doesn't think like me is automatically a wanker."

"Women aren't an Enema."

"It's not a man's world and it doesn't take a frilly necked lizard to fill it."

Hysterically, they laughed and clapped their hands together, and even though Luke felt a slight tinge of disloyalty for taking the unreserved piss out of his friend, it still felt great and what's more it felt even better to be with Katie. It had been about four months since they had last spoken, and although they were still on very good terms, he had been getting over Jennifer, which for some reason he had never told Katie about, while she seemed happy enough with her new boyfriend, James. However, despite the over-polite texts, and the funny emojis, it was pretty obvious, that they both wanted more, and so they continued to sip their drinks and look over towards the London Eye on the other side of the river, until the small waves lapping against the side of the boat, gently rocked Katie's face into Luke's chest, and then, without warning, he leaned across and finally kissed her. He smiled, she kissed him back, he laughed, she laughed, he kissed her again.

"I have a boyfriend," said Katie.

"So, do I," replied Luke, as they giggled and then kissed some more, until deciding that they were way too sober to make any kind of a considered decision about what to do next, they trooped off, arm in arm, down the gangplank of the floating bar and headed off towards the centre of town. From the Tattersall Castle, they walked up Villiers Street and drank in a few local pubs, until Katie declared that she wanted a martini in the Savoy and as a result, Luke soon found himself in the American bar of the celebrated hotel, staring at a long-stemmed glass with an olive floating in it. As far as Luke was concerned, it was basically a triple vodka, and therefore wincing at the bitter taste of cocktail, he immediately ordered a JD and coke, before the pair of them, sat under a Terry O'Neill print of the actor's Paul Newman and Lee Marvin and listened to a piano player sing Cole Porter songs for the next hour or so. It was the cat's meow, as his mother would say, and they drank and cheered loudly after every song, until somehow Katie persuaded the pianist to play *Rock the Casbah by the Clash*, and as he sang, "Sharif don't like it" in a lounge style, and everybody in the bar mouthed "Is this the Clash?", Luke and Katie smiled at each other, as if they were the coolest couple on the planet.

By 8 pm they had taken a taxi to East London, and by 10 pm they were in 93 Feet East in Brick Lane, drinking Margaritas and slurring how much they loved each other. A little trip to a club, called Cargo then followed, until at about 3am, they found themselves kissing like intoxicated seals in the back of a taxi, to *Foreigner's I Wanna Know What Love Is,* as Heart FM provided the customary soundtrack to the end of an evening.

It was bound to happen, and what's more Luke probably knew it from the moment Katie's text had appeared on his phone ten hours earlier. It was, as if, the great architect had sent her to him, and after the near misses of the crisp aisle of Sainsco's and Burning Man, in the silence of Katie's flat, there was no ceremony, no reflection, no official statement, as Luke's self-imposed sex ban finally came to an end.

Suddenly, he felt guilty.

How would he explain this to his right hand?

Still, it was done, the fast had been broken, and so now, there was not only a good chance that his eyesight would improve, but also, he could probably walk into a Wetherblakes again without thinking about a wank. Whoever said that alcohol, "provokes the desire, but it takes away the performance", obviously hadn't been without a shag for 28 months, thought Luke as they talked, fucked, smoked, made love, talked, had sex, until both of them collapsed into a drunken sleep. Exactly four hours and twenty-three minutes later, Luke blinked through a savage hangover, as he pawed around on Katie's carpet for his phone, only to find, to his horror, hundreds of messages now appearing in front of his drunken eyes.

"Nice one, bro – Fitz."

"Hope you took your time – Ravi."

"Any comment – Lucy Worrell – Jones, the Daily Sun."

It turned out that the uber driver who had driven them home had recognised Luke, and after filming the entire scene in the back of the taxi on his phone, he had then uploaded it online for the whole of the world to see. Apparently, he was a Mithras member, and as he would later tell a reporter, he had been so disgusted by his leader's blatant hypocrisy of breaking his celibate promise, that he felt duty bound to record and release the video. Therefore, for the next few days, Luke's love life continued to grab all the media attention, with headlines like 'Luke gets back in the saddle', 'Women are so not the enemy' and 'He wants to know what love is' referencing the Foreigner song which had been playing in the background of the video, and as a result, now re-entered the charts after a 40-year absence.

For another week, at least, the media frenzy continued, as the story refused to go away, and therefore to avoid further controversy, Luke and Katie, decided that it was probably best to avoid meeting each other for the time being, until everything had died down, plus Katie wanted to do "the right thing" and explain things properly to her boyfriend James.

In this regard, Luke did feel a slight twinge of guilt for cuckolding a fellow male, but consoled himself with the thought that it wasn't really his problem, as it was Katie's boyfriend, and anyway, he'd seen her first.

"They say we are the new "It couple" and we have single-handedly saved romance. Send me a cock shot where you can 😊 xxx" texted Katie, as Luke smiled and then placing the phone on the bed, he turned his body to one side and stared blankly at his bedroom wall again.

Chapter 33

Luke looked up from the table and for the third time in as many minutes, he'd caught his mother staring at him again, so now, it was actually beginning to unnerve him. *It had been a hell of lot easier being celibate*, he thought as he placed another spoon of his favourite Eton Mess ice cream into his mouth, and found temporary relief in its creamy loveliness. Back then, there were no enquiries, no conspiratorial winks, just pity, and the assumption that he was going slowly insane from pleasuring himself too much. But now he was back in the fold again, he was no longer a freak or a holy man, just flesh and blood, and so, almost inevitably, the questions started again.

"Why don't you invite her over?" his mother enquired putting more ice cream into his bowl before he was forced to fabricate another smile. That could be his very idea of hell, thought Luke, as an image of an exhibition of photographs from his awkward youth being produced on a coffee table for Katie's benefit suddenly flashed into his mind, and therefore deciding to avoid another afternoon of his mother skipping around the house, like a half-crazed teenager whilst asking him for the fiftieth time, what Katie's father did for a living, Luke shoved another two spoons of ice cream into his mouth, before racing out of the door, in the direction of Mithras HQ, to seek some solace there.

It had been two weeks now, since his libidinous liberation, and he was still getting nods in the street from men, as well as warm smiles from women on the tube, all happy that he was doing what a healthy young man should be doing and getting laid. However, despite the good intentions, Luke was beginning to tire of all the focus on his personal life and just about everything else for that matter. It was draining, to say the least, and so, as he stepped onto the Piccadilly Line, more toxic thoughts fizzed around his unsettled mind, until by the time he got to Leicester Square, he'd nearly had enough and consequently decided to get off a stop early, to walk the rest of the way and maybe clear his head. Wearily, he trudged up the steps from the station onto the Charing Cross Road and was just about to take a right turn towards Covent Garden when from somewhere behind him, a voice called out his name, making him stop and turn around. In an instant, the familiar sight of a large mop of red hair and piercing blue eyes, made Luke wince, before his survival instincts kicked back in, and he quickly scanned the street for a possible getaway.

"Well, lovely to see you too, Romeo. Anyway, what you doing here, I thought you would be in a Travel-lodge somewhere making up for lost time," declared Suzanne Burke, now walking up to him with her arms folded.

"Yeah, yeah, very funny, well err I've no comment and I've gotta go," replied Luke, lowering his head as he tried to step around the reporter, but to his surprise, she stood her ground and halted his progress.

"Hey look, please don't go. I'm sorry, really. I don't know when to turn it off sometimes, I actually think it's a form of Tourette's. Look, please stay Luke, I'd like to talk," said Suzanne, as Luke remained motionless in front of her raised hands for a second or two, until the gentleness in the journalist's voice seemed to trigger a release from all the pressure, and he swayed a little, before Suzanne moved forward to grab his arm.

"Oh honey, you look exhausted. C'mon, let's go for a drink somewhere, I know a great place, if you don't mind drinking with men wearing red braces and hair sprouting from their ears."

"No, I'm good, really," replied Luke trying to pull away, but Suzanne quickly grabbed his arm and now gently rubbing it with her hand, she guided him, a few hundred yards to a wine bar called the Cork and Bottle, who's chintzy interior immediately reminded Luke of those awful sitcoms from the 1980s that his mother loved so much, and for some reason he started to feel a little bit more relaxed.

"Hidden gem," said Suzanne over her shoulder, before she got some drinks from the bar and they settled down at a table in the corner.

"I hear some lunatic has just blown up a sperm bank in Australia, as a protest against women surviving without men. Apparently half of Melbourne is covered in two-year-old cum "said Suzanne with a cheeky grin, as she took a big gulp of her vodka and tonic.

"Beats sitting in the wet patch I suppose."

"Oooh that's very good."

"For a man?" replied Luke, raising his eyebrows in mild irritation as he took a sip of his drink.

"You know Luke, I shouldn't really say this, but entre nous, I never thought Mithras was that bad actually," confided Suzanne in hushed tones, as she leaned across the table towards Luke.

"Pardon!" replied the younger man, now nearly spilling his drink.

"Well, granted the name was a bit dramatic, and some of the slogans were little too obvious, you know it's not a man's world and all that, but your basic aims weren't so awful. I mean sorting yourselves out, stopping being mummy's boys, very laudable really. But keep that to yourself though Casey, I have a reputation as a first-class misandrist to protect."

"That's a man-hater, right?"

"Yes darling."

"So why didn't you say anything?"

"Well, us girls have to stick together, you know," said Suzanne smiling.

"Tell me about it," replied Luke, sarcastically.

"Now hold on a minute, Buster. This sisterhood thing is only a recent phenomenon you know. Wasn't that long ago when, women would claw each other to death before extending a helping hand to a fellow female. That's how you lot kept us in our place."

"Well, I don't think you're doing too bad these days."

"Poppycock," replied Suzanne.

"Whatever. Anyway, looks like you will get your way now, after the Vaughan thing, the male strike, me and Katie and of course that fucking bomb."

"Ooh yes the bomb," replied Suzanne suddenly sitting up.

"Still can't believe someone would do that. Especially one of our own members. I mean we had rules, no violence and we even employed mentors and therapists to help young guys who had issues with women"

"INCELs?" confirmed Suzanne.

"I fucking hate that word. Most of these men that you brand as INCELs, are all right, you know. A bit pissed off that they can't get a date, which is fair enough I suppose, but basically, they are good blokes. I mean you ever see the algorithms for those dating sites? If you aint perfect, you've got no chance. That's why men hire Ferraris for the day, so they can get pictures taken, standing beside them, to impress women, it's sick."

"I get it," replied the journalist, now a little taken back by the force of Luke's rebuke.

"I don't think you do actually. All you women do, is take the piss out of men, who get rejected, don't you? No wonder they are so lonely and angry, and if they complain, it's all, you're a fucking misogynist or an INCEL."

"But some do harm though, Luke."

"Yeah, fair enough some do, but not most of them."

"What was it Margaret Atwood used to say? Men are afraid women will laugh at them and women are afraid men will kill them," replied the journalist with a slightly smug grin.

"And when did she say that? Thirty years ago, I bet. Jesus, it's so general. Don't you people understand? Men have changed so much since then! These days, most guys don't mind the piss being taken out of them by women. In fact, I can't think of one man I know, who would say anything if a woman laughed at him. We're used to it, bro'! Seriously, look at any Film or TV programme you like, and it's usually, some stupid man being shown up by an empowered woman innit? Yeah, yeah, and before you say, like everyone else does these days, there are fucking psychos out there, we all know that, don't we? and most men hate them more than anyone; but they are a tiny percentage, on the margins, any stat will tell you that. Most of the men you call, INCELs, wouldn't hurt a fly. I mean it. I have met loads of them, done meetings, had group therapy sessions; they are just guys who want a girl and a normal life, know what I mean, it's fucking bullshit."

"Okay, I guess it's hard sometimes for men" replied Suzanne softening her eyes and suddenly feeling a little more empathy than usual for anyone with an XY chromosome.

"Hard?! It's a fucking nightmare. Do you know how rare it is for a man to get any encouragement from a woman? Like any, at all? Virtually impossible. In fact, the other day, I nearly found myself starting to cry, proper tears, when I heard this woman online, say something vaguely positive about men. Pearl, her name was. Such a surprise to get it from a woman. It's crazy! You know, most of the guys I met in Mithras were great; working through their shit, trying to get better, being more noble. Course, you lot on the left, fucking hate that idea, don't you? Be noble. Have honour. Be masculine. That's just something to take the piss out of, innit? but it means something to men, it really does."

"Well, I think there's a bit of a difference between Patriarchal norms and doing the right thing Luke," replied Suzanne, trying to stick to her side of the argument.

"Patriarchal norms? What does that even mean? Oh yeah, sorry, I remember. That's the one where, one minute you're all She Hulk, going on about men being toxic all the time and being empowered and all that shit, and then the next you're clutching your pearls cos some guy looked at you twice in a bar and made you feel a bit uncomfortable. It's a fucking joke bruv! Yeah, but you are first ones to complain, when a woman gets beaten up in the street or nearly raped on the tube in broad daylight and everyone is just standing around filming it, ain't ya? or when those cops did fuck all in that school shooting in Texas, years ago, then it's all, where were the men! where were the men! Such fucking crap. How do you think it gets to that, hey? That's what happens when you call men, animals, brutes, savages, all the time, mock them for being men, for doing the noble thing, no wonder we don't step in now."

"Well, yes, you have a point, but you have to get the balance right. I mean…."

"So many guys trying their arse off to get it right, you women have no idea, seriously! not a fucking clue! But you just love giving us your valuable input though, don't you? You're watching too much porn, you're too aggressive, you need to check your privilege. Actually, I don't even know what I'm complaining about, men have known this shit for years, so, it's no surprise to us, what you do or say, that's why we formed Mithras, in the first place, to give us some space, know what I mean? And then just when we were actually getting somewhere, finding our way a bit, some arsehole joins up and plants a bloody bomb," interrupted Luke, now nearly close to tears, as he raised his eyes in deep frustration to stare at the ceiling of the bar for a moment.

"I get it, I know, it's all being going too far, recently, hasn't it?" replied Suzanne, with some genuine sympathy in her voice at what Luke had just said, until, after an awkward pause, her inner journalist, elbowed its way to the front again.

"Weird about that bomb, though, wasn't it?"

"You taking the piss again." snapped Luke.

"Not at all. Look, it wasn't a coincidence that we bumped into each other, just now. I followed you from your mother's house," revealed Suzanne, suddenly.

"What?"

"You walk very fast, young man, I nearly lost you on the escalators. Look, forget about all that now, because I desperately needed to talk to you about something. Do you know a guy called Simon Pinner?" asked Suzanne, lowering her voice and moving forward across the table again, while Luke shook his head at the question, and also tried to get his head around the fact that he'd just been followed for the last hour.

"Oh, okay. Are you sure? This guy?" replied Suzanne then showing Luke a picture on her phone.

"Oh yeah, I know that guy, but that's not Simon Pinner. His name is Carl, Carl Morgan."

"Oh, so that's what he is calling himself now? Well Carl or Simon as I knew him, did an interview with me five years ago, when he was the spokesmen for an extreme male group called Men Walking Their Own Path, you know advocating women getting back to just being mothers and wives again"

"Yeah, I think he mentioned something about that, but Vaughan checked him out and said he wasn't into that kind of thing anymore."

"Well, that's as maybe, but guess who I saw him with in Soho just over a year ago?"

Luke's face looked blank.

"Alex McDonald," said Suzanne.

"The newspaper editor?"

"Oh, I wish. He's way, way more than that Luke. Basically, the most powerful man in British media, maybe the world, even Elon Musk is scared of him. Shapes opinions, destroys any politicians who annoy him, just for fun. I mean he's the guy who took us into a war in Iraq without blinking an eye," explained the reporter.

"I thought he was your boss?"

"Journalists are whores, darling, we work for anyone who will pay us," replied Suzanne laughing.

"So, what's he doing with Carl?"

"Exactly. It's all very dodgy as far as I am concerned. So, I looked into it and this Simon or Carl, as you call him, joined Mithras about thirteen months ago, right?" asked Suzanne.

"Yeah, sounds about right," agreed Luke.

"About the same time Mithras started becoming more aggressive. Before that, it was all 'No women February', helping out in women's refuges, sunglasses on the tube, but after Carl joins it gets increasingly more militant, you know, men and women working in separate work-places, male strike, all that nonsense."

"I never agreed with that, by the way."

"I believe you, but all of this starts happening, just after I saw Alex McDonald meeting Simon Pinner aka Carl Morgan in Soho. Funny that, innit?" said Suzanne.

"So, what are you are saying that this Anton guy who tried to blow up that conference centre was working with Carl?" asked Luke, still unconvinced.

"I wouldn't put it past him. Simon or Carl was an extremist, his ideas had nothing to do with yours, and with Alex McDonald involved, I would wager a large packet of Haribo's on the two being connected. The bomb never went off, did it? So, no damage done really, except to you and the geeky fascist who was caught; and surprise, surprise, when he was caught, he was wearing your T- Shirt and your literature was everywhere, in the bag he was carrying, and all over his bedroom. I bet you anything that Simon and his mates joined him up without him knowing. I rang his nearest branch in Portsmouth and they said they had never seen or heard of him," replied Suzanne, clicking her fingers.

"But the explosives they found in his bag were real? Surely, he wouldn't go that far, would he? replied Luke, now sitting back in his chair.

"You don't know Alex MacDonald. He has to win, and after the failure of the court case against Vaughan, I think, he got jittery," replied Suzanne.

"Nah, I can't see it. Alex McDonald is like Bezos or Gates; he wouldn't get involved in stuff like that." replied Luke, shaking his head again.

"So, what was he doing with Simon Pinner in Soho?" asked Suzanne, as Luke shrugged his shoulders and returned a blank stare.

"Exactly," replied Suzanne, as she finished her vodka and tonic and then walked over to the bar to get another two drinks.

Chapter 34

"Ha! I still can't believe people go so crazy for all the nonsense that I talk," said Jake walking into his dressing room, as the applause from the studio audience echoed down the hallway and he quickly turned around to lock the door behind him.

"That's because you are a superstar, darling," replied Antigone moving off the edge of the makeup counter and walking over to kiss him.

"Mmm... you're the superstar," whispered Jake tasting her lips and feeling her hand gently stroke his face. So different from his wife, he thought as he continued to kiss her, before Antigone, realising that she was in the middle of another threesome again, pulled away and walked back to the counter once more.

"Oh, by the way, I managed to speak to your agent cupcake, and he says the Americans are very, very interested in doing something with you."

"Really? do you think the yanks would get what we do here?"

"My God! Of course! Everything is global these days. My New York friends, Nora and Keisha fucking love the show. It's like James Corden but with a degree, smart and funny, just like you darling," replied Antigone, as the chat show host moved forward to kiss her again. He loved it when she complimented him, and now pushing her back against the ledge of the work-top, he was just about move his hands underneath her blouse, when suddenly there was a large knock at the door and the handle started to move up and down as if someone was trying to get in.

"Hey Jake, what are doing in there? Banging the makeup girl? Come on, let me in, I wanna take you out for an over-priced Hendricks and Fever Tree tonic, or whatever you millennials like to drink these days."

"Fuck! Alex!" whispered Jake to Antigone, as she squeezed his love handles and his startled eyes urged her to be quiet.

"Oh, err hi Alex. Yeah fella, was just gonna have a shower, err give me a few minutes, and I'll meet you in the Francis Dashwood across the road, yeah?"

"Come on, Jakey boy, let me in, I've seen a small cock before."

"Err ha! yeah, err no, I'm err, I'm err just about to get in the shower," replied the chat show host as Antigone whispered "Jakey Boy?" and Jake mouthed "arsehole" while the two of them pressed their foreheads together and giggled silently, like naughty school- children, before the voice outside the door spoke again.

"Okay, see you over there in ten minutes then, and don't take too long, I've got be back at the paper in a couple of hours. Great show by the way," said the media mogul in a disappointed voice, as he tried the handle one more time before quickly walking away.

Fifteen minutes later, Jake sat staring at a bottle of tonic water, with a sizeable erection in his pants and was wondering whether he should pour all of it into his double gin or just bugger off to the gents for a wank. *Is there anything worse than coitus interruptus?* he mused, as he waited impatiently for his mentor to return from the toilet and tried not to yelp,

"After all these years, I still can't get used to the taste of it," declared Alex placing himself on a high stool before bringing a huge bowl of soda water, lime and ice to his lips.

Jake grinned.

The glass didn't quite fit, the suit and the crumpled face and a bit like an elderly person eating a Big Mac, some things should definitely have an age bar, thought Jake, while he continued to try and take his mind off his semi erect penis that was now lolling around unemployed, in the dark reaches of his underwear.

"Liked the show, as always Jake, you're a natural. You have the right energy for the modern age."

"Oh, thanks."

"Yeah, it was great. Only thing is, I thought, you could have increased the pressure on that Mithras guy, a bit more."

"Err really? Thought I did a pretty good job. Got him to admit that Mithras' response to the Dolores Brady case was deeply misogynistic and the main aims of the organisation had caused unnecessary divisions between men and women."

"Well, no disrespect, Jake, but I think we all know that, don't we? The thing is, we still need to hurt them, destroy them, and this type of intellectual approach is just playing straight into their hands. They love it, when the whole damn thing descends into some kind of whataboutery and no-one gets to land a punch."

"Err well yeah maybe, I suppose, but they are finished now anyway, don't you think?" replied the chat show host, a little irked by the criticism.

"I wouldn't be so sure about that."

"You think? Their support is draining away by the minute. They used to have millions in their movement, now it's in the thousands. Josh Middleton has said sorry, Mason Meyer has bought his mum a house in Dartford, because he criticised her parenting skills, and even Levi Jones has said he was misguided and they are looking to give him his Oscar back. It's over. Seriously Alex. I just think we should let them die a slow death, like the Lib Dems."

"Well, that's the great mistake Jakey boy," replied Alex taking a sip from his drink, while Jake returned a weak smile before looking out across the bar.

God, he hated that name.

Like being back at school and called Jakey-Wakey or something similarly hilarious by the older boys. What a total fucking wanker Alex McDonald truly was, he thought as he glanced sideways into media mogul's watery blue eyes.

Self-made monster from a Norfolk Comprehensive.

Could there really be anything worse?

Loud, boring men, who took the Tory's advice and got on their bikes in the eighties, before making a shitload of cash, crushing or sexually molesting anyone who came within fifty feet of them; and then to make matters worse, simply loved having well-bred lackies around, so they could remind them every ten minutes, in whatever crap dialect they were raised in, how they had made it out of the swamp. Bet he and the wife never missed an episode of Only Fools and Horses on UK Gold, with a bargain bucket from KFC, and a nicely chilled bottle of Asti Spumante, Jake thought as he folded his arms on the distressed wood of the pub table and pretended to listen some more.

"When a man is down Jake, never, ever, EVER give him a chance to get back up again. Just simply put your foot on his neck and drill a hole into his cerebellum with a nice Black and Decker or a Bosch if you are looking for real quality," continued Alex with a slippery grin.

"Well, yes, I suppose that could work, but I don't think you have to go that far fella. Have you seen the headlines recently? The wind is changing, romance is back. Even Luke Casey is getting laid and any bloke wearing one of those "women are not the enemy" T-Shirts, now looks a bit weird. Six months ago, it was the norm. I'm telling you Alex, it's over. People have just moved on. It's like fashion, happens all the time," said the chat show host, before taking a sip of his drink.

"Well, I think it took a little more than fashion."

Oh, the bomb you mean?" replied Jake shrugging his shoulders.

"Well sometimes you have to give things a nudge," added Alex cryptically as he wiped away some spilt drink on the table with his hand.

"Well, that was just chance, wasn't it? A random nutter." said Jake, now a little confused.

"Of course," replied Alex hurriedly, "but it did change the narrative, didn't it? Before that, Mithras were still a viable concern even if you disagreed with them, but after Anton whatever his name was, they became a quasi-terrorist organisation. MithrISIS and all that. You have to take advantage of luck Jakey boy, and then make sure you finish the bastards off. If I have learned one thing in life, it's that…."

"Well, you know Alex, with all due respect, but maybe, I am a bit bored with Mithras, Luke Casey, Vaughan 2Late and the rest of the circus. I mean, I have been at it, for nearly three years now and to be honest it's fucking exhausting. I really think it all needs to move on," interrupted Jake, in a firmer voice, which was quickly followed by an uneasy silence, as both men looked out into the bar and took a sip from their drinks, before Alex broke the silence again.

"I hear you've had a few offers from the States."

"Err yeah. Err, how did you know that? It's supposed to be confidential," replied Jake a little shocked.

"Don't get your Calvins in a twist, Jakey. Head of the network, is an old friend, and wanted to sound me out. It's normal practice. You're not gonna invest millions of dollars in someone unless you're sure, are you?" said Alex with a grin.

"No, I suppose not."

"Exactly. And I don't mind by the way," added the billionaire.

"Well, of course, I was going to tell you, when it was more certain"

"Of course. Look, don't worry, Jake. I get it. Do you think I got to where I am today without ambition? Of course, you wanna try your luck across the pond, do a James Corden, great idea, you'll do very well, but I just don't think we are finished here just yet, that's all. Trust me. Another six months of shoving and the whole Mithras caravan will go over the cliff," said Alex now edging his body closer towards his protégé.

"Look I do get it, but to be completely frank Alex, I think that I have come to end of the line with the whole debate. I really do and what's more I think the whole country has too. Ultimately, we have to trust the people on this. I mean they know best."

"Jesus, what the fuck do people know, Jake? only what we tell them for God's sake. They are mildly intelligent sheep, and that's putting it politely. Look, my people are putting together another expose on Vaughan and some of his highly dubious dealings in the nineties. I mean the guy was heavily into drugs and some very violent practices and…"

"Look Alex, I am extremely grateful for all you've done for me."

"I just recognise talent."

"Thank you, and I would like to think that you've got a return on your investment. My show is the biggest chat show on UK terrestrial TV, and my articles sell your newspapers but I want new challenges now."

"And I want them for you, but like I said, the job isn't done, Jake," replied Alex more resolutely.

"Well, I'm sorry, but I think it is. And if it isn't, then it's not my job anymore, someone else will have to…"

"Fuck me, you snowflakes are all the bloody same, aren't you," broke in Alex, now no longer able to contain himself, as he sat back in his chair and shook his head.

"Pardon," replied Jake, looking a little shocked from the sudden change of tone.

"A little work, a little reality and you fold and go for the easy option, don't you? I have always said it; you pricks will die from politeness and convenience in the end, I'd put my last penny on it," said Alex with a grin.

Look, I don't think insulting me will…"

"How do you think things work, Jake? Mmm…? Jesus Christ! You lot actually believe that you have reinvented the wheel, just because you can't pinch your secretary's arse and get away with it anymore. Really? Its who has the power son. An ex-public school-boy like you, should know that, bred to lead and all that crap."

"Ha! think you can do better than that Alex surely? Private school privilege, a bit lazy, don't you think? I can get that kind of tosh from half my listeners, any day of the week," replied Jake with a smug smile.

"You know, for all your wokeness, blue check marks and pronouns, you're bigger fucking snobs than your fathers even were. At least they had the decency to look down their noses at you; you lot are much, much more slippery, aren't you? Kill you with a hug, isn't that the way? You know I have a friend and he's got a son, a little bit younger than you, thick as mince, no use to anyone. His father bought him a restaurant a few years ago for two million quid in Shepherds Market, fucked that up of course, then he bought him a boutique hotel in the Lake District and that went to the wall as well, so now I have the halfwit working for me, writing a weekly column, which I had to teach him how to write, by the way. I mean that's all I see traipsing through my office's, day after day. The sons and daughters, or grandsons and grand-daughters of people who were once exceptional. Nepotism doesn't even come close to describing it."

"So, Alex if you know all this, why do you bother then?"

"For only one reason, because it basically works. The world, whichever way it spins, doesn't really operate too well with too much democracy. We need an oligarchy. A one percent, who know what they are doing and know each other. It's simple really. Everyone keeps calling for a revolution, but that's the last thing we fucking want. Ever read Orwell's *Homage to Catalonia*? It's all there. Forget *Das Kapital*, if you wanna know how the world works, just read that. When the Spanish civil war started, it was all, let's be equal, waiters turning down tips, and everyone playing at being in the perfect society, but then after a few weeks, human nature took over, the monkey spirit was back, and the boys who were in charge before, took charge again, just this time, they made sure they wore a different hat. You do the same thing sunshine. I've seen you. Bit of mockney here, send your kids to a good catholic state school there, so you can keep on "the right side of history", but it's all lovely camouflage, isn't it? because the result is still the same. You keep the power," said Alex, leaning forward to take a sip of his drink.

"You know I have heard this crap a thousand times before, and it never gets any less boring," replied Jake, finally losing his patience and glaring straight into the eyes of the media mogul for the first time.

"People like you don't run the world, Alex, you just think you do. Narcissists, who should be in jail, or under some kind of medical supervision, and not anywhere near a proper job. You dinosaurs have no idea how fast the world is changing do you? Lunatics, who clawed their way out of some housing estate, are no longer relevant, I'm afraid. Those days are over, thank God. Now, what we need is pure intelligence and sophisticated management, not tough guys from dodgy backgrounds with that "1977 spirit" and we can definitely do without your thuggish insights into how everything 'really works'. Kinda last century, fella, if you don't mind me saying so. But if we are going to be honest here, which I assume we are, from the rapidly diminishing tone of this conversation, then no, I don't want to work for you anymore, Alex, and you can chase Mithras over all five continents and stick as many electric drills into their heads as you want, because, as far as I am concerned, it's time for me to move on, and I think I will definitely take that job in the States now."

"Good grief, Jake, are we breaking up? Very sexy. Have you spoken to your wife about the job in America by the way?" replied Alex resisting the urge to smash his glass into chat show host's face before calmly clasping his finger together on the table in front of him.

"Yes, I have and she is very supportive."

"Really? and what about Antigone?" asked Alex.

"Who?" replied a startled Jake.

"Well surely, you must have cleared it with your young mistress first? Or were you banking on getting an American version once you found your feet in Los Angeles?" said the billionaire with a grin.

"Err, look, Alex, erm, it's getting very late, isn't it?" replied Jake now looking frantically around the bar.

"I would watch it, Jake. Miss Partington-Wise looks the vengeful type. Might have to keep her on side. Bet the sex is good, though, isn't it?"

"Err, err, you know Alex, I just forgot, I have to prepare for tomorrow's radio show, so, err thanks again for the drink, but I think I'd, err better go, you know, get back," replied Jake and with that, he quickly pushed the huge fishbowl of gin and tonic to one side before fleeing in the general direction of the door.

Alex now laughed as he watched Jake's dramatic exit momentarily stall, when the chat show host somehow found himself caught behind a huge guy in the middle of the bar, and now looking like a little boy, he started to swing his arms about wildly for a few seconds until eventually finding a gap, he managed to squeeze his way past, and then hurry off into the night.

What a cunt, thought Alex, and wincing once more as he took another sip of his soda water and lime, he brought the mobile phone up to his ear and began to speak.

Chapter 35

"So, you're sure," asked Vaughan leaning against the edge of his kitchen counter as he watched in mild horror while Luke poured orange juice into a glass of his best rum.

"100% bruv," slurred Luke. "Suzanne seen him over a year ago, having a meeting with Alex McDonald, and his real name ain't Carl Morgan neither, lying fuck, it's Simon Pinner."

"Well, anyone can change their name. Maybe he owes the bank a load? I knew a bloke who did it once to avoid council tax arrears."

"Well, I don't think this is about council tax bro', know what I mean. And anyway, why is a nobody like Carl meeting up with one of the most powerful people in England, hey?" asked Luke.

"And she was definite," replied Vaughan.

"Suzanne? Just seen her, I told you. That's why I come over straight away. She done her research; found out that Carl or Simon or whatever his name is and his mates were up to their necks, in all that far right bollocks. Loads of shit on twitter. And you know Suzanne, she don't mess about, she just wants the truth."

And the rest, thought Vaughan, as he tried to expel the reporter's face from his mind for the thousandth time and just concentrate on the matter in hand.

"Nah, Luke, I don't buy it. The geezer told me himself that he used to believe in some extreme views, but that was years ago."

"Not sure about that mate. He believes in it now. Suzanne showed me some posts that he did recently under his real name. Really fucked up stuff. Maybe the Handmaids Tale should be a template for men, rare good idea from a woman, build the new Gilead."

"Nah, it's a smear. I know Carl, he's a bit pushy, but he is loyal, I am pretty sure of that. Suzanne is just fishing," replied Vaughan shaking his head.

"Dunno bruv, its very dodgy."

"Just words innit. I used to believe in all sorts of revolutionary bollocks when I was a kid, but I don't believe it now." added the older man.

"Yeah, but all the crap we've been getting recently has only really happened since Carl and his crew have joined. Think about it?" replied Luke pointing a drunken finger towards his temple, while Vaughan placed his hands on the counter and ran some of the data over in his mind again.

"Carl was here before you went to San Francisco and everything was okay then, right?" declared Vaughan after a few seconds of contemplation.

"Well yeah, but he ain't gonna start causing problems straight, away, is he? No point being a double agent if you are gonna be fucking obvious is there? he's sneaky, bruv," replied Luke before pulling a face as he took another sip from his drink.,

"Ain't you got no diet coke, bro?"

Vaughan shook his head, and then turning to pour himself a glass of water from the sink, he took an anxious sip, while a hundred thoughts crowded into his mind. Could it be true? Where was the proof? Instinctively, he hated conspiracy theories, they were almost always wrong, but then again, why would Suzanne lie? He needed to know, and so after listening to Luke ramble on incoherently for another twenty minutes about his new on/off love interest, Katie, and how he really wished that he had been 18 in 1993, Vaughan led his near comatose friend to a couch in his front room, before quickly retreating to his bedroom to discover the truth about what he had just heard.

He had previously made a few checks on Carl, when he had started to get more heavily involved with the movement, which was standard procedure, especially after the infiltration of the organisation by Mark Eastwood and his undercover reporters, but aside from a few angry posts about women having double standards and romance being a bit unfair to men, he had found nothing serious. Then again, he had been looking for Carl Morgan, not Simon Pinner and it would have been relatively easy for one of his techy mates, like Big Phil or Paul to plant those quotes under a false account, thought Vaughan, as he bit nervously on his lip before he tapped "Simon Pinner" into google.

Bingo.

Same face, different name, and from the look of it, linked to every loony male group on the planet, most of whom were explicitly banned by Mithras. Take back Control, a pro male group, which advocated the end of female contraception and an INCEL community which actively encouraged violence against women, where two of its former members had already carried out mass slaughter on American campuses. Vaughan slumped back into his chair and stared at the ceiling. He hated this. All those pats on the back, morning boss, another drink Guv? you're the best, don't worry, I'll sort it.

He'd been played.

"Dick," he mouthed to himself.

Suzanne had called him Iago, what a joke.

He was Othello.

Did that make her Desdemona?

God, how he wished she was here now.

No chance of that now though.

She wasn't coming back; she'd already made that plain enough.

Did men love women more than women loved men?

He had his suspicions.

They seemed to dust themselves down quicker and get back to living again.

Unlike men.

No wonder he had spent his life, gripping the handle of the door, ready to bolt.

Much safer than walking into the middle of the room.

Who knows what dangers lurked there?

Anway, who gives a fuck?

You come into this life alone, you leave alone.

Good title for a Musical, thought Vaughan smiling to himself, before an image of his son suddenly came into his mind and he glanced at the ceiling again. Long-time no see, Brandon? Any advice for pops? No? They had stopped talking years ago, the last revenge of his mother. Taken him to live in America, and filled his head full of lies; made him support Spurs as well, by all accounts. That wasn't nice. Could you take an ex-spouse to court for doing that? Should be a law; at least it wasn't Millwall he mused, as his fingers moved slowly across his face, and explored the deep lines running across his skin. For once his aged flesh gave him some comfort, and now seeking some spiritual nourishment, Vaughan rose from his seat to place the soundtrack of an obscure British film called *That Summer* on the turntable before moving the needle to the last track on side two. *Blank Generation by Richard Hell and the Voidoids* on yellow vinyl. Very Seventies, thought Vaughan as he returned to his chair and started to nod his head to the scratchy punk guitar. Nostalgia was indeed the dirtiest narcotic, but sometimes it brought a savage clarity, and so after listening to the rest of the song, he now reached over for his phone on the coffee table to quickly tap out "bell me in the morning" before turning off the record player and going straight to bed.

The next day, he rose early, and not wanting to waste any time, addressing some of the outstanding issues that were still unresolved between himself and Luke since the big row they'd had a few weeks earlier, he quickly hustled his severely hungover friend out of the door, with a slice of toast and a can of diet coke, before sitting quietly in his front room for the rest of the morning to consider his options. Ever since his arrest and subsequent release, he hadn't really been himself. Ruminating too much on the unfairness of public condemnation, and retreating into his usual comfort zones of Vodka and Cocaine, he had let go of the rudder, and allowed others make the decisions for him. That was always fatal. However, now, was not the time for recriminations or self-pity, Epictetus, the great Stoic philosopher had told him as much, and anyway, he was back on familiar ground once more. Betrayal. He knew how to deal with that dirty transgression and so after sending a text to Carl, Luke and some of his oldest friends, he rose from his seat to set about making preparations for the evening's events.

By 6.30pm, everything was in more in less place, and he was just about to prepare some little nibbles, when the doorbell sounded and Luke appeared again.

"So, what you gonna do?" mumbled the younger man as he ambled into the kitchen, sucking on a bottle of Lucozade and still looking a little worse for wear.

"We're gonna have a party, bruv" declared Vaughan with a grin, before placing some chickpeas in a blender.

"A what?"

"A little gathering."

"But what about, what Suzanne said," asked Luke.

"Don't worry about all that my son, I'm making hummus, pass me the tahini will ya," replied Vaughan with a cheeky wink, as Luke handed over a jar from the side of the counter, before taking a seat at the kitchen table and taking another sip from his bottle. For the next half an hour or so, the two men chatted away about nothing in particular until the doorbell rang again and Carl, Big Phil, Paul and Stevie turned up, who after each being handed a cold beer, were immediately taken on a tour of the flat by their host.

"Now, that's *The Raft of the Medusa by Gericault*, and on the other wall is an original poster from the film *Bladerunner,* personally signed by the director, Ridley Scott, no less, while over there is a self-portrait by an ex-girlfriend of mine, after she spent the whole weekend on ketamine," declared Vaughan pointing to a picture of four huge eyeballs and a bulbous nose drawn in black marker pen. His new guests laughed and continued to marvel at the cultural treasures contained in the older man's flat, while every now and again, Vaughan would wander too close to Luke, who would then hiss from his seat at the table "when we gonna talk to them about the bullshit Suzanne found out."

"Soon hombre," assured his old friend as he proceeded to hand out more red stripes to his guests and crack more jokes until the doorbell sounded again, and Andy Papps, Jimmy Jazz, Davie B and Ray walked into the kitchen and duly introduced themselves to everyone.

"Guv, I thought this was just a meeting for us?" whispered Carl, moving beside Vaughan and now looking a little unnerved by the new arrivals.

"It is, mon brave, but I thought we'd have a party as well, you know after all the fucking nonsense of the last few months," replied Vaughan with a warm smile, as both sets of friends started to mingle and the music was turned up.

This boisterous bonding session continued for about another hour or so, while Luke, remained stuck on his chair in the corner of the kitchen, and continued to issue concerned looks in the direction of his friend, only to receive a cheeky wink, each time in return. Luke felt as if he was about to burst, and in frustration, after the climax of yet another story from Vaughan about something vaguely criminal from the last century, he was seriously contemplating walking across to hm, to ask what the hell was going on, when Carl suddenly pointed towards a poster at the end of the kitchen.

"Oh fella, I love this picture, who are they?"

"Way before your time, mate, or even mine for that matter," replied Vaughan as he motioned his head towards a print of Sean Connery, Jimmy Greaves, Bobby Moore and Yul Brynner standing together having a drink, outside the entrance of a Country House.

"Nice," replied Paul.

"Yeah, I have seen that poster before, wasn't it taken during the filming of the fifth Bond movie, *You Only Live Twice?*" added Big Phil, authoritatively, who fancied himself as a bit of a film buff.

"Close Philip, but alas no. A lot of people think that, cos it was made in 1966, just before the World Cup, hence the presence of Bobby Moore and Jimmy Greaves, who were in the England squad at the time and were visiting the set. However, it was, in fact, taken during the filming of a little-known movie called *Double Man*, starring Yul Brynner, would you believe."

"Oh right," replied Big Phil nodding his head towards Vaughan, whilst making a mental note to file that fact in his obscure film data base, just in case it ever came up in a pub quiz.

"Proper geezers," declared Carl.

"Yes, indeed Carl, you are not wrong there my son. Proper geezers, mensch's, men you could rely on," confirmed Vaughan.

"Definitely," agreed Paul and Stevie.

"Here's to men you can rely on," said Vaughan raising his can of beer.

"Absolutely," replied Carl banging tins with Vaughan.

"Because, it's a fucking betrayal, when you can't trust your friends innit?" said the older man.

"Of course, most important thing," confirmed Carl, taking another sip from his can.

"Well, I'm glad you agree there, Carl, or is it Simon, I can never remember?" enquired Vaughan causally, before reaching up to the top of a kitchen cupboard and pulling down a folder.

"Err pardon, fella?" replied Carl, now taking the can from his lips.

"Well, that is your name, isn't it?"

"Err," replied Carl, now anxiously looking around the kitchen.

"Are you telling me that isn't your name?" asked Vaughan again.

"Ha! Come on Vaughan fella, what's this all about?"

"Man doesn't even know his own name, Danny," broke in Andy Papps.

"That is a serious problem, Papps. So, what is it then? Carl Morgan or Simon Pinner?" queried Vaughan looking straight into the eyes of his shocked guest.

"The sinner called Pinner," joined in Ray.

"Well err, yes. I mean Simon Pinner is my actual real name, but well I've had a few tax issues, you know?" replied Carl, with a re-assuring smile.

"Mate! You don't need to tell me about the HMRC. I've spent my whole life dodging those jokers. But what I am really referring to, is these pictures of you and the power rangers here, at all these white power demonstrations. Hardly in the spirit of Mithras, is it?" replied Vaughan, as he carefully placed pictures of Carl, Big Phil, Paul and Stevie at various Far Right rallies, onto the kitchen table.

"Well yeah err, like I told you, that was a long time ago, you know," said Carl looking very unnerved at the sight of the new evidence, while the rest of his crew eagerly nodded their heads back in agreement with their leader.

"Err yes, people change," added Big Phil.

"Yes, they do Phillip, and don't get me wrong, I am completely on board with all that, especially in today's cancel culture, where some poor sod who said something vaguely offensive 9 million years ago, ends up getting shafted and losing his job. Offence archaeology, I think they call it. Nasty business, so yes, my son, we certainly need a bit of redemption in this cruel and heartless world, but I am not talking about that, am I? You say that this was years ago, yeah? So, then how do you explain, exactly nine months and three days ago to be precise, you, Stevie and Paul tweeted and I quote "Yeah Mithras is a total fucking joke! The pussies of the male protest movement. They are nothing but piss. I would rather deal with a Feminazi any day of the week and anyone who joins Mithras is total filth and deserves executing," declared Vaughan reading from a piece of paper in the file.

"That sounds a bit disrespectful, Danny," said Davie B.

"I can't lie Davie, I was a little hurt," replied Vaughan.

"Well, we had a bit of a conversion," laughed Carl, nervously looking around the kitchen again.

"Sounds like a fucking Damascene conversion to me, Carl, and the thing is, you'd already joined Mithras for nearly six months at that point. So, one minute you were persecuting Christians and the next minute you are helping to direct Mithras policy and being my best mate?" replied Vaughan now quickly stepping forward to pinch Carl's cheek with his fingers, while Ray grabbed Big Phil and pinned him against a full-length poster of Audrey Hepburn.

"Or was it when you were contacted by Alex McDonald and he told you to cause as much chaos to the organisation as possible?" said Vaughan leaning into Carl's face.

"Oowww, no, ahhh, you have it wrong Vaughan."

"I thought it was Guv. Ain't I the guvnor no more, Simon?"

"Ow, ow, Hey Vaughan, come on," screamed Carl,

"I should have guessed, but I am the trusting sort, in' I? All those mysterious nasty posts to celebrities, the pigs head to Portia Ramone, the nutcase journalist who interviewed Luke, the male strike, and of course, let's not forget that fucking bomb. That was all you, wern it?" snarled Vaughan now releasing his grip on Carl's face and taking a step back.

"Err no, no, of course not Guv, err I mean Vaughan," replied Carl, as his eyes now darted about the kitchen in pure terror.

"You sure? Okay, here's another question you might be able to answer for me then. Did Alex McDonald tell you to join Mithras?"

"Err who's Alex McDonald?" enquired Carl innocently, before Vaughan took a step forward and then punched Carl on the bridge of his nose.

"Ow, Jesus, aarghh."

"Say who is Alex McDonald again, I fucking dare you," shouted Vaughan over Carl's screams of pain, while Ray started to squeeze his fingers around Big Phil's throat and Audrey looked very unimpressed.

"Bruv, come on," said Luke now becoming increasingly concerned at the new turn of events, as he put down his bottle of beer and quickly rose from his seat.

"Come on what, Luke? Let's be reasonable? I seriously think that time has passed, mate," replied Vaughan, as he punched Carl on the nose again, this time breaking it.

"Alex McDonald?" repeated Vaughan.

"Aarghh, what about him? Christ, I don't know anything," pleaded Carl as he raised his hand to the pain in his face, while Luke recoiling from the violence, now stepped forward towards his friend.

"Come on Vaughan, that is too much."

"I agree, it is too much," replied Vaughan as he hit Carl on the nose for a third time.

"Aarghh, ow, ow," bleated Carl, feeling the blood starting to pour out of his nose while he stared back at Vaughan with terrified eyes.

"Right, you cunt, I will keep hitting you on the nose until it is a stump and you will need a pair of tweezers to fucking pick it. So again. Alex McDonald?!," repeated Vaughan, who was visibly starting to lose his temper, while Big Phil looked over towards Luke with absolute fear in his eyes.

"Get him to stop, he knows nothing, he knows nothing," pleaded the big man, as Luke, now stood motionless behind Vaughan, and uncertain what to do amidst all the shouting and violence, he found that he was instantly transported back to the night of his attack in the club again. Now his hands started to sweat and feeling as if he was going to scream, he felt his heart thump like steam-hammer inside his chest, until unable to bear it anymore, he walked straight in front of Vaughan to shout, "Fucking stop it, just fucking stop it now," However the older man was in no mood for a discussion and easily brushed Luke to one side, before leaning across to press the switch for the George Foreman grill that was sitting on the kitchen counter.

"Now usually, I only bother George for a late-night cheese and baked bean toastie, but he also does a nice steak or chicken"" replied Vaughan with a vicious grin.

"Yeah, I've done a sirloin in there, very healthy, no fat," replied Jimmy Jazz.

"It also does a nice hand. Oh, and don't bother about the neighbours hearing anything. There are visiting relatives in Bangladesh for a few weeks, so you can scream as much as you want darling," said Vaughan raising his eyes towards the kitchen ceiling.

"Jesus Christ, no, what the fuck, no, no mate, no," screamed Carl.

"It's mate now, is it? not fella? how very old school of you, Simon, dear boy," said Vaughan, before Luke walked into the middle of the kitchen once more to try and put an end to the increasing violence.

"Look Vaughan, Papps, Davie, this is ridiculous. You can't do this!"

"We need to know Luke. All he has to do is tell us the truth," replied Davie B, staring at Luke, who now shook head in disbelief, before turning all his attention back towards his old mentor again.

"Look Vaughan, stop this now! Stop this or I am walking out. I'll leave Mithras, I mean it,"

"Well, that's your call, Luke. Maybe you've left already, I dunno, but I'm gonna find out what these fuckers have been up to, if it takes me all night," spat back Vaughan as he continued to look at the terrified, bloody face of Carl, while Ray punched Big Phil in the solar plexus causing him to bend over and vomit on the floor.

"Jesus, this is so fucked up," replied Luke, looking desperately around at the older men but their eyes were steady. No compassion, no compromise, no going back.

"Don't leave!" Carl suddenly screamed, but it was in vain, Luke had already walked out of the kitchen, and now widening his eyes in terror once more, he shook his head in silent denial, before Vaughan grabbed his hand and brought it slowly over the hot grill.

Chapter 36

"Well, you'll have to get a job or sign on or something. love, but you can't sit around here all-day watching Netflix and eating crisps," declared his mother as she started to clean up around the coffee table, while Luke stared blankly at the TV screen and started to crunch.

"You know, I remember once, when your uncle Paul tried to stay in bed and not go to work and your Nanna, god rest her soul, went downstairs filled a saucepan with water and then came back up and threw the whole lot all over him," continued his mother, laughing to herself, as she walked back into the kitchen to put the kettle on.

"She sounds delightful," said Luke shaking his head.

"She was tough, right enough, but fair play, he never dossed in bed again."

"Oh right, so you gonna lob a pan of water on me every morning from now on, then?" enquired Luke, craning his head over the top of the sofa.

"Of course not, love, but it's been weeks now since you left that Mithras lot, and you have to do something," replied his mother, before reaching up to take two cups out of the cupboard.

His mother was right.

It had been weeks, but despite his present inertia, he knew that whatever he was going to do next, he had definitely made the right decision to leave. You can't go around beating the hell out of people like that, not even scumbags like Carl, thought Luke, and after storming out of the flat, he had every intention of going straight to the Police, until Andy Papps caught up with him and said that he shouldn't worry, as it had all been pre-planned and, they'd pulled a similar stunt before, with a promoter who had stolen money off them, back in the nineties. "Mate, the worst they'll get is a broken nose and a few pairs of soiled boxer shorts. You should come back," urged Papps in the middle of Harlesden High Street, but for Luke it had been the last straw, and even without Carl and his bogus little circus, he hadn't really been happy with the direction Mithras had been going in for some time now. More political, more mainstream, it definitely wasn't the movement Luke had envisaged a few years earlier and although Vaughan had texted to say that it was all a joke and he should come back to work, it wasn't enough.

He was leaving, and so the following week, his departure was officially announced on the Mithras website, where in a strangely moving tribute, Vaughan credited Luke as the real reason for the existence of the organisation in first place, and likened his influence to that of Iggy Pop in the creation of Punk back in the last century. This comparison had made Luke smile, as even up to the last, his old mentor still couldn't resist getting another reference to his beloved Punk in there somewhere, but despite the nice words from Vaughan and the thousands of glowing comments from countless Mithras members, he still couldn't escape the undeniable fact, that the co -founder of one the biggest male empowerment organisations in history, was now pot less and still living at home with his mum.

It was depressing to say the least, and in recognition at the terrible irony of his new circumstances, Luke was just about to lean forward to open yet another bag of Ridge Cut, Flame Grilled Steak flavoured crisps and commence a weary crunch when "You know, I could get you a job doing some building work with Desi, if you fancied it" suddenly wrenched him from his latest bout of mini-despair. Now, as he looked across from the sofa at the smiling face of his mother, gradually, a strange sensation began to grow in the pit of his stomach causing him to immediately discard his packet of crisps and stare into an ungrateful void. All through the madness of the last two and a half years, his mother had stuck by him and just carried on, while all he did was bang on again and again about what was going wrong in his life.

But what about her?

How many times, had he seen the sadness in her eyes?

Had she done something wrong?

Was she responsible for his attitude towards women?

A guy stabs someone to death, or cons thousands in a Ponzi scheme, or just wants to live his life in a different way, and society whispers "Probably because of the mother," as they jab out their fingers in lazy judgement. They had more or less said as much in the press and social media, and Luke would wager most of her friends thought the same thing too, but despite this, she had kept believing in him. By rights she should have slung him out or chucked a saucepan of water over his head a long time ago, but here she was, trying to help him again, and as he stared through to the kitchen and watched while she bounced a tea bag up and down in his favourite cup, in that precise moment, he suddenly felt a giant, unconditional, and enormous love for all women, everywhere.

Their soft eyes, their courage, the way they pushed on and still smiled, even when the roof was falling in or the sky turned black. Men were not fucking worthy, not worthy at all, and equality was a sick joke, when women had to endure all the pain, all the responsibility, all the shame. We are pointless compared to them, not even the spit on their shoe, Luke concluded, as his body now fizzed with so much appreciative energy, that he feared, at one point, his heart might actually stop. And then, as quickly as it had arrived, this "sensation "suddenly passed, and after taking a deep breath, Luke picked up his bag of crisps again, before accepting the tea from his mother, strong with a little milk, just as he liked it.

"Yeah, I suppose I could do that," said Luke, taking another sip from his mug.

"Better than sitting around the house all day, feeling sorry for yourself, love," replied his mother as she walked back to the kitchen while Luke rested his head back against the sofa and considered his new choice of career.

Ever since he was a kid, Luke had heard stories from his uncles of the centuries-old path from school to shovel for young men from an Irish background, and although his generation had been lucky enough to head for the civilisation of an office space and so the heaviest thing, he'd ever have to lift was a packet of photo-copy paper, it was still in his basic DNA. Even his dad, who he vaguely remembered, had worked on the sites, and been good at it, by all accounts, and so deciding that it was probably better than doing nothing, two days later, Luke made his way to the corner of Askew Road and Uxbridge Road for 7am, where he was picked up in a white van by heavy set guy with a big grin, and duly handed a cup of milky coffee.

"Hey Luke, seen youse on de telly, giving dem old birds some fair stick," declared Desi Lynch, an old schoolfriend of his mothers and married to her best friend, Lorraine, as he winked at his new employee before speeding off towards a job in South Harrow.

"De two bastards in de back are Pav and Chris, Polish and Romanian," added Desi, while Chris shouted back, "Bulgarian, you Irish prick," and the three men then exchanged happy insults for the next ten minutes or so, to let Luke, know that they were all good boys here and everyone got on well here.

227

"I voted leave," cried Desi again as he pulled up at some traffic lights.

"Good, we want you to leave," replied Chris, before Luke sipped his coffee and laughed along in the front, while his mind prepared itself to join the real world once more. It had been about eighteen months since he had been officially fired from Drake and Sanderson's for holding, as Amber Jones had stated in her original email, "beliefs that were incompatible with the views and aims of a modern employer". It was standard fare, and at the time, Vaughan had urged him to appeal, but Luke couldn't really see the point of going to all that trouble for a job that he didn't care about anyway. But now he was back, an average Joe again, not only having to make some money after his salary from Mithras had been stopped, but also needing to move on with his life.

So, he was quickly handed a shovel and although for the first three or four days, Luke feared his body might collapse from eight hours of lifting bricks and shovelling cement, once his hands and shoulders got used to the rigour and the repetition, there was an exhilarating release in the toil. Of course, Mithras was always there, lurking in the shadows, and he watched, with genuine fascination, as the organisation tried to rebuild itself from the wreckage of the previous few months. Carl or Simon and rest of his toxic entourage seemed to have left without as much as a murmur, while any reports of late-night Reservoir Dogs torture scenes or implications of Alex McDonald in the attempted bombing on the South Bank, failed to surface in the press or anywhere else for that matter. This surprised Luke, as he had heard from Andy Papps, who he still kept in touch with, that Vaughan had finally "persuaded" Carl to spill the beans that night about the media mogul, so it was a mystery to him why he wasn't using the information. Maybe his wily old friend was just biding his time and holding it as his ace card, in case Mithras got into any more trouble further down the line, Luke reasoned but whatever the outcome, elsewhere, things were also taking a new turn.

For a start, there was definitely less sunglasses on the streets and it was quite a rare sight to see a T-Shirt with the Mithras brand anywhere in towns and cities, as after nearly three years of bitter acrimony, it seemed an uneasy peace was starting to settle between the sexes. Now encouraging articles around the theme of "What I like about men" or "What I have learnt from Women" started to appear by degrees in various newspapers and magazines, while a Documentary by Mark Eastwood about a Mithras member and a radical feminist, falling in love and trying to make a life together, became the surprise hit film of the year.

Then, in early Spring after an ultra-feminist group had photographed random males swaggering about on empty tube platforms in an attempt to shame them for their "patriarchal, hetero-normative behaviour that suppresses women on a daily basis", a group of women called Sex United quickly formed and arranged a march through the centre of London to recognise the positive impact that "the male of the species" has brought to life in general over the past millennia.

"Let's recognise the enormous good that men have brought to our lives, because without their incredible ingenuity and industry, quite frankly, none of the many advantages of modern life would exist today. Who built the roads, lost their lives constructing skyscrapers, tunnelled out the sewers, brought light and warmth into our homes and workplaces?" their website declared, echoing the famous words of the American academic, Camille Paglia who once said "If civilisation had been left in female hands, we would still be living in grass huts". Meanwhile, Polly Dworkin, a co- founder of the new movement, went even further on Radio 4's today programme when she stated that, "It was actually men who gave women the tools to set themselves free in the first place. The Pill, IVF and the Internet, which amplified the ideas of the Me-Too movement, were all invented by men and therefore women should be eternally thankful to them for these indispensable contributions to our lives."

Naturally, many feminist groups hit back, saying that women could have just as easily made similar contributions to society if they hadn't been "chained to a kitchen sink, to bring up the kids for thousands of years", but despite these highly credible criticisms, the demonstration went ahead and succeeded in attracting hundreds of thousands of women who marched seemingly without irony, as they held up pictures of Martin Luther King, Albert Einstein, Nicholas Winton, who saved Jewish children on the Kinder Transport in World War II and strangely one of 6ft 5' Rugby Union superstar Ade Hodges, recently voted, most the handsome man in the world. These events were soon replicated all over the globe as women seemed genuinely interested in celebrating the historic input of men, while at the same time seeking a way to finally end hostilities between the sexes.

Similarly, Luke, since the ending his "love ban", was also seeking greater accommodation with the opposite sex, as he continued to see Katie, and over the next few months, they slipped, without even realising it, into the comfortable paradigm of boyfriend and girlfriend. Oxytocin was indeed a dream drug, and so still in the honeymoon stage of their relationship, her love of Coldplay and Reality TV, were met with tolerant smiles from Luke, while his love of Greggs and football hooligan films received a loving smirk from Katie. Of course, every now and again, he might find himself a little irritated by the something that the "centre of his universe" had said, especially when she explained to her well-spoken friends that he was "exploring lots of interesting avenues after leaving Mithras, and was just waiting for the right opportunity to turn up."

On these occasions, Luke fought valiantly to bite his tongue, as he resisted the urge to declare in his best cockney accent, "Well actually Cordelia, I shovel cement and look at the crack of a Bulgarian's arse all day", but in reality, he wasn't really that fazed, and anyway it was probably par for the course. *Love between the classes was about as easy as climbing the Shard in your flip flops,* Vaughan had once observed and as usual he wasn't wrong.

One day she would probably say something unkind about poor people without thinking or he might get caught making a crisp sandwich with salad cream and all hell would break loose, but for the moment, they seemed to have enough affection, curiosity and desire for each other to surmount most obstacles, and for the moment, at least, that was enough for Luke.

Chapter 37

Months passed, and slowly, life for was beginning to slip back into its pre-Mithras rhythm as Luke's weekends were now either spent enjoying boozy Friday nights out in the company of Fitz and Ravi or wandering around farmer's markets on a Sunday beside Katie with an over-priced bacon roll in his gob. Initially this suited him fine, as after the craziness of the previous few years, the humdrum proved to be a very pleasant distraction, but as time wore on, having glimpsed a different life, gradually, the initial thrill of the everyday started to lose some of its lustre, and therefore, it was with some relief, that out of the blue, he received a text from his old mentor.

"How's tricks?"

Luke smiled as he looked down at the message.

That was so Vaughan.

Last time he'd seen him, he'd been threatening to grill a man's hand on a George Foreman grill, but now, its "let's forget all that, how's tricks?"

"So, you don't want the Klingons to wipe us out then?" Luke texted back with a grin, recalling his old friend's previous comment in their argument at the old Mithras HQ, and when Vaughan replied "only the influencers" the two men quickly slipped back into a familiar dialogue, apologising here, justifying there, until they finally agreed to meet in a bar called Bradleys one Friday night in early June. Predictably, it took Luke an age to find one of Vaughan's "many favourite bars", but once inside, he was greeted with a big smile and a pint of lager, before being swiftly directed towards a large glass cabinet thrust against the back wall of the bar full of 45-inch vinyl singles, with the words "the only proper juke box left in London."

Instantly, pound coins were plucked from trouser pockets, as they both nudged each other out of the way to press the buttons for their favourite songs. E24, *Gimme Shelter by Merry Clayton* (Vaughan), E79 *Live Forever, Oasis* (Luke), E42, *Mr Blue Sky, ELO* (joint decision), were selected while they laughed, slapped shoulders and generally beamed at each other for the next hour or so. Now, as the music continued to play, Vaughan explained that, since the departure of "Carl and those other assholes", Mithras was, not only, far less political these days, but also, because most of the money had run out, they had moved to new premises in Hounslow, which was more in keeping with the low-key profile, the organisation wanted to project.

"You should come back, mate," urged Vaughan taking another sip of his lager, but Luke just grinned and shook his head, explaining that as he had a girlfriend now, he didn't think she would approve of him joining an organisation that stated "all relationships have an end date". Vaughan laughed and quickly gave his former protege a cheeky wink, and after singing the chorus of *Mr Blue Sky* at the top of their voices for the fifth time, they both decided, that the best idea was to head out of the bar towards Soho, and go in search of a bar crawl.

The Toucan, the French House, the Coach and Horses, the Admiral Duncan, all received a visit, as Luke and Vaughan weaved their way through the narrow streets of the decadent hamlet, so by 10 pm, they were nicely drunk and standing outside the Crown and Two Chairman having a cigarette and watching the world go by.

"You know when I was a kid, all the blokes tried to look like women, but were fucking lunatics and would punch you in the head as soon as look at you, while today all the geezers look like men, with regular haircuts and massive beards and can't wait to give you a hug. Fucking nuts, innit?" declared Vaughan, looking at a group of young guys walk by across the street, as he took another drag from his cigarette.

"Progress bruv," replied Luke, smiling back at his older friend, who seemed to be in a more whimsical mood and a little less sure of himself than usual. Luke wasn't completely surprised, as the diminishing influence of Mithras, over the previous year, from an organisation with one hundred and fifty million followers on twitter and the ability to call a global strike to one banned from most of social media and being considered a fringe entity, would affect anyone's confidence. However, despite this, Vaughan was still Vaughan, and after being recognised in the street, which always cheered him up, pints of lager were soon replaced by vodka shots and cocaine, while the two men continued to roam around the centre of town for the next few hours, until running out of places to stagger into, they decided to head back to Vaughan's flat, in search of a nightcap.

"Don't worry, I never did anything, just scared the crap out of the little prick," declared Vaughan as they walked into his kitchen and Luke stared over at the George Foreman grill sitting on the counter.

"Still wasn't right, bro'."

"Probably not. But fuck it, we all know, what I'm a dick, I am, don't we?"

"Nah, you are solid bruv" replied Luke with a big smile, as he and Vaughan sat down at the large oak table, in the middle of the kitchen.

"You think.? You know when I was your age, I had a nervous breakdown," replied Vaughan quickly changing the subject, and snapping the ring on a can of red stripe.

"What? Really?" replied Luke slightly amazed at the sudden revelation.

"Yeah, quite a bad one, actually. Haven't really told too many people about it, only Davie B and Papps know. I was approaching thirty and living in a squat in Camden Town, and I happened to be smoking some very good hash oil one day, when I thought, what the fuck have I done with my life? Shagged a couple of birds, organised a few Raves, did a year at Goldsmiths, doing an English lit degree until I gave it up. I mean Paul Weller had written all his great songs by the time he was 24 and Alexander the Great had conquered the most of the known world before he was 28, and what the hell had I done? It totally freaked me out. I mean, I was being persecuted by Paul Weller and Alexander the Great in a shithole in North London, probably singing a duet called Town called Persepolis, just to annoy me."

"Very good, Vaughan," laughed Luke, taking a sip from his can of beer and appreciating his old mentor's little joke.

"I thank you, just made that one up, actually; anyway, I shit myself, didn't I? Couldn't leave the squat for a week, was curled up on a dirty mattress, scared out of my wits for days, didn't know what the fuck it was? You see, we didn't have a vocabulary for it back then, so I didn't know that it was just a panic attack, but I was terrified. I wanted to kill myself. Seriously. Thought about it for ages, you know how I would do it. Slit my wrists in a hot bath? maybe jump in front of a tube train? but anyway, thank Christ it's pretty hard to top yourself, cos if there was an off switch, I would have definitely pressed it then. It was awful, I can still remember the fear, and of course twenty-five years ago you couldn't tell anyone, could you? they would just take the piss, wouldn't they?"

"Yeah, I bet," said Luke sympathetically, before he added, "I get them as well."

233

"I guessed. Shit innit?"

"It is," replied the younger man, staring into his can of beer for a second.

"You know, Lukey boy, for all my positive man- up, be a stoic, take control of your life bullshit, I still spend most of my time living in the past, where it's safe and warm. Where you always know what's gonna happen next, like Xmas. But you know the past is the worst narc…"

"Narcotic," chimed in Luke.

"Ha! I say that a lot, don't I?"

"Just a bit."

"Ha! Fuck it. I have so many regrets."

"That's normal," replied Luke.

"Not really. I have done some shit, mate. Some nasty stuff."

"Well, it was different, when you were young wern it?" reassured Luke.

"Maybe. You know the thing I love about you lot, is, you don't have the bullshit of my generation. I mean you're typical snowflakes, of course and say "to be fair", "bruv" and "iconic" way too much," said Vaughan.

"Oh cheers," replied Luke slightly raising his eyebrows in mild protest.

"Yeah, well, I'm only taking the piss, aren't I? But what I mean is, you lot don't have all this useless rage lying around, like me and my mates have. Davie B, Andy Papps, Jimmy Jazz, Ray, me, everyone up for it, no one backing down. You know in twenty years' time, fucking idiots like me and Davie B will be tearing around Morrison's in our Motability scooters lobbing tins of fruit cocktail around the place cos someone looked at us the wrong way."

"Boomers," laughed Luke.

"Oi Gen X, thank you very much, born in 1971, I'll have you know," protested Vaughan.

"Sooooo gammon," sniggered Luke.

"Ha! I like that expression. Lot of the fuckers I grew up with were gammon, including me. Bashed and ignored. Our five a day were clips around the ear. Made us selfish though. I think your generation are a lot better."

"Not really Vaughan, only in some things."

"Nah, in everything. I was a cunt, mate," said Vaughan bitterly, as he leaned forward on the kitchen table, to light a cigarette.

"Nah, you are just old school, bruv."

"No mate, trust me, I was," said Vaughan, now looking much more serious.

"Don't believe it, Mr 2Lose, you're a good guy. On the side of the angels."

"Oh yeah, am I? What about Dolores then?"

"Dolores?" replied Luke, a little confused.

"The girl I was supposed to have punched."

"Well, yeah, but that was sorted, wasn't it?" confirmed Luke, taking a sip from his can.

"Wasn't for her." replied Vaughan.

"Well, yeah, of course it was bad what the press did to her after the video came out, and all that. But that wasn't your fault bruv, that was nothing to do with you, was it? you were innocent," said Luke, taking a sip from his beer.

"Was I?"

"Well yeah, 'course you were," replied Luke firmly, while Vaughan stared down at his can of red stripe and shook his head.

"I fucking did it, didn't I? replied Vaughan before rubbing his face with his hand and sitting back in his chair.

"What?" replied Luke, now lowering the can from his mouth, in complete amazement.

"We was down Bagley's in Kings Cross, and Dolores was a proper party girl back then, fucking right up for it, know what I mean. I'd kind of known her since my early twenties, when she used to hang around with all the DJs from the clubs and raves. She knew everyone, and so we started going out, off and on, nothing serious, you know, ring each up when we fancied a fuck, spend a few Sunday afternoons watching old movies and eating yoghurt covered raisins, that sort of thing. So, anyways we are down Bagley's, this one night and doing loads of pills, Charlie, booze, the usual, and she starts dancing with this guy in front of me and I kinda laugh to start off with, but then she starts taking it further, you know to piss me off. Fucking typical. I mean, we'd already had an argument earlier in the evening, about some bollocks, I can't even remember now, but then she gets the arse with me, and starts kissing this guy, so, of course, I know where this is going, so I piss off to the bar. Anyway, she comes back half an hour later and starts telling me about this geezer, and I don't wanna fucking know, do I? so I say whatever and go to fuck off home, but then she follows me out. Anyway usual business, big argument in the middle of the street, and I say I am going and then she says she wants to come too, yadda yadda, so she comes back to my place and then the rowing starts again, and she starts telling me about another guy, she's been fucking, and I shouldn't really be pissed off about this, cos I am doing the same thing myself, if not worse, but then she starts to get to me, and starts pointing at me and I can smell that fucking awful perfume she wears and I just want her to shut up and then I look at her and I think fuck it, so I punch her. I mean I couldn't believe it when I did it, cos I'd never hit a bird before, I fucking hated men who hit women, and I used to step in all the time whenever I saw it, but then I punched her again and it felt amazing, just to shut her up, know what I mean? And so, I punch her again and again, really hard, I mean really hard, and I reckon I've probably hit her about eight or nine times, maybe more and then she goes really quiet, and Dolores always had some come back, but not this time and she looks at me with this fear in her eyes, and you know what? It felt great, it felt really good because I wanted her to feel that fear. I wanted her to shut the fuck up, and watch her mouth but then the next minute I look down and she's on the floor, and I'm breathing hard and then she starts to cry, and I realise what I've done."

"Are you sure, I mean you were pissed and…"

"I know what I did, Luke! I fucking battered her, cos she pissed me off, and I just wanted to shut her up," bellowed Vaughan now smashing his fist against the wooden table.

"So, she was telling the truth then?" replied Luke, as he sat back in total shock whilst staring at a poster of Malcom X on the opposite wall of the kitchen, before Vaughan slowly nodded his head and took another sip of his beer.

Chapter 38

"Jesus, that was some night, weren't it?" declared Vaughan placing a cup down on the Moroccan coffee table, while Luke peered out from underneath the duvet, and his eyes blinked painfully into the morning light.

"Yeah, Bradleys?! Fucking love that place, like walking back into the eighties innit? especially the bogs, ha!" continued Vaughan as he paced manically about the front room, before stopping to tell a story about some guy they had come across the previous evening who said that he'd given Pete Doherty from the Libertines, his first joint.

Instinctively, Luke reached over for his coffee while he stared at his old friend for a second.

He had never seen Vaughan like this before.

Uncool, unfunny …guilty, he thought before forcing out a polite smile.

"Yeah, yeah, God I was totally fucking arseholed last night! Mate, gotta stop doing Charlie! At my age?! Jesus! And the shit I talk! Apologies. I mean you ain't seen me in over six months and all I do is talk bollocks, all night."

"No, it's fine, we drank a lot," replied Luke coolly.

"We did, didn't we? Oh, and mate, all that crap about Dolores at the end? I fucking hope you didn't take me seriously? Ha! geezer! I was just talking total bullshit. I mean couldn't hit a bird, even if I wanted to, you know that? probably doing all that fucking Gianluca, made me feel sorry for her."

"Yeah sure, no problem," Luke replied, as Vaughan suddenly put his hyper-animated performance on hold for a second, to stare into his friend's eyes, and plead for selective amnesia, just for old times' sake, until Luke looked away and the older man exploded into contrived bonhomie once more.

"Lovely jubbly, best forgotten innit? Right then, only solution to a massive hangover like this, is a monster fry up and I know this great place on the high street. No frying in olive oil, no stupid looking plates and it's all under seven quid for a blinding slap-up including toast and a cup of splosh."

"Err you know, mate, I'd err love to but I err promised my mum to help her move some stuff today, so I'm gonna have to go take a rain check on that one, if that's okay?" replied Luke, now quickly moving from underneath the duvet and preparing to leave.

"Ahh, mate, it's gotta be done, I'm paying."

"Err, yeah, it sounds great, Vaughan, but Jesus, oh look it's 11 o'clock already, bollocks, I'm gonna be late," continued Luke now grabbing his phone, and putting on his shoes, so in less than a minute, he found himself out of the door and heading towards the Willesden Junction tube.

That wasn't completely obvious, was it? Luke grimaced to himself, as he continued to speed down Manor Park Road, as if pursued by an unseen entity, until feeling at a reasonably safe distance from Vaughan's flat, he placed some head-phones into his ears and started to listen. He had no idea, why, when Vaughan started to tell his story about Dolores, he had pressed the record button on his phone, but he did. Maybe, after years of encounters with aggressive journalists or feminist activists, it was some kind of reflex action or perhaps it was his meddlesome conscience, interfering as usual, but whatever the reason, when Luke heard the words "And so I punch her again and again" played back into his ears, he felt nothing but guilt. Minutes later, he entered the underground station and after quickly finding a bench at the end of a platform, he sat down and replayed the recording again, in the faint hope that his friend had been doing that "guy thing" and just making stuff up to sound impressive to another male, after a night of heavy drinking. However, as the drunken confession came to an end and Luke slowly removed the headphones from his ears again, he realised that this excuse wouldn't fly.

There was absolutely no doubt.

His friend had beaten up a woman and resting his elbows on his knees, Luke narrowed his eyes, as a voice in his head started to speak, in an effort to bring some order to the situation.

"Of course, it was horrific, of course it was awful, and violence against women could never be condoned, in any circumstances. Never. Then again, it was years ago, another time, different values, and anyway, who was he to judge? She had survived, had a kid by all accounts, and Vaughan seemed to be genuinely upset; he knew what he had done and he was sorry. His punishment was his conscience and although he was flawed, he was essentially a good guy. A really good guy, and nothing would be achieved by saying anything to anyone,

especially the Police, so the best thing now, was just to delete it. Definitely," his thoughts confirmed again and momentarily relieved at the rationality and balance of his decision, he was just about to press his thumb down on the little dustbin beside the recording on his phone, when a second voice, started to crash its way forward from the back of his mind.

"Oh well as long as he is a good guy, that makes ALL the difference then, doesn't it? I mean if he was a tosser, you could give him up with a clear conscience, couldn't you? but not a good guy? Oooh, heaven forbid! I mean aren't they a protected species or something? Grade 1 listed? How the hell are we supposed to go forward if the so-called good guys just stand by and do nothing while the other good guys just get away with it?"

Shut the fuck up, screamed the other voices in his head, as every cell in his body now swarmed together to denounce this solitary heretic, but the louder they shouted, the more Luke realised that he really had no choice, and bowing his head in shame, he kept staring blankly at the smooth concrete of the platform floor, while his traitorous fingers completed their dirty task.

"Hey Suzanne, please give me a ring ASAP, have something really important thing to tell you about Vaughan and Dolores," he texted and so two hours later, he found himself sitting in a coffee shop in Farringdon, feeling slightly sick, while Suzanne slowly removed the ear buds and handed back his phone.

"This is unbelievable."

"I know."

"What are you gonna do?" asked Suzanne, while Luke turned his head to watch the rain beat down outside the coffee shop onto the passing umbrellas. Grass! Snitch! Traitor!

The voices from 3.5 billion men seemed to whisper in his ear, as continued to stare out of the window, seeking some kind of relief, until reluctantly his eyes found their way back to the journalist again.

"You have to go to the police Luke."

Now her voice made him flinch.

Men never liked being told what to do by women.

His time in a hundred Mithras meetings had told him as much.

This is why mothers could never stop their sons' taking drugs, or using knives, or riding motorbikes. It was the oldest rule in the book.

Only men can tell men what to do.

"Yeah, well I'll have to think about, won't I?" snapped Luke, as he quickly grabbed his mobile phone back from the table in front of him and glared at the wall opposite.

"I know it's difficult, Luke. Vaughan is someone I cared about too, you know, but we have to do something about this. We need to talk to Dolores."

"What? Dolores? Err, why her?"

"Well because she has to press charges," replied Suzanne firmly.

"Err, I'm not so sure," replied Luke shaking his head, as he gripped the phone tighter in his hand.

"She needs justice! Bloody hell, you have to Luke! Otherwise, why the hell did you bring me down here in the first place?"

Good question, and as usual Luke had no answer, and so instead he chose to stare blankly into his cup, as the rain beat harder against the window of cafe.

"Oh great, so all that stuff about women not being the enemy and men being emotionally self-sufficient was nothing but empty words, was it?" continued the veteran reporter, while Luke stared at his nicotine-stained fingers for a second, and desperately searched his mind for another alternative.

"Vaughan is my friend, Suzanne. In fact, he is probably more than that. My old man pissed off when I was four and didn't really come back and then he died, so, I suppose Vaughan is like my dad in a way," replied Luke desperately.

"He's not your dad."

Luke looked away again.

This was useless, of course Vaughan wasn't his dad, that was just something to say, to justify whatever he was trying to avoid. The truth was that he had contacted Suzanne to outsource his conscience, but now, when the chips were really down, he didn't want to go through with it. Did he want to betray his friend? No, he didn't, but he also knew what had to be done, and so for the second time in as many hours, Luke tried not to look, as he went against his better judgement again and slid his phone across the table towards Suzanne.

Chapter 39

The following day, Luke and Suzanne went to see Dolores, who, after the collapse of her last, highly publicised, court case, had been forced to move to Woking with her son. At first, she had refused to even open the door until the formidable Suzanne screamed "It's your fucking duty," through her letterbox for five minutes, and so after two cups of tea and three Bacardi and cokes, together with assurances that this time it would be different, twenty-four hours later the story was splashed across the front pages, as the whole world proceeded to go completely insane once more.

"Casey drops bombshell", "Mithras at war" and "Vaughan 2Lose, again" boomed out from every news stand and laptop screen, as the usual media storm raged on for days, until Luke reluctantly handed in his mobile phone to the Police, and Vaughan 2Lose, formerly known as Danny Ward, was re-arrested for the physical assault of Dolores Brady.

The next few weeks were particularly challenging for Luke as he tried to carry on as normal and even returned to work, but the subsequent long silences in the van and at tea-breaks from Pav and Chris forced Desi to say that although "he admired his nuts" for doing what he had done, it was causing problems with the job and as a result, he would have to let him go. Luke nodded that he understood, as Desi stuck £200 in his hand and slapped him on the shoulder, before adding, "Tell your mum I'm sorry." Unfortunately, his mother was in a less forgiving mood, as she declared that Desi Lynch "had always been a yes man and a fecking coward and vowed never to let him or any of his mob into her house again, as long as she lived."

This was harsh to say the least.

At least Desi had the decency to say it to his face, unlike a lot of his friends, who now kept a safe distance and were treating him as if he had a combination of the bubonic plague and a child sex conviction. Even more than "don't steal your friend's girl", "don't grass on a mate" was the very cornerstone of male friendship, and may have actually been present in the code of Hammurabi, which were the first laws ever written down or whispered into the ear of Moses by God on the top of Mount Sinai. Therefore, as a result of crossing this forbidden line, his fellow males no longer nodded at him in the street, but rather stared off into the distance, or nearly walked into lamp-posts to avoid his treacherous gaze whenever they encountered him. Others, were less diplomatic and simply muttered "wanker" or "grass" as they sauntered past, forcing Luke, in a further ironic twist, to wear sunglasses everywhere he went from now on, to avoid the hostile looks from his fellow man. Thankfully Fitz, Ravi and Imran, remained true and provided their usual help and support during this period, but Luke could see, even in their eyes, that they were conflicted regarding the decision that he had made, as predictably, the abuse, especially online, soon reached epic proportions.

"Who tapes a friend's conversation?", "Sounds like a setup to me" and "Snitches get stitches" screamed out of the Twittersphere, Instagram and even Tik Tok while conspiracy theories abounded that Vaughan's voice had been doctored from previous interviews, as the establishment was up to old tricks again, fabricating evidence to clamp down on honest dissent. Initially, Luke chose to ignore all the abuse and stay off social media completely, so as not to add any more fuel to the fire, but despite this very sensible strategy, the denunciations just got worse and after receiving numerous "credible" death threats, Luke decided not to put his mother through any more stress, and so with the help of Suzanne, he decamped to one of her friend's flats in Tufnell Park and tried to sit tight until everything blew over.

Obviously, the location was kept secret, but every now and again, when it was considered safe, Katie would be allowed visit to keep his spirits high with soft kisses and stories of support from Hollywood celebrities and various politicians, as even her previously hyper-critical friends were suddenly overcome with a new admiration for what her boyfriend had done.

"Wow he is so brave."

"Totally amaze, you must invite him to my next party."

"I love him. He is such a fucking role model."

However, as much as he appreciated all the encouragement and kind words, the very thing that Luke had wanted to avoid at all costs, was now happening again; except this time, it was his reputation that was broken instead of his nose. Weren't the last few years with Mithras supposed to have been an antidote to the agonies of female approval? but here he was, once more, "A Decent Man" trapped by the same process and just about to destroy a friend, thought Luke as Katie whispered "You're such a hero," before she snuggled up to him on the sofa and started to remove his T-Shirt.

Is this how he got to feel good?

Please the girl and you get a biscuit? and feeling like a complete sham, he hated the fact that his girlfriend's kisses had become more urgent just because her privileged friends or a few celebrities online had said something nice about him. Now, as the back of his head pressed against the soft fabric of the couch, and he felt Katie's lips press against his once more, the words of B-Nard, the American Postman bounced into his mind again.

Hey Luke, if I had a better job, I'd have a nicer girl and a better car.

Suddenly, his heart started to beat like a drum, and at one point, he thought that he might actually have a panic attack in mid snog, until Suzanne thankfully walked into the front room, and saved him from further anguish.

"Oh my God, young love," the reporter declared as she pretended to put her fingers down her throat, before flopping down in the large chair opposite.

"Cynic," replied Katie, disentangling herself from Luke and resting her head on his chest.

"Whatevs. Anyway, that cock McDonald had me in his office again today, telling me to calm down on the abuse aimed at Vaughan; well, we all know what's that about, don't we?" declared the journalist, as Katie looked back, confused, while Luke began to shake his head vigorously, thus prompting Suzanne to immediately change the subject and start to tell a story about a famous soap star, who she'd heard, had, recently, been admitted to an A & E department "with a bottle of HP sauce rammed up his anal passage". Katie started to laugh, while Luke looked away and his mind tried to process what Suzanne had just said about Vaughan.

The trial was only a week away now, and his old mentor's top prosecution team, crowdfunded by secret wealthy donors, were still defending the case based solely on Dolores' allegations.

Why wasn't he using his ace card against McDonald, about Carl and the bomb plot?

Surely now was the time to use it? he thought and was nearly upset with his old friend for not taking this option, as deep down, despite the seriousness of the offence, he was secretly hoping that Vaughan might still get away with it. At least, with that outcome, it might help expunge some of the guilt that seemed to follow him everywhere like a dark, brooding cloud. In fact, when the story first broke in the Press, Vaughan had actually contacted him, to ask him to reconsider his decision, but when Luke texted back that he couldn't, his old mentor had simply replied, "fair enough" and even added a smiley face. Luke wasn't surprised at his reaction; as it was typical of a man whom he still respected more than anyone he had ever met but of course it only served to make things worse. Thankfully Davie B, Jimmy Jazz and even his beloved Andy Papps were less reasonable in their assessment of his decision and had called him every nasty name under the sun from the eighties, some of which he'd had to google to understand, so at least, he could still feel some anger, retain some solidarity with himself.

For the next few days, Luke continued to struggle with these toxic thoughts, until in no time at all, the dreaded court date soon arrived, as journalists from every part of the world now gathered outside the Old Bailey to watch the drama unfold. Not since the Male Strike of 2027, had so much of the world's attention been focused on one event, and for the first week of the trial, Luke, sensibly kept away from everything and just followed events through the normal news outlets or updates from Suzanne.

However, by the second week, it was Luke's turn to testify, as everyone held their breath, while the one-time ally and friend, now turned traitor, made his dramatic entrance into the proceedings. It was like a plot from a Shakespeare play or a Hollywood thriller, and as the cameras flashed from all sides, Luke, surrounded by fifty or more police officers, tried to approach the court steps, as his former comrades in the Mithras organisation, Femi, Angus, and Perry all stared back in total disgust. Now shouts of "Don't do it, Luke", "You're a fucking traitor, Casey" and "You're better than this" echoed around outside the old courthouse, and despite the heavy police presence, at one point, it seemed they might not be able to make it through at all, as hundreds of angry male protestors surged forward again and again towards the star witness, while eggs and other projectiles rained onto their heads from the dirty London sky. It was pandemonium and to make matters worse, a large group of female demonstrators had also gathered outside the court holding placards, that read "Justice for women," "Women have no real rights "and "You're the one of us Luke", which just seemed to compound his misery further, until finally, he was hustled up the steps and into the main entrance.

An hour later, after he had cleaned all the egg splatter from his suit, Luke stepped into the witness box to give evidence, while everyone in the gallery leaned forward in their seats to make sure they didn't miss a second of the spectacle. To the uninformed observer, it might have been difficult to assess who exactly was on trial, as the defence team immediately went on the attack and tried every trick in the book to discredit Luke's testimony.

How many drinks did you have?

You take drugs, don't you?

You didn't really like Vaughan, did you?

Each accusation, was greeted with a slow shake of the head from Luke, as he repeatedly denied that he had any axe to grind with his former colleague, and that he was only acting in accordance with his conscience. However, when the defence barrister, Nick Nottingham asked why had he taped a conversation with a friend in the first place? the courtroom gallery suddenly erupted into righteous male fury as the Judge had to order that the courtroom be cleared and at least twenty men were ejected for shouting traitor and shame at the former hero of Mithras. During the whole ordeal, Luke repeatedly rubbed his face with his hand, as his mild OCD returned with a vengeance, and everyone in the courtroom, except Vaughan for some reason, were now dressed in stockings and suspenders and engaged in all manner of sexual impropriety. It will pass, it will pass, he repeated to himself, as somehow, he managed to keep it together and when the prosecution finally asked him if the accused had told him that he had punched Dolores Brady, he took a deep breath and simply answered, yes.

A few days later, Dolores' testimony completed the job, as she bravely recounted the events in question and calmly rejected the contention of the defence barrister that she was too influenced by drink and drugs to know what had really happened. "I think, I know when I am being punched, mate," she had said defiantly, as all previous fear now seemed to depart from her eyes, and this particular quote would later become a global rallying call for women's groups around the world, for years to come. For Luke, this one image of a confident and empowered Dolores, made his betrayal nearly worth all the trouble, and so after three days of further testimony, and final summations from the defence and prosecution teams, the jury was then dispatched to a back room, where forty minutes later, they came back with their decision.

Guilty.

The courtroom gasped, and then gasped again, as Vaughan received a sentence of five years, which was at the top end of the tariff for such a crime. Luke had decided not to attend the last day, but Suzanne told him later that when the sentence was handed down, Vaughan remained motionless in the dock for a few seconds, and amidst all the shouts and jeers from the various opposing groups in the gallery, he seemed to look over to Dolores as if to say he was sorry, before he was led away towards the cells.

Back in the flat in Tufnell Park, Luke rubbed his damp palms against his jeans, as he watched the evening news and pictures of the police van, with Vaughan inside, driving down Ludgate Hill on its way through the London traffic, before he suddenly rose from the sofa to angrily shove his clothes into a sports bag that was sitting on the table.

"I still don't hate him, you know," he declared looking over to Suzanne, who was sitting by a breakfast bar.

"That's no crime, mate," the journalist replied, now unscrewing the tops of two miniature bottles of vodka before pouring their contents into an empty glass.

Chapter 40

"I don't wanna say I told you so, but, hey, the facts don't lie, unless, of course, this is fake news, but thank you Wes from Cheshunt, I think we know people like you are never going to be satisfied, unless we live in the rubbish world that you and others like you would like to create. Keep hating fella. So, listeners, Vaughan 2Lose, was there ever a more appropriate name for a demagogue of hate? has just been sentenced to five years in jail for savagely beating up a woman. A Mithras member called Anton Phillips tried to blow up a group of peace-loving feminists and is now in a secure mental institution, probably for the rest of his life, while anyone who disagrees with their patriarchal dogma receives an avalanche of death threats. In fact, I have received so many, that I feel as if I am not actually doing my job properly, unless I receive at least one an hour. Even their founder Luke Casey, after testifying very bravely in court, it must be said, yes hats off to him, has disappeared from view, so all in all, I think we can safely say, Mithras is dead. Yes, the Persian god is no more, his power has gone, and maybe he will reappear in thirty years' time as the brand name for a pair of jeans or a new hybrid car. Oh yeah, the Mithras, makes you feel like a real man! Who knows? One can only dream. So, to celebrate this excellent news, I have the great pleasure of inviting on the programme this morning, the woman who broke the story and the scourge of misogynists everywhere, the very wonderful Suzanne Burke. Good morning to you, Suzanne."

"Good morning to you Jake," replied Suzanne brightly.

"So first up, great news about Dolores, she finally received justice."

"Yes Jake, she did. Finally! But as usual, for women to get the normal justice that most men get by right, she has had to pay a huge personal price. She is still getting horrendous online abuse and has had to move again with her 7-year-old son."

"Oh my god, that is so horrible. Please pass on my sympathies to her." replied the radio host.

"Well, yes I am sure that will keep her warm at night," said Suzanne with deadpan eyes.

"Ha! yeah," replied Jake, frowning a little at the sarcasm of his guest before diplomatically looking down at some ideas for the interview that he had previously scribbled down on a writing pad. He had been warned that the veteran journalist could be a "tad spiky", but it was nothing, he couldn't handle he reasoned, as he raised his head again and cheerfully pressed on with his questions.

"So, Suzanne, you must be very happy with the passing of Mithras. Membership down to err, what is it now? fifty thousand from a high of thirty million, a year or so ago. Centres closing by the day, a bit more sanity on the streets, people starting to work together again, what do you think?"

"Yes, back to the status quo again, hey ho. Well thank God for that, eh?" replied Suzanne, now glaring at the radio host.

"Well err, yes, I mean, of course, there is still lots to do, obviously."

"Actually, some of what Mithras did was quite laudable," shot back Suzanne.

"Well, err…"

"They worked very closely with women's refuges, and at least ten women I know of personally have their kids alive today, because someone from Mithras talked down an ex-partner who was threatening to do something awful to them."

"Of course, but, at its core, it was still a very malign organisation surely? Okay, they may have done some good things, but that was just mere chance, wasn't it? I mean you could argue the Nazis built the autobahns, and ISIS gave food to people in Syria," replied Jake with a grin.

"What the hell are you going on about, you fool? Jesus! A few blokes running around in sunglasses and being angry about modern romance is hardly a genocidal terror state, is it? Luke Casey has just testified against his friend and will probably spend the rest of his life getting hell for it. What have you ever done, Jakey boy?"

"Err, well,

"No seriously what have you done to actually help the cause of women, in general, I mean?" asked Suzanne, folding her arms.

"Well, err I think, I have done my best through my platform in the media, you know constantly highlighting the problems with Mithras and…."

"So basically, building a career," interrupted Suzanne.

"Now, hold on a minute, that's a bit unfair, I…"

"Really? Two years ago, I'd never even heard of you and now you're a big chat show host and ready to go off to the States to make a few more bob," broke in Suzanne again.

"Well err, actually, that's just a proposal at the moment."

"Of course, it is, darling. Come to think of it, as we are here, Jake. Can I ask you a question for a change?"

"Erm, okay," replied Jake now looking around nervously at his staff behind the glass screen in the radio studio.

"Do you think you are good to women?"

"Well obviously, society is still pretty patriarchal, but err, you know I do what I can, I mean we can all…"

"Really? So would you consider yourself, to be a good husband for instance?" asked Suzanne, leaning forward in her chair.

"Well, I like to think of myself as…"

"Good? Well of course, there's only so much a man can do, isn't there? But I definitely respect my wife, help with the chores when I can, but you have to remember I have a busy life, chat shows, book launches etc, but I do try my best. Am I close here, Jake?" replied Suzanne imitating the radio host.

"Well, err…"

"Well err, except, when you are having an affair with a member of your staff, of course. I mean other than that incey wincy, little faux pas, you're basically man of the year, aren't you?" continued the journalist.

"Err, pardon, err, excuse me, now look, I totally reject…"

"Yes, I bet you do, Jake, or should I say Jerk. You are an unfaithful husband, sunshine! With your researcher, Antigone Partington-Wise, 28, tutt, tutt, shame on you. Twenty years younger than you, but of course, you love your wife, she's so special, but you do deserve a little treat at the end of the day, as well, don't you? of course you do, cupcake, I totally understand."

Jake now stared back at Suzanne in total shock and was just about to lean forward in his seat and completely deny the allegation, when suddenly the veteran reporter lunged forward across the short desk between them and grabbed some of the chat show host's long shaggy hair.

"Aarghh, Jesus."

"How does that feel, Jake? Uncomfortable? Painful? Humiliating?" asked Suzanne, now increasing her grip.

"Yes, yes, oh my god, ouch, owwww."

"Not in control?"

"Ooww, aaaghh, err yes, err no." shrieked the radio host.

"You see, that's how most of us feel all day, every day. You know the ones, who don't get the chances that bloody people like you get every second of your greedy lives? The privilege that you and your type try so desperately to cover up, by hiding behind identity politics, supporting women, people of colour, LGBTQ rights, and anything else to keep us distracted, keep us off the scent. Just as long as we don't take, what scumbags like you really value - your money and your power. Isn't that right, Jakey Wakey?"

"Yes, yes, I get it, I get it, owww, let me go, ooww," pleaded Jake.

"Horrible creep," declared Suzanne, as she held onto his hair for a few seconds more until loosening her grip, the radio host slumped back onto his desk, before the journalist rose from her seat and casually walked out of the studio.

Probably blown the chance of a regular spot on his show now grinned Suzanne, as ten minutes later, she was sitting in a coffee shop and sifting through the contents of a large brown envelope, which she had just taken out of her bag. Pictures of the radio host kissing a young woman, having sex in a hotel room, his wife and family, all the evidence of middle-class hypocrisy laid bare, together an attached note, that simply said "the young woman is called Antigone Partington-Wise, 28, she is a researcher for Radio and TV shows and has been having an affair with Jake O'Callaghan for the last eighteen months".

"Fucking Alex McDonald," she mumbled to herself as she sipped her coffee and stared at the photographs again. She hated that she was doing the bidding of the media mogul, but when she received the envelope thirty minutes before going on, she had no choice but to use it. Of course, she could have waited until the end of the show, and written another breakthrough piece, but after the Luke Casey phone tape, she was already the toast of Fleet Street, plus the smug face of the talk show host had finally tipped her over the edge.

She had always disliked him.

Phoney, third way, bourgeois fraud. Scratch a little deeper and you will always find the same conceited, greedy ambition that you found in Bono or Blair who despite all their nice speeches and worthy causes, essentially wanted the world to stay the same way as it had always been, so they could carry on making their money and talking shit to anyone stupid enough to listen. Take a knee or fly a pride flag, which costs them nothing, whilst gleefully putting up prices in the worst cost of living crisis in four decades, *the privileged class had indeed built a world that only they could live in,* she thought remembering a line that she had written nearly twenty years before, following the banking crisis, but this time it might not be so easy to get away with it. The penny was beginning to drop with ordinary people about late-stage crony capitalism and many were starting to seriously bite back against the neo-liberalism/feudalism of the past few years and if there was one thing that she had learnt in "her totally fucked up life", it was, in the end, everything had to be paid for.

And pay Jake O'Callaghan most definitely would, as over the next few weeks the radio host's face was rarely off the front page, while his former lover Antigone Partington-Wise quickly joined the pile on as she tearfully revealed in various interviews with the mainstream media, how the TV celebrity had cynically used his power and fame to gaslight her and ultimately destroy her life. Moreover, after his wife had unceremoniously thrown him out of the family home and immediately filed for a divorce, the radio host remained unavailable for comment as he retreated to an undisclosed address, and awaited his fate. He didn't have to wait long, as not only was he suspended from his daily radio programme and Friday night chat-show, but also his prospective TV deal in America was now cancelled due to the unfortunate publicity and concerns about his behaviour around women.

"Horrible fecking wanker, God forgive me for saying so, but he never liked normal people you could tell by the way he spoke to them on his radio show," commented Luke's mother while she shook her head at the front of the newspaper and took another sip of her tea. *This was indeed true,* thought Luke sitting at the breakfast table and although he wouldn't be shedding any tears over Jake O'Callaghan, he didn't retain the same brutality of the older generation, like Vaughan, Suzanne or even his mother when someone got what they deserved. They were still a person, and even after all the nonsense he had been through, he actually felt a little sympathy for his former nemesis, especially a few days later when someone called Marcus gave him a call, to ask if he would be interested in hosting Jake's old radio show on a temporary basis, with a view to making it more permanent if "things worked out".

"That's got Alex MacDonald written all over it," replied Suzanne when Luke told her of his offer, before adding, "but do it, we need someone like you doing stuff like that." Katie encouraged him too, but to Luke, it seemed a bit too contrived, a bit too 21st century, plus he had been here before, as he amusingly recalled the prediction of his old boss, Amber Jones, "I can see you being an

251

assistant team leader by Christmas, Luke, just as long as you don't take any more sick leave, of course."

Err don't think so Bruv.

He'd had quite enough of shallow inducements for the present and craving something with a little more substance, he gracefully declined the offer and instead concentrated on developing a web-site for men who suffered from Pure O, with a friend from his Mithras days, while helping out now and again at a local food bank.

Naturally, Suzanne had no such conflict of conscience, as, after being fined for her attack on Jake O'Callaghan and sentenced to a hundred hours community service, she was then hired by Alex McDonald to take over the late-night slot of the man she had just assaulted. Her TV chat show, simply titled "Suzanne", soon proved a huge success, especially an interview with Portia Ramone, where after a particularly fractious back and forth between the two women, the journalist had finally accused the actress of being nothing more than "a social tourist and an enemy of real women", thus prompting the Hollywood actress to storm out of the studio and into the arms Denzel Beauregarde, an American actor, fifteen years her senior, and star of the hit Netflix show, Deranged Antelopes.

Meanwhile, outside of all the on-going drama, Mithras had been quietly taken over by two long-time members, Femi and Angus, who, after all the adverse publicity of the previous year, had decided to change the name of the organisation to Global Man. This new launch, together with the tag line, "Supporting independent men in a modern world", started to attract more members, and as the months passed, Global Man, although remaining faithful to the general themes covered by the Book of Mithras, were now also augmenting the message with some ideas of their own, in particular something called *"The Rubric of Dating"*.

These new directives regarding the rules of relationships were devised after a symposium of a thousand men and women agreed to meet and decide on such conventions as "who buys the drinks on a first date?", "the etiquette of approaching someone you find attractive" and "the correct way to end a relationship", whilst also enthusiastically adopting "Luke's Law" to reduce street harassment, encouraging both sexes to simply turn around and check each other out to initiate a romantic interaction in public, thus recalling the now well publicised manner, in which their former leader Luke first met his girlfriend Katie. These proposals proved to be very popular amongst men and women as it seemed, at last, there was a written code of conduct that everyone could refer to, thus providing general guidelines of accepted behaviour between the sexes, while "The Symposium" also agreed to meet every two years to update the regulations in the ever-changing world of relationships.

Now, after more than three years of fractious debate, it was clear that politics between men and woman had moved on a great deal and so the idea of finding true happiness in a significant other, also required a new definition for a new age. No longer would men accept the lazy stereo-types regarding their sex or being preached at by a hostile establishment, as advertisers and the film industry studiously avoided pointlessly disrespecting and ridiculing men, as had been the norm for the previous thirty years, and most easily exemplified by the cartoon character, Homer Simpson, who's perennial ineptitude could only be rescued by the intervention of a "much wiser woman". This was now considered outdated thinking and extremely discriminatory by a majority of heterosexual males, and prompted further discussions around this issue, especially, as regards, the age old convention of men needing to be saved by "the love of a good woman" The general conclusion from these various conversations, was that men should seek for the answers within themselves rather than rely on some kind of "mother substitute" whilst a few of the more extreme voices within Global Man, even advocated having children with a total stranger by IVF, thus addressing the joint problems of a declining birth-rate and the potential fallout from any failed relationship in the same breath.

However, most men opted for something more inclusive, and in a bid to improve relations between men and women, Global Man also branched out into the hospitality industry, as bars and clubs were quickly established in the UK and some other European countries, specifically designed to encourage adults to meet outside of dating sites, and interact in more traditional and personal settings. Here, general guidelines of good behaviour were again encouraged, as even "the last dance", i.e. a half hour of slow dancing to cheesy love songs at the end of an evening, was revived from the previous century, to bring a little healthy awkwardness back to romance. Incredibly, it was very well received, particularly amongst Gen Z'ers, who after years of the lockdowns and Mithras controversy, started to crave relationships, based on fun and flirting, rather than constantly searching for micro-aggressions or reasons to criticise the opposite sex.

In saying that, it seemed as if men, especially younger men, were still not looking for a relationship with a woman to solve all of their problems, and increasingly, as the decade neared its end, the emphasis, for many males, was now firmly on personal development outside of the female gaze, rather than seeking a solution to their complicated lives in some abstract notion of an "emotional joint account". As a consequence of this, after years of denial, especially in the mainstream media, a majority of the adult population were now finally coming around to the idea, that there was, indeed, a clear difference between men and women and, despite the presence of Jung's "Animus and Anima" lurking under the surface in every human being, these contrasts were real and more importantly, completely normal. Women, too, were broadly of the same opinion, as both sexes started to realistically conceive of societies where the relationship between a man and a woman was no longer seen as one of the main building blocks of modern life, but rather just one, of many, other, equally valid options on offer.

For Luke, things started to change too, as after six months or so of voluntary work, ZZP, the second largest online news website in the world, offered him a job as their newly created male correspondent. It was a perfect fit, and for the next few months, he started to make a name for himself, as he railed against society's narrow view of what a man should be, whilst challenging his own sex to break free from their own emotional idleness. Furthermore, his article regarding the upcoming new James Bond movie, written by the comedian Dolly Butler-Crisp, which controversially had 007 committing to a long-term relationship with Miss Moneypenny, was now, itself, up for a prestigious press award. It stated that maybe women shouldn't always write male characters and maybe men shouldn't always write female characters, as more often than not, they produced, stereo-types like Mr Darcy or Madam Bovary, that simply reflected, how they would like the opposite sex to be. This article proved very influential, and prompted the hugely popular lead Devon Flannery, the first black actor to play the British secret service agent, to refuse to do any more movies of the franchise until a more authentic version of the Ian Fleming character, obviously without the blatant misogyny of the past, could be found. "Luke Casey is fast becoming the new male Suzanne Burke", joked a national newspaper, and as well as enjoying success in his new found career, he found at the age of thirty-one, that he was now making enough money, to finally move out of his mother's house and relocate to a nice rented garden flat in Manor House.

"Oh, there's a letter for you over there, love," said his mother after kissing him on the cheek on one of his mandatory bi- weekly visits, before pointing her finger towards the coffee table in the middle of the living room. "Oh Thanks," replied Luke and walking over he picked up the envelope and after pulling out a sheet of A4 paper, he started to read.

Dear Grassing Bastard,

I trust I find you well.

I do hope so, and after all the bollocks of the last year, I thought I should write a letter to clear the air - well, you weren't gonna do it, were you?

So, immediately addressing the three-legged hippopotamus in the room, when you first taped our conversation and handed it to the police, obviously I wasn't too happy. I felt betrayed, to say the least, I mean who wouldn't, but as the cliché goes, what is done, is done.

Anyway, fuck it, feeling bitter, isn't going to help, is it? Therefore, I have decided to spend my time in my cell, with a bloke from Cornwall who seems to smell permanently of Parma Violets for some reason, to really THINK for a change.

Thing is, you were right.

Yep, it was definitely the right thing to do.

I did it.

I knew it then and I knew it twenty-five years later and you have to pay for your mistakes and that was a big one.

Dolores deserved justice.

It's weird, every woman I'd ever dated, flirted with or spent any time with, all had horror stories where they had been pushed about, punched or mentally tortured, and I used to think who the fuck does that? I mean, I knew a lot of geezers and I couldn't imagine any of them doing half the shit I heard from these women. I used to think they were exaggerating, you know the usual, making a big deal about it, playing the victim all the time, but then I did it myself.

I DID IT.

A decent geezer, or so-called, and I ran from this thought for twenty-five or more years of my life.

Well, time has a habit of catching up with you, doesn't it? so, I got what I deserved.

I see that now, and therefore what I really want to say is, no hard feelings, mate. You did the right thing, and don't take any notice of anyone who coats you about this. They are wrong. Very, very wrong.

The "mate's code" doesn't extend that far.

Lying for your mate when he is having an affair? Maybe? Covering up if he hits a woman? err no.

Right, lovely, glad that's out of the way now.

So otherwise, you will be happy to hear, that I have not been idle, and I am cracking on with the next big thing that is getting up my nose.

Housing.

Especially in London, but also in Manchester and elsewhere. You've probably seen all these private developers building flats all over the place, costing £400,000 a pop, which of course no fucker on a normal wage, can afford. So, I say, don't build them in the first place then, and build some council houses and proper affordable housing instead, and as a result, I am mobilising a bunch of beautiful loonies to picket these building sites on a full-time basis, until we get what we want. Anyhoo, there is a big private development going up in Finsbury Park right now, called Renaissance Villas and I was thinking, it could be a good story for your website? Yes, I am reading your stuff online and it's very good by the way, so maybe you could look into it?

Obviously, I am doing all this under another assumed name.

How does Daryl Raspberry grab you? Too eighties?

Anyway, look after yourself, BRUV!

Carpe diem kitty kat.
Danny

Luke came to the end of the letter, and after smiling at it for a moment, he quickly tore it in two and placed it in an ashtray on the coffee table before picking up his phone and tapping Renaissance Villas into google.

Chapter 41

Ravi looked like he was about to be shot, as he glanced sideways in the direction of his father, who was standing mournfully amongst the leaves and the fox poo and looking like he might actually start to cry.

Poor guy.

All he had ever wanted, was a nice reception in a posh hotel with a few hundred guests and not standing in the middle of the New Forest with thirty people he didn't know from Adam and the odd hedgehog. Still, after three break-ups, twenty sessions with a relationship counsellor and another stag night, he and Emma had come to the blindingly obvious conclusion that they couldn't live without each other, and so finally he was here. *Maybe love does conquer all*, he thought, as the rays of the afternoon sun suddenly seemed eager to answer his question, as they streamed through the branches of the trees, and warmed the side of his smiling face.

"Why a forest?" whispered Katie into Luke's ear.

"He's really into Lord of the Rings," replied Luke, as she gave his arm a little punch to demand the truth.

"Well, this is where he proposed to her, and they both liked it so much, that they decided to get married here as well. Plus, her parents are Catholic and his are Hindu, so this was seen as a compromise," explained Luke, while from a few feet away, Imran now pressed a key on his lap-top and the wedding march suddenly erupted from a speaker leaning against a tree, and everyone shuffled through the leaves to get into their places.

"It's so romantic," said Katie.

"Fuck that, he looks terrified," laughed Luke, as the bride now walked on her father's arm, through a gap in the congregation and stopped beside her husband to be, before everyone craned their necks to get a better view. For the next few minutes, the humanist celebrant, spoke the words of the service and smiled benignly as the happy couple promised to love, respect each other, and try, as much as possible, to be the very best of friends, before "You can now kiss the bride," provoked a loud whistle with his fingers from Fitz and spontaneous applause from everyone else, while a small group of men and women milling about at a near -by dogging site, now raised their heads in mild confusion.

To his surprise, Luke found himself clapping too.

Obviously, being the former co-founder of Mithras, he wasn't the greatest fan of weddings. If two people were in love, why did they need the validation of their friends and family yadda yadda? But then again, it was his best mate, and as he watched Emma laugh and Ravi roll his eyes, while their hands move tenderly along each other's arms, he thought that maybe these two had a chance, whatever that the hell meant. Soon, the sun disappeared behind a large cloud, and as the light started to fade, everyone quickly gathered around the Bride and Groom to engage in the normal chitchat you have after a formal occasion, until having had enough of the horse-flies, the happy couple decamped to the nearest decent hotel, where all the conventions of an English wedding were then faithfully observed.

Nervous speeches were heard, vegetarian options were given to the wrong guests, children hid under tables, before everyone gathered on the dancefloor, to watch Emma and Ravi shuffle around to the strains of *At Last by Etta James,* a last-minute replacement by Emma's mother for her daughter's original choice of the feminist anthem *You Don't Own Me by Lesley Gore.* Together, Luke and Katie stood by the bar and laughed, as they watched their friend's pull increasingly drunken faces at each other, while Ravi's mother leaned across to enquire, "When are you two going to do the decent thing then?"

"Ha! never," they both chorused, prompting the older lady to smile and squeeze Katie's arm, before leaving the bar to congratulate her son and his new wife.

"I really hate that," observed Luke as he quickly swallowed a shot of tequila and looked around the room.

"What?" protested Katie.

"The way she squeezed your arm, as if to say it's your job to persuade him."

"Ha! You should be so lucky. My God, Luke! she was just being nice," said Katie, shaking her head.

"Maybe."

"It's a wedding, you idiot, people say stuff like that all the time. It doesn't mean anything."

"Fair enough," replied Luke now sinking his hands into his trouser pockets.

"You take everything sooooo seriously, don't you?" scowled Katie, now angrily walking away from the bar, while Luke grimaced and turned to order another drink.

Meanwhile Alex sat in his office on the thirty fifth floor of the newly completed McDonald Plaza in the middle of the City of London, while he looked at the shaven head of the man standing in front of him, and wondered how he had managed to acquire the large scar that ran down the side of his forehead.

"So, what did he say?"

"He said he was okay with that, but now he wants another million pounds for Dolores Brady," replied the man.

"Does he now?"

The man nodded.

"Very noble, but we agreed four hundred thousand, plus I gave him Jake O'Callaghan, so no deal."

"He says she needs to be properly compensated for all the trauma that he has caused her, you know with moving twice because of the video and the trial," replied the man.

"And what about for himself?"

"He said he doesn't want anything."

"Wow, what a role model. Maybe more woman beaters should take a leaf out of his book? replied Alex.

"Err, yes Sir. Err he says he will give you the recording."

"What guarantee do I have there isn't any more? I won't be fucking blackmailed."

"I think he is kosher on this one, sir," replied the man, before Alex looked away and tapped his fingers on the desk.

"I have heard the recording sir and it's pretty damning; Simon Pinner admits to everything," said the man, breaking the silence.

"Jesus, I have already paid out a million to his fucking noddy mates."

"Be cheaper than losing everything, sir."

"Mmm... okay tell him I'll pay it," replied Alex.

"He also asks sir, that she gets it now."

"Fine, but tell him that's it."

"I will, I am visiting him next week, he will be happy. It's a good decision sir," replied the man.

"Wow, thanks for your input, Gulliver. Maybe next time I have a big decision to make, I'll give you a tinkle first, yeah?"

"Err sorry sir," replied Gulliver, bowing his head, before he added, "Err…shall I tell Simon to come in now."

"Oh Christ, I forgot about him. No tell Pinner to go back to the house and wait for me there."

"Sir," replied Gulliver as he nodded his head and then turned to walk out of the room.

He'd had to employ the little prick and his shiftless crew after they had been battered by Vaughan 2Lose and his gang and forced to confess their involvement with him on tape. Still, it wasn't all bad and once you stripped away the mental misogyny, Simon, in particular, was actually quite clever, got things done. In fact, all in all, things hadn't worked out too badly in the end, Alex thought as he leaned back on his chair and clasped his hands across his flattish stomach.

£ 2.4 million, wasn't exactly a king's ransom to ensure his safety.

He made that in a few hours, plus he had got what he'd really wanted.

The end of Mithras.

Now the world was back on its axis, where it should be, until of course, the next bright spark raises his head, and tries to fuck everything up again, he thought as his eyes settled on a picture of himself with Tony Blair and Noel Gallagher, that was hanging on the wall opposite.

Good days.

Suddenly, he fancied a drink. When didn't he? he thought as looked back affectionately at the photo again for a few more seconds, until Sergeant Kelly David came marching towards his desk with a big smile for his daily visit, and now desperately reaching for the pills in the top drawer of his desk, Alex felt the inside of his mind start to melt, as it screamed out in terror once more.

Chapter 42

Luke looked up at the full moon, which now stared back inscrutably from the blackness of the summer night, before he sucked slowly on his cigarette.

"Not dancing?" asked Katie walking out from the hotel bar.

"Not really."

"Are you okay?"

"Yeah."

"I thought you were giving up?" said Katie moving towards him.

"I'm not a very good role model, am I?" replied Luke.

Katie sighed.

"Am I gaslighting you?" added Luke with a grin.

"This is a bit exhausting, darling," said Katie.

"I know."

"You wanna leave it?" suggested Katie.

"Yeah, maybe it's for the best."

"Love is a drug,"

"Most relationships have an end date." confirmed Luke.

"Did you write that on Ravi's wedding card?" asked Katie with a smile.

"No, I got him a 'You don't complete me' T-Shirt."

"He will never wear that."

"No," replied Luke.

"What's wrong with us, Luke?" said Katie, after a brief pause, as she reached over and took the cigarette from his hand.

"Absolutely nothing."

"So, we can still sleep with each other tonight?"

"Of course, if you want."

"Commandment 6?" enquired Katie taking a drag from the cigarette and handing it back.

"Actually, I think it's 5," replied Luke, as they moved closer to each other and kissed tenderly for few seconds, until Katie stopped and pulled away.

"And will you still want me in the morning?"

"Will you still want me?" replied Luke, as Katie laughed and stared into his eyes again.

"Drink?"

"Brandy and Lucozade," said Luke, before she stuck her tongue out at him and then turned to walk away.

Now the crunch of her heels against the gravel of the car park was the only sound in the warm night air, as Luke placed his hands into his pockets and looked up at the moon again.

It was full and bright.

Just beautiful, he mused, and now running his fingers over his palms, as he always did, when lost in his thoughts, he suddenly stopped and began to smile.

They were dry.

CPSIA information can be obtained
at www.ICGtesting.com
Printed in the USA
BVHW031010251122
652759BV00013B/472